"The author keeps you on edge; needing to know what comes next.
I highly recommend this book."
- 5 stars Amazon

"I really loved the premise of this story. It had everything I look for
in a great book... My only complaint would have to be that I wanted
to know more and didn't want the story to end."
- 5 stars Amazon

"A fast-paced book which you can easily lose yourself in, with a
romantic turn at the end."
- 5 stars Amazon

The Lost Art of Magic

Jonni Jordyn

Jordyn @ Large

Other books by Jonni Jordyn

The Lost Art of Magic Series
The Lost Art of Magic
The Untold Prophecy
The Old Child
The Orb of Destiny

The Mother of All Viruses Series
The Mother of All Viruses
The Queen of All Viruses

The Valley of Hope Series
The Calling of the Grull
The Hammer and the Chain

The Beat of a Different Drummer
The Diva of Mud Flats
Something About Nobility

A Sonnet About Magic

What comes from knowing more than senses touch?
What makes the unforeseen to someone known?
What makes the unbelievable too much
For educated people to be shown?

Beyond our senses lies a world of fear
Of those who know a pinch more than we do
About the nature of the powers here
Around us, in the world we thought we knew

The scientists love taking things apart
Evangelists like making answers up
The politicians think that they're so smart
But none of them drink from true powers cup

If magic was, then magic is, for just
The gifted few of whom we'll never trust

— Jonni Jordyn

"Here you leave today and enter the world of yesterday, tomorrow, and fantasy."

— Walt Disney

The Lost Art of Magic

Chapter 1

Michelle Boutin busied herself around the home setting charms and talismans strategically along the ley lines where their power was the greatest. She yearned desperately for the kind of faith in her witchcraft that would leave her feeling safe, but she knew that she didn't have that kind of power. Her charms were from the old times, passed down through the ages, but true magic had disappeared centuries ago and her talismans were little more than shadows from a bygone era. They wouldn't provide the protection she wanted, but she hoped and prayed they would help.

The Boutin residence was an old country home built upon a small plot of land poking up out of the bayou. It was an aging home with peeling paint, but it was built with strong wood. A snake- and alligator-infested swamp circled the small island like a moat around a castle, and she still didn't feel safe.

A dread like none she had ever known grew deep within her bosom. She had never seen any of this coming. For the first time since she had gained the sight when she was a young girl, she was unable to see into the future. What was coming was unknown to her.

Not for lack of trying. She consulted the cosmos to see what would be, but this wasn't her future to see; it was her grand-daughter's. She stared at Destiny, and maybe for the first time, she didn't see her as a little girl, but rather as the young woman she had become. Michelle felt a measure of pride as she watched Destiny calmly prepare for the coming danger.

Destiny stood at the window, staring out into the swamp. The moon shone down on the cypress trees, casting beams of light through the thin mist that rose from the swamp, lighting up the small ripples in the water into a dazzling field of twinkling diamonds. This would be the night. Destiny could feel the power in the air as her unseen future hastened to converge upon this spot and either kill her or die in the attempt.

Michelle cast her gaze around the room at her charms and portents and sighed. They weren't enough. She would never be, could never be satisfied with her preparations. "Come on, Cherie," she said, "we should get out of here. It's not safe here. I can't make it safe.

Destiny never deflected her eyes from the scene outside, but coolly replied, "It's too late, Nana. You. That should go find a safe corner to hide in."

"What do you mean it's too late?" Michelle sprang to the screen door and stared out into the swamp, but all she saw was the bayou. "I believe you, and I can feel it in my bones, that it's not safe here, that's why we should go."

"It's too late," Destiny repeated herself. "They're here." She pulled her grandmother from the door and tried pushing her into the center of the house. "Hide yourself."

Michelle pointed her thumb to the kitchen table, where their guest was sitting and asked, "What about him?"

"Don't worry about him."

"Don't worry about him? He's a stranger who shows up outta da blue and then in the blink of an eye, you says they is here and we be in some serious trouble? You don't know squat about him. He looks shifty to me."

"Shhh!" Destiny closed her eyes and cocked her head in different directions. She whispered, "Get in the corner like I told you! They have us surrounded."

Michelle bottled up her fear and shrank into a corner next to the armoire, where she kept her herbs and powders.

Destiny spread her senses well beyond the confines of their home. There were four men surrounding the house. Three soldiers with guns, and one very dangerous man who had hired them. Sorcerer or wizard is what they prefer to be called, although they haven't existed for over a thousand years, but he had the power. And there was the boy sitting inside at the table.

He sat quietly at the table, pretending to be a witch like Destiny; pretending he was their friend and was on the same side as Destiny and her grandmother, trying desperately to hide the real truth from her. Destiny knew that he was like her. He could do the old magic and he had both witch and sorcerer powers, but she didn't know that he had come with the men outside, that he was one of the sorcerer's men. The sorcerer, who had come to kill Destiny, had only recently developed his true magical powers, all in just the last couple weeks. All since Destiny first discovered her power and unleashed a wave of energy upon all the magical races and their descendants. The boy, who had also developed the old magic, had no idea how powerful the sorcerer had really become, and thought himself to be the most powerful magician the world had seen in centuries, but he didn't want to reveal himself until the last moment; so he waited.

Michelle scanned the room, cataloging all her talismans, afraid she may have missed a spot. She muttered prayers and incantations, hoping they would boost the power of her charms. There was little else she could do to help. She could make potions and talismans, and she could see into the past and the future, but only Destiny could make war. Destiny had learned a magic long extinct, a magic relegated to the annals of myth and fantasy. She had the real magic, the awful frightening power of children's tales and horror stories.

The leader of the mercenaries approached the house from the direction of the island's dock. His men were in place, and he was no longer concerned about stealth. He approached the house and took his stand in front of the porch. Clouds of dust stirred up from the dirt path by his boots. It mixed with an obnoxious odor coming from the fire pit and swirled around him, wafting past his nose. He waved his hand in front of his face to fan the stench away and yelled out, "You in the cabin, we have you surrounded! Come out with your hands in the air, and nobody will be harmed."

That's how it began. Destiny felt them approaching long before she saw them. She heard their words and heard the deceit in their voices. She knew what was coming. She had seen this much of her future, but she never saw how it ended.

The mercenaries stood ready with their weapons trained on the house. They were professionals. They kept their cool. They thought they were the great firepower on the scene. They had no idea what was about to transpire. It was the sorcerer that started everything. He stepped out from behind the leader of the mercenaries he hired and approached the house, pretending all the time to be a government official. He boldly stepped up onto the porch and said, "Just give us the boy and we'll go, simple as that."

"Liar! Liar!" Michelle yelled from her corner. "I sees straight through your lying tongue!"

The sorcerer hated the old woman. He hated all witches. It was an ancient hate that bubbled in the pit of his stomach. He threw open the screen door, prepared to rain fireballs all over the room, but especially towards Destiny.

She was ready for him and landed a barrage of spells on him, expelling him back out into the yard. She leaped out of the house and started directing fireballs and lightning at the sorcerer. He was quick to his feet, and started returning fireballs to Destiny, where they impacted upon her personal shield and fell to the ground in a shower of ash and embers. The two of them exchanged spells, with neither having an advantage over the other. The mercenaries opened fire, but their bullets were equally ineffective against Destiny's shields. The sorcerer's only advantage was his unadulterated ruthlessness.

Destiny may have known how to make fire and lightning, but the sorcerer knew how to make mayhem and destruction. He had an evil soul. He was born evil, and was trained to be even worse. He fired a giant fireball into the ground below Destiny. The explosion threw her into the air. Her protective shield dissipated as she slammed back to the ground. The mercenaries carried her limp form up to the house and tied her to a chair.

The sorcerer had felt his power grow the whole time they had closed in on her. Now, standing over her, he felt more powerful than ever. He extended his arms towards Destiny and spread them out at shoulder height. Thin blue filaments of electricity slowly extended from his fingers and wrapped themselves around her torso. The coils squeezed in on her. They were like hot razors against her skin. Her spine went cold, and the inside of her mouth tasted like metal. She screamed. At first, it was one long agonizing scream, then it was panting gasps and short sobbing.

He leaned his head backwards and breathed in deeply, savoring the smell of sulfur and electrical discharge in the air. "I want to thank you, little witch. You unlocked the box that has held our power bottled up for all these centuries. You should be very proud of yourself. I think, maybe, I will write songs about you. This is a time to rejoice. It's a time of victory! Well, not for you, little witch; you're going to die. This is my victory." He glanced over at the boy at the table and gloated. "To think, of all the centuries we wasted trying to breed a super witch, and all we got was you. All we really had to do was wait for her to unlock the power, and for me to accept my place as our people's messiah."

The sorcerer reared back to inflict the final blow. Destiny's vision retreated back into her mind. She could hear the sound of her nana's sobbing fade away behind her. She blamed herself. She thought things would end differently, and now, all she could do was close her eyes and beg the cosmos for mercy, wondering where she had gone wrong.

Two Weeks Earlier...

It was a beautiful morning in the bayou. The oppressive gloom of winter was gone, and the warm spring days were already shifting towards the even warmer summer temperatures, allowing the swamp to hold in some of the heat from the previous day. Destiny hopped out of bed and threw on a short jumper and some sandals so she could help her nana with the morning chores. Not that she was so eager to do chores, but picking eggs from the henhouse outside was better than being cooped up inside doing schoolwork.

Her grandmother was in the garden picking through the leaves and flowers, pulling the pests off her crops. She carried two bags with her; one for the bugs she would keep, and the other for those with no use. Her garden was filled with all the common vegetables that are found in family gardens everywhere, including tomatoes, peppers and corn. She also had an assortment of odd herbs and plants whose names sounded like something sold by an apothecary in a Shakespearean play.

Destiny went straight to the chicken coop. She slipped her fingers into the chicken wire, careful not to catch any splinters from the weathered grey wood, and swung open the spindly old gate. A fox would probably have no trouble getting into the coop, but the gators kept the predators away from here, and they never bothered venturing this far into their tiny island themselves.

Michelle sang out, "Good morning, Cherie, you sleep well?"

"I slept fine, except I had that dream again."

Michelle kept picking through her crops while she responded, "The dream where you was shootin' fire and lightning from your hands?"

"Yeah, that's three nights in a row now."

"It's just a dream. Sometimes the nightmares can haunt a soul like that."

Destiny fished fresh eggs out of the shallow straw nests and left the coop to join her nana. "Are you sure? Weren't you having the dreams long before you was my age?"

"Yeah, you right. You be a bit behind me there."

"So why do you think they's just regular dreams? You always told me I'd be having the dreams when I come to be a woman. Well, I'm fifteen now, and these are the dreams I've been having!"

"They cain't be the dreams," Michelle said. "We never be the ones that has the fire and lightning coming from our hands. Now, if you was dreaming that you was fighting against someone and they had the lightning, then it might be different, but our people don't do that."

Destiny frowned. Her sixteenth birthday was almost upon them and life was whizzing by, leaving her behind. She was descended from a long line of witches, going way back to the days when they held real power and did real magic, but she showed none of the signs that she would be one of them. She was afraid that she might be the odd generation that gets skipped by the gifts.

"Oh, stop with the long face," Michelle said with a big reassuring smile on her own face. "Your time will come. You just gots to be more patient with it."

"Yes'm."

Michelle stopped harvesting bugs long enough to stand and face Destiny. "Look," she said, "I know it's a nice day, but don't you got some schoolin' to get back to?"

"Yes'm." Destiny carried the eggs inside and put them in the cooler. Her nana had already left her lessons laid out on the table for her. The morning that was so beautiful, just turned into the same dreary morning she'd been having since winter started.

Destiny sat hunched over her books. They were the same books her mother and nana had learned from, which made them seem even more boring to her. She pulled the top book off the stack and wondered how a fifty-year-old textbook could still be called 'Practical Applications for Modern Geometry'. The school board had suggested new books to Michelle, but they also knew the financial situation for these remote kids, and as long as Destiny continued to pass her tests, they were willing to allow the old books.

Destiny cracked the book open to the page with the bookmark. The binding barely held the book together, and it didn't concern her any if it fell apart. She set the bookmark aside and started going through the lesson. Learning wasn't difficult for her, but she didn't like math too much, which was why her nana always put that lesson first. At the end of each lesson was a test. She may have dawdled through the reading, but at the ends of the lessons, the tests were completed as quickly as possible. She didn't always show her work, and sometimes counted on her fingers, but her answers were good, or at least good enough. She closed the book with her answer sheet and the bookmark inside, and set it aside. Her nana would check her answers later. Before opening the next book, she went to the cooler and poured herself a glass of lemonade. Destiny held the glass up to the light and counted the seeds.

"I hope you ain't puttin' no toe nails in there for me," Michelle teased from the doorway.

"No, Nana, one seed find your mate, two seeds adventure await s..."

Michelle finished for her, "and three seeds, guard your fate. Whatcha got?"

"Three seeds. It's the dreams I been havin'. I'm sure of it."

Michelle peered into the glass and said, "That one's broke clean in half. You only gots two and a half there."

Destiny frowned. "So, I'm going to meet my fate on an adventure with the man of my dreams?"

"Not your dreams, I hope."

A mockingbird warbled in the distance. Its melodious song easily pierced through the swamp, adding to the cheer of the dawning day.

"Nana, it's too nice a morning for schoolin'. Can't I go out for a walk and do my lessons later?"

Michelle smiled. "Nice try, missy, but you don't think I can tell the difference between a bona fide mockinbird and your friend Antwan?"

"It's Anton."

"Whatever. Ever time you goes off with him, I never sees you again till supper."

"Not every time."

"Enough."

"Sometimes his mama takes us up to Kingston."

"The two of you loose in that town? Doing God knows what!" Michelle knew what they did, but wasn't inclined to make it easy for the girl.

"We just goes to the library! You know how much I like to read. It's almost the same as school work!"

"Fine then. Go on with yourself, but you better be minding your manners. You thank his mama and make sure you do what she tells you. Ya hear?"

Destiny sprang to the porch and inserted her thumb and finger into her mouth. She let out a loud whistle back to Anton.

"I axed you if you heard me!"

"Yes'm. I heard you. I'll be good."

Destiny ran down the path to their small dock. The dock was little more than a wooden walkway with pontoons on the end to keep it afloat. Michelle followed her down the hill at a more leisurely pace. Anton motored the small pirogue up to the dock.

"Hey, Destiny."

"Hey, Anton. Where's your mama?"

"Hey, Ms. Boutin, my mama says 'hey' too. She's throwin' a party and she wanted me to spread the word."

Destiny was disappointed that she missed an opportunity to go into town.

Michelle reached the edge of the dock and said, "When is this party?"

"Tonight! I spect she's makin' ready right now."

"Tonight? Gahlee, that's too soon! What's the occasion?"

"Can't say. Mama has an announcement to be makin'."

Destiny couldn't contain her enthusiasm. "Please say yes, Nana! Mrs. Planchette throws the best shindigs!"

Michelle started to answer when Destiny grabbed her arm and pulled on her sleeve. She jumped up and down, chanting, "Say yes. Say yes. Say yes."

Michelle held her fingers to Destiny's lips so she could get a word in. "Tell your mama we'll be there, but that hardly gives us time to fix nuthin to bring."

"Mama says 'don't worry 'bout no food'. She's got enough for the whole dang parish. I gotsta go spread the word some more. Bye, Destiny. See y'all later."

Destiny returned to her schoolwork, but her mind was on the party. Mrs. Planchette's parties were famous. She always had good food and good music to go with it, plus everybody showed up for her parties. There weren't many chances to see everyone all in one place.

Destiny worried a bit about getting ready. She only had two dresses to choose from, so that would be easy, but she would have liked a chance to pull a brush through her hair. Knowing her nana, they'd be going early so she could lend a hand. She tried concentrating on her lessons so she could get them out of the way.

"Nana, are you sure this history book is still any good?"

"Why? You think the past has been changed since that book was writ?"

"It keeps calling Russia Prussia. It's very confusing."

Michelle was picking through her special bottles. Just because Mrs. Planchette may have enough food for everyone didn't mean she'd go empty-handed. "Prussia is not the same as Russia. Look at the maps."

"I'm lookin' at the maps. It looks like Russia to me."

Michelle stopped what she was doing and went to look over her shoulder. She pointed at the map and said, "Look, there's Germany to the left, and Hungary down below. Russia be way up here. That there is where Poland ends up being."

"Then why don't it just say Poland?"

"Because this is history, and they has to go through some wars before it just says Poland."

"I'm confused."

"I think mebbe you're distracted. Could be you should put your books away for today and go get yourself ready for the party."

Destiny hugged her nana and said, "Thank you, Nana. I love you."

She closed up the history book and dashed to her room. She already knew which dress she wanted to wear, but still had her hair to deal with. She brushed her hair every day, but didn't always force the brush through the deep matte that formed underneath. She struggled now to regain control over the underneath hair, bit by bit.

Michelle returned to her storeroom and selected a pink bottle with lead veins crisscrossed across the surface of the glass. She took the bottle to the kitchen and poured one of her best skin creams into it. She completed her gift with a matching ribbon around the stopper. Now she could get herself ready to go.

She was no longer blessed with Destiny's youthful hair; it turned white on her ages ago. She had a lotion that could return a creamy blond color to her hair, but it did little to make her hair as soft and manageable as it was in her youth. She put on her Sunday dress and checked on Destiny.

She found her granddaughter fighting against her hair and tried taking the brush to help her.

"No thanks, Nana, I got this. It hurts less when I do it myself."

"It will hurt less if you put some of my tonic in your hair, too."

"I know, but it smells so sweet that I would have to chase the bugs away all night."

Destiny finished fussing with her hair and joined her nana, who sat waiting on the porch, enjoying the weather. Seeing her granddaughter dressed and ready to go, Michelle grabbed her big purse with the gift inside and headed down the hill to the boat. She pulled the small craft closer to the dock and climbed into the back. The skiff had three seats and Michelle placed her purse on the middle seat in front of her, leaving the front-most seat for Destiny. Once inside, Destiny pulled the rope off the hook that held it and they pushed the craft away from the shore.

It was early in the afternoon, and the weather had warmed considerably. Winter was behind them, and the bayou was itself again. The large cypress trees provided patchy shade that flickered on them as they passed beneath the giant boughs. Michelle knew the way by heart and easily poled the boat between the great trees. Destiny patted a wet cloth around her neck, then paused as a slight breeze blew across the swamp and licked the moisture from her face. The breeze combined with the shade made the weather at least somewhat tolerable. Michelle hummed a light tune as they pushed past some disinterested gators and wary heron. A little past the half-way point to Cricket Bend, they emerged from the shade and into the full light, where they were pelted with the full brunt of the mighty sun.

The swamp wasn't particularly attractive, but it had its moments. As they crossed the tree line and emerged into the sunlight, the surface of the water turned bright green from the thick carpet of duckweed, broken only by the ever vigilant eyes of patient alligators waiting for an unfortunate crane or careless duck.

They could see Cricket Bend in the distance. It was home to the general store where Michelle did business, and the post office which provided them with an address. Michelle turned the boat to the left and headed up around the edge of the swamp.

The Planchette plantation was on the edge of the swamp on the mainland side. At one time, it was a thriving sugar farm, but Mr. Planchette had sold most of the farmland to a neighboring plantation, and sold the mineral rights for a few select parcels to an oil company. The Planchettes retained the home and were comfortably set for life.

Michelle leaned on her pole, pushing the small boat up the long branch of water that ran the full length of the bayou. Destiny heard a motor approaching and turned to see who it was. She waved and shouted, "Hey, Danielle!" Michelle turned also and saw the Pinet family in their full size motor boat.

Mr. Pinet slowed his boat and pulled alongside them and said, "Bonjoo, Madam, and Mademoiselle; your boat can tow?"

Destiny grinned broadly and bobbed her head up and down while throwing them the bowline. Michelle pulled her pole up and laid it on the side of the boat, grateful for the assistance.

Mr. Pinet tied off the rope and put his boat back in gear, pulling the rope taught. He towed them the rest of the way. Mrs. Pinet leaned over the back of their boat and tried shouting pleasantries to Destiny and Michelle. Destiny could see that she was saying something, but could not hear her over the din of the motor, and simply shrugged. Seeing they could not hear her, Mrs. Pinet considered trying again, but ultimately decided to simply shrug back and smile. There would be plenty of time to socialize.

Mr. Pinet kept the throttle slow enough that Destiny and Michelle weren't jarred about by his wake, but Destiny didn't care. It was much faster than her nana could push the boat, and she was thrilled by the sense of speed and the cooling breeze in her face. The shore on the right was lined with a thick carpet of grass, broken by an occasional dock as they passed a modest home here and there. Most of the homes along this stretch of shore were vacation rentals where city people could come see the bayou. On the left, the cypress trees still marked the edge of the deep swamp.

The water narrowed. Mr. Pinet slowed the boats a bit more as they started gliding over another layer of duckweed. The carpet of duckweed was made of tiny little green things about the size of mosquitos. They floated on the top and stuck to your skin if you swam in them, but the only danger they posed was to plants below that may have wanted some sun to poke through. The surface of the water became clogged with more life than just the obnoxious little green weed. The Pinet boat thumped now and then, as it ran into the more substantial hyacinths. The hyacinths produced beautiful flowers summer after summer, but they were voraciously hardy plants and grew into a web of inter-connected plants that not only shaded the water, but also made navigation difficult. The gators and many waterfowl of the bayou helped keep the hyacinths from forming large nets, but the local lakes were threatened by the plants, resorting to herbicides to keep them in check.

Mr. Pinet pulled the boats up to the Planchette dock and tied his rope to the pier while his wife hopped up onto the dock and offered to take Michelle's purse. Mr. Pinet then helped Destiny and Michelle out of their boat and pulled it around the dock and up onto the shore with the other pirogues and smaller craft.

It was apparent from the music that they weren't as early as Michelle had hoped. Mrs. Planchette's get-togethers attracted a fine crowd. She should have expected as much.

Anton was the first to greet them. "Hey Danielle, Destiny, come see what my mama got us!"

A nod of Michelle's head was all Destiny needed to go running off with Danielle behind the slender boy. Colored lights were strung from poles, marking the perimeter of the yard, with many tables and benches prepared for eating and drinking. The girls followed Anton through the tables and past the flagstone dance floor where the band was already playing. He led them past the back porch and off to the side of their house.

The Planchette home was the largest in the parish. It was an old plantation home with a wide porch that circled around all sides of it. The porch eaves were supported by large columns and provided shade to the home year round. Anton slowed his pace as they started to dodge the many young children running around playing.

Destiny could see where they were heading and pulled to a stop. "Anton, that's for kids!" Mrs. Planchette had rented one of those big, inflatable dinosaurs that the kids jumped around inside. Danielle never stopped and had already disappeared inside the large purple monster.

Anton came back and took Destiny's hand. "Not dat," he said, "she got us one for just us, and not for the teet bebs." He pulled her past the dinosaur to the large trampoline that was securely anchored to the ground. "Pretty cool?"

It still seemed kind of babyish, but Destiny didn't hesitate to climb aboard and start jumping.

Michelle and Mrs. Pinet crossed the dance floor to the kitchen door. In some respects, the home had two front sides; one with a road lined by oaks that leads out to the highway, and one that leads to the dock, which was actually used more than the road.

"Ahhh! Michelle! Julia! Welcome, welcome." Arlene Planchette welcomed her latest guests. They each handed her their respective gifts, which she took and placed on a table with the others. She kissed

Julia on both cheeks, followed by Michelle. Michelle whispered into her ear, "It's a skin lotion. You can use it to hide that scar on Anton's leg if you wish. I uses it to hide my liver spots." Arlene had no intention of wasting it on Anton's leg, and Michelle never really intended for her to.

Arlene put her arms around both women and said, "Now I must insist that you two leave my kitchen. The cooks are far too busy. I do believe you will find quite a bit of new gossip collected around the lemonade cooler, and you might find the men folk collecting around the bar by the dance floor. I'm counting on you, Julia, to drag that good lookin' husband of yours out on the dance floor and make this party happen."

Julia hugged Arlene and added, "I might just let him have a drink or two before I gets him to dance."

The women were, as Arlene had said, talking and sipping lemonade. They stepped quietly to join in the outside of the circle and catch what was being said.

"...so, my boy takes a stick and whacks that gator on the nose and sends him back where he come from. Oh, hey Michelle, did I tells you how my boy saved his baby sister with just a stick and his bare hands?"

"Give it a rest," Zeline interrupted, "nobody wants to hear no more about your son whacking a baby gator on the nose." Zeline was always the loudest and most obnoxious, and she seldom thought before she spoke.

Ezora was incensed. "Baby? It warn't no baby, it be four feet if it was one."

"That be a baby," Zeline retorted, "My boy works for the government catching dem eight foot monsters for the zoo. He caught a white one once. Made them pay extras for that one."

Ezora ignored Zeline's boast and took Michelle aside to retell her story.

The sky turned a brilliant pink as the sun slipped down below the tree line. The lights strung around the property came on, casting a warm, cozy glow to the yard. Mrs. Planchette called everyone to attention from the bandstand and announced that the food was ready.

A small squad of men and women dressed in neat white coats carried domed platters from the kitchen and set them on a long table next to the bandstand. Two of them with chef hats stood ready at the table, carving meats for the guests. The line formed quickly. Destiny and Anton were near the front of the line, while Michelle was towards the back with Mrs. Thibodeaux. She had no worries. There was always enough food to go around twice over.

The line moved quickly. Guests carrying plates piled high with meats and skewered giant shrimp in one hand, and bowls of gumbo in the other hand, arranged themselves at the many tables. Pitchers of beer and lemonade were already arranged on all the tables. Most parties around these parts were potluck affairs, and even though the Planchette's were more prone to have them catered, they never sacrificed on the home-cooked quality of the food. Mrs. Planchette gave her guests plenty of time to finish their meals and even have second helpings before the chefs brought out the crème brûlée and ice cream. During desert, she centered herself in front of the band to make her announcement.

"Friends, if I can have your attention for just a moment, I have some news. I'll keep it brief so the party can continue. As most of you no doubt know, it's been three years now since I lost my dear husband to the swamp."

More than one head turned in the direction of Zeline, afraid she would yell out that he was eaten by a gator, but she said nothing.

"They been lonely years, but the time for loneliness is passed."

This was not part of the gossip, and a small amount of tittering erupted from the guests.

"No," she continued, "I'm not taking on a husband..."

"Why not? Heck, I'll marry you!"

She smiled and said, "Thank you Rene, but as romantic and charming as that proposal was, I don't think I'll be marrying the oldest gigolo in the parish this year; but ask me again in a few more years."

"In a few more years?" he said, "I'm eighty now. I might not have a few more years!"

Everyone laughed and Arlene continued with her announcement, "I've asked my sister to come live with me. She just lost her husband to the war and..."

"Not the war," her sister slurred. "I said I lost him to the WHORE." Arlene's sister had spent the evening at the bar drinking, and showed no signs of slowing down. "That son of a bitch got his whore knocked up, and he left me."

Arlene tried to hide her embarrassment and said, "That be my sister, Margot; everyone say 'hey' to my sister!"

The guests lifted their glasses and shouted, "Hey!"

"Now that everyone has met my sister, I think she's had enough party for one night." Arlene went to her sister and got one of the men to help take her inside. As they reached the porch, she turned and yelled to the crowd, "Laissez le Bon temp rouler!"

Rene lifted his glass and shouted out, "Oui oui! Let the good times roll!"

The band struck up a lively Chank-a-Chank and couples appeared on the dance floor, with beers in hand and a genuine lust for life on their faces. Several of the mothers packed up the children and put them to bed in the Planchette family room. It was time for the Fais do-do, the party that comes after the children are asleep.

Destiny sat at the table sipping on her lemonade when Anton sat next to her and playfully shoved her towards the center of the bench. He showed her his beer and asked, "You want me to get you something a little stronger?"

"No thanks, I'm fine."

The two of them tapped their toes to the music and watched the couples gyrate across the flagstone. He took another gulp of his beer and asked, "You ever feel like life just passed by you? Like it was a train you forgot to get on?"

"All the time," she said, "My nana keeps telling me my time will come, but I feel like I'm already missing something."

Arlene came up behind them and tapped them on the shoulders. "What is you two sitting around for? There's music, there's dancin', and you makes such a cute couple." She nudged her son towards Destiny. "You axe her to dance."

"Mama! She don't like me like that. She gots her beau already in her mind and he ain't me."

"So what if she gots the ahnvee for some other man? You be here now. Be a man and axe her."

Destiny laughed and said, "No use fighting it. We should just go get it over with."

The two of them left the table for the dance floor just as the band finished one song and started a slow dance.

He took her in his arms and danced with her. "You know," he said, "if things was different, I would like you that way."

"I know," she said, "but they're not different. He's out there some-where. I just hope I'm in the right place when it's time to meet him."

He lifted his beer and said, "Here's to your Mr. Right being Mr. Right on time."

"Thanks," she said, "yours too."

"Yeah, mine too."

Old Rene caught Michelle by surprise and asked her to dance. She shouldn't really have been surprised, he was always catching her unawares at these affairs, and she didn't really want to dance, but she was too kind to turn him down. He had always been very agile for his age, and was a far better dancer than most people gave him credit for. He swung her around the floor for a couple songs, but when he excused himself to refill his beer, she snuck off to find Ezora crowded around a table with a handful of other women. As she approached, she could hear Zeline reading the bones to the small group. As far as Michelle knew, Zeline was just a crazy old woman who thought she was a witch.

"...the bones be telling me that we're gonna have a good spell of weather clear to June. They also says someone will come dat will change how some of us think on things."

Ezora spotted Michelle joining them and said, "Give it up Zeline, you never could read dem bones. Let Michelle give them a real read."

Michelle shook her head and pleaded, "I'm just here to have a good time."

Except for Zeline, the small crowd of women began chanting, "Bones...bones...bones..."

"Gracious, alrighty then," Michelle caved, "give me the bones."

Zeline wasn't inclined to hand the bones over, so Ezora snatched the bones and the tin that kept them, and handed them to Michelle. Zeline glared at Ezora and stomped off, uninterested in anything Michelle would see in the bones.

Michelle stood at the end of the table and looked at the bones inside of the tin. She turned the tin three times in her hands and blew lightly into the cup. She turned it three more times, then placed her hand over the opening and shook it five times. She closed her eyes and held the tin high over her head, then lowered it and spilled the bones across the table. She stared at the bones, but did not speak. She didn't like what she saw, and passed her hands over the bones, feeling their energy. "Something's wrong with these bones. This ain't right." She started to scoop up the bones, but Ezora stopped her.

"Tain't nothin' wrong with dem bones. Read da bones."

Michelle had never felt this much fear or anxiety over reading bones before. She looked at the faces that surrounded her, hesitant to continue.

"Go on with it!"

"Very well," her lower lip trembled as she spoke. "It says something is going to happen. A stranger is coming, and...and...well, that's what it says."

Michelle tried scooping them up again, but Ezora stopped her a second time. "What is it you be holding back?"

Michelle saw all their expectant faces, but it was not good news.

"Tell us."

Michelle stood up to leave the table. All traces of gaiety from the party had been erased. Her voice was low and solemn as she said, "A stranger is coming. And someone is going to die."

The crowd gasped, "Who?"

"They don't tell me that."

Ezora sat Michelle back down at the table, then sat directly across from her. "Then you gots to read each of us one at a time."

Michelle read them one by one, but the bones didn't reveal who would die. "I'm sorry ladies, I've read all of you, but the bones aren't telling us who."

Destiny had finished dancing with Anton and came to see what her grandmother was up to. She sat down next to her nana and saw the bones on the table. She also saw the curiously anxious expressions on everyone's faces.

"You haven't read everyone," Ezora said, "you haven't read yourself, or Destiny, or anyone else at the party except us."

Destiny jumped up and seated herself across from her grandmother. "Read me! Read me!"

"No," Michelle said, "I'm tired."

"Aw, Nana, please?"

"Read her," Ezora insisted, "you can't drop that on us and leave it unfinished."

Michelle relented and prepared the bones one more time. She spilled them onto the table and looked horrified at the results. She refused to speak, but her voice read the bones without her command, "Someone near you is gonna die. If you is not careful, you could die too."

CHAPTER 2

A hush came over the women as Michelle stared at the bones on the table, and the smile eroded from Destiny's face. Ezora was the first to break the silence. "You know what? I think you was right. These bones is broke. They must be tainted from that fake Zeline." She wrapped her arms around Michelle's shoulders and continued, "This don't mean nothing. We'll all just forget this ever happened." But they wouldn't forget, none of them.

Michelle slowly pushed herself up from the table and said, "Thank Arlene for me. I think I best be going now. Where's my purse? Come on, Destiny. Has anyone seen my purse?"

Mrs. Pinet, who had joined the women in time to see Michelle's reading of Destiny, said, "You ain't goin' nowhere like this. Ezora, don't you let them leave. I'll fetch my husband to take them home." She ran off hollering, "Danielle! Carl! Come on now. It's time to go."

It wasn't time to leave. These parties went on till near sunrise, but Carl Pinet knew his wife well, and recognized from her voice when it was no time to question her. Seeing her walking Michelle to the dock, he tied the Boutin skiff to the back of his boat and prepared to make way. He started up the motors and lit the searchlights that pointed forward so he could navigate the bayou in the dark; and it was dark.

The skies were overcast, turning the half-moon into a mere glow in the clouds. Michelle was visibly shaken as Mrs. Pinet walked her to their boat and helped her into one of the captain's chairs mounted behind the pilot's seat.

Destiny and Danielle sat in the back and waved goodbye to Anton, who stood at the end of the dock, waiting for them to leave.

Danielle saw how serious her mother was and whispered to Destiny, "What happened?"

"My nana was reading the bones."

"So? They always end up with the bones, eventually. What happened this time?"

"It got kind of scary. You should have seen her face. She looked like she had just seen the most horrible thing in the world, and then she said someone was going to die. Someone near me was going to die."

Danielle stiffened slightly, separating some from Destiny.

"Don't worry," Destiny said, "I don't think it's gonna be tonight. She said something was going to happen, and someone near me would die, and..." Destiny swallowed hard. Her eyes wetted with the revelation of what her nana had really said.

"And what?" Danielle pleaded.

Destiny's voice choked slightly as she finished, "...and I might die too."

Danielle gasped and thought about it a moment, then put her arms around Destiny, holding her. "Maybe it's a trick; a cruel play on words. Maybe you're just going to dye your hair. We can do that, you know. My mama can get us some dye and we can do your hair. Then you'll be safe. What color do you want to be?"

Destiny wiped the tears from her cheeks with the back of her hand. She smiled weakly but shook her head. "I don't think that's gonna work, but thanks for trying. It's probably best I stay by myself until I figures this out."

"No!" Danielle ran their conversation back through her mind. "Your nana said you MIGHT die. That's what you told me. Well, you might die if you don't have your friends around you. Maybe you need us to keep you safe!"

"She also said someone near me would die. I don't want that to be one of my friends."

Danielle felt trapped by her own logic. "Maybe we'll figure something out."

"Yeah, maybe."

Carl pulled the boat up as close as he could to the Boutin dock. He used a pole to push the boat's stern around close enough so Michelle and Destiny could step out onto the dock. He untied the skiff and tied it to the hook on the dock. He started climbing back into his boat when Julia stood in his way, waving her hands and shushing him away. He shrugged back at her.

"Go on up to the house," she said, "and make sure they're safe before we go."

He started to ask, "What's goin'..."

She stopped him with her fingers to his lips and said, "I'll explain later. You just go be sure the house is safe."

He tied his boat to the dock and briskly walked past Michelle and Destiny, who had stalled at the end of the dock. Julia and Danielle jumped out of the boat to walk with their friends up to the house. Carl went from room to room, not knowing even what he was looking for. There were no intruders, so he went to the porch and called out, "Everything is fine in here." Julia and Danielle escorted Michelle and Destiny inside and ended up staying a spell, drinking tea and catching Carl up on the incident with the bones until Michelle was near herself again.

Michelle's eyes had barely cleared when she looked around the table at her friends, and they were misty again. "I'm so sorry to be such a bother to you folk. It's late, an' you needs to get yourselves home."

"You're no bother," Julia said. "You'd do the same for us."

"Just the same, you needs to get back to your lives while we got us some figgerin to do."

Julia shook her head. "Right now, figgerin is the last thing you needs. Sleep is what you ladies have to do. You can't be worrying about dem bones. How many times have you told me the bones could be tellin' on next year or something in thirty years? You needs to get past it."

"Thank you Julia, sleep does sound good."

"And, I tell you what, we'll just come call on you once in a while."

"That be nice. Maybe bring your dominoes and we can play a spell."

Julia frowned and said, "Maybe I'll just bring some cards. I think we've all had enough of dem bones for a while."

A light, halfhearted laugh escaped everyone's lips, and the Pinets left down the hill and out on their boat.

Carl put the boat in gear, leaving the motors low, and puttered out into the swamp. He stood behind the wheel, slowly picking his way through the Cyprus trees and the sandbars. Julia and Danielle stood near, leaning against his shoulders, treasuring their family just a little bit more than they might have earlier that day.

The bayou outside the Boutin home played a soothing symphony, with crickets and cicadas providing a steady background for a lone frog's solo song. A pair of owls silently hunted rodents, occasionally adding their own counterpoint to the frog's song. Even the alligators who hunted at night melded the splash of the kill into the soothing sounds of the evening.

Destiny and Michelle both slept soundly. Were she younger, Destiny might have crawled into bed with her nana. Even without sharing her bed, she felt like she was wrapped in a cloak of love and comfort, and slept without any further dreams or interruptions.

The moon passed overhead and slipped down into the western world. The first rays of the sun woke the early birds, and the bayou was filled with a new song.

Michelle was already up planning her day when Destiny finally joined her. "Hey, sleepyhead, how you feeling?"

"Tired mostly."

"You have that dream again?"

Destiny shook her head. "Not last night, but that don't mean nuthin. I still been having it often enough."

Michelle looked at her granddaughter with a critical eye and said, "I don't know what's goin' on with your dreams, but after last night, I'm not gonna fight it no more. I left you your lessons on the table. I'm goin' up to Bend for some supplies, and we's gonna start your other lessons tomorrow."

Destiny's spirits jumped up a couple levels. "Can I go with you? Please?"

Michelle shook her head and explained, "You already missed your lessons from yesterday. Don't you got some studyin' for a big test next week?"

"We won't be gone that long, will we? Besides, I can bring one of my books and study on the way."

"Well, I gots to admit, I ain't so keen on leaving you alone here. You make sure and bring that book, ya hear?"

"Yes'm. I love you, Nana."

Michelle fixed a modest breakfast for the two of them and started pulling her wares from the pantry while she inventoried her ingredients.

A voice called from outside, "Yoo Hoo! Michelle? Where y'at?"

She recognized the call of Mrs. Thibodeaux.

"Morning, Ezora," Michelle shouted out, "we be here."

"You gots time for me? I tink dat witch Zeline put da voodoo gris-gris on me."

"Oh, Ezora, you always be tinking you got dis curse or dat curse."

"And you always be makin' it better."

"I was on my way to be makin' groceries, but come on in, I can spare a moment."

"Nana!" Destiny shouted. "I'm still in my jammies!"

"Well, you best pull some pants on over your drawers then, we has visitors."

Destiny jumped into her short jeans and pulled a blouse over her head. She peaked out of the screen just in time to see Ezora reach the porch and take her first step up the stairs.

Ezora was followed by her son, who stopped at the bottom of the stairs when he saw Destiny in the screen door. "Hey, Destiny."

"Hey, Gilbert."

Gilbert kept his hands in his pockets and said, "I spect my mama's gonna be a spell. You wanna see my new snake?"

"My nana's taking me into town today."

"Oh," he said, disappointed, "dass OK."

"But, I s'pose your mama will be collecting you before we have to leave."

Destiny pushed the screen open and sprinted down the steps just as Mrs. Thibodeaux reached the door. Ezora caught the screen, then turned to her son and said, "Shah you two! Git you down to da bank before you pulls dat nasty teet critter from your pocket."

"Destiny, Cherie," Michelle said, "Would you collect a fresh egg for your nana before you runs off to play?"

"Yes'm."

Mrs. Thibodeaux found a seat at Michelle's table mumbling to herself, "Da egg. Da egg. It always works when she does da egg."

Destiny retrieved the egg for her nana, then skipped around the house with Gilbert and down the bank to a special spot where they have played since they were little. Gilbert was a few years younger than Destiny, and she found her tastes regarding fun and play were different from his, but friends were too few for her to be picky about how old they were or what they wanted to do for fun.

Gilbert reached into his pocket and pulled out a small, slender snake. It was almost a foot long and less than half an inch across. It wriggled in his hands as he held it up for her to see.

She pointed a finger and touched it on the nose. "I like how it flicks its tongue out at me. It tickles."

"Yeah, you right." Gilbert put the snake back in his pocket and sat down on a log they had set up years ago.

Destiny sat down next to him and skipped a stone across the water.

Gilbert waited for the ripples to die down before saying, "My mama's feelin' poorly agin."

Destiny picked up another stone and felt the weight in her hands. "Seems to me she's always feeling ill."

"Yeah," he said, "but she says Ms. Zeline be hexin' her."

"She always thinks that, too."

The conversation stalled. Destiny and Gilbert took turns skipping stones across the water.

"Destiny, can I ax you somethin?"

"What?"

"Is your nana a witch?"

"Why do you ask?"

"I dunno. Jest that Mama always come to her when she be tinkin she got da gris-gris."

"What if she was? Would it be such a bad thing, if my nana was a witch?"

Gilbert shrugged his shoulders and said, "It seems to me that witches are ugly and do bad tings to people, but I ain't never seen your nana do nuthin bad, so I guess I'm just bein' silly."

"I don't think Zeline is that ugly."

"Yeah, she is."

Destiny laughed. "What if my nana's a good witch?"

"I ain't never heered of no good witch."

"GILBERT!" Ezora's voice bellowed through the swamp, causing ducks and heron to launch themselves into the air.

"COMING!" Gilbert yelled back.

Destiny walked him back up around the house and down to their boat. She wondered what he would think about her if he thought she was a witch.

"See ya, Destiny."

"See ya."

Michelle put the slab of bacon that Ezora had left as payment into the icebox and resumed packing up the lotions she had pulled from the pantry, placing them into a burlap sack. She hefted the sack and carted it down the dirt path to the small dock. Michelle set her wares just aft of the pilot's seat and held the craft steady while Destiny climbed into the seat up front with a carrying bag that held her school book and a few school supplies. Michelle settled herself in and poled the craft away from the dock.

As they approached Cricket Bend, they could see the general store's dock, larger and sturdier than their own little floating walkway. It stretched out into the swamp, where it serviced the many locals who lived in the bayou. The dock was the only structure on this side of the road that ran along the shore where the mainland met the swamp. Michelle poled up to the dock and threw a rope around a piling. Destiny climbed out of the boat and helped her grandmother lift her merchandise up.

Michelle wagged her finger at Destiny and said, "I want you to take your book and sit yourself down in front of the general store. You can get yourself a soda, but I expect to see you readin' your book."

"Yes'm."

Michelle flung the sack over her shoulder and followed Destiny across the road to the red and grey building.

The proprietor opened the door for them as Destiny reached the porch. "Bonjoo, Bonjoo bebs. Gahlee, if teet Cherie tain't growed up some today? Wontch you come in out o' da sun dare?" He held the door and asked, "I can be gettin' you sumpin today?"

Destiny skipped into the store. "My nana said I could have a soda."

"Sure, sure," he said, "but might be you has to reach back dare if you wants a cold one."

"Morning, Henry." Michelle flung the sack onto the counter. "I only got you the regular lotions today."

Henry counted the bottles and checked the stock on his shelves. He scribbled some numbers on a piece of paper and announced, "How thirty two fitty be?"

Michelle handed Henry a list of spices, oils, and animal parts she required. "I be needing some more jars, too."

He started collecting the items into a small basket. "Dare be some new tings on your list today. You mekin up sompin special for next week?" He pushed some of his products around in the cooler, looking behind and under what was there. "Tsk, tsk. Looks like I only has four pound of the beef tallow, but I can get you an extra pound of sheep tallow if you likes."

"It will do."

He scratched some more figures out and said, "Dat be six fitty lef for you and Miss Destiny."

Michelle caught sight of Destiny dawdling at a rack of postcards and shot her the evil eye.

"Nana, can I send my mama a postcard for my birthday? Please! I just know it will brighten her day!"

Michelle exhaled a parent's sigh of frustration. "What on earth am I going to do with you, child?"

"Please Nana? I won't ask you for nothing else."

Henry mumbled, "Dat be one fine day when da young'un not axe for nuttin."

"Fine," Michelle said to her, "You send your mama a postcard, but then you get yourself to your schoolin'. I mean it now, ya hear?"

"Yes'm. I promise."

Destiny selected her postcard, showed it to Henry, and skedaddled through the door to the porch.

Michelle started browsing the small aisle of clothes, looking for a birthday gift for Destiny.

"Pahdonne moi, Cherie," Henry said, "I lef me sompin in da cellar. I be right back."

Michelle looked through the small selection, and picked out a short white blouse that tied at the waist, the way she sees the girls wearing them these days.

Henry returned with another burlap sack that he plopped up onto the counter next to Michelle's. "I nearly forgot my mind. Mr. Woolsly sends you a big tanks for dat potion you done him. He says his wife was up 'n' around in no time at all, and he sent over dis special bag o' bones and a half quart of elk tallow for you."

"Gracious, that be mighty kind of him. Please convey my many thanks to Mr. Woolsly."

"Take care wit dat one. He put some poo-yee smells in dat jar."

"I'll be careful." Michelle showed him the blouse and asked, "How much for this?"

He closed one eye and scratched his head, as if that would help him remember, and then announced, "Three fitty, dass how much dat one is, three fitty."

"That can't be. Are you sure?"

"Coo-yon me! I buyed me too many o' dem," he lied. "I swear you be doin' me a jie-yon favor by takin' dat off my hands."

He wrapped the blouse to keep it clean, and packed the new merchandise in her sack, along with the bag of bones.

"Thank you Henry." Michelle accepted her change, hefted the sack over her shoulder and headed for the door.

"Always a pleasure beb. Y'all come back now."

Michelle exited the small store, and Destiny was not where she was supposed to be. She walked the length of the porch and found Destiny around the corner, leaning against the railing, looking at the diner.

"Destiny Faith Boutin, what did I tell you?"

"Sorry, Nana, the bus come by, and I was just lookin' at all them people gettin' off it."

"And what did you see that was more important than your studies?"

"I don't know. I just be playin' a game, lookin' at dem all, and wonderin' where they come from and where they be goin'."

"You stop dat. I teached you to talk better than yo' old nana."

"Yes'm, but sometimes I just wonder what it's like to be one of them, goin' in the diner to eat and all."

"Someday, maybe, you and me will go in there for our supper, if you ever does your schoolin', that is. Did you send off your postcard?"

"Oh, NO!!" Destiny pulled a pencil out of her bag and wrote on the back, "Hi Mama, it's me, Destiny. My birthday is coming up. I'm gonna be sixteen, and Nana says we can come visit you. Love, Destiny." She scribbled an address on the other side and ran the length of the porch to where the postal station was.

The general store, the diner, and the postal station were all that there was to Cricket Bend. The postal station was just a bunch of post boxes with key locks and an outgoing mailbox. Michelle and Destiny's mailing address was simply Cricket Bend, Louisiana, no street name or house number. If it weren't for the post boxes, it probably wouldn't even have a name, and it certainly wouldn't have been called Cricket Bend. It was originally called Crooked Bend, named after the waterway that runs through this spot. The water is shaped like a long bend in a river, but it doesn't flow like a river, and is really just a branch of the swamp. It was a government man that named it Cricket Bend. He was the same man who told someone to build a post office here. Maybe his hearing was bad, or more likely, he just couldn't understand everyone's accent well enough, but it'd been Cricket Bend since around the big depression, and most everyone had come to accept it.

Destiny ran back and grabbed her things. She nodded her head to her nana and started back to the dock. Michelle watched her run and saw all the signs. She recognized the restlessness and the wanderlust in her granddaughter. She had felt the same tug to see what was out there when she was younger, too. Her mama saw the same signs, but didn't cry when Michelle packed her things to go see the world, because her mama, like almost everyone in her family, especially the women, had the sight. She knew her baby would return, just like she had already known she would leave. She also knew that when she returned, she would come back a new woman.

As a young girl, Michelle had already demonstrated the sight, and was much further along in her training than Destiny was. She knew her destiny was out there somewhere, waiting for her to find it, and she was ready to meet it. Things were different in those days. It was the '60s, the war raged on, and young people everywhere rebelled against the values of their parents and experimented with new family and community models. Michelle lived the life of a gypsy. Her sight made her an oracle among the hippies. She didn't just turn on, tune in, and drop out, like so many others of her generation. She was already tuned in to the universe in ways few of them could ever understand. She was wise beyond her years, because she came with the built-in wisdom of her ancestors. She never adopted a new name for herself, because she wasn't searching for a new identity, but as word spread of the girl with a link to the cosmos, she had become legend, and her legend carried the name Crystal. Her closest friends still knew her as Michelle Alliene Boutin. Life was good for Michelle, but when she felt the calling to return home, she did so without hesitation, and she did not come back alone. She brought a small baby girl, Tempest Storm Boutin.

Michelle's mother raised an eyebrow when she first heard her granddaughter's name, but she sensed the troubled path that lay before the child and knew it was apt.

Tempest's early years were much like any other young girl's. She played with dolls, had imaginary friends, and begged for a puppy dog.

Her mother and grandmother could sense that her future would be filled with mental turmoil and anguish, but for all their combined powers, neither of them could ever glimpse an actual picture of that future. They could feel great chaos and confusion, and even greater terror, but all their attempts to see what lay ahead for Tempest were blocked, as if by a curtain beyond which they could not see.

The child before them, however, could not be more different from the horrific shadow they perceived from her future. She was a sweet, vibrant child who adored them and loved playing with them, but she did not like their magic and would disappear out into the yard whenever she found them staring into their candles. She even shied away when they were just making the lotions and potions that they sold for the tourists. Many times they had tried, but failed to get her to sit down with them so they could allay her fears of their craft. Most times, when they wanted to have the talk, she just was never around. On those few occasions when they found her to have the talk, she squirmed and fidgeted and made excuses like her tummy hurt or she was too sleepy, anything to avoid the subject, but eventually the subject itself became unavoidable.

Her innocent years only lasted ten birthdays until the middle of her tenth year when puberty struck, and with the onset of puberty, her mind exploded with thoughts from her mother and grandmother. She covered her ears and wrapped her pillows around her head, but they only grew worse with every passing day.

When Michelle and her mother tried to explain the need for her to learn to control her abilities, she didn't want to listen to them and could barely hear them over the din, anyway. Michelle accessed her ancestral memories, searching for a cure, but there were many memories, covering thousands of years. Tempest was almost twelve before Michelle discovered the ancient ways to settle Tempest's mind and bring her peace, but there wasn't enough magic left in the world. Michelle hadn't the power to use the old techniques, anyway.

It was very old magic from times long forgotten, when witches and magicians were commonplace; from a time long before using or even believing in such abilities branded you as a simpleminded fool.

Michelle had exhausted all avenues and had lost hope of ever curing Tempest with the old magic. She renewed her efforts to see into her daughter's dark future. What few glimpses she did manage were short and chaotic. A veil surrounded Tempest's future, and Michelle found it nearly impenetrable.

Tempest's desperate desire for peace led her out into the swamp to get away from her mother and grandmother, but still, she was never alone. Her mother and grandmother were always in her head, and now she found that stranger's thoughts from miles away also filled her head. She hated the voices and would try anything to stop them, anything except her mother's magic.

Tempest quit her regular school lessons, and started sleeping late, and after waking up, she would just go back to sleep. She'd sleep all day if it were possible. Her fondest wish was to have thoughts that could be her own, but thinking was like trying to speak in a crowd when nobody else would stop talking long enough for her to get a word in. Her mind was so full of other people's thoughts that there was no room for her own, and even if she ever did manage to squeeze a thought in, she might not recognize it as being her own voice. Sleeping, however, did not provide the answer for her. Sleeping brought on the dreams. Tempest had dreams of the past, and dreams of the future. Her dreams were filled with monsters and demons, and the dreams were even more terrifying than the voices.

Sleeping was a failure. The dreams were so frightening that one day she decided to try the complete opposite, and never sleep. From the age of fourteen on, she was seldom seen without a cup of coffee. She tried staying awake forever, but couldn't sustain that, and it did absolutely nothing to silence the voices she heard. Life was unbearable for young Tempest. Her futile attempts to have thoughts of her own turned to ways of ending her life, hoping that death would bring her peace, but she could never bring herself to act out those ideas. Something deep inside of her told her to be patient and persevere. The solution will present itself.

Michelle continued trying to see into Tempest's future, hoping that if her cure could not come from the past, perhaps she could find it in the future. The veil that surrounded Tempest grew stronger every year, until finally, when she was sixteen, Michelle found that she could barely even sense her feelings anymore.

It was Tempest who eventually found her own cure when she stumbled upon a neighbor's still and his stock of home brewed spirits. She finally discovered something that could quiet the voices. Alcohol brought her enough silence that she could finally hear herself think. She would slip out in the middle of the night and pilot her mother's skiff to a neighbor's plot and take just a small amount from his still. But, even a small amount at a time had not escaped the neighbor's notice. So, one night, he decided to hide in the bushes and find out who'd been stealing his brew. He wasn't angry, he just wanted the thief to either stop or pay him something for what was stolen. When Tempest showed up and filled a small jar, something unexpected came over him. He saw she was just a girl, and a pretty one too, but he was overcome with a feeling he could neither understand nor explain. His feelings started as a discomfort in the pit of his stomach, spread into an irritating heat on his skin, and ultimately grew into an uncontrollable rage. He didn't know where the anger came from, but he went out of his mind. She stole from him, and she was going to pay. She was going to pay the only way a pretty girl could.

She heard the rage in his mind and recognized it from her dreams. She had seen the monster that had overcome him before. It was an ancient monster that had preyed on her kind for thousands of years.

She couldn't stop him any more than she could stop the voices or the dreams.

He hit her across the face with his fist and then followed it up with the back of his hand. He knew he was going to rape her, and there was nothing he could do to stop himself.

Again and again, he hit her. Her face, and her mind, were on fire. She could hear and feel his rage, the same rage she had heard so many times in her dreams. She could hear something else, too; they weren't alone. She heard him tell his sons to back off and wait their turn. He stopped hitting her and surveyed her for a moment before he pulled out a large knife and cut her dress from hem to neck. Her vision narrowed, and her senses dulled as her mind retreated into itself, escaping from the relentless pounding of the crazed man, and then of his sons.

Her eyes glazed over, until she couldn't even see them anymore, as they took turns climbing on top of her. They kept taking turns until they could take no more. The father had considered keeping her, and locking her up in the henhouse as a pet, but the rage was wearing off. Without the rage, he didn't have the heart to keep her as their toy, but he couldn't leave her here next to his still either. He briefly considered dropping her off in town by the dry goods, but she might talk, and even without the rage, he still had the grits to avoid that. So, he took her deeper into the swamp, away from anyone. He couldn't find the courage to kill her or even dump her in the water, so he dumped her on a small patch of land. If she lived, she lived. If the gators got her, then it wasn't his doing.

Michelle and her mother knew she was in trouble, and were already looking for her. They could almost sense her location, from time to time, but it was slow going and was not until sunrise when the veil finally lifted long enough for them to really sense her, and find her on a small mound that surrounded an ancient cypress. She was still unconscious. Even with the bruises that had begun to form, a mottled pattern across her body, her alabaster skin reflected the rising sun and shone, as a beacon, in bright contrast against the dark roots over which her body was draped. Her feet dangled in the water, but the alligators that circled the scene did not approach. The remains of her torn dress were bunched up under her waist and the rest of her clothes were gone. Michelle wrapped her coat around Tempest's shivering form and carried her into the boat to take her home.

Tempest slept for two days, and when she woke, they couldn't tell if she was angry, scared or just crazy, but she went wild, screaming incoherently, and lashing out at everything in the room, breaking whatever she could break. None of the old remedies helped. Michelle searched her memory, and she searched her ancestors' memories. There was nothing she could do to help her daughter. Tempest was like an animal, completely untamed. She wouldn't talk or dress herself. She shoveled her food into her mouth with her hands, and wiped them on her clothes.

They removed anything breakable and locked her in her room. Michelle continued to search her memory for a cure, or at least for something to end the torture she could sense within Tempest, but nothing came to her. She found ancient memories of ancestors being able to reach into the minds of troubled people and guide them out as if they were locked in a maze, but again, it was old magic, and she was unable to find the power within herself. Whether it was because she wasn't powerful enough, or more likely, Tempest was too powerful for her to overcome, she was unable to penetrate Tempest's mind. She couldn't even see what had happened to her daughter, or who had done this to her. She could only feel her pain.

As the days passed, progress was made. Tempest calmed down some. She no longer acted like a wild animal trapped in a cage. She remembered simple things like how to use a chair and the bed. She made eye contact with Michelle and her grandmother, but she hadn't spoken. They unlocked the door to her room, and she freely moved about the home, still withdrawn and silent, but it seemed like only time would be her cure, and in a sense, it was. Time did not bring Tempest back to her mother, however, it did bring her back to her wits, and the first thing she did was walk out and take the boat to Cricket Bend, and a bus to anywhere. Alcohol was the only cure she was interested in, and now she knew how to get as much as she wanted, because she knew what men wanted, too.

Months went by without any word, and without even any sense or dream of how or where she was. All Michelle could do was pray and meditate, and search her own mind for clues to her daughter's location. Finally, after eight agonizing months had passed, Michelle found her. She could not see her clearly, only that she was in a bed and seemed to be in some trouble. She followed her feelings, which led her out of the Bayou and north of Cricket Bend to a hospital. Even in the hospital, Tempest was hard to find. Nobody knew her name, and all Michelle could offer was her age and general build, which unfortunately, described a lot of young women. When she admitted that her daughter may not be right in the head, they led her to a different wing of the hospital where Michelle identified Tempest as the girl staring out the window.

The nurses wouldn't let Michelle visit Tempest until she spoke to a doctor first, but she could see her through the glass, sitting in a wheelchair, at peace, watching the world outside. The doctor was a pleasant fellow and explained that she was a very sick girl. She suffered from numerous psychological problems, and she had suffered from a very traumatic experience. In fact, it was only recently that she was able to speak to them. Only after they had given her very powerful doses of psychotropic drugs to control the voices in her head. He explained that they could not give her the drugs at first, for fear they would harm the baby. Michelle had barely even noticed the newborn in the nurse's arms at the doctor's side.

She was a healthy young girl, and all indications were that she was perfectly normal, with ten fingers and ten toes. The doctor was satisfied that Michelle was indeed the grandmother, and explained to her that if she had not come forth as she had, the young girl would have ended up in foster care.

Michelle was led in, with the baby in her arms, to see Tempest. Tempest spoke. Her voice was light and airy, and her words sounded like they were traveling down a long tunnel to get out. The doctor was encouraged that she recognized her mother. She asked her mother to take care of her baby, to name her, and bring her up. She said she belonged in a hospital and needed their medicine. The truth was that after months of experimenting with drugs and alcohol, she finally found a drug that completely quieted the voices she constantly heard. The doctor said she would be moved to a permanent facility. It would not be a great place, but that the county would see to her needs.

And so, Destiny Faith Boutin was born. Michelle's mother saw her great-granddaughter, and even though she knew she would not live long enough to raise her, she had seen her future. Together, she and Michelle had named her.

Chapter 3

"Nana, tell me again how you found my mama and rescued me in the nick-of-time."

"Hush child and concentrate on your lessons."

Destiny squirmed in her chair. She sat at the table surrounded with her books, tablets, pencils, a short tallow candle, and a dark bowl filled with water. The sun shone brightly outside, and the cypress danced in the breeze, casting shadows through the blinds and teasing the young fifteen-year-old who would much rather be outside romping through the glades.

"Lessons, lessons," she cried out, "all you ever care about anymore is lessons!"

"You've come into your womanhood now, and your lessons are more important than ever before."

"Dang, Nana, it's not like I just come into my womanhood yester-day. I'm almost sixteen years old now!"

"That's right, child, you is almost sixteen. You are a beautiful young girl with no experience in the outside world. You been beg-ging me 'bout when you is going to get your other lessons, tellin' me you already has the dreams, so here we is. Maybe now you's having the dreams so we be here starting your lessons."

Michelle was right. Destiny had been begging for this, but now, faced with the reality, she was afraid she might not be able to do it. "I still don't see why I can't get my learning at a real school. Danielle says the bus stops at the Bend every day to pick us up and drop us off."

Michelle sighed. It was a frequent and tiresome conversation. "You know perfectly well that you ain't like them other children. They only gets your mornin' schoolin'. They don't never learn what you learns after lunch."

"Well, maybe I don't want to have no learning after lunch neithers."

"Since when? You been begging me since you was ten. You wants to end up just like your mama?"

Destiny stood up from her chair and announced, "I love my mama. She's so beautiful."

Michelle stroked her hair. "And you should love your mama, but look where she is."

"I know, I know, she's in the crazy house. But she's not really crazy."

"Them doctors sure think she is, and let me tell you, without her afternoon schoolin', she sure acted plenty crazy."

Destiny sat back down and surveyed the items arrayed around the table for her. "Well doctors ain't so smart, are they? They think that just because she hears voices, she must be crazy. But hearing voices don't make you crazy, or you'd be locked up beside her!"

"No child. Hearin' voices doesn't make me crazy, but hearin' voices sure as hell did make your mama crazy, and if you doesn't concentrate on your afternoon learnin', you'll end up crazy just like your mama. I don't want to see you all shot up with drugs just so you won't be hearin' them voices no more."

"When can we go see Mama again? It's been so long now!"

"Didn't I already tell you we could go see her for your birthday? What's gotten into you today? Why is you squirmin' so much?"

"Do you ever think about how maybe some people might think you being a witch might be a bad thing?"

"People always be gettin' some purty strange notions in they heads. I spect there be some bad persons puttin' those notions there too, but right now, you needs to stop your fussin' and git back to your studies. Concentrate on the flame. Stare at it as if you are pulling yourself into it and the room disappears around you. Listen to the voices. Pick out one voice and see if you can identify who it is. Find a voice from our past. You need to find your ancestors. Then your real learnin' will begin."

"Yes'm." Destiny stared dutifully into the flame. She felt a slight dizziness behind her eyes as her mind opened to the voices. It was like standing in the middle of a party hearing all the different conversations at one time.

She searched for voices that sounded old, not like the speakers were old, but like they spoke in older words than people use today. It helped to imagine herself cocking her head from one side to the other, turning slightly, as if she were adjusting the rabbit ears on the TV they had at the diner in Bend, only it was more like turning the dial on the radio.

As she started to focus in, she would only hear snippets of a conversation, and by adjusting her head, she could zip through the different conversations.

Michelle had told her that she was supposed to choose one of the voices and focus on it, but she didn't really understand how yet. Following them as they seemed to float past her proved difficult. She couldn't hang on to any of them yet.

Destiny continued to stare into the candle flame, but she really didn't see it any more. Her nana said that was a good thing, but now, she felt that her opportunity was slipping away. The voices that were sliding past her began to fade away, and she was aware of the flame dimming out of her sight. Destiny felt like she was falling asleep. This exercise was exhausting her, and sleep sounded better than this, so she let herself go.

"No sleeping on the job! Wake up, you sleepyhead."

Destiny felt a nudge in her side. "Huh? What? Oh, sorry."

She opened her eyes to see a young man, maybe even a boy, with short dark hair that fell loosely around his head in big curly wisps. His eyes were dark brown, and he had remarkable dimples when he smiled. He wore a white apron covered with blood, like a butcher would wear.

Who are you? She thought the words, but they did not come out of her mouth.

What she heard instead was, "Stuff it, George. You know how tired I am. Let me sleep a bit." Destiny tried to look around the room, but could not.

"Sorry, I would have, but I thought you should know that they're questioning him again."

"About what? About why he is a better surgeon than the rest of them?"

"That's just it." George sat down in front of her and continued, "They've been observing him all week and determined that he is not a better surgeon, yet his results are so extraordinary."

She lifted herself from the small cot and crossed the room to the mirror. She poured fresh water into the bowl and splashed some on her face. She stared at her reflection, and finally Destiny understood.

She saw someone else's face in the mirror. A girl, slightly older than herself, with light blue eyes and long red hair dangling from a plain white cap. Her eyebrows were barely visible, they were so pale and thin.

Destiny realized that she was watching and feeling this girl's life unfold before her. She was not a participant, only an observer. She felt a chill, and the girl in the mirror pulled her shawl tighter around her shoulders. Destiny and the girl were one, and she saw her world as she would watch a movie. She relaxed her hold on her own thoughts and let the memory take her where it would.

She rolled up her fists, slammed them onto the table and yelled, "It was that bastard Dr. Bernard. He thought he was the golden boy the moment he arrived. He's been jealous ever since."

"No doubt," George replied, "and his record is probably below average, too. But he is rich, and he knows people. He could probably arrange to transfer all the surgeons to other units until he was the best one left in the compound. But he just can't fathom what your Dr. Westin has done, nobody can."

"Why? Because our patients live?"

"Yes, Rebecca, because your patients live. All of them live. The other surgeons are hacking off legs and arms, and still many of their patients don't survive, but yours all recover with their limbs intact. It's not natural."

"You? You too think it is unnatural? You would prefer that some of our patients died?" Rebecca sat back down on a cot. Destiny could feel the tears welling up in her eyes. "Why can't everyone just appreciate the fact that we are saving our soldiers? Isn't it a good thing that we send our men home on their feet instead of sticking them in the ground?"

"Oh sure, sure, it's good to save the boys." George got up and paced the room. He was uncomfortable where this conversation might lead. "We all want to save them, so why can't he share his secret with us so maybe we can do the same?"

"He has," she said. "He shared all his techniques. It's not his fault if they can't do it as well as him."

"That doesn't work," George said. "They are good doctors. Something is going on here in this tent that they can't replicate."

"So you assume it must be unholy? I thought you were my friend here. Have you considered that maybe it's something holy?"

George sat down next to Rebecca and took her hands in his. "If it's holy, then why can't Dr. Pearl do the same? He is an ordained minister as well as a surgeon. If anyone should have a holy advantage, 'tis him."

The tears started to escape from her eyes. "What will they do with him?"

"I don't know. I need to go change some bandages. We'll speak on this again."

Rebecca took a deep breath. She needed to free her mind from of all her fears and tend her own patients. She returned to the mirror. Her face looked tired. Dark spots were forming under her eyes. She cupped her hands together and scooped up some more water from the bowl and dipped her face into it. The water was cool and refreshing. She straightened up and adjusted the dress she wore. Destiny didn't recognize the style, but it looked old, and the material looked like linen or muslin. Rebecca frowned at the sight of her rumpled shift and reached under her vest to pull the wrinkles out. She pulled her cap off her head and tried vainly and unsuccessfully to pull a brush through her hair. Disgusted with what she saw, she rolled her hair and wrapped it in a net that held it in place under her cap. Small ringlets of red hair poked out from under the cap and curled down her cheek. She liked the curls.

Next to the water was a stack of fresh aprons. She pulled off the top one and slipped it over her head, wrapped the cords twice around her waist and tied the knots in front of her. The aprons were supposed to be white, but after so much use, even with bleaching, they still showed faded traces of blood.

When Rebecca exited the tent, she had to shield her eyes from the sun, but it still reflected brightly off the snow pack. She guessed it was around ten in the morning. She waited for her eyes to adjust, then she trudged through the trampled snow to the infirmary. No matter how much snow fell at night, it never remained white within the compound itself. Foot traffic, horses, and wagons repeatedly cut into the snow and stirred up bits of mud from below. The snow in front of the infirmary was mottled with blood, which was bright red at first, but eventually dried to a dark brown which blended into the reddish clay color brought up from below.

She crossed the compound to the front of the infirmary, put on her best smile, and popped in. "Good morning, boys. How are we feeling this morning?"

A young boy in the nearest cot responded, "Much better, thank you, ma'am."

Another added, "Me too! I feel like I'll be up and about in no time."

Still another asked, "Is it true, what they say?"

Rebecca looked at the last boy. "Forgive me, is what true? What are they saying?"

The boy looked barely seventeen. He pushed himself up in his bed. "Well, I hear that the Doc was in league with some witches and used unholy powers to heal us all. To be honest, I don't care if he made a pact with Beelzebub himself, but Blanchard there," he pointed his thumb to indicate the scowling figure in the corner behind him, "he says we're all going to hell for this, but I don't see's how doing a good deed could ever be mixed up with the Devil."

"Ye mark me words," growled the cowering figure in the corner, "Tis the devil's work. We were all marked for death, and now we just be the devil's pawns."

"Mr. Blanchard!" Rebecca stood up tall so all could see and hear her. "Don't you think the devil would revel in your wounds and misery rather than aid in your recovery? Seems to me he'd be more interested in your souls, and not your flesh."

A commotion brewed up from the other side of the tent. Rebecca heard her friend George raise his voice, "Rebecca, look out, I couldn't stop them all!" She turned and saw the angry patient hobbling towards her. His right leg was a bloody mess. The blackened foot already showed signs of gangrene. He didn't use the leg and instead leaned heavily on a single crutch.

He hobbled to the center of the room and turned toward Blanchard, yelling, "Why don't you stop your damn whining and carrying about? You've got all your arms and legs, yet you're complaining about how healthy you are? How many of us would like to carry that burden for you? I expect I'll be losing me leg tomorrow. I tell you now, I'd trade with any one of you that's unhappy with living."

He tried raising his crutch to point at them, but instead started to fall. Rebecca caught him before he had completely lost his balance. She held him up on his left leg long enough for George to come and take the place of the crutch.

Rebecca felt for him. Losing a leg was a tragedy. "What's your name, soldier?"

"Patrick Thomson, ma'am."

"I'll include you in my prayers, Patrick Thomson."

"Thank you, ma'am."

George turned him around and started guiding him back to his cot. "Come on now, Pat, me boy, stop flirting with the beautiful Miss Rebecca. I saw her first. How am I supposed to catch her eye if you swoon her with your sad story?"

Patrick tried to laugh as they made their way across the tent, but all he managed to get out was a wince.

Rebecca felt a hand on her shoulders. She spun her head around and saw it was her Doctor Westin. "Oh, good God, am I glad to see you! What happened?"

"It's not good. I think their suspicions linger, but they let me practice because I am putting boys back in the field for them."

"There must be something we can do to prove that it's just providence and pure luck on our part."

The doctor shook his head. "I don't think so. I tried to explain to them that they just aren't giving me the most severe patients, but they claimed otherwise. I think the only thing that would satisfy them is for some of our patients to expire."

Rebecca gasped, "No! We couldn't."

"No. I wouldn't do that to a healthy young boy, but maybe, next time they come in, you pick some of the worst ones, ones we can't save, and just make their last hours more comfortable."

"Oh, no doctor, I couldn't."

"You are kinder to these boys than any of the other nurses. I don't think any of the surgeons here would do anything to endanger any of the patients, but I think they concentrate their efforts, as they should, on the wounded they can actually help. As a consequence, some of the patients they lose are just those boys they couldn't help who just die in their cots. You would be doing them a service by making them more comfortable, even if you just talk to them so they don't die alone."

She didn't relish the thought of dealing with death or dying, but she felt for them and nodded her head in agreement. "Aye. I can do that."

She bit her lip and thought about what lay ahead. It wouldn't be long; most of their wounded came from the morning skirmishes, and arrived shortly after they served lunch. Fighting raged on through the afternoon, but those injured late in the day rarely survived the freezing night to be found in the morning.

Stewards brought lunch to the tent. Rebecca doled out portions for each patient in her care. Some might only get broth, while others might get some morsels of meat or vegetables. Nobody in the camp ate well, the officers included. Supplies were hard to come by. The camp was well fortified, surrounded on two sides by steep and treacherous hills, and thick forest on the other. Only one side was open, and it opened to the well-traveled road, but even in times of peace, a well-traveled road in the dead of winter was a difficult and slow journey. During war, supply shipments were a valued target and so a rare commodity out here.

As expected, shortly after lunch, the wounded started to arrive. First were wagons bearing men who couldn't walk. The wagons were cargo wagons, built for hauling bales of hay, and not built for comfort. The driver's seat, which could also accommodate one passenger, sat on springs, affording them some small measure of comfort against the harsh roads, but the bed of the wagon did little to ease their journey. There was little the drivers could do to make the ride more comfortable, except for going slower, which was not in the best interest of the most seriously wounded. Not all of the men in the wagons survived the trip. Less serious wounded would crowd into the remaining wagons, if any, often sitting around the edges with their feet dangling over the side. Those that could not fit on the wagon had to walk behind it. These wagons took at a more leisurely pace, with a procession of wounded men following behind, their feet sometimes sinking deep into the snow.

It was unfortunate, but unavoidable, that the men most vulnerable to the rough ride had to endure the worst ride, but it did get them to the compound first, allowing the surgeons to get right to work with them before the others arrived.

At this time of year, the war only accounted for about half the casualties. Winter was credited with the rest. Many soldiers suffered frostbite, especially those that had to walk to the compound. There were even some soldiers that did not suffer wounds in the war, but had to report to the infirmary solely due to frostbite.

Rebecca was first out to receive the wounded. The wagon held ten men in two rows of five. She quickly checked off those that had died en route, leaving them in the hands of their chaplain, Pastor Williams. Rebecca selected those she thought had lost the most blood, and indicated which ones she wanted the bearers to take to her area of the infirmary. George raised a curious eyebrow. This was uncharacteristic for her, but it was certainly her right as much as his, or anyone else's.

Another wagon pulled up, and she was quick to board it and select the most serious chest wounds she could find. A thought festered in the back of her mind. What if Dr. Westin really was better than all the other doctors? If he spent all his time caring for mortally wounded men, then other men who they could have saved might receive less adequate care from the other doctors, and either perish, or survive without all their limbs intact.

The final wagon pulled in, but George raced into it before Rebecca had climbed out of the second wagon. "Save some for us, Becky."

She had not intended on being so obvious. "I just didn't want anyone accusing me of only selecting the easy cases for Dr. Westin."

George had never told her that he selected the easy ones and left the obviously mortal wounds for her. As the thought crossed his mind, he realized that he had never noticed before that all those mortally wounded men survived. He had never before entertained any suspicions about Dr. Westin, but in that moment, he looked around the compound and found Dr. Westin standing outside his tent. He was smoking a pipe, but never took his eyes off of them. A chill ran up George's spine as he watched the doctor's dark eyes staring at him through the rings and curls of smoke.

"Oy, George, back to it," yelled one of the other nurses behind George, waiting for him to take one of the patients off the wagon.

George nodded to Dr. Westin and said, "Look at him, Shamus, just standing there staring at us."

"Aye," Shamus said, "they're all talking about him."

"What am I saying? I have no time for such superstitious nonsense."

"You said it yourself," Shamus said, "Look at him standing there staring at us."

George was unaware that Rebecca was standing just below him, listening. "He's not looking at the two of you," she said. "He's looking at the wounded. He's a good doctor."

"I know he's a good doctor," Shamus said. "They're all good doctors."

"Sure," she admitted, "they're all good, but he's just a bit better than the others."

"Nobody is that good," Shamus said. "Look at his eyes. He doesn't even have pupils."

Rebecca pushed him aside to get another patient, and said, "You're daft. He just has really dark eyes."

"Dark, like the Devil's."

"So, you've looked into the devil's eyes?" she replied. "Maybe they should be talking about you and the company you keep?"

"I'd keep better company," Shamus chided, "if you'd just find your way to my cot tonight."

Dr. Pearl, who had been leaning over a dying man offering last rites, heard the offensive remark and said, "That will be quite enough from you, Shamus O'Callahan. I'll be seeing you in my tent tonight, where you'll be saying your Hail Marys until your throat goes dry."

"But you're not even Catholic," he protested. "How can you give me penance?"

"I'll be giving you a switch on your back if you don't rein in your mouth."

"What'd I say?" The boy was crimson red. "You know I didn't mean it like that. I've always loved Rebecca, but she..."

Dr. Pearl held up his hand and said, "Quiet lad, she probably can't stand the stench coming from your mouth. Some Hail Marys might do you a bit of good washing that filth out." He turned and winked at Rebecca, who by now had weathered Shamus's insult.

"My apologies," Shamus said to Rebecca, "truly, I did not mean it to sound as vulgar as it came out."

Rebecca caught Dr. Pearl's eye and returned his wink. "Well, it certainly was a vulgar remark. Too bad though, I was feeling a bit lonely today and could have used the company. Too bad you'll be spending your evening with Dr. Pearl, saying your Hail Marys."

Shamus held his hands over his heart as if an arrow had struck him. "Now that truly hurts. What would your mother say if she heard you toy with me like that?"

George shot a look to Rebecca. She didn't respond, but simply jumped off the wagon and followed the wounded to the infirmary. He turned his attention back to Shamus and slugged him in the arm. "Will you never learn to shut it, Shamus?"

"What'd I say?"

"Let's just say that she's sensitive about her parents."

"Why?" Shamus asked. "What's wrong with her parents?"

"Nothing, 'cepting she never knew them. She was raised by the parish priests."

Shamus's mouth hung open. He was blushing bright red from chin to forehead. "I didn't know. I didn't mean nothin' by it."

Rebecca entered the tent and started her preparations. In addition to making the wounded comfortable and keeping them warm and fed, her duties also included cleaning the wounds before the doctor made his examinations. She used two standard salves to treat the men. She always mixed a fresh batch at the start of the day. Both salves started with beef lard and baking soda. The lard was only used to deliver the ingredients in a paste, which could be rubbed into the flesh. In one salve she added camphor. This paste was spread on the chests and helped to reduce coughing diseases that so often followed such serious wounds. The second paste was mixed with citrus juice, lemon, and lime worked best. This was administered to the wounds after cleaning.

Rebecca went to the first cot. She scraped off the snow that was used to pack the wound and peeled his pants away from what looked like a blade wound. She had to cut part of the pant-hem to expose the whole wound. It was actually a musket wound that had torn into his flesh and lodged somewhere deep in his thigh. She picked out some large pieces of debris, mostly bark and dried twigs, then rubbed some of the lemon and soda mixture into the wound. Rubbing the salve mixed the baking soda and citrus, creating a fizz that helped clean the wounds. She felt a familiar tingle in her hands as she gingerly rubbed the balm into the wound. The doctor would be here soon, and the wound wasn't bleeding too much, so she didn't bandage it just yet. She moved up to his chest and opened his shirt to rub the camphor in. He was sleeping and stirred a bit, cracking his eyes enough to see her, then dropped back asleep. Her hands were still tingling and warm now. She cleaned her hands and moved on to the next patient.

She opened up the boy's shirt and exposed a bayonet wound to the chest. She cleaned out the wound and packed it with the soda solution, but couldn't administer the camphor solution so near to the wound.

Dr. Westin was usually right behind her, tending to the wounded. She saw him standing at the entrance, watching her. He had a frightfully strange look on his face. She felt an unfamiliar twisting in the pit of her stomach. The tribunal must have really shaken him up. She worked her way from patient to patient, while he just stood there and watched. She guessed he would rather let them die than suffer the retribution of the tribunal. She wondered how much comfort she could give them if he was going to let them die.

She finished preparing the last patient and approached Dr. Westin. "You can't just stand there and let them perish."

"No, no, of course not. I was just watching."

She heard some low voices just outside the entrance and realized he wasn't actually alone. The doctor's face contorted and his eyes welled up with tears. She thought he was going to say something, but he held himself back. His face was pale. He lunged forward as if he were shoved in the back before he spoke again. "Rebecca, they want me to ask you, what's that thing you do before each patient?"

She was confused and didn't know what he was asking. The twisting feeling in her stomach grew worse. The room started to swirl around her. She was barely audible when she squeaked out, "Who wants to know? What thing?"

"With your hands? You make some kind of signs with your hands as you approach each patient."

"Signs? I don't know what you are talking about, Dr. Westin. I just clean their wounds, sometimes I have to remove some of their clothing, and then I apply the salves. You know that. Who is it that's asking these questions?"

"I know you clean the wounds, but between patients, you dip your hands in water and make some kind of signs with your hands."

One of the gentlemen who had been standing outside pushed his way inside, shoving Dr. Westin completely out of the way. He was a repulsive man, short and stocky, with a large round face and thick bushy eyebrows that nearly met in the center. His face was dark red, and featured a huge dark mole, which sprouted five dark, wiry hairs. His hair was oily and his skin was sweaty, and he obviously hadn't bathed recently. When she had seen him from across the compound, she thought he was revolting. Up close, he was absolutely vile. Her stomach twisted into an even tighter knot as he approached her. He moved without grace, but with the kind of bearing that showed he must believe every move he made was completely graceful. He moved directly into her face and stared her right in the eyes. "Who do you pray to when you dip your hands in the water? We saw you make the signs. You did not fold your hands as a Christian. You never looked up in prayer, so now you must tell us. What heathen god do you sign with the water?"

"With the water?" The room spun around Rebecca. She felt the fear and loathing of this man wrapping tightly around her soul and squeezing the consciousness out of her. "I make no signs. I wash my hands, then wave them to rinse off the water."

"Why not use a towel to dry your hands?" the repulsive man demanded. "You will tell us what signs you are making."

"The towels get quite foul with the two lotions, especially the camphor, so I try to dry my hands in the air."

"Everyone else uses towels. Why are you the only one making signs?"

"I am not making any signs," she protested, "and if it's true that everyone else is using towels, then they must be rubbing camphor into the wounds."

The short stocky man leaned forward and squinted his eyes, looking her directly in the face. "Are you a doctor, miss? Why should you care if some camphor is worked into the wounds?"

"The camphor burns," she argued. "I feel it burning my hands. I could never apply it to an open wound."

"Nobody else complains of it burning, and nobody else makes signs to the Devil." The stocky man signaled two soldiers to come in. "You are hereby accused of witchcraft and heresy. You will be tried by tribunal, and when you are found guilty, you will be burned at the stake until your unholy soul leaves our world and returns to your master."

Rebecca's mouth fell open. She wanted to protest, but she was unable. The room was gone from her vision. She felt as though she were about to fall faint on the spot. All she could see was the vile little man's dark eyes staring into hers.

Two soldiers grabbed her by the arms, careful to control her wrists so she could make no signs against them. The doctor started to attend his patients, but the short man stopped him. "Leave them. We will have our proof soon enough if they live."

She was led to a tent on the far side of the compound. She was bound, hand and foot, and tethered to an anchor in the ground. There was nothing gentle or compassionate in their handling of her, nor was there the least bit of concern for her comfort or well-being. Her hands were shackled together with an iron bar holding them a foot apart. Her feet were shackled to chains, which held her firmly to the cold, hard ground. Not even straw was offered between her and the frozen dirt.

She was allowed no visitors. The guards preferred to keep their distance and call her names from outside the tent. When her food was delivered, they held it in front of her while they spat into it. She thought she heard George try to visit her, but they refused to allow him in, chasing him off and warning that if he insisted on visiting her, he would burn alongside her. Only the vulgar, sweaty pig of a man was allowed in the tent. He always came alone. He always crowded her face with his own ruddy excuse for a face. He would demand, in a loud commanding voice, that she reveal her demon lord, but then he would speak the most humiliating things in a voice that only she could hear. He never tired of telling her what a horrible end she would come to at the stake. He would reach under her tunic and roughly squeeze and pull her breasts. Throughout his abuse of her, he would suggest ways for her to earn an easier, quicker death than the burning. She no longer fought to remain conscious. She didn't know whether it was his odor or just her fear and hatred of him, but every visit brought her closer to fainting, which was far better than enduring his presence.

Days passed; Rebecca didn't eat, and barely slept. She no longer cried; she had given up all hope and did not understand what was happening to her. She couldn't fight off her tormentor's abuses. Even if the shackles had been removed, she no longer had the strength to fend him off. He took whatever privileges he dared, and she lay dead to him, unconscious and dreaming of another world.

She lost count of how often he came to visit, or how many days had passed. She had never before in her life hated anyone as much as she hated that awful, fat little man. She dreamed that she lived in a magical world where she had the power to share her pain and misery with him. In her dreams, she made him feel sorrow and emptiness instead of the hate and loathing he expressed towards her. She could make him hate himself instead of her. This is exactly what she was dreaming when he visited her one final time.

Rebecca was somewhere between consciousness and sleep, and was aware when he entered the tent with two guards at his side. He ordered them to stand her up. They grabbed her by the arms and briskly flung her onto her feet. She no longer cared what they did to her. Nothing could ever compare with her humiliation by the wretched little toad that now stood before her.

He closed in on her face. He smiled as he slapped her face to rouse her from her dreams. "Wake up! Wake up, little witch! I have good news for you today. We no longer require your confession. No more questions about your unholy practices. Your patients have told us all we need to know. You'll be glad to know that we'll be transferring you from this location to a facility that was specially designed to handle your kind." He leaned and pressed his lips to her ears and whispered, "We'll be sending you back to hell now."

He stepped back and assumed a more commanding posture. "Take her outside and hang her on the stake."

Rebecca knew this would be coming and had resigned herself to her fate. She did not know how anyone could be so cold and uncaring that they could order such a fate for another human being. She couldn't understand how they could possibly come to such a horrendous conclusion. But she was beginning to understand hate, and had concluded that the evil little troll had orchestrated this whole affair. She didn't know why he hated her so much or why he took such perverse pleasure in her suffering. She had never done anything to him, but had learned to hate him back in equal shares. More than ever, she wished her dreams could be true and she could share the pain before her with that pathetic little worm.

The guards dragged her through the compound, not because she resisted, but because her legs wouldn't walk for her and their pace was too swift. In the center of the compound, she saw her destination. A tall wooden post surrounded with a rather large pile of wood. In the center of the bar that kept her hands apart, there was an iron ring. They pulled her to the top of the pile, turned her to face outwards, away from the stake, and raised her arms over her head, slipping the ring onto a hook atop the stake. She fell slack, hanging from the hook as the guards quickly jumped down from the pile.

She saw the reason for their haste. The wicked little devil of a man was already setting a torch to the pile of wood. An evil smile spread across his broad, dark face. The flames spread around her. Spectators started to form a circle around the pyre. The guards stepped back to a comfortable distance, but the fat little runt stayed close, still looking her in the eyes. She could see the flames reflecting off his pupils.

Smoke encircled Rebecca and soon filled her lungs, burning her every breath. The flames reached the top of the woodpile and started to lick her flesh. She wished for the unconsciousness that accompanied his unwanted visits, but she could not find that peace, so she tried being brave. She pretended she was the girl she dreamed of and tried pushing her pain on to the round little bastard standing just outside the flames. He pumped his fists up and down in the air, egging the flames on. Lowering her gaze into his eyes, she focused on all the strange feelings she dreamed of, opening his mind and pouring her pain into it, forcing him to feel feeble and wracked with unforgivable sorrow. The flames grew, catching the hem of her dress and searing her legs. She didn't want to give the repugnant little insect any satisfaction at all, but she could bear the pain no longer. Her legs were pinned down and could not retract from the fire, her mouth stretched wide to scream and the compound echoed with the words, "It burns! It burns! The pain!" But it was not her voice she heard. An instant before her flesh blistered and fried, she could see the horrid little man, and instead of the wicked smile, he was screaming at the top of his lungs, "It burns! It burns!"

***

Michelle was making more candles for Destiny's training. She varied the ingredients for different candles so each could produce a different intensity, and sometimes a different color flame. This batch used kerosene to enhance the intensity of the flame. They also tended to burn rather fast, which kept her busy making them. She sat at the table, watching Destiny while she worked. Destiny's face was expressionless. She was consumed with her vision and completely unaware that her grandmother was even in the room. Michelle remembered when her own mother taught her how to access her first ancestral memory. She could only recall small fragments. Her early memories only lasted a few minutes. Destiny had been in this one over an hour now. It took Michelle years before she could stay in her trance that long. She was mixing kerosene in with the tallow she used for the candle's core when she began to sense something was wrong with Destiny.

Destiny screamed and flailed her arms about. Michelle dropped the wax she was working and rushed to her granddaughter's side, trying to console her, but Destiny accidentally knocked over the candle she was staring into. The candle bounced on the table and rolled in a round arc back to Destiny and Michelle, touching Michelle's kerosene-soaked sleeve, immediately igniting her arm and hand.

Michelle yelped and ran to the sink, screaming, "It burns!"

The long-term indigent care ward at St. Austin Mercy Asylum erupted in a cacophony of screams and rambling. It all started with Tempest Boutin, who leapt out of her seat screaming, "It burns! It burns!" Other inmates, either frightened or simply startled, began parroting her screams while running around the ward flapping their arms in the air.

In downtown Phoenix, homeless souls standing on the curbs dividing the roadway stopped panhandling and begin running out into traffic, screaming, "The pain! It burns!!!"

Further northwest, in Las Vegas, a psychic convention was interrupted when the lecturer and a few select attendees began screaming, "It burns! It burns!!!"

Outside Portland, Oregon, a small, little known, private asylum was beset with the screams of its inmates. This was no ordinary asylum, however. Unbeknownst to the general public, its inmates were handpicked for study by the doctors who themselves were handpicked to work here. Unlike the St. Austin Mercy facility, where the inmates merely imitated Tempest's screams, the inmates here all shared a common pedigree, and all erupted in unison, "It burns! It burns!!"

The doctors here were specially trained to recognize unusual events such as this, and act upon them, but it had been centuries since the last recorded event of this type, and the staff was unprepared for anything of this magnitude. One by one, their eyes widened, and their hearts raced with fear. To a man, nobody here had ever exhibited a shred of true care for the patients. They treated them more as lab rats, but now, their hearts opened to them in pity. They could see their pain and do nothing about it.

The staff corralled the inmates into a huddle and gathered in a circle around them. The patients' screams had eventually muffled down to simpering and whimpering. The inmates huddled together, facing the center, holding their heads against each other.

One bewildered staff member turned to another and asked, "What are they doing?"

"Beats me; never seen this before."

Their voices blended into a single voice, chanting, "Burn! Burn! Burn!"

Fear enveloped the doctors and spread around the ring until all the staff was chilled to the marrow.

The huddle turned around suddenly, united, holding hands, and stared deeply into the eyes of the staff members encircling them, and continued their chant, "Burn! Burn! Burn!"

The frightened doctors and aids started to squirm.

"Fight it," one doctor said. "It's all in your mind! Don't fall victim to suggestion!"

But it was no use. The doctors, nurses, and aids tried to focus their minds on reality, blocking their minds from the chanting, but, one by one, the staff fell victim to the intense burning and screamed out, "It burns! The pain!"

Across the country and around the world, the strange event rippled until select persons from every corner of the planet were infected with this fearsome sensation. Especially the dark asylums, which all experienced an inmate uprising similar to the one in Portland.

Destiny came out of her trance. She was exhausted and in tears. Flames still filled her eyes and her whole body shook from the terror of the experience. She panted in rapid shallow breaths and tried to scream, but her voice was too hoarse and dry. As she looked around the room and began to recollect her own identity, her pulse began to calm and she gulped in larger breaths of air. She saw her nana at the end of the table, holding one of her arms in a large bowl of water.

As her systems returned to normal, she found her tears and her voice. "Oh, Nana, it was awful. They killed her, only it was me! They killed me, and I couldn't do anything about it."

Michelle lifted her burned arm from the water and wrapped a towel around it, but said nothing.

"What happened to your arm?"

"Nothing child. I had a little accident makin' dem candles."

Destiny reached out for her nana's good hand and held it. "Oh, I'm sorry. You burned yourself? That explains the dream then. I was burning in the dream too, but it was so real." As she caressed her grandmother's hand, she felt a strange but familiar tingle.

Her nana was astonished. "What was that?"

"What was what?"

"That thing you just done."

"I didn't do anything. I was just holding your hand. It felt kinda funny though, kinda like in my dream when I was helping all those soldier boys."

"That warn't no dream, child. Here, touch my hurt hand."

Destiny carefully took her nana's burned hand and lightly held it, tracing her fingers across it. She felt the strange tingling again, then the tingle transformed into mild warmth. "What's happening?" Destiny asked. "What does this mean?"

Michelle felt a momentary pang of fear of the unknown, but it was quickly replaced with a pride in how special her granddaughter really was. "It means you has the power. You learnt yourself how to heal. The pain in my hand is gone now. So, tell me about what you been rememberin'."

"I wasn't remembering anything. It was someone else."

"Of course it was someone else. You was rememberin' one of your ancestors."

"That can't be Nana. She was so young, and they killed her. She didn't have no babies."

"She still musta been family. We probably come from a sister of hern. What can you remember? What was her name?"

Destiny proceeded to tell her nana all she could recall. She recounted the tale of Rebecca, the nurse who was burned at the stake, accused of being a witch. Talking about it helped quell the fear in her heart. Seeing her nana swell with pride almost made Destiny feel brave about the experience, but not brave enough to do it again.

Michelle knew Rebecca's story, and had lived the memory, but never came away with the power to heal. She had recalled thousands of memories and never had a single memory of anyone having such a power for over 200 years, and very few, in fact, for over a thousand years.

"You done good, child. We'll continue again tomorrow."

Tears returned to Destiny's eyes. "No, Nana, don't make me do that again, it was horrible."

"You gots no choice. I cain't teach you how to use your new gift, and if there's one thing I learnt from our ancestors, it's that those who gots the gifts have to learn to control them or they's looking at trouble somewheres down the line. So, you see, if I cain't teach ya, then your ancestors will have to do it for me."

"It's not fair," Destiny cried. "I didn't ask for this. I don't want it."

"But you got it. Could be, the Almighty has some plan for you. It's best you be ready."

Destiny saw the truth in her nana's words. She didn't like it, but she understood it. She hugged her nana and held on to her for security.

"Everything will turn out just fine, Cherie, you'll see."

"Yes'm."

Exhaustion trumped distress and stretched Destiny's mouth into a lazy yawn. She plopped onto the sofa and sank her head onto a throw pillow. Her eyes unfocused as she reflected on the day. She had her first ancestral memory, and apparently returned with the ability to heal, the same ability that resulted in Rebecca's death at the stake. She had lived over a week, and died, all in less than two hours' time. She feared what she might dream. She now held images and feelings in her head that she never wanted to relive, but she was so tired that consciousness fled from her mind and sleep came easily.

CHAPTER 4

B rian Bernard Grupp arrived at the asylum in Oregon to find his world turned upside down. His staff was making the patients comfortable when they were supposed to be keeping them sedated and under control, and the patients were roaming about freely.

Brian grabbed the arm of an orderly walking by and asked, "Henry, what's going on here?"

"What do you mean? Every thing's right as rain here."

"I see. Have you seen Marshall?"

"I think he's in Records."

"Thanks." Brian headed towards the records department. Marshall was his head of security. If anyone could shed some light on things, he could. As he walked through the halls, nothing he saw was as it should be. This kind of change had been foretold long ago, but few believed it would ever happen. He suspected that it must be a supernatural event, but he would look like a fool if he made such a claim before investigating it.

Marshall was in the file room, as Henry had said. He was pulling a box of old records off a high shelf when Brian entered the room.

Brian started to speak, but then held back and watched what Marshall was doing. He saw him carry the box over to the back of the room and start feeding the contents into a shredder.

"Marshall, what the hell are you doing?"

"What does it look like I'm doing? I'm shredding everything. We're finished here. We don't want to leave anything behind."

"Don't you think you should investigate what's going on here before initiating a complete shutdown?"

Marshall glanced up at Brian, but kept feeding documents into the shredder. "I don't need to investigate," he said. "I just need to destroy."

"Have you considered, maybe, that's not your call to make?"

"Oh, sure, sure, I wouldn't make that call myself."

Brian hit the power button on the shredder so he could get Marshall's full attention. "Well, I didn't tell you to destroy all the records, so tell me again why you are doing this?"

"Because I have to, that's all. It must be done, and I'm the right one to do it."

"Well, I want you to stop. I order it. Stop right now!"

Marshall laughed. "That's a good one. Yeah, a real rib-tickler."

"I'm serious. I never issued orders to destroy these records. I want you to stop."

"That's not my call, not yours neither."

"Whose call is it?"

Marshall turned the power back on and said, "Theirs."

"Whose?"

"You heard me. I'm kinda busy. I don't really have time to chitchat."

"Who are they?"

"You know. Them. Take it up with them if you want me to stop."

This was more serious than Brian had suspected. Whatever was going on had infected his chief of security. He was going to have to handle this himself. He left the records room and took the elevator to his office on the second floor. He locked the door behind him, picked up the phone, and dialed a sister facility in Utah. The phone rang once, twice, three times. "Come on," Brian pleaded, "pick up."

The phone kept ringing. Brian was ready to slam the receiver down when he heard someone pick up and answer, "Hello?" He could hear that the voice was out of breath.

"Dr. Schaefer, please. Tell him it's Grupp."

"One moment, sir." He could hear the woman cover the phone with her hand and yell out, "Richard? It's Grupp!"

The woman placed the phone down and all Brian could hear was muffled chaos until Richard picked up the phone, also out of breath, and said, "Brian, is that you? It's about time you returned my call."

"Sorry, I didn't know you called. Listen, I have a situation here and I need to borrow you and your best investigator."

"No can do. We have our hands full here."

"Well," Brian said, "you can drop what you're doing. I think I have a prophecy level event here. I need you guys here, stat."

"You're kidding, right?"

Brian clicked on the security monitor and watched the madness below. "No joke. This facility is out of our control. I think we've been hit big time with some real dark ages stuff."

"Yeah, well, we really do have a problem, then. We're seeing the same stuff here. The inmates are running the show. I've only been able to identify four people, so far, who are unaffected by it."

Brian groaned. "I haven't found any yet. This can't be a coincidence. We need to combine forces and find someone who can look into this for us."

"Agreed. I think we need to get some troops in here, too."

"How'd they ever manage to counter their meds?"

Brian could hear Schaefer put his hand over the phone and yell, "Marcy! They're getting into the scissors!" Brian heard some scuffling before Schaefer returned to the phone. "Sorry about that, Boss. Near as I can tell, they are still medicated. The drugs are supposed to inhibit all higher brain function, yet somehow they managed to link up with each other. The real problem is that they aren't getting any more meds now, so they will start to resume real consciousness within a week."

"So," Brian suggested, "maybe when the troops get in we just separate them, or thin out their ranks a bit."

"Hopefully," Schaefer said, "if we can weaken them, our people will snap out of it."

"We need to get them back on their meds and under our control. I also need you to start checking with the other facilities and see how many were affected by this."

Destiny slept well. She didn't have the nightmares she would have expected after such an ordeal. Instead, she had a deep, quiet sleep. She slept a little longer than usual, and woke up feeling perfectly fine, unaware if she even had dreamt at all. She was tired, but not from lack of sleep. She had the kind of run down feeling the body sometimes gets after too much sleep. Her nana, on the other hand, was feeling phenomenal. She was up at the crack of dawn, fluttering around the house like a butterfly, rearranging furniture, and cleaning those hard to reach spots she kept putting off for another day. She felt young, strong, and full of energy. There was no sign that her arm was ever burned at all, no pain, no scars, nothing.

She looked at her granddaughter with a measure of awe and pride. She always believed Destiny was special, but then, all parents and grandparents probably believe the same. Michelle had something more tangible to believe in now. Her granddaughter had a gift which hadn't been seen in centuries. Michelle set up a candle on the table and sat down to consult the ancestors. She could teach Destiny to recall ancestral memories, like her mother had taught her. She could teach her to view the past and future and even show her how to mix herbs into potions. Those were her gifts. She couldn't teach her anything about healing. Nobody could; at least, nobody alive today. Destiny required training that she wasn't prepared to offer. She needed to find an ancestor who could teach her how to train her young prodigy.

Dr. Richard Schaefer had never been more than a business acquaintance to Brian. He had risen in rank to head the Utah facility. He reported to Brian, and had met with him many times, but he had never been part of the inner circle. He saw this as an opportunity to advance himself and join that select group. He spent all morning contacting other sister facilities. The more of them he had reached, the grimmer the outlook was. Initially, as he began to realize how widespread this phenomenon was, he thought this might be his ticket to skip a few levels, but when the reality of the global nature of the event struck him, he worried that there might be no organization within which he could rise.

He dreaded the call he had to make now. He only had bad news, and could offer little in the way of suggestions to improve the situation. He picked up the phone and dialed Brian's office.

Brian was reviewing some ancient texts, but was quick to answer the phone, "Dick, what did you find out?"

"It's not good. As far as I can tell, this event has affected every single control facility we have. It didn't affect our training facilities, only the holding wards. Do you think we are under attack?"

"If it only affected the control wards, then it must have something to do with the inmate population. They must need them before they can attack us more directly."

"Brian, have you considered who they are, and where they came from?"

"I can only guess. We've always known there were rogue witches out there, but we had no clue that they ever organized, or that there were enough of them to cause this. I don't know how they could keep themselves a secret from us."

Schaefer cleared his throat and said, "The thing is, I was thinking about the prophecy. 'A child will come of all their strengths and all our wisdom.'"

"I know the prophecy. That's why we've been keeping them all these centuries. That's why we've been trying to breed them to produce this child."

"But what if the child is born to them?"

Brian swiveled his chair around, leaned back, and stared out the window. "There can't be many of them left out there. We've been weeding them out of the general population for centuries, and those we didn't keep, we terminated. Besides, where would they get our bloodline?"

"I don't know," Schaefer said. "The ancient texts tell us that they lost their power at the same time we lost ours. All magic was gone from the world. Since that time, we have lost many of our people, especially those not privy to the prophecies."

Brian sat up in his chair. "Do you think the witches have breeding programs like ours?"

"No. They would never do that."

"Are you suggesting that some of our own kind have started their own breeding program?"

"No," Schaefer said. "Not without our knowing about it."

"Do you realize what you're suggesting? The only other possibility is that they have accidentally created the messiah that we have been unable to produce on purpose."

"It was their prophecy. We stole it from them and tried to make it ours."

"I know, I know." Brian chewed a stick of gum while he puzzled it out. "But even if they did produce a child, how could they become this powerful? The magic is gone, and it's been gone for centuries. I guess we need to find them before we can answer that."

"I have an idea," Schaefer said. "Let me get back to you tomorrow. I may be able to come up with a location."

Destiny emerged from her room to find her nana at the table, staring into one of her candles. This was nothing new. She had seen her do this since she was a baby, but she saw it differently now that she had done it herself.

She sat down at the table, wondering how long her nana would be. She watched her face for signs, wondering where she was, whose life she was reliving. Seeing no clues in her nana's face, she looked into the candle, wishing it could reveal something to her.

"Come on in, child."

Destiny blinked her eyes and looked at her nana. She heard a woman's voice, but not her nana's. She looked into the flame again.

"Do not be afraid," the voice said, "we have been expecting you."

She held her gaze into the flickering flame and spoke back, "Who are you?" She felt the world melt around her, and a new world opened up before her. She blinked her eyes, only they weren't her real eyes. Destiny found herself staring into a small fire on the floor in the center of what appeared to be a dome shaped room. The hut looked like a very old style structure, the kind you would see in a museum of natural sciences. Also sitting around the fire was an old woman and her nana.

The old woman was dressed in skins and had wild, unmanageable hair. Her face was adorned with either tattoos or paint, and she had small animal bones piercing her ears. She spoke a strange language Destiny had never heard, but English filled Destiny's ears. It was like watching a dubbed foreign movie. Even though Destiny heard English, the old woman's words came to her with an accent and a texture that fit the image of the wild-looking woman.

"Hello, Destiny, welcome."

Destiny sat quietly. Her nana began to speak, but the old woman held up her hand to stop her. Destiny gathered her wits and returned the greeting, "Hello."

"Very good," the old woman said. "You speak, I understand. I am Mala, medicine woman for my people. Your nana has told me much about you and your people and the strange times you live in."

"I don't understand."

"My words are not right?"

Destiny shook her head. "Your words are fine, but they aren't your words. And how is it we can speak, if this is someone's memory?"

"Ah. That is a question. Indeed, this is a very special place, which I have created for us to meet. It would seem that much has been forgotten, and your people have neither the power to pierce the veil of time, nor the training, but I do. I foresaw this meeting many thousand years before you were born and left a memory to invite you here. Your nana heard my invitation, and here you are."

"But how is that possible?"

The old woman chuckled softly and said, "Many things are possible, things you have not even dreamed. Do you know what means your name, Destiny?"

"It means the future. What you are meant to be in the future."

"Ahhh, that is a good meaning. I think it is a pretty sound too, Destiny. In my tongue, it sounds like a word we use, distinak. Can you say dee stee nock? It means to complete something that was long and hard. It also has another meaning, to bring a string of things that happen back around to the beginning. We believe that circles are very strong, and to make important things work in circles is very good to do. A person who works distinak magic is very powerful. It is a very special thing. Maybe this is your destiny."

Mala turned to her nana. "Thank you, Michelle, for bringing her to me. I must see the child alone. Go now."

Michelle bowed her head in respect and faded away.

Destiny's mouth fell open, shocked to see her nana dismissed like that.

The old woman looked at Destiny, sizing her up for a moment, then said, "I have many children brought to me for training. Of course, in my time, they are brought to me much younger, and I have so many gifted candidates to choose from, but it seems that you are a lone candidate from your world. All the same, I won't show you any special treatment. I teach. It is in you to learn, or not to learn."

Destiny was overwhelmed. She was still reeling from yesterday's adventure, and now this. How could she trust this woman? How could she even trust that this was even happening? It might have been better if her nana had remained, so she could be sure it wasn't just some silly dream.

"You do not need your nana to tell you it is not dream."

Destiny's mouth fell open again.

The old woman threw her arms in the air and exclaimed, "How do you expect to learn the magic if you continue to be amazed by the magic? You are practically a non-believer. I cannot teach a non-believer."

"No," Destiny said, "I want to learn. But you have to understand, there's no such thing as magic. In my time, I mean. Nobody in our world believes there ever was magic, and those few who do believe can't prove it. Even those with the gift of sight have no control of what they see."

"There's no magic in your world? Does your nana lie to me? She tells me you have the old magic."

"Nana wouldn't lie, but it only happened once. Maybe it was just a fluke, left over from the memories I had just witnessed."

"Magic no fluke. I show, you watch. You take magic back to your time. You see."

Brian sat behind his large walnut desk, waiting for the phone to ring. He read through the historical archives about the old wars and the last known prophecy-level events. Events like this were rare, and the texts were old, and as he searched back in history, the language became ancient and grew more difficult to read. He knew it would be Richard when he heard the phone ring. He was anxious to hear if they had learned anything yet. "Hello Dick. What do you have for me?"

"I don't have a location yet, but I'm pretty sure we can locate the origin of the event. I'm collecting the security tapes from all our centers and comparing the event time from each of them. So far, it looks like we'll be somewhere in North America, probably between the Rockies and the East Coast, and possibly in the southern US. I'll need to get some mathematicians to pinpoint the exact location."

"So we can track the event spreading across the country? What is its speed?"

"The speed is faster than sound and much slower than light, but it seems to vary. It looks like it picks up speed as it goes, and it's not just across the country, it's around the world."

Brian spun his chair around to look out his window. He imagined seeing the wave spread across the sky, like a tsunami crossing the heavens. "Have some of our computer geeks put that data into an animation so we can watch how it spread."

"What do we do when we find the origin? Send in a team to neutralize it?"

"No," Brian said. "We need to learn who we are dealing with and where they came from. If it is the prophecy, then we need to know who is the chosen one, and how many are following him."

"If this is an attempt to free their people, they must have a plan, one that needs more of their people."

Brian turned his chair back to face his desk, where the old texts were still displayed on his computer. "The archives suggest that an event like this would be followed by a gathering. I didn't think there were enough of them left out of our custody to gather, let alone produce this."

"If they are planning a gathering, we could let some of the inmates escape and follow them."

"Let's save that idea. I think we have some people we might be able to use to find them."

"We do?" Schaefer asked incredulously. "Who? They can sense our people from a mile away."

"True. They can sense us coming. I can't tell you who we'd send in, at least not yet. See how close you can get to locating the source of the event and I'm sure we'll be looking at a new grade for you. Then I can let you in on some secrets."

"Yes, sir."

Carrots and sticks were how this organization operated. Dr. Schaefer was right all along. This could lead to advancement for him.

Chapter 5

Michelle was beside herself. She was simultaneously filled with pride over her granddaughter's prospects and worry for what might be happening to the young girl now. She had the greatest respect and reverence for Mala, but those were different times. Children grew up tougher than they do today. She feared Destiny may not be prepared for the harshness that she might face. The old people's ways were sometimes cruel.

She busied herself around the house, never leaving Destiny out of her sight for more than a few moments. When she had finished dusting and cleaning everything a second time, she moved on to re-arranging the furniture. She knew she didn't have enough furniture to keep her occupied for long and planned to polish the silver when she finished. She didn't have much silver either, and was running out of ideas.

Michelle checked Destiny again. Her face was completely blank. Her eyes stared off into space, well beyond the candle. A fly flitted around, landing on her cheek now and then. Michelle shooed the fly out the window, careful not to disturb her trance. She hated flies.

Moths weren't so bad, at least they were more attracted to the flame, but flies liked to lick the sweat off your face, and here in the Bayou, sweat was always on your face.

Michelle went to the sink and mixed up a small potion of water, sugar, and salt. She poured the mixture outside the window, hoping it would be more attractive to the flies than Destiny was. There were other ingredients she could have used, but they tended to be a more putrid concoction, and she was hesitant to smell up the place for just a solitary fly.

Mala focused her attention on Destiny. She narrowed her eyes and chewed on nuts and seeds that she pulled from a pouch hanging from her waist while she watched her new pupil. She stared deeply into Destiny's eyes, which completely unnerved the young girl.

Destiny was unable to look directly into the old woman's eyes. She tried focusing on her mouth, but found her eyes drawn to the deep ruts that marked Mala's wrinkled face. There was no feature on Mala's face that she was comfortable to focus upon, so she tried looking around her. She could see bent wood poles tied to large animal bones that formed the frame of the hut. Animal furs of different colors formed the skin over the frame, tied to it with leather straps.

Destiny had seen enough of the domed hut and looked at her hands. She thought she detected an eerie glow to her skin, but they looked normal otherwise. She turned her hands over to see the palms of her hands.

Mala spit a seed shell out into the fire and tossed a nut skillfully into the side of Destiny's head. "Pay attention, child. Normally we start you out learning your herbs and plants, but that takes years and you already showed the power. We need to jump ahead for you. This is not our way, but I am told I am to teach you. Come closer."

Destiny was still sitting on the ground with her legs crossed. She pushed and slid herself closer to the old woman.

"Closer."

She wiggled and inched a bit more until she was right next to the woman.

"Turn and face me, look into my eyes."

Still with her legs crossed, Destiny firmly planted her palms on the ground beside her, and lifted herself up, then swiveled around to stare into her new mentor's face.

"From now on, when I say closer, I mean CLOSER!" The old woman reached up and grabbed Destiny around the back of her head and pulled, crashing their heads together. The vision of the hut and the old woman began to spin out of control, then faded from Destiny's mind.

Destiny found herself kneeling in the dirt, bowed at the waist, with her forehead pressed to the ground. She could hear footsteps passing by. There were many footsteps, all walking in unison. She wanted to look up, but was unable. It sounded like marching with the sound of metal clanging in time to the stomping of boots. She heard voices approaching against the flow of the oncoming soldiers. They spoke Latin as they passed her.

Destiny did not understand a single syllable of Latin, yet she clearly heard one man say, "These are the recruits you bring to serve me? I thought you were to present your finest men for the church?"

"Oy, stand tall there, lad." The second man clearly spoke English as he addressed one of the men marching by, then switching to Latin, said, "I assure you, they will serve your eminence with distinction. They will stand against any man you put before them."

"Ah, but there's the rub. We won't be pitting them against men, but against myths and superstitious ideas whose time has come and gone."

"What's that you say?" the Englishmen asked. "These men are soldiers, not scholars. What have they to do with myths?"

"I intend to use them to put down, once and for all, the primitive notions of magicians and evil spells. Then we can finally lead Britain into the modern age."

The soldier bristled at this remark. His back stiffened, and his hand fell to rest on the pommel of the sword at his waist. "So, the church has sent you to mock us, then."

The prior ignored the commander's stance. "No, not at all. I merely wish to enlighten you. The days when men cower in fear at the mere suggestion that their enemy has magic are over. You will see. In fact, I will show you." The dark-haired monk pulled a rather large coin out of his pocket and held it in his left hand. He flipped it around in his hand so all could see. He passed his right hand over the coin, taking it from his left hand and blew into his hand. The coin vanished into midair.

"You are a wizard, and yet you mock magic?"

The prior smiled while he dipped his left hand into the commander's vest and pulled out the coin. "I am no wizard, and this is no magic. It is merely a trick of the hand that fools the eye. Magic is nothing to fear, once you understand just what it is."

"But sir, you're newly arrived here. Perhaps you should be here a while and see a bit more before you proclaim all magic to be fool's tricks."

"Nonsense. On the one hand, I am a spiritual man devoted to the one true God. On the other hand, I am a man of science. In neither hand do I have room for such ridiculous superstitions as magic and magicians. If there be any magicians present, I dare them to strike me dead with a bolt of lightning to my chest."

Destiny's head popped up at that remark and she could clearly see the old soldier backing away and making numerous signs against evil magic. He was a grizzled old veteran with broad shoulders and a tangled brown beard sporting streaks of grey. A scar on his right cheek left him looking mean and angry, but she could see a much friendlier man behind the scar.

"I'll make you a deal," the prior continued. "You bring me a true magician and show me some true magic, and see if I can't explain what it is."

"Aye, that I can do, but best you don't be boasting about lightning bolts striking you down when I do."

The pompous prior chuckled softly, "Agreed."

Destiny felt a sharp rap on the back of her head followed by an old woman's scolding voice, "'Ow many times ave I told you to keep your bloody 'ead down afore someone lops it off yer pretty shoulders?"

Destiny stood up, rubbing the back of her head. "Have you taken leave of your senses and forgotten who I am? They're gone now, anyway. You've no cause to accost me like that."

"Cause? I needs no cause. Our deal was I gets you into the castle as me servant, and while you're in here, I be your master, and you best be gettin' used to it missy."

Destiny stood tall and looked the haggard old woman square in the eyes. "Let you get this straight. I appreciate your help getting me in here, and providing me with a reasonable purpose to be here, but if you insist on interfering with my business, I'll be forced to make some changes. Perhaps I'll start with your species. I think you might make a very fine rodent. What do you think?"

The old woman's eyes widened with fear. "You wouldn't! You couldn't! 'Aven't I treated you like me own daughter? If I's 'ard on you, it be just cause that's 'ow a master's spected to treat a servant, and the walls 'ave ears, they do."

"You think you have treated me as your own daughter? I pity any fruit of your loins. You have been simply awful with me, and the time has come for it to end."

"My apologies to you then, mum. I warn't meaning no 'arm, it were all just meant in jest. You knows that, don't ye? Asides, I was only tryin'ta remind ye not ta let 'em catch ya listenin' to them."

"Enough of your excuses. I will overlook it just this once and attribute it to stupidity."

"Aye, mum. I'm terrible stupid, ask anyone."

Destiny grunted. She would have dismissed the old hag, but they were both heading to the same quarters.

"It's been my great fortune," the old woman said, "having you stay with me. I loves 'earing you talk You 'ave such a pretty and well learnt tongue. It'd be a awful shame if you turnt me into a rat and I wasn't able to understand all yer big words."

"Relax, Mrs. Thatcher, I won't be turning you into a rat now. At least not yet."

Destiny let the memory play out in front of her. She still had received too few clues to her identity, except that she was apparently a witch of some power who was undercover in a castle occupied by Englishmen. She wished she had paid more attention to her history studies now. Everything, including Mrs. Thatcher's clothing, pointed to the Dark Ages, or Middle Ages, or maybe Renaissance. Destiny wondered how she could understand two men speaking Latin and yet not know what time period they were in. She remembered the medicine woman, Mala, and wondered why she was even here. What does all this have to do with the gift her nana insisted she had to heal?

Any large organization, whether corporate, governmental, or even religious, is going to have their secrets. In Brian's case, where a whole race of people has been driven underground and their very existence is forgotten, the secrets they keep tend to be deep.

Brian hated witches. He was raised to hate witches. The ancient texts told him to hate witches. It was witches that banished magic from the Earth. The ancient texts tell tales of witches threatening to rob his people of all magic if they did not end the war between them. When the war did not end, the witches followed through with their threat. It was their fault his people were forced underground. How fortunate they were, able to live in society, side by side with mundane men, waiting for the day when they could once again take their places as the ruling class.

His people, once proud mages and wizards able to command fire and lightning with their hands, were now reduced to weak, pathetic scholars clinging to their past. The witches at least maintained some psychic ability, but his people could barely conjure the strength to bend a spoon with their minds. They hadn't lost their cleverness, however, and over time were able to convince the naïve mankind that they never actually existed, and thus relegated themselves to the class of myths and legends.

"Excuse me, sir, can I offer you some champagne?" The stewardess held a tray with three filled glasses of bubbly.

Brian waved his hand. "Just some white wine, please."

The mages' hatred for the witches ran deep. Just being around them incurred a discomfort that rose up from their bowels and filled them with anger and fury. Destroying the witches was as much a matter of self-preservation as it was a matter of dominance. For the witches to destroy all magic was just evil. It served no purpose for either of them.

The only hope for his people was in the prophecy. How ironic that the hope which they clung to would spring from a witch prophet. The mages had no prophets. Their magic was physical. The witches had command of the spirit world and people's minds. Only they could see into the future and the past.

So the prophecy said a child would be born of both worlds, and the Banus project was born. Even stripped of their powers, the mages were still gifted scholars. The Banus project was the highest secret their people had ever held. Only the most elite leaders, of which Brian had recently been inducted, knew of its existence.

"Ladies and gentlemen, the pilot has started our descent. Please fasten your seat belts and bring your chairs and your tray tables to their full upright and locked positions. Crew members, prepare for landing."

Brian finished his wine and held the glass out in the aisle for the stewardess to collect. His heart was pumping. Though he had known about the Banus project, this was his first time meeting one of its products. The Banus project was the breeding experiment designed to cross their bloodlines with the witches. The goal was to develop a new bloodline that had all of their strengths plus the witches' abilities. The project did not go well. Most of the boys conceived showed no signs of the witches' blood, but the girls tended to go mad soon after puberty. Even if they did not go mad, the girls could never be controlled, and exhibited all the anger and madness that struck them all whenever witches and sorcerers were in the same room. The assumption was that most went mad from lack of proper training, since nobody in the cult knew how to train the witches' powers.

The jet landed with a slight bump and a powerful application of brakes and reversing thrust. It was a small airport, without the familiar jet ways used by larger airports. Brian stepped off the plane and onto the tarmac in Missoula, Montana. It was a bright, sunny day. He shielded his eyes with one hand and unfolded his dark glasses with the other. It was noon now, and he was early. They must have picked up a tail wind. He still had another leg to his journey. His next destination was a forgotten little airfield outside White Hall, Montana. The airfield was too small for a jet, so he had arranged for a pilot and a small aircraft to meet him here. Dr. Schaefer still needed some time to put his data and the animation together, and Brian hoped he might find something extraordinary here.

"Dr. Grupp?" A man in tan overalls with dark aviator glasses and an enormous smile approached Brian with his hand already extended.

"Just Mr. Grupp."

They gripped hands. "Oh, I thought all you guys were doctors and scientists."

"Nope, I work for a living."

The thin man had heard the same joke a million times during his tour in the air force, but he smiled all the same and gestured towards a row of hangars and led Brian to a section of the airport reserved for private craft. "A bean counter then?"

"Yeah," Brian lied, "I have to visit the site every now and then and make sure they are putting the money to good use."

"I hear ya. These guys may be geniuses and all, but seems to me sometimes they aren't all so securely tied to the ground."

"Fortunately for us, sometimes their dumbest ideas can be more brilliant than us mere mortal's best ideas."

"I don't know anything about that," the pilot said as he pressed the button on the hangar which engaged the door openers, "but I'm glad enough to get their business now and then."

"How remote is this place, anyway? Outdoor or indoor plumbing?"

"I guess you'd call it indoor plumbing, but the water comes from a water tower on the compound, and is pumped up from ground wells. They have regular electricity though, so it's not like you'll be completely in the wilderness."

Brian checked the reception on his phone and frowned. "I suppose cell phones would be out of the question?"

"Don't know about that, but they must have a phone. They call me when they need me."

Brian nodded as they entered the hangar. He was relieved to see a modern twin-engine plane and not a beat up old crop duster. He was equally relieved that it appeared clean and shiny, and generally well maintained.

"Well now, milady, 'tis 'bout time you waked. Maybe now the rest of us can get some sleep."

"Speak plainly, Mrs. Thatcher, what are you saying?"

"Oh, nothin', nothin' at all. It was just such an awful racket ye made last night."

"If I have not made myself plain before, let me be perfectly clear with you now, Mrs. Thatcher. Speak your mind clearly and be coy at your grave peril."

"You talks at night. When you sleep, you talks."

"Loud?"

"Loud enough, I should say."

"What did I say? And be as precise as your humble mind can possibly manage."

"Beggin' your pardon, ma'am, but me 'umble mind gets forgetful when I's scared."

Destiny's host rose to her full height and glared down at the incompetent old woman. "Mrs. Thatcher..."

"I remembers now. I remember you spoke funny. No accent I ever 'eard before. You said somethin' about your destiny and you wantin' to go 'ome."

"Are you certain?"

"Certain I is. Certain as I'm standin' 'ere talkin' to you, I is."

She puzzled over it a moment. "Your words mean nothing to me. I must have been dreaming."

"Oh, and you screamed too, you did."

"I screamed?"

"Yes, mum. Curdled me blood too, let me tell ye."

"Did it rouse anyone else? Did anybody come to the door?"

"No mum, maybe they thought I was beatin' ye."

"Well, I must admit I'll be glad when this cursed business is done and I can leave here, though I know not what home I may have spoken of in my sleep."

Mrs. Thatcher was a strange woman. Fearful of reprisals, yet she couldn't help saying just the wrong thing to the wrong person. Her back was crisscrossed with lash marks commemorating the many times her masters had taken the whip to her for her defiance. It was her defiant nature that led her to sneak a stranger into the castle, that and the coin she was promised when it was over. She left a basin of water on a rickety table and exited the room.

Destiny got up from the bed and crossed the room to the basin of water. She peered into the water and saw a young girl's face with dark brown hair. Her face was plain, almost boyish, but pretty. "Nimisen, you dolt. What have you gotten yourself into now? I sure hope you're as good as you think you are."

She went to her bags and pulled out a bright green vest and put it on over her sleeping gown, fitting it around her waist, and pulling the laces snug. Next out of the bag was a dark red and brown skirt that wrapped around her waist where it just overlapped the bottom of the vest. A brown hooded cloak fastened around her neck with a green and gold brooch and hung over her back and shoulders. She wound her hair into a loose bun and placed two metal spikes through it to hold it in place. The last item she pulled from the bag was a small piece of parchment, folded into a small envelope. She slipped it into a secret pouch she had sewn inside her skirt.

Nimisen's job, provided by Mrs. Thatcher, was delivering water and spirits to the many guests throughout the castle. Eating was generally discouraged in the private quarters, largely due to the inherent pest problems associated with having food all over the place, but also because the castle had a rather large and gracious dining hall which served both as a social hall and a source of information. Occasionally, minstrels would pass through and entertain the guests, and at other times bards would share songs of the news from the far reaches of the empire.

Water was plentiful and made the perfect guise to give Nimisen access to restricted areas of the castle. She easily moved about the castle as if she were invisible. Nobody ever took notice of a servant maiden carrying water.

The English were somewhat mixed on the presence of the monks. Nobody in the English royalty relished the thought of them meddling in affairs of state, but the church had gained an enormous amount of sway with many monarchs, and they had deftly instilled the fear of everlasting torment to any who opposed them.

Nimisen reached the quarters given to a brilliant young monk engineer who came to learn from the castle's architect so he could build a new abbey for the church. The young engineer stood over a table facing a window overlooking a great river that ran just north of the castle. She moved silently to the smaller table behind him and poured fresh water into his pitcher. He never paid her any notice. She pulled the parchment from her skirt and tapped it over his pitcher, releasing a small dust into his water. She swirled the water to help the powder dissolve, slipped the parchment back into her skirt, and left the room as quietly as she had entered.

———

The runway was unmistakable for anything else, but it lacked any of the support structures normally associated with an airstrip, and it was in dire need of maintenance. Brian saw rebar in the ground, off to the side, where a tower might have stood at one time, but was now taken over by weeds and bushes. This was a dead airfield.

A jeep and a driver waited for Brian at the end of the runway. The small plane kept some distance from the jeep so it wouldn't overwhelm them in its prop wash. Brian was grateful for the opportunity to get his ground legs back as he walked the short distance to the waiting vehicle. As soon as he climbed into the Jeep, the plane had turned around and started to taxi down to the other end of the runway to leave.

"I'm Jensen," the driver said, "commandant of the farm."

"The farm? That's what you call it?"

"Yes, sir."

Brian nodded as he climbed into the vehicle. "It fits."

The commandant put the jeep into gear and pulled away from the airstrip and down a small hill towards a paved road. "Sir, may I ask you now, why you are visiting us?"

Brian looked the man up and down, wondering if he was really who he said he was. "You're the commandant, you said?"

"Yes, sir, here." He reached into his inner jacket pocket and produced an I.D. card with his picture.

"Very well," Brian said. "I need to find someone we can send on a mission; someone who won't be detected."

"A mission? Has something happened?"

Brian didn't answer.

Commandant Jensen wasn't a particularly intelligent man, nor was he especially experienced. He was a middle-aged man who had proven himself very capable in the handling of people. He had also displayed a willingness to be ruthless when it was deemed necessary. He did, however, know when silence was all the answer he was going to get. "Our students are just kids. Can you tell me why you want one of ours instead of an outsider?"

Brian was silent again while he considered whether to share with the commandant. He finally decided his interests would be served best if he shared what he needed. "Very well. Your instincts are correct. Something has happened. We don't know any details about the source or its strength, but we are concerned about the threat this event represents. We need someone who can search out the source and relay back enough information for us to determine the threat it poses."

"I see. Just one person then?"

"Honestly, I don't know yet. The more we send, the more chance we risk exposure. Perhaps we need to consider some outside contractors as well?"

"I don't know how much we can help you there. We are mostly a training facility for our own kind, and we don't usually see much talent in them. We only have one of the others here. We're not quite sure what to do with him, and I'm concerned he may have inherited some of their compassion."

"Can he command a couple contractors?"

"He's just seventeen, and no, he can't command mercenaries. He's an awkward, geeky kid, a nerd, but he has shown some promise in detecting their presence without being detected himself. I think he might be able to sense their thoughts, or at least their moods, at times."

Brian sat back in his seat and contemplated his options while the jeep wound its way through the heavily wooded valley.

The Banus project was centuries old. It started with kidnapping and then raping young witches, who remained held against their wills until the offspring were born. The babies were then raised in isolation until puberty, when they were examined for any signs of magical abilities. The first brood was a dismal failure. None of the subjects exhibited the least bit of cross abilities, and the females quickly became quite hostile and difficult to handle. Even the best minds of the 17th century were not sufficiently educated to understand the intricacies of breeding, or how human breeding differed from farm animals. Failing to produce the desired results, the project was almost scrapped. Some would like to believe that the experiment was continued because of the prophecy, and because so much time had already been invested in it, but the truth was that the men running the experiment were lusty old men who saw this as an opportunity to have their way with some young girls. Over time, the experiment graduated to more of a private brothel for the privileged elite. That ended when the girls began to exhibit super witch abilities. They failed to create the sorcerer they yearned for, and instead had new, more powerful witches to contend with. It wasn't until the early to mid-19th century, that science had learned enough about heredity and genetics for them to map out a plan to breed a super sorcerer, who they thought would save their kind and rid the world of witches once and for all.

Towards the end of the 20th century, they began to see subjects who didn't trigger the witches' defenses, and who themselves did not feel the anger or hatred towards the witches. This was progress, and this was exactly where Brian thought he could find someone to scout the source of the other day's event.

<hr>

The prior stared out the window overlooking the training grounds where his monks were trying to teach the English rabble how their prayers would be heard by God, and how the power of God would shield them from heathen magic. Some soldiers ignored their preaching and trained themselves in sword and shield, while others listened and laughed, but a few disciples heeded the monks' words. A handful of converts was all the prior expected. He absentmindedly ate from a bunch of grapes and listened to the clang of weapon play outside.

An aide rushed into the room and approached his table, something they rarely did without his invitation. The aide was breathing heavily and gasped out, "Sir, forgive the intrusion, but something dire has happened."

"What was that? What has happened?"

"The engineer, sir, the one who came with you, we think he's been poisoned."

"Nonsense," the prior said. "What assassin would be bold enough to ply his trade in this fortress? And upon a servant of God, no less? The engineer probably just came ill from the food here."

The aide blanched at the thought that the food could be tainted. "Sir, we've all been eating the same food, and only he lies near death."

"Near death? That serious? Very well, take me to him." The prior followed the aide to the engineer's quarters.

Nimisen stood in the hallway near the engineer's quarters. She whispered in others' ears about what had happened, knowing a crowd would collect. She stood calmly among the gathering crowd while the prior brushed past her and entered the room. His voice could be heard from within the room. "Has anyone sent for the lord of the castle? He should be here."

The lord of the manor entered the room just as the prior's words had faded away. "I am here. What is this we have here?"

The prior stepped aside and motioned to where the young monk lay on the floor. "It would seem that somebody does not like my engineer."

"Who could be so foolish?" the lord barked. "This castle is impenetrable. It must be something else."

"What would it be?" the prior chided. "Evil spirits?"

"Aye."

The crowd outside started to stir. "It's a hex!" and "Evil magic!" could be heard throughout the hall.

The prior heard the crowd outside. "Nonsense," he said for all to hear. "Someone inside the castle has done this. I understand the king has a wizard who is knowledgeable in the properties of poisons and herbs."

"Take care what you say next, Priest. If you slur the wizard, you slur the royal family, and I will take that very personally. Besides, not only is he as honorable a man as you will ever meet, he is also an engineer and was somewhat fond of your man."

The prior waved his hands back and forth. "You mistake me. I suggest no complicity towards your wizard. I merely ask that you send for him, please. Let him tell us what happened. Let us see if he has magic to set this straight, and we shall also see if I cannot explain his magic as something else."

The lord of the castle yelled out into the hall, "Someone fetch the wizard! Bring him here directly!"

Nimisen waited for an aide to sprint down the hall, then left the crowd herself and started to cross the castle, staying mostly in the shadows and walking undetected to the famous wizard's room. With him busy in the engineer's room, she would have plenty of time to find what she came for.

She kept her hood pulled over her head as she slunk through the servant's hallways. He would surely take the main halls, but still she kept to the shadows. She maintained the pretense of delivering water even as she entered his room, but finding it empty, she closed the door behind her. The apartment was dark, which suited her well. Most of the room was a standard living quarter with a bed, a night table, a desk, and some storage. The far end of the room, however, was quite different. There were animal skins and heads on the walls, but not those of a hunter. They were a scholar's display. There was a display of butterflies pinned to a board with their wings beautifully preserved. A table stood away from the wall with odd glass items and jars of various colored powders and liquids. Next to the table, against the wall, she found several trunks and boxes, where she started her search.

Mostly she found and set aside small bottles of various ingredients, ground herbs and odd animal pieces. She came to the last trunk. It was a large trunk reinforced with brass straps and had a large lock securing the lid to the trunk. Nimisen pulled her hood back and extracted the metal spikes holding her hair up. She went to the lock, inserted the spikes, and started to manipulate the tumblers until the lock sprung open.

Inside, she found a much better assortment of items. She shoved some items aside, but pulled a few out and slipped them into the secret pockets inside her skirt. Anything with jewels made it to her pocket. She kept digging, deeper and deeper, looking for the one prize that brought her here.

"Looking for this?" She heard the voice booming inside her head. She sprang up and spun around to face him. He stood in darkness but held a perfectly round crystal globe that glowed from within, dimly lighting his dark beard and pale face against the gloom behind him.

She stammered a moment, trying to think of an excuse, but he raised his free hand and she was unable to speak.

"It is beautiful, is it not?" He was young for a wizard of such importance. His eyes were bright blue, even in the dim light from the orb. They pierced her eyes and held her stare locked with his. He stepped towards her and waved the orb back and forth in front of her. She was frozen, completely helpless. She felt like one of those butterflies, pinned by his gaze. He stepped closer and brought his face close to hers. She stared at his face. It was young with flawless skin. His beard was dark brown and neatly trimmed. His eyes were light and happy, and when he smiled, his whole face was bright and soothing.

Nimisen blushed. "Yes, very beautiful."

"It was a clever distraction, and it might have worked had I not seen it coming beforehand. I've been expecting you, for quite some time, you see. Waiting for you, actually."

He led her to a chair and released her. "You've been waiting for me?" she asked. "Why would you do that? Where are the guards? Why didn't you just have me arrested when I arrived here?"

"As you can see, I have no need for guards, and having you arrested would not serve my purposes at all. Besides, it would have been far too complicated to try and arrest you for a crime you had not yet committed."

"I've heard about you before," she said. "I've heard how you try and twist people's words and actions as if they all served your grand design. I only serve my own needs."

"Do you?" he asked. "Clearly, you are not here to serve water, so, pray tell, why are you here?"

Nimisen didn't respond, preferring silence to admitting her crime.

"Come now, surely you can speak in your own defense? Most thieves are quite vocal. Perhaps you have young children to feed? No, that wouldn't be it. You're practically a child still yourself, and those thieves usually are caught stealing food. What would have brought you here now, if not to serve my needs?"

"You tell me," she replied defiantly. "You seem to be the man with all the answers, the man who sees all and knows all."

"Yes," he said, "I do know. So now, if you are through with your idle wit, perhaps you can tell me if you know why you came here?"

"I was just looking. That's all, just looking."

"And you tried to poison the engineer because you just wanted to look at my belongings?"

Nimisen began to formulate an excuse in her mind. "I was looking for something that was my mother's, if you must know."

"So, now you claim that it is I who is the thief here?"

"No, sir, not that." She tried to laugh lightly. "I caught the thief, and he claimed he sold it to you. It was quite old, and he said he often sells old heirlooms to you."

"And I suppose you were taking all those things home so your mother could identify them for you, at which time you would promptly return the rest back to me?"

"It's like you could read my mind, almost, except my poor mother is no longer with us. My aunt, Mother's half-sister, was going to assist me with the identification."

The wizard took the orb, which he still held, and let it roll down his arm to the crook of his elbow, then back up his arm to his hand, like a jester might with juggling balls. Nimisen's eyes were transfixed on the orb as it traversed back and forth on his arm. "And once recovered," he continued, "you planned to keep this missing heirloom, for sentimental value, no doubt."

Her eyes remained focused on the orb. Her voice was weak and hollow when she answered, "Again, you read my mind. What they say about you and your mystical powers is true. I see that now."

He let the orb roll all the way up his arm and across his shoulders, then down the other arm. "It must mean a lot to you, the heirloom, that is."

"Yes, sir," she said, somewhat haltingly. "It means the world to me."

He let the orb spin in the palm of his hand. "I think I know just what you mean. It must break your heart to be separated from it."

"Yes, it does, sir. It's like I lost my poor mother twice, it is."

He wrapped both hands around the orb and rubbed his hands on it, first this way, then that, until he separated his hands and the orb was gone. "Truly, it must be a profound item for you to miss it so terribly, and yet not know what it looks like."

Nimisen blinked at him, trapped by her own lie.

He held up his hand so she wouldn't speak. "I know, I know, don't tell me. I shall read your mind again." The young wizard stroked his long, thin chin whiskers. "You know the item you are looking for, but felt you needed to keep a few extra trinkets to compensate you for your troubles."

With the orb gone, her voice returned to her, and she began weaving a new set of lies. "You are absolutely amazing, except I wouldn't keep anything for my troubles, were it not for my expenses, which are truly enormous. I had to pay a mighty bribe to get the thief to talk, not to mention the bounty I paid to find him."

"Certainly," he said, "that makes complete sense. I wouldn't want to stand between you and your heirloom. Perhaps you could describe it to me, and I could help you find it."

"Thank you, sir, but why would you want to do that?"

"I wouldn't want it to be said that I was in possession of stolen property. I am the king's adviser, after all."

"Well, if you are quite sure, I came for that trinket you were playing with just a moment ago."

He reached behind her ear and pulled the orb from her hair. "This thing?" He waved the orb in front of her. It spun in his hand and seemed to float, just barely suspended over his hand. "Your mother must have been a most intriguing person. This is no ordinary item. In fact, it is extremely rare, and quite powerful."

"She was truly gifted, sir, and very powerful indeed."

"She must have been. This item does not serve the weak. A woman of such power would have surely passed on her abilities to her daughter, especially one as doting as you."

"Who me?" she said. "No, not me. I'm just an ordinary girl."

"No," he argued, "I am quite sure of it. A woman powerful enough to wield this orb would have surely guaranteed its safe keeping by passing its secrets on to her beloved daughter."

"Perhaps, but I was terribly young when she died. She probably never had the time or opportunity to share its secrets with me."

"Or perhaps she did, and they are buried secretly within you. Surely you have come into your abilities by now. Show me some of your witchly powers. I have always enjoyed learning from others."

"Witchly powers?" she asked. "Me? I've never had any of those. No. I'm just a plain, ordinary girl, reduced to thievery trying to regain her mother's prized heirloom. Nothing more."

The orb flashed for a moment, and she could hear Mrs. Thatcher's voice from the wizard's mouth. "But warn't it you what was goin' ta turn me into a rat?"

Nimisen was now terrified. Her hands and legs shook uncontrollably. She saw no escape. Her voice warbled as she spoke, "The truth, sir, the truth is that I'm just a thief. I heard you had something of great power and some mages were willing to pay a generous ransom to get it from you." Nimisen heard what she said, but didn't quite understand why she spoke the truth.

"My dear girl," he said, "you are hardly just a thief. There are very few thieves who would brave operating in this stronghold, let alone go up against me. Do you not fear me?"

"No, sir," she said, "well I mean, yes, sir, I do now, a little, but I didn't before."

"You didn't fear my reprisals?"

"No, sir. I'm not superstitious. I don't believe in magic."

"And now? Now, do you believe in magic?"

"I don't know, but I think I fear you a little now. I mean, that is, I'm sure I fear you now."

He chuckled. "No matter. I give you a choice. I suggest you think well before you respond. Were you to be tried for thievery, you might be facing some very unpleasant months doing slave labor deep in the bowels of the castle. As an assassin, however, you will probably find your pretty head separated from your shoulders by the executioner's axe, but probably not before some vile and loathsome nights in the jailor's bed."

"I'm a thief," she cried out, "not an assassin!"

"Well, you're not a very good assassin anyway, I'll grant you that, but then again, you're not a very good thief either. But, as I said, I offer you an option. The chopping block, or you can agree to give up your livelihood and start a new life as my apprentice."

Her mouth parted, but nothing came out.

"I trust you are thinking about it. If words fail you, then perhaps you could simply nod or shake your head so I know your intention."

She slowly nodded her head.

"Very well, but know this, should you betray me, you may find that the jailor's bed and the executioner's axe are not so unattractive an option after all."

She swallowed hard and pushed that thought aside. "How is it a thief such as myself could be of assistance to you?"

"Well, strangely enough, many of the fanciful tales you have spun to get your way with other people have a grain of truth. You are descended from a long line of witches, as was I. Our line was scattered to the winds after the last great war, when we were defeated by the vilest practitioners of the arts the world has ever seen."

Her head spun with the news. He lit a pipe and blew smoke circles into the air. "The time has come for us to plant the seeds that will unseat the black mages from their thrones of power. This is our destiny, yours and mine."

Her mind was suddenly crystal clear. "It was all a trick. You lured me here! You tricked me to come here and seek out that orb."

He nodded. "Does that upset you?"

"No," she said, "I think I should be furious, but I'm not. What else do you see in my future?"

He just smiled and blew more smoke rings.

Chapter 6

The jeep pulled off the main road and headed down a narrow dirt and stone track. The road was completely surrounded by a forest of Lodgepole Pines and Douglas Firs, with an odd Spruce or Cedar mixed in here and there. Occasionally, the road would run alongside a meadow full of grasses and mustard plants with stands of quaking aspen visible on the far edge of the meadow. A short distance off the main road, they pulled in between two pine log fences that stood as the entrance to the remote camp. The first thing Brian saw in the facility was five spartan cabins with a flagpole surrounded by a ring of small boulders.

Brian said, "It's smaller than I expected."

"Just wait. This is just for visitors."

The jeep circled around the flagpole and between a pair of cabins, then descended down a small hill that opened up into a wide meadow. Across the meadow, Brian saw a large beige building which looked like a minimum security prison.

"I have a room prepared for you. Will you need some time to get settled in?"

"Settled in? No, I won't be staying. I just need to see this boy. Depending on my assessment, I may give you instructions on what to do with him, but I will be heading directly back this afternoon."

Destiny's head hurt. She didn't know if the headache was just a side effect of recalling ancestral memories, but she suspected it was from cramming days and weeks of memories into her head in just a few hours.

"Here, child, drink this." Her nana gave her a cup of tea. She sat down at the table across from Destiny and waited for her to take a few sips. "So, tell me, did you learn anything new?"

"I learned that one of our ancestors was a thief. I don't think she was very good though, she got caught by some wizard. You know what was really strange? She was really smart, she even knew Latin, but she tried stealing from the wizard guy, and when he caught her, he wasn't mad at all. He just wanted to keep her as an apprentice."

Michelle nodded and smiled while she listened. "But did you learn any new magic? Did you learn more about healing?"

Destiny cocked her head now, remembering how Mala had given her that memory. "No, now that you mention it, there was nothing like that. This Nimisen girl kept threatening this old woman that she would turn her into a rat, but she never did. I think she was only pretending that she could do it anyway, just to scare the old woman. It's all really confusing, because in the end, I think maybe the old wizard made up the old lady in her mind or something."

"Hmmm. Mala must have had some reason to show you that. You probably need to know it later on."

"I dunno. That Mala is kinda scary. I'm just glad it's over and behind me, and I'm real glad they didn't behead her for being an assassin. I don't ever want to go through another execution again."

Michelle chuckled. "It's not over. She's your teacher now. You'll have to find her again tomorrow afternoon. You hungry? I can fix you a sandwich if you want."

Destiny nodded her head and took another sip of tea.

Brian waited in the commandant's office. The room was dominated by a row of file credenzas on one wall, and several shelves of books on the opposite. The commandant's desk was a modest but serviceable piece, covered with an array of papers and other work. There was a minimum of personal touches on the desk. He appeared to be a man dedicated to his work.

Brian looked out the window onto the compound, which was dry and dirty, but he could see a grassy meadow and a tree line beyond that. He heard the door open, and the boy was ushered in.

"This is Blake," the commandant said, "the boy I told you about. I'll leave the two of you alone to get acquainted." He left the office, closing the door behind him.

Brian offered his hand. "Hello, Blake, my name is Brian. Why don't you sit down?"

Blake sat gingerly in the large chair facing the desk. He had no clue why he'd been called here, but usually when students were called in, it wasn't good.

"How are your studies here coming along?"

"Good, I guess."

"I trust you've already been instructed in the history of our people?"

"Yes, sir."

"And what are your thoughts on that?"

"I don't know, sir. What do you mean?"

Brian sensed that the boy was reticent to speak openly. "Are you afraid of me?"

Blake nodded.

"Don't be," Brian said. "I'm here looking for someone with special talents. I'm recruiting for a special mission, something very important to people like us. I need someone who is willing to be a hero, and do whatever it takes to help our people."

Blake started to tremble.

"What's wrong? Your commandant seems to think you might be able to handle the task. Why are you afraid?"

"I don't want to sacrifice myself, sir."

"Sacrifice?" Brian asked softly. "I wouldn't ask you to."

"I'm sorry, sir, when you said you needed someone to do whatever it takes, I thought..."

Brian summoned up his most reassuring voice and said, "You may need to get your hands dirty on this job, but I don't want to lose you. I need someone to do a fact-finding mission. Somewhere, right here in the USA, there is a witch we don't know about. We need to locate him and find out what he's up to."

The boy nodded. A wave of relief washed over him, relaxing his posture. "I get it. You asked for me because sometimes they can't sense me."

"Exactly. We aren't really sure what skills we are going to need, but we know that most of our people can't mix with them without being detected. Your commandant seems to think you can do that. Can you?"

"Yeah, they don't seem to be affected by me like they are with the other boys."

Brian sat for a moment, looking at the boy. The program was devised centuries ago to provide them with a new line of wizard that blended their powers with the witches, but the centuries had seen the total decline of magic. There were still a select few who could summon some power, but none of them could do anything even half as impressive as the illusions performed by ordinary theatrical magicians. It bothered him that the witches had somehow been able to conjure up so much power while his people remained completely impotent. Brian was questioning his decision to find someone within their own ranks. What was the point of sending someone who was completely powerless against the witches? Maybe he should just send a mercenary. The witches can't sense them. This boy was so young. How was he supposed to determine if the boy was fit for this mission without knowing how to measure his abilities?

"An excellent question, sir. A mercenary could destroy the target, but could never answer the question."

Brian was momentarily stunned by the boy's outburst. "Pardon me? What question?"

"How the witches discovered the power when we haven't."

Brian cocked his head and measured up the boy again. "Go on."

"Okay. You should give me a test. I know, how about Sparky, Sad Sack, and Tuxedo?"

Brian was catching up. The boy had heard his thoughts. He might have been put off by having someone hear his thoughts, if it weren't for the overwhelming satisfaction that the Banus project may have succeeded under his watch.

Blake continued, "You were trying to think of a test to give me, which I think is a good idea, so I listed the three dogs you had as a child. Want more?"

"I wasn't thinking about any of my childhood pets."

"I know. I searched your memory."

"You can do that? Well, obviously you can." Brian tried to suppress his thoughts. It was dangerous for the boy to read his memories, but he couldn't allow himself to think about that. "Why are you able to summon up the witch's powers, yet our people can't seem to find anyone still able to do the simplest magic?"

"I don't know. Maybe I'm just better than they are."

"Hmmm. I'm satisfied, but it's going to take more than just some witch's powers to complete this mission. We don't know where this will take you. We'll need some experienced trackers to help find him, and a commander to lead them. As far as they are concerned, you will be a special tracker, like a bloodhound."

Blake nodded. "When do we leave?"

"I'm leaving in an hour. I'll send for you in a couple days. You keep practicing your skills. You may need to infiltrate their coven and get to know him. Do you think you can pass for one of them?"

An evil grin spread across the boy's face. "I don't know if they can sense me or not, but I can do their magic, and sometimes I have dreams that I think come from them. I see them in my dreams, and it's like I already know some of them, even though I've never actually met any."

"I don't suppose you recollect hearing or sensing them recently?"

"Actually, I can pretty much sense them all the time, but mostly they're kind of hazy, like they were in a dream, but the other day I started hearing some of them really clear."

"Do you remember anything about burning?"

"Oh, yeah!" Blake said. "How weird was that? For an instant there, I thought I was on fire. You mean that was them?"

Brian nodded. "Yes. That was them. You'll do well. I think you may have a pivotal role in our future."

Destiny's sleep was rocked with a myriad of dreams all jumbled together. She pictured herself as a cat burglar sneaking in and out of windows, only to be caught by Nimisen's mysterious magician. She had dreams where she was sneaking across a field being chased by men with hounds, or she was a warrior waiting to ambush a single rider on horseback. She was a bird flying high over the ramparts of a castle, spying on the troops waiting in defense within the castle walls. The dreams kept coming all night long, and they all ended the same way, with her falling into the arms of the mysterious magician. Even the bird flew back to land on his arm. By the time she woke in the morning, his face was etched in her memory, and not just a single face. She had dreamt of him at different ages in his life, and she could picture him from many different ages.

Michelle had sensed her restlessness throughout the night and knew she was dreaming, but couldn't determine how her spirits had coped with her dreams. Sensing that she was waking, Michelle sang out from the kitchen, "Good morning, Cherie. How you feeling this morning? It sure looks like it's going to be another magnificent day. I fixed you some eggs and toast."

Destiny sat up in bed and rubbed the sleep from her eyes. She looked around the room and out the window and decided her nana was right. It did look like it would be a nice day. "Good morning, Nana. You sound just a bit too cheerful for this early in the morning." She yawned and stretched her arms wildly over her head. "You know something? I feel pretty good. I had strange dreams all night long, and some of them were scary, like nightmares, but in the end, everything always seemed just fine."

"Well, everything is just fine. You are a very special child, and you can handle anything the world dishes out to you. By the way, it's not so early in the morning, Miss Smarty Panties. You slept quite a spell there, and you're late for your schoolin'. Why don't you go ahead and have some breakfast, then you can get on with your learnin'. I got everything setup for you to go see Mala when you be ready."

"Again? What about my morning schooling? I can't be skipping that, you know. Can't I take a break? I don't seem to have any time for my own life these days."

"Oh, shush. Don't you worry 'bout nuthin. You got plenty of life in front of you, but right now you gots things to be learnt, and this be the only way."

The commandant chose again to personally drive Brian back to the airstrip. He prattled on about the various programs he was running and some of the innovative ideas he had to advance the program. He clearly saw this as an opportunity to hitch his wagon to the boys' rising star, but Brian wasn't interested in the commandant's personal agenda. His mind was focused on how he could use the boy's talents to track down the source of the disturbance. He hadn't yet devised a plan to enact once he found the source.

The plane was waiting on the strip as the jeep pulled up alongside it. Brian climbed out and offered his hand to the commandant. "I want you to know that your efforts have not been unnoticed, and will not go unrewarded. You have done an excellent job with the boy, but in the future, you might consider delegating menial jobs, like ferrying VIPs back and forth. You're far too important to our cause, and I'm sure you have much more important things demanding your attention. You'll be hearing from me soon."

"Yes, sir, thank you, sir."

Brian climbed into the plane. He reclined his chair and sat back, rubbing his temples. He'd like to talk to Dr. Schaefer, but he'd have to wait until he was in cell range at the larger airport.

Destiny was not looking forward to her training with Mala. She was a brutal and harsh woman. Rationalizing that in Mala's time, a person's actions carried life and death consequences was of little consolation for the young girl. She sat at the table, taking deep breaths, while her nana lit the candle in front of her. She held her breath slightly, then exhaled slowly, and focused on the flickering flame.

Mala was sitting next to a large man with a salt and pepper beard. She was looking quite displeased already, and Destiny had just arrived. "You're late. Half the morning has passed already. This is Ishun, one of our elders. He wants to meet you himself before we continue your training."

Destiny stared at Ishun, confused how a man could be a witch's elder.

Mala threw a small stone that landed squarely on Destiny's head. "Why shouldn't a man be an elder?"

Destiny rubbed her head and replied, "Because he's a man, and witches are women."

"Who told you such nonsense?"

"Nobody had to tell me. My nana is a witch, her mother is a witch, and my mother would have been a witch. It's just a girl thing."

"Bah! Women better know their feelings. Some men never learn their powers, but some men do, and are just as powerful as we are."

Destiny nodded her head, but Mala's face screwed up in a new expression. Mala wagged her finger at Destiny and spat out, "Why you change the subject? I not like waiting for you. You be on time when you see me."

"If I'm coming here from the future, why would the time of day mean anything?"

Ishun chuckled. Time paradoxes had always confused and amused him.

"Ayeee!" Mala exclaimed. "I am too busy to wait for students who don't come early in the morning."

"I'm sorry, Mala," Destiny said in a calm, but somewhat condescending voice, "but I just searched out your voice and came to you. If you want me to come earlier, you'll either have to teach me to control time or you'll have to send out your voice earlier in the morning."

Mala was not accustomed to students talking back to her and was visibly displeased with the course of this conversation. She turned to Ishun and started ranting, "You see? You see? She no respects her superior. She's rude to me, and it seems she's a little baby princess who can't be disciplined like normal students!"

Ishun just nodded his head toward Mala. The expression on his face was all he had to convey to her. Destiny thought she detected a mentor relationship between them, as if he was her teacher at one time, or maybe he's her boss here. Destiny looked at him, then at her, and back to him again. If he were older than Mala, the whole elder thing would make a lot more sense to Destiny.

Mala was frustrated with his reactions. "What?" she screeched. "You can't be agreeing with her? Stop with that look on your face! Say something!"

Ishun nodded. "Very well then. Her thinking is correct. She does not know our ways. She is not one of us, and you can't train her as if she were. She appears to be a very bright and talented young lady, not unlike you in your youth. You need to recall your innocent youth and treat her as a new friend. Then you can share your world and your knowledge with a new friend, instead of training her like she was a new warrior."

His voice was calm and soothing, and his advice was always impeccable. Mala closed her eyes and took a deep breath. She suddenly looked younger to Destiny, years and years younger. She opened her eyes and turned to Destiny. "We start new. I have much to show you. Come."

She jumped up and pulled back the hide that covered the door to the hut, and waited for Destiny to exit.

Destiny stepped through the door, but did not find herself outside the hut. She stood in the middle of a broad, flat desert. She could see mountains far off on the horizon. Nearby around her were assorted cacti and an endless sea of dirt. She spun around and saw that Mala had followed her there, too. Mala was now barely older than Destiny. She giggled softly and spread her arms wide. Destiny thought she looked like one of those models on a game show when they show the fabulous dinette set that the contestant was going to try to win.

"This," she said while turning her head right and left, "is all a dream of our world that we have created for you."

"You mean this, and the hut, are not actually real?"

"They not real to you," Mala said. "All this not real, is it? Are you not sitting somewhere in the future staring into some shiny object?"

"Is this different from the other memories I have experienced?"

"Yes. Those were someone else's memory. It was real place and real time. This place is not a memory. It is a projection of my world that we make for you. It exists outside of the boundaries of time. It is a place where our kind can come together from all the different ages.

I am not actually here. I am in my home, staring into the flames. We share this world with you, as we do with many people, so we can get together from across great distances, and even across time, as you have."

"So," Destiny said, "that must be how you were able to change your age so easily."

"Yes. It is sometimes very convenient to change yourself when dealing with other people."

"And that must be why I am myself here, but in my other memories, I was always someone else."

Mala nodded. "Yes."

"Why did you give me that last memory? I didn't learn any new powers or anything there."

Mala started walking through the desert. Her pace was slow, and Destiny easily kept with her. "That memory was part introduction and part test." Mala said, "You met him, no?"

"Met who?"

"The Great One. He who is the most powerful of our kind. He saved our people. You descend from his line. He took Nimisen as not only his apprentice, but eventually as his bride. There is great power in your blood."

"I met him," Destiny said, "but he didn't teach me anything. He caught Nimisen trying to steal something from him, but it was all a trick. He lured her there, caught her, and forced her to be his apprentice."

"He may have tricked her, but she was willing enough. As powerful as he already was, his power only grew when they were together. Hers, too. They were each more powerful as a team than either of them was alone. I think their power came from their love for each other. I think they loved each other all along, before they even met. Love is a powerful and mysterious thing, young Destiny. Do not let it be a distraction to you, but do not let it slip through your fingers, either. Love is like a blanket. The blanket not really make you warm, but when you wrap it around you, it doubles the warmth inside you."

"Well, I didn't see any love, but he was kinda cute. Will I meet them again?"

"When dreams not bound by time," Mala said, "you will find that there are those you will run into."

"I see."

"No, you don't yet, but you will. You saw the Orb of Destiny?"

"Is that what it was called? I have an Orb named after me?" Destiny laughed softly.

"Not joke. Not named after you. Maybe it was made for you. Maybe not."

"What? You think that some orb that was made a thousand years ago was made just to wait for me to come along? That's crazy."

"The universe is full of mysteries. That is just one of many possible truths. If the orb is for you, then it will find you."

Destiny's eyes glazed over with the thought that a magical orb waited over a thousand years for her to be born.

"No day dreaming. I have things to show you." Mala jumped up on a boulder. It was the size of a picnic table. It had a few smaller rocks piled around its base, and was one of the very few landmarks to be seen in this flat, desolate desert. As soon as she landed on the boulder, a rattlesnake hastily slid out from under one of the smaller rocks, rattling its tail to alert all nearby of the danger it presented to them.

Destiny shrieked and jumped up on the boulder, clinging to Mala for balance. "Are you trying to kill me?"

"No. I not kill you. See? I am your friend now. I share things with you." She jumped off the rock and approached the serpent, holding her hands out. The snake turned around to face her and coiled up into a small pile, but instead of threatening Mala the way snakes do, it simply calmed its tail and rested its head on its coils.

"See?" Mala said. "Calming snake is like healing hurt. Instead of fix injury, you fix fear. When snake not afraid, snake can relax with us."

"Why would we want the snake to relax with us?"

"You prefer snake bite us?"

Destiny shook her head. "No, relaxing is better than biting."

"You try." Mala released the snake from her influence and jumped back up on the rock. The snake was annoyed for having been interrupted, but was unable to comprehend what had happened to it. It did, however, detect two warm-blooded bodies moving on top of the rock. It reared up in its coil and hissed and rattled at them.

Destiny held out her hands and tried to exude calmness, but had no effect whatsoever.

"You must believe. Feeling come from deep down."

Destiny tried again, but the snake just continued to rattle and rock back and forth on its coil.

"I not convinced. Snake not convinced. Do like you mean it."

Destiny shifted her position, breathed deeply, and tried pushing a feeling of calm from her to the snake.

"No. No. NO!" Mala shouted. "Do like your life depend on it!"

Mala pushed Destiny off the rock. She fell to the ground just a couple feet from the snake. It was clearly unhappy that she would approach this close and took a couple threatening strikes towards her. Her heart was thumping in her ears. She held up her hands to block any upcoming attack while she brought her feet under her so she could get up again. The snake started to strike again, but then pulled back into its coil. It stopped rattling and rested its head again.

"Yes!" Mala shouted. "That's it!"

Destiny backed away from the snake and hopped back up on the rock. She was naturally furious. "You are crazy! That snake was going to kill me!"

"No, it not kill you."

"Were you going to jump down and stop it from biting me?"

"No," Mala admitted, "I not stop it. It would bite you. But I heal you before you die."

"What happens to me if I die in this world?"

"I told you, I not let you die."

"But," Destiny repeated, "what would happen to me?"

"It be better you don't die here. I teach you to stay alive."

"Oh, that makes me feel so much better."

"It good you feel better. You stop snake. Well done. Some lessons are hard."

"Great," Destiny said bitterly, "I'm safe from a snake attack. Like I was ever worried about being attacked by snakes." In truth, snakes were common place in Cricket Bend, but Destiny was far too angry to let either truth or logic enter into the conversation.

"What work for snake work for bear, lion, almost all animal."

"What about people? Can it work on people?"

"Some maybe," Mala said, "not all. It might only help calm some people, but it still good to know. It more easy to plant idea in calm animal."

"Why would I want to plant an idea into an animal?"

"Maybe bad man attack you, and there is animal near. You not want animal help against bad man?"

There were lots of critters in the Bayou. Destiny might find this useful and asked, "You can make an animal attack someone?"

"Not exactly. You not control them, but you make them dislike someone, and you make them think that person is threat."

"And then they attack him? Cool."

"Sometimes they run away too. It still good to have as option I think."

The snake leaped out of its coil and straight up the rock where it sank its fangs into Mala's right ankle before it jumped down and slithered away.

Mala fell off the rock, landing on the ground with a thump. She was holding her ankle, straining to remain in control, fighting away tears. "You did that! You make it attack me!"

"You said I could not control it like that. But don't worry, I won't let you die." Destiny jumped down off the rock and crouched down beside Mala. She wrapped her hands around Mala's ankle, not being particularly gentle around the bite. She brought up the healing waves from the pit of her stomach. Her hands warmed and tingled.

Mala looked at Destiny warily.

"I'm sorry, Mala," Destiny said. "I guess you were right. Some lessons can be hard."

"Lesson over. You go now."

Destiny came out of her trance, visibly upset. Michelle wanted to console her and calm her down enough to learn what happened, but Destiny was pacing this way and that, turning at odd and random intervals. Michelle just got winded and dizzy, trying to catch her, and sat back down at the table to catch her breath.

"Child!" Michelle shouted. "Child! Slow down and tell your nana what be goin' on in your mind!"

Destiny stopped pacing momentarily and faced her nana. "Ooooooh!!!!" was all she managed to say, and then she was pacing again.

"I'm sorry, Cherie, but I'm not up to date on the vernacular of today's youth. Can you please translate 'Ooooooh' for me?"

"That woman is so infuriating! I hate her! She tried to kill me! But I got her back. I doubt she'll be wanting to see me ever again."

"Nonsense. You'll see, tomorrow is a new day. I'm sure she still wants to train you."

Destiny sat down at the table. She was still seething, but as with dreams, the emotions her body was feeling were quickly dissipating. Unlike dreams, she could still vividly remember the experience, and she was still angry with Mala. She just didn't have the racing heart and clammy skin to add oomph to her hatred.

"See that?" her nana said. "I can tell already, you is feeling better."

Destiny looked into her nana's face. It oozed with love and compassion. She wondered maybe if her nana did have a power to calm her down, and just didn't know it.

Chapter 7

Destiny's head swooned with a jumble of images. She had never been particularly afraid of snakes before, but tonight she had to check in her bed, under her bed, under her pillow, everywhere. She lived in the Bayou and snakes were everywhere, like ants.

It was a warm enough night that she could have worn her short pajamas, but she was feeling anxious and exposed, and nervous about everything, so she just felt more comfortable pulling her long jammies on. She turned off the lights and sprinted to the bed. She pulled the blankets around her a little tighter than usual. She was tired, but her eyes did not want to close. She listened to her heart reverberating in her ears and wondered why she hadn't just left the lights on. In the dark, snakes could slither all over the floor, and she would never know it.

She rolled over to face the window. The window was open, but the shade was pulled down. The moon was nearly full outside, and it cast shadows of the trees onto the shade. A bare branch was cast prominently in the center of the shade. It was a gnarled branch with three spindly twigs spread out from its end like a claw that pulsated as the shade flexed in and out of the window with every breath the house took.

Destiny rolled over again, facing her back to the window. Sleep seemed hopeless to her. A hole in the shade cast a narrow beam of light onto the wall that swayed back and forth in a hypnotic dance. She stared at the light, dazzled by the arcs and loops it traced on the wall. Sleep finally started to pull her eyelids shut until she felt the presence of someone watching her. She was paralyzed by the thought that she may not be alone. She tried to convince herself that she was just being silly; nobody could possibly be there. She closed her eyes and tried bravely to ignore the beating of her own heart, which now thundered through her whole body in a throbbing pulse.

She heard something move behind her. Still frozen, she opened her eyes and glanced over at the mirror on her wall. There was a face in the mirror. She sucked in her breath as her body tensed up, but the face smiled down upon her. Destiny stared into its eyes and saw something familiar. She spun around in the bed again and gasped, "Mama?" But nobody was there.

She settled back down in her pillows and saw something move on the branch outside. A snake had wound around the claw-shaped branch. It beckoned to her. She wrapped her pillow around her ears, but still she heard the snake call for her. She went to the window and pulled the shade aside. The snake lifted its head off the branch and smiled at her. As she watched the snake, its head transformed into the weathered face of Mala's old appearance. The smile had turned sinister and menacing. The head morphed again, this time into the young Mala's face. The smile was friendly and inviting, but her eyes were angry and threatening.

Destiny let loose the shade and jumped back into the bed, pulling the covers over her head. She started to cry little baby tears, and was angry with herself for being so immature, which only made her cry more. She was losing her ability to tell dream from reality. She was going to end up like her mother.

Her mother's voice floated into her head, "No dear, I will never let that happen to you."

In the morning, Michelle had already gathered up the fresh eggs and was fixing a plate of scrambled eggs for Destiny. "Don't worry about your regular schoolin'. You go right in and see Mala. You'll see that today is a new day and you'll start the day fresh."

Destiny dallied over her breakfast. She sat in front of her plate, pushing the eggs around with her fork.

Michelle stood over her, hands on hips, and asked, "What's gettin' into you? How long do you plan to pretend you're chewing those eggs?"

Destiny looked up at her nana and shrugged. "What's the point? She doesn't like me. She thinks I'm spoiled and undisciplined. She didn't teach me nothin' about healing. You can teach me to explore our ancestors just as well as she can."

"What's this really about? You never has told me why you was so upset yesterday. What you not tellin' me?"

Destiny didn't answer.

Michelle cleared her plate and set a candle on the table. "If you ain't gonna confide in your only nana, who raised you from birth, then you might as well git to your schoolin'." She lit the candle and sat at Destiny's left hand, watching her stare into the flame. "What's the matter, dear? You didn't take this long before. Are you sure you're trying?"

Destiny avoided looking at her nana. "Sure, I'm trying. It's just hard for some reason today."

"Go ahead, try again."

"I am!"

"No, you ain't! You think I can't tell when you is really tryin'?"

"But it's hard."

"Sure," Michelle said, "it's hard, it's hard for me, and it's hard for others. Most of the folks out in the regular world don't even know it can be done. And if you told them, they wouldn't believe you. That's how hard it is. But, tain't hard for you. I watched you. You learnt it like a fish to swim."

"Maybe I just got lucky, or maybe it comes and goes, you know, like other stuff that come once a month."

Michelle chuckled, "Nice try missy, but don't you think I woulda noticed if it came and went with my monthly visits? Now try again, for real, she's waiting for you."

"But she's so unpleasant. I didn't like her at all."

"No matter if you don't like her, she's your teacher, and it's time you go to school." Michelle pointed at the flame.

Destiny saw that arguing would be fruitless. If she was going to get out of this, she would have to try a different approach. She stared into the flame and drew her mind into it. Voices immediately began to fade in and surround her. She heard Mala's distinct voice calling for her, but she turned her mind in another direction. She thought she heard a child laughing and latched on in that direction. The world wrapped around her, like a fog bank, and then the fog lifted and she was standing before a long wooden table with a variety of plants and odd items displayed upon it.

She walked down the length of the table, poking a child's finger into the various piles of leaves, twigs, and bark saying, "No," for each one she poked. As she reached the end of the table, she came to a glass jar with a frog inside. She leaned in close and stared at the frog.

It stared back at her. She was about to say, "yes," and pry the lid off the jar when she heard the clang of metal upon metal and felt her heart tugged away from the table.

She crossed the stone floor, leaned over the wall, and found herself staring down upon the world from atop a castle rampart. She saw boys of many ages practicing with sword and shield. They were like ants from this dizzying height. They wore simple leather tunics, but Destiny could see other, older men walking up and down the rows of boys in ring mail, stopping occasionally to correct a boy's posture. She didn't understand why, but she desperately yearned to be down there among them.

She heard footsteps on the stone behind her as someone new entered the rampart, and an elder gentleman's voice said, "My apologies for being late, princess, let us continue from where we left off yesterday. Kindly identify this plant."

A young girl standing before the table said, "That's Dwale. No wait, it's Wolfsbane."

"Very good, and this one?"

"That one's Dwale."

"Excellent," he said, then raising his voice slightly, asked, "and what would you get if I added it to your meal?"

She started to answer, "It..."

"No," he said, "Not you." He coughed a very loud and false cough.

Destiny spun around and found him staring at her. She walked back to the table where he stood. His long white beard scraped the surface of the table and had some of the herbs embedded in its snowy mass.

Staring directly at her, the old man asked, "Would you kindly tell me what would happen if I mixed some Dwale in with your meal?"

Destiny heard a young boy's voice respond from her mouth, "I expect you would find yourself in some trouble, as I would most likely be dead."

The old man inhaled a shallow breath, then closed his eyes and exhaled as he shook his head in exasperation.

"I suppose, however," she continued, "that if you gave me a small enough amount, I might only sleep."

The old man nodded his head, grateful that his lesson wasn't completely lost on the child.

"Of course, I would be sleeping the sound sleep of death, and people would believe I was dead, and you'd still be in trouble."

The princess giggled while color rose in the old man's features and his hands rolled up into clenched fists.

"But," Destiny's host continued, "you would not be in nearly as much trouble as you will be if you ever dip your beard into your tea."

"Enough!" the old man growled.

"I suppose," she continued, "that if you were in the habit of consuming Mithridate, you might be immune to the particles you carry in your beard."

The teacher's stance softened. "What else can you tell me about Mithridate?"

She walked up and down the table, toying with the various specimens, before she answered. "First of all, if you are not careful, mixing and using Mithridate is probably just as likely to kill you as this dwale is."

"Yes, go on."

"And even though it has a reputation as a universal antidote, I believe that if you were to use Mithridate, and then you did ingest some Dwale, and by some chance you survived, I would probably be more inclined to attribute it to your cantankerous personality than the Mithridate."

The old man's face turned dark crimson. Destiny thought he was going to burst a blood vessel. He gripped the edge of the table until his knuckles turned white and growled to them, "Class dismissed."

Destiny pulled the princess aside. "Auntie, can we talk?"

"Shhh," she said, "not here."

They each ran off, taking separate paths to their favorite meeting place. Destiny's path took her down the spiral steps, which lined the walls of one of the towers. She flew down the stairs and out the main gate, past the boys she had seen training with swords. She stopped and watched them train for a moment, but the two youngest boys on the end nearest her stopped when they realized they were being watched.

"Hey you," one of them yelled out, "this here is for noble born lads like us, and not meant for fatherless bastards like yourself. Scat now, or I'll lay a welt upon your backside."

Destiny hesitated, and the boy stepped towards her, but before he had made two strides, one of the instructors laid his rod forcefully on the boy's back, knocking him down. The boy got to his feet, his ego bruised even more than his back, and muttered, "I'll get you."

The instructor barked out, "Did you not learn your lesson from the first blow? Must I administer another?"

The boy glared at Destiny, but went back to his training while she ran off across the field to the edge of the forest where the ground rolled downwards into a small valley. She could hear water gurgling down below and skipped down to their secret spot.

The princess was there already. She sat on a chair-sized boulder, with her light blue gown spread perfectly across the rock.

"Goodness," she chided, "I thought you had lost your way."

"It was those boys again." Destiny dropped to her knees at the creek's edge and grabbed a loose twig that lay on the ground. She poked the stick into the water, stirring up bugs from the bottom. Through the ripples, she stared into a young boy's reflection. She thought he looked like he was about ten or twelve years old and had deep blue eyes and windswept dark brown hair that hung nearly to his shoulders. He parted his lips as if about to say something and then chose to stir the muck beneath his reflection instead. Having contemplated his situation, he looked up at the young girl, who was maybe a couple years older than he, and said, "You're a good friend. I'm lucky to have you."

"No, I'm not. If I was really a good friend, I wouldn't sneak out here just so nobody would see us talk."

"I still think you're a good friend. I just don't know why those boys have to know I'm a bastard. Why couldn't they discover that I was the King's grandson instead?"

Princess Saffir picked a small flower and inhaled its fragrance. She carefully plucked the leaves off the stem and slipped it into her hair at the top of her braids. "Do you think it would make so great a difference if they knew, and you were Prince Marvalaine instead of Master Marvalaine?"

"It might make a difference to them."

"I'm sure you are correct, but, unfortunately for you, Master Marvalaine," she emphasized his name, "they don't know, or they would hold their tongues."

Marvalaine returned to stirring his stick in the mud. Destiny could feel his great longing for acceptance. He had many questions, and he could tell that his mother knew the answers, but was unwilling to share them with him. "Well, at least they are allowed to get training in weapons and stuff while my own family keeps me hidden away."

"Or maybe the King won't allow his only grandson to become someone's squire? Have you thought of that? You can't have regular training with those boys."

"Sure, but what about what I want? I'm not getting any training at all!"

"Nonsense," she said, "we both get the same lessons in languages and herbs from the same tutors."

"So, I'm being trained as a princess instead of a prince?"

"Stop being so dramatic. You are being trained as a scholar. Do you think those louts ever have an original thought between them?"

"They're being trained for action," he responded. "What need have they for thinking?"

"Ask yourself what need has a king for thinking? Or should a king only be trained in action?"

He thought about it for a moment, but it did not help his mood. "It seems to me that the monks and friars are also trained in the scholarly arts. Perhaps I am destined for the abbey."

"I doubt the abbey would take you. You are far too proud for them."

"That's me," he said. "I'm the proud family embarrassment."

"Oh, hush."

Destiny heard a loud rustling behind her, followed by the two boys from the practice field crashing through the brush.

"There you are!" the first one said. "You got me a fat welt on my back, and I intend to return the gift to you double!"

Princess Saffir, who had been hidden from their view, sprang up off the rock in defense of her nephew. "What are you doing here?"

Startled out of his wits, the young bully couldn't find his tongue.

The princess did not wait for him to regain his composure. She had been trained to put on airs and deal with people below her station. "You are intruding upon my privacy. I demand that you leave at once!"

The boy took a step back, then did a double take and said, "Wait a minute, your privacy? You're with him! And I means to deal with him."

Marvalaine stepped aside from his aunt's shadow and said, "I'm not afraid of you!" In truth, he was, and Destiny wasn't too thrilled with where he was taking her.

The young bully stepped towards Marvalaine with his hands raised, preparing to either grab or push him.

The Princess stepped in front of her nephew again and slapped the bully hard on the face.

He stopped in his tracks and stared at her. A deep red rage filled his face. "Princess or not, there is only so much I am willing to take from a girl!" Instead of grabbing Marvalaine, he now grabbed the princess by the arms and started to push her backwards towards the creek.

Marvalaine jumped up and grabbed the bully's arms. He was younger and smaller than the bully, and wasn't very strong, even for his age. He had little chance of prying the bully's arms off his aunt, but Destiny felt a strength well up in his arms. His hands tingled as he gripped the bully's arms. His aunt squirmed free and backed away, watching the two of them struggle. Marvalaine stepped squarely in front of his antagonist, staring him straight in the face. The ruffian was paralyzed. His mouth fell open, and his hair stood straight up around his head. His eyes rolled back in his head and he fell backwards onto the grass behind him.

The princess grabbed her nephew's shoulders from behind. "What did you do to him?"

"Nothing, I mean, I don't know."

"Come, let us make our escape before he comes to his senses. We had better tell your mother about this too, I think." She took him by the hand and led him back to the castle. They both stared down the other boy, who was content to back out of their way and let them pass.

The turbulent skies did not allow Brian to get much sleep. He didn't suffer from motion sickness, but he was grateful to get back on solid ground when they landed.

The airport was busy, as all large airports usually are. Teams of airline workers hustled about keeping the planes and the terminals clean and tidy. Security guards stood at various access points, watching the people come and go.

Brian made his way to the terminal where he would catch a departing plane and found a bank of phones alongside a row of arrival and departure monitors. Dr. Schaefer was ready for his call. "Richard, I hope you have good news for me."

"Not all good, I'm afraid. Assuming the event moved radially and at a relatively uniform velocity, we should be able to triangulate its location, like we do with global positioning satellites. Unfortunately, none of our locations are tightly synchronized on the correct time, and that introduces considerable error in the calculation, but that only makes it a larger area to search. We can still narrow it down. Unfortunately, though, it gets worse. The wave also appears to travel at different speeds over different terrain, and get this, I think that our inmates accelerated it. I wish we had a way to measure it with equipment."

"Dick...Dick...You haven't said where it is yet."

"Oh, sorry, I've narrowed it down to somewhere in the mid-south United States. But that's still an area about eight hundred by eight hundred miles. I'm hoping we will be able to refine that number down to about one quarter the size, but I don't think we will be able to get much closer than that."

"Good job," Brian said. "I think I've located someone from within our ranks who might be able to track them down once you get your final numbers. Now, what's the status of the facilities? Have we regained control of them yet?"

"Yes, we've regained control. We've accounted for all the inmates, and the effects of the event have worn off all our personnel."

"Excellent. Do me a favor. When you think you've started to narrow down the area, see if you can find me a short list of contractors who know the area. I doubt we're looking for an urban area, so we'll want some guys comfortable living off the land."

"Military?"

"Yeah, but Dick, let's try and find guys that look more like deer hunters, and a little less like Rambo."

"Sure, I'll see if one of our local groups in that zone can recommend anyone."

Blake did his exercises in solitude. He never made many friends in camp, and when he did, they usually didn't remain his friend for long. This wasn't a camp where they maintained breeders. He'd been weeded out as a young boy of significant potential and sent to this camp for training. The camp wasn't designed to train young witches. Its goal was to find a promising youngster who could harness the lost power. Their training was mostly in the malevolent arts, bending things, starting fires, where Blake was being trained in the benevolent arts like reading minds, seeing the future. Unfortunately for him, there were no instructors who could really train him, other than offer encouragement to seek out his own inner abilities. The other trainees had no clue who he was or what his talents were. They only knew he wasn't in their classes training with them, so they assumed he was inferior to them. Such assumptions were a particular problem with their kind in general. They treated him as a freak and always drove away anyone who would befriend him.

He wanted to tell all of them that he had a special mission. He wanted them to know that the future of the clan might well rely upon him, and that he was in fact, far superior to them. He wanted to, but a small voice within him told him to keep quiet, that he would have far better opportunities to deal with them in the future. So, he practiced in silence.

None of the instructors had worked with him in years. They couldn't understand what he did, or how he did it, and certainly they had no way of evaluating his performance, so they just let him go about his studies on his own. Consequently, nobody knew what talents he had developed. His first gift, when he was young, was his ability to hear people's thoughts from time to time. He eventually learned to focus on people's minds and even to search their memory. He had developed a pretty uncanny ability to make good decisions by intuition. Best of all, he could, if he tried really hard, give headaches to those boys that went out of their way to torment him. His favorite ability, and least developed, was dreaming the future. He had no control of this whatsoever, and he was still struggling to tell the difference between an ordinary dream, and one that was a reflection of the future.

For now, though, he needed to practice listening to other minds. Among his favorite targets were the other trainees while they were in their class. He set a small figurine in the middle of the table where the sun was shining. The figurine was a Sea Gull, which had no special significance, but it was covered in glitter. When he hung it on its stand, it twisted and swung with the slightest breeze. He stared at the glittering light and narrowed his focus only on the figurine. The room retracted and faded from his vision until he found himself in a small circle of trainees. Each boy sat cross-legged on the floor, holding a plain spoon in their left hand while tracing the spoon's shape with the tips of their right hand fingers.

The instructor walked around the circle. His footsteps were silent, and his voice was soothing and almost monotone. "Feel the spoon. Feel the warmth from your fingertips transfer into the spoon." He stopped occasionally if he felt one of the students wasn't concentrating properly, and rapped the student sharply on the ear with the horse whip he always carried.

It was a familiar exercise. They didn't have very many different lessons. These lessons are the lessons that students have learned for thousands of years. Blake found their persistence amazing. None of the boys ever succeeded in bending the spoon, or even warming it up. Once, a boy bent one with his thumb and tried passing it off as the real thing. He was never seen again. These are the same boys that thought they were so superior to Blake, and yet, they couldn't even bend a spoon.

Blake snapped out of his trance. The spoon lesson was boring. He picked up a spoon from the table, gave it a quick glance, and watched it bend over in the middle. Nobody had ever given him any interest. It had never occurred to them to train him in the dark arts, but that would change. They didn't need to know about his abilities. He was going out on a mission, where he would be able to prove himself. For all he knew, the rest of his kind were as inept as these boys, and if he played his cards right, he could become the most powerful person in the clan, maybe even in the world.

Princess Saffir and Marvalaine ran through the main hall, out the side exit, and up the stairs to the balcony, where Princess Avaliene sat writing letters for her father.

Princess Saffir was still in mid-stride when she shouted across the room, "Sister! Sister! Wait till you hear!"

"Woah, you two," her older sister said, "slow down. It's not seemly for a princess to be seen running about the halls like a wild animal."

"No!" the young princess insisted. "Listen to what happened!"

"I'm listening. Slow down! Take a deep breath, and talk calmly to me."

Princess Saffir continued, "We were down by the stream, just talking and stuff."

"Do the two of you go down to the stream together often?"

"Yes, Mother." Marvalaine had been standing with his head down, staring at his feet, but looked up now to speak. "Well, we don't go there together, if that's what you mean, but we meet there sometimes."

Princess Avaliene put her quill down and picked up a brush to run through her younger sister's hair while they talked. "I see, so you met there today and were talking."

"Sister, you must understand, that's one of our secret places. We meet there and talk about things we can't discuss here."

Princess Avaliene smiled. Children always found life so dramatic. "Oh, I think I understand. And what happened today, when you were discussing your secret things, in your secret place?"

Princess Saffir pulled away from her sister's brush and turned to face her. "Those boys are always so mean to Marvalaine. Today they came down to our secret place, and I think they meant to hurt him."

Princess Avaliene's posture stiffened slightly. "Did they?"

She nodded her head. "The lead boy tried, but I stepped in front of Marvalaine and stopped him. Then he attacked me instead!"

Princess Avaliene dropped her brush and started for her father's office.

"No, sister, wait, we haven't told you what happened yet!"

She turned and asked, "There's more?" The mirth of the children's little drama, and even the concern over the rough handling of the princess was now replaced on her face with an expression of quizzical concern.

Princess Saffir tugged at her sister's sleeve and tried to return her to her seat. "Much more!"

Marvalaine turned sideways, slouching slightly. He stared at his feet and traced circles on the floor with his toes.

Seeing his posture, Princess Avaliene steadied her voice and said, "Son, tell me what has you so agitated."

Marvalaine twisted right and left, clearly hesitant to answer.

"Marvalaine?"

The stern tone of her voice mixed with his own fear of being discovered left him torn, unable to decide what he should do next. He looked up at his mother, his eyes wide with fear of disappointing her.

She returned to her bench, taking him with her. She wrapped her arms around him and said, "You can tell me anything. I know your arrangement here has been difficult for you, but I do love you."

He took a deep breath and said, "Something happened. One of them attacked Auntie. He grabbed her arms and started to push her backwards. I think he was going to push her into the water. That made me so mad that I grabbed his arms and forced him to let go of her!"

"Well done, son!" Princess Avaliene's face brightened as she shouted, "Bravo! You defended your aunt's honor! I should tell your grandfather about your noble deed."

"No sister, you don't understand." Princess Saffir stepped up next to Marvalaine and took her sister's hands into her own. "He grabbed the bully's arm, and something happened. Something happened to the bully. His hair stood up, he turned very pale, and he collapsed backwards, just from Marvalaine's touch!"

Princess Avaliene recognized the significance of such an event and summoned up her own faerie powers to calm her emotions. She smiled at her son, hiding the concern from her face. "Oh my, now I understand. That is something to get excited about. It seems, my son, that you may have some faerie in you after all. I should consult with the elders about having you properly tested."

"But Mother, you have tested me before, and I never showed any talent for faerie magic."

"True, son, but you may have been too young, or I may have given you the wrong tests. We don't speak of your father, but he was from the other faeries, and you may have some of his blood in you after all."

Marvalaine's eyes wetted uncontrollably. "I've only heard bad things about the other faeries, and I don't want to be like them! I want to be like you and your mother!"

She wrapped him again in a warm embrace and said, "Don't worry, son, you are nothing like your father, but you may have inherited some interesting abilities from him. The black faeries, which are what my mother called them, have magical abilities different from our own. Our people can see into the future, or the past, or even into other people's minds. The black faerie people could control things in our world, things we can touch, and see, and smell. They can harness the power of fire, and they can pull lightning down from the sky."

"Fire and lightning? How did we win the war if they could do all that?"

"The war? We haven't won any war. Nobody wins wars. The war between the faeries has only hurt both sides, and now we find ourselves outnumbered by the simple folk who live in our lands."

"I don't see how they didn't wipe us out with fire and lightning."

"Our ways are also very powerful, son. Our warriors would get into their heads and confuse them, so they would use their powers against each other."

She held her lips to his forehead and gave him a gentle kiss. Destiny felt the now familiar sensation of being drawn into a memory, only this time it was Marvalaine, and he was taking her with him.

When focus returned to their eyes, they were riding in a magnificent carriage. It was a beautiful day, with a deep blue sky mottled with thin white clouds. The carriage had an open top with a high back and front, hiding them from the road and sheltering them from the dust stirred up by the horses. Destiny could hear the clink and clop of horses both before and behind them.

A rider pulled up alongside the coach. He was dressed in a regal looking uniform with light armor on his legs and chest. "Your Majesty," he said, "our scouts have spotted a clearing ahead with a stream where we can water the horses. Perhaps you and the princess might like to stretch your legs?"

"Thank you, Geoffrey. That would be nice. Let us have our mid-day meal as well. I don't believe your knights have enjoyed a meal out of the saddle since we left."

"Yes, Your Grace."

The woman next to Destiny turned to her and said, "I guess we had better finish this so we can enjoy some fresh air ourselves." She was a beautiful woman whose blonde hair fell down around her face from a black and saffron hat, but it was her eyes that captured their attention. They were bluer than the sky. She held a ball of yarn, which she was winding from the yarn wrapped around Destiny's outstretched hands.

Destiny could feel Marvalaine's confusion as a young girl's voice escaped their lips and asked, "Mother, what do you mean when you say it is time for me to be trained by our own people?"

"It is our way. When a child reaches a certain age, it is the time of the training. It is what our people have done since time began."

"Our people? Is Father not our people?"

The queen smiled warmly and explained, "Your father, the king, is a great and powerful ruler, more fair-minded than most from the world of men, but he was at war. Our people, too, were at war. He had soldiers who could aid our people, and we had a different kind of soldier who could aid his, so we formed an alliance. I married your father to seal the bond between our people and his."

"I thought you and Father were in love."

"So we are. I grew to love him."

The queen finished rolling the ball of yarn and tucked it into her bag just as the carriage pulled to a stop alongside a grassy meadow. She handed the bag to Destiny and waited for the coachman to open the door. Geoffrey sat tall in his saddle, directing half his knights to stand guard around the camp while Romney placed a stool at the foot of the carriage and offered the queen a hand while she stepped down.

"Thank you, Romney."

Romney nodded his head and turned to offer the same hand to the princess. "And for you, Princess Avaliene?"

She handed him the bag with the yarn and said, "I'll be fine, but the queen will be wanting this."

Destiny could feel Marvalaine blanche as they reached down and grabbed hold of the full skirt and underskirt that flowed around them, and then jumped down to the step and on to the grass below.

The princess followed the Queen to a place near the brook where the valets had already set a large blanket on the ground with a parasol to provide shade. A stuffed bench was placed on the blanket so the queen could sit higher than the rest. The queen sat down, arranged her skirt around her feet, and accepted her knitting bag from Romney. Princess Avaliene, on the other hand, threw herself onto the front edge of the blanket and rolled to her mother's feet. She loved the softness of the meadow grass crushed beneath the weight of the blanket.

The queen shot her a scolding eye and said, "Are we ten years old all over again? I'm not so sure I can go through that again, young lady."

The princess sat up like a proper lady and arranged her skirt modestly around her. Marvalaine cringed again, thinking she had just started to get interesting.

Having settled down, the princess looked to her mother and asked, "Do you think they will like me?"

The queen returned to her knitting, one of her few passions, and answered, "Of course they will like you. They will love you, as I do."

Princess Avaliene scrunched her mouth while she thought how she would form her next sentence. "If you married Father to bond our people together with his, why are our people still kept secret?"

"Truly, I think your father wishes it weren't so, but the world of man is not so open-minded as he. There are those who believe the faerie people are an abomination."

"That's just ridiculous," Destiny said. "We are not so different from them."

"No, sweetheart, we are actually quite different."

"Well, we certainly are no abomination, especially you. You are the nicest and most beautiful person I know."

"Thank you dear, but not all the faerie people are like us. Our war was with those other faeries, and they are an evil lot."

The princess reached down for her stomach. "Where is the food? I'm so hungry it hurts!"

Marvalaine and Destiny felt it, too. It started deep in the bowels and rose up uncomfortably into their hearts.

The queen dropped her knitting and yelled, "Geoffrey! Raise the alarm." She waved her arms in circles until she and the princess shimmered like glass. She grabbed the princess's hand and led her back to the carriage, but it was too late. Fire rained down from the sky, destroying the carriage and one of the horses.

She turned and pulled the princess in the direction of Geoffrey, whose sword was finding its target in the shoulder of a hooded man. He wheeled his horse about and was about to come down on another hooded figure when lightning bolts filled the air and converged on his sword, throwing him from his mount.

The queen turned away from the brook and headed deeper into the wild woods, but lightning filled the air once again and struck the base of the trees. The crack of thunder shook the ground below them, nearly knocking the princess's hand from hers, and cleanly felling the trees all around them. A large tree landed squarely on top of them, crushing the queen, and as her life ebbed from her limp body, so did the cloaking spell fade away. Princess Avaliene tried to run, but found herself in the grip of an invisible force, unable to escape.

Three hooded figures came to collect her. They inspected the queen, but she was dead.

"Damn," one said, "I wish she hadn't died so fast. Tie this one up. We'll see what Patyr wants to do with her."

"What is he going to do with this one?" another asked. "She's too young to know anything. I say we just leave her."

The largest of the three, the one most in charge, grinned and said, "I'll take care of this one. You two scout for more guards."

He led Princess Avaliene beyond the felled trees to the edge of the remaining forest. He stepped close to her. She convulsed as his body odor assailed her nostrils. She tried taking a step backwards, but found her back against a tree. He took another step forward and leaned his face in close to hers. His breath was like dead fish. She turned her head to the side and tried not to breathe while she gripped the tree on each side behind her. He stepped back and erupted in a deep, menacing laugh. She had to look. His eyes weren't black like his companions; one was blue and the other green. They twitched in their sockets as he removed his tunic.

He pumped his arms up and down, clenched his fists, and spread his fingers widely. A cool breeze brushed against her skin as her dress shredded apart and fell to her feet. He stepped forward, reaching for her naked breasts.

***

Princess Avaliene pulled her lips from her son's forehead. "Oh no, you don't," she scolded. "There are some places you may not venture."

Marvalaine's mouth fell open and matched the roundness of his eyes. The fear from his mother's memory filled his soul and began to manifest itself in his quaking limbs.

Princess Saffir cocked her head to the side, unaware of what she had just seen, but certain she saw something. "What just happened?"

Princess Avaliene hugged her son.

Marvalaine's fear melted away in his mother's embrace. He wiped the tears from his eyes with the back of his sleeve and looked up at her. "Mother?"

"Son?"

"Was that man my father?"

"He is the one that made you, but as I think on it, I don't think we should call him your father."

"How could anyone be so horrible? I hope, someday, I can become a powerful wizard and avenge what he did to you."

She just hugged him, preferring that they never meet.

Princess Saffir threw her arms in the air and demanded, "Will someone please tell me what just happened?"

"Ease yourself, Saffir, your nephew just had a vision, a memory of when our mother was killed."

Princess Saffir shrunk in shame for intruding on such a personal moment.

Marvalaine pondered his situation. "If I do become a powerful faerie wizard, do you suppose that Grandfather would invite me to his table as an advisor to the king?"

"Well, that's a very interesting question. Have you seen this for your future?"

"I don't know, but I have had such a dream. I think I would like it to be so."

He had one more question he wanted to ask, but held back, afraid of the answer. He turned and started towards the door, afraid he might just blurt it out. He couldn't seem to control his thoughts; the question kept rolling around in his mind. *What if it turns out I'm a black faerie, and I can control fire and lightning?*

His mother heard his thought as clear as if he had spoken it. "Well, it would certainly seem that we need to spare no haste in adjusting your education. I will contact Mother's people immediately."

"Yes, Mother." The prospect was both pleasing and terrifying to him. He dreaded the thought that he could grow up to be the enemy, but at least he would get some answers and some training.

He decided it was a good thing, and smiled, thinking his future just brightened up a bit.

Blake grew restless with his exercises and started finding ways to spice them up. He became increasingly brazen and risky, and started playing harmless pranks on the other students. He liked to scan their minds to find one walking in the hallways, and just before going through a door, Blake would reach out and try to lock the door before they went through it. This stuff was getting easy for him. He didn't understand why more of them couldn't do it. It was easy for him to rationalize that these skills would be useful for him out in the field.

"Did you hear that?" Princess Saffir was even more excited than Marvalaine. "You're going to be trained by the faeries and come back a great and powerful wizard. I just know it!"

"Too bad you don't have your mother's faerie powers, or I might believe you had seen it in a vision, and you weren't just trying to console me."

"I don't need faerie powers to know when my sister is impressed with someone's potential. I've certainly seen my fair share of disappointment every time I am tested and show none of Mother's faerie abilities."

The two of them had been scampering out of the business quarters of the castle towards the private quarters, when they stopped short in front of the same two hooligans that had accosted them earlier.

The large one shouted out, "You two! Again! How can you stand to be seen with this fatherless whelp? I've already told me uncle that you've been consorting with 'im. It's probably best you said your goodbyes now. He'll be gone by morning, I think."

She laughed out loud, which irritated the bully tremendously. "You actually think your uncle will stand for you after he learns how you accosted the princess? Do you actually believe he'll stand against anyone who came to my rescue? You must have taken complete leave of your senses!"

"Oh yeah? Well, what about what he did to me? How do you explain that?"

"Explain what? He wrestled your arms away from me and forced you to submit to him. That's what I saw."

"He has the devil in 'im. His bastard father must have been a faerie wizard, and he hexed me!"

"You stupid, ignorant oaf! Leave my sight before I have you locked up and whipped for touching me."

"I told you before, I won't take that kind of talk from any girl!" He started to step towards her, but Marvalaine stepped in front of her, with a rekindled sense of confidence.

"You still think you can protect her? You don't think I'm ready for you this time?" The bully pulled a large knife from its sheath and started to sprint towards the two of them.

Marvalaine saw the knife coming towards him. His eyes widened. He wasn't prepared for this. He raised his hands in front of him, palms out, and yelled, "STOP!"

His voice boomed unnaturally through the hallway, but was drowned out by the thunderclap as a bright blue thread of lightning bolted out of his hands and straight into the bully's dagger. The bully's body seized up with the electric jolt and fell in a lump. The smoking knife skittered harmlessly across the stone floor.

Destiny snapped out of her trance, her hair was on end, and silver threads of electricity flowed from her fingertips out to the walls of the room. Another clap of thunder startled her, and the threads dissipated from her fingers.

Michelle heard the thunder from the garden where she was tending her herbs. She could see the lights flashing inside and knew it could only be Destiny, but she knew nothing of the lesson her grandchild was now learning. She had never had any lessons involving lightning or thunder, and thought only the ancient evil sorcerers could call up the powers of electricity.

Brian sat at his desk, on the phone with Schaefer, discussing methods of better observing the inmates. He wanted to more accurately identify the correct time should there be another event. Hopefully, better information could be used to triangulate the position of the source.

"Just capturing the correct time may not be sufficient," he said. "I want the data to be immediately distributed to at least three other locations. I don't want to worry about the data being corrupted or destroyed by them. Maybe you can…" Brian stopped speaking. A shiver went up his spine. He felt his hair follicles twitch up, and his face went clammy. He felt faint and reached for his drawer, where he kept his vitamin pills. A large spark discharged from his hand to the drawer handle.

"Hello? Brian? You still there?"

"Huh? I'm sorry. I just felt a little faint for a second there. Probably low blood sugar, but you should have seen the size of the static spark that just popped off my fingers."

"Are you kidding me? That just happened? I had the same sensation right before you called. I popped a huge spark, reaching for the phone."

"Could it be a coincidence? Did we just register another event? Check the inmates there and get back to me."

Blake was lying on his cot when the wave reached him. His eyes were closed, and his breathing was shallow. He'd been casually spying on his classmates when he began to feel a bit nauseous, but that passed when he sat up. His hair stood on end, and he could taste the electricity in his mouth. He felt chilled and rubbed his hands together. When he separated his hands, a thin blue thread of electricity flowed and undulated between them. "Cool."

Michelle waited for the light show to die down before running into the house. She could sense that Destiny wasn't in any immediate trouble, or she might have panicked. She went straight to Destiny, who still sat in her chair with her mouth hung open.

"Lord, child, what has Mala been learnin' you?"

Destiny barely moved, but shifted her eyes over towards her nana. The rims of her eyes were wet with tears pushing to get out. She closed her mouth slightly and simply shook her head no, rather than try to explain.

"You are alright, aren't you?"

She nodded her head, but her trembling hands suggested otherwise.

"Tell me, child, tell me what happened."

She didn't want to tell her nana the truth. She didn't want to relive the experience, and she surely didn't want to admit that she didn't go see Mala.

Michelle went to Destiny's side and stroked her head. "You'll start to feel better just as soon as you starts to tell your old nana what happened to you."

Destiny started to speak, but stopped and simply wrapped her arms around her grandmother. She closed her eyes and leaned her head against her bosom.

Michelle sat down and took Destiny's hands in her own. "This is important. You had lightning and thunder coming from your hands. This be no time for keeping secrets."

Destiny's tears flowed freely down her cheeks. "I didn't see Mala. I ran away from her. I ended up in a small boy who didn't even know he was a witch, but he learned to make lightning from his hands."

"You saw the memory of a boy witch who could make lightning, and just like that, you is making lightning? I heard tell of witches who could do the fire and lightning, but that was in them olden days, and they was evil witches. We must got some bad blood mixed in us."

"Not we," Destiny said, "just me. I'm the one this is happening to. Don't you see it? I'm not like you. This is probably what my mama went through, and I'm going to end up just like her."

"Stop that. You're your own person, and we're getting you the trainin' your mama never wanted. I think you needs to see Mala more than ever now."

Destiny wrapped her arms around her nana again. Tears still stained her cheeks and sniffles had formed in her nose. "Nana?"

"Yes, Cherie?"

"Who's my daddy?"

Michelle had dreaded this question ever since Destiny was born and she knew she would have to raise her. "Well, I don't rightly know who he was. I'm not even sure your mama knows."

"But you know what he was?"

"I don't tend it much mind, but I guess I knows, alright."

CHAPTER 8

Brian dreamed of great power coursing through his body. In his dream, he controlled the elements like his kind did centuries ago. When he woke, he could still feel the tingling in his hands from the day before. There was no question in his mind that this was the second in a series of epic events, and this time, he had shared in it. He wasted no time getting to his office and picking up the phone to dial his friend. The phone was answered on the first ring. "Dick, tell me you have something."

"Well, yes, and no. It was definitely another event, and it was as big as the other, but I'm afraid that it didn't lead us any nearer to the source."

"Why not?" Brian asked. "Didn't we synchronize the tapes onto a standard time signal?"

"Sure, we did that, but we were watching the wrong places. We were focused on the inmates, and they were unaffected by this one. The effects of this event seem to be limited to our own people, and while we have plenty who can testify to what they experienced during the event, none of them could be very specific about the time, and even if they were, they wouldn't have been synchronized on the same time."

"I don't care how much it costs. I want you to put cameras everywhere, with time clocks on them."

"Sure," Schaefer assured him, "we can do that, but that is going to be a lot of cameras. Are you sure you don't want to see how much before you don't care how much it costs?"

"This could be an attack, and if it is, then we can bet there will be another."

"An attack?" Schaefer asked. "Who could be doing this? I can't believe it could be a witch. They've been powerless for centuries. They lost their powers the same time we did. Why would they suddenly find this kind of ability when we haven't?"

"Those are all good points, and the only way we're going to be able to answer them is to be prepared and learn as much as we can from each event, assuming there will be another event. Besides," Brian added, "if it's not us, and it's not the witches, then who could it be? Has there been a third sect lying dormant all these centuries?"

"Have you ever heard the rumor that the witches used to be able to communicate through time?"

"Sure," Brian said, "we've all heard that one. I think the evidence in the archives presents a pretty strong argument supporting those rumors. Do you think they could have figured out how to cause these events through time?"

"No," Schaefer said. "What would be the point for them to reach forward in time and do this?"

"I wasn't thinking forward. I'm wondering if they recovered their powers in the future. Maybe we did, too, and they decided to reach back in time and eliminate us in their past."

"Now you're scaring me. Especially since, if it is the witches, future or past, they seemed to have stolen some of our secrets to control electricity. What about the boy you found? Is he able to shed any light on the source?"

"I have to send him out into the field, but I don't know where to send him."

"For now, try Alabama. We know it's somewhere in the south, maybe the south east. The last event was less specific than the first, but it still seemed to generally aim at the southern US."

Brian was glad to have a target, but still said, "I thought you didn't have it figured out yet?"

"I don't. It could easily be three or more states away from there, but it's as good a place as any to start."

"Good enough. Maybe the kid will pick up something on his radar."

Blake wandered off the main grounds. He liked to find private spots to practice his abilities, and this spot was one of his favorites. It was tranquil and surrounded by trees with a small creek running down one side. The ground was flat and smooth, which gave him room to experiment.

The regular students were all quite excited this week, when one of them managed to move a tennis ball about three inches across his desk. Blake dropped a tennis ball on the ground. He held his hands out in the air and batted the ball back and forth on the ground. He could pretty much move it in any direction he wanted. He could even push it down against the dirt, but he hadn't figured out how to pick it up and levitate it. When he tried, it rolled off to the side and bounced across the ground.

He tried again to pick it up, but it shot off away from him and rolled down the embankment into the creek. He tried scooping it up off the water, but it only skittered and splashed across to the other side. He reached out with his mind and pulled it back through the water until he was standing over it. It bobbed in the water, just inches from his feet. He wanted to lift it up out of the water and concentrated on surrounding the ball with a sphere of energy. He held his gaze for a moment and tried to picture the ball inside a snow globe as he tried to lift it up and out of the water. The water surrounding the ball bulged upward slightly, then fell back, splashing water all over him. Frustrated and wet, he cursed at the ball. A large bolt of lightning shot out of his hand and went directly into the poor yellow ball. The ball exploded with a loud pop, and was reduced to bits of confetti falling through the air, some of which smoked and smoldered as they fell to the ground.

Blake turned his palms up and stared at them. "Very Cool."

Michelle shook Destiny's bed. "Get up, you lazybones. I won't let you lounge in bed, you gots to call the Mala."

"Mala, Mala, Mala. What's so great about Mala, anyway? If you ask me, she's a couple cards short of a full deck. She's kinda scary, in a mean sorta way."

"Stop being a baby. Mala is wise in ways you don't even understand yet."

Destiny sat grudgingly at the table and stared into the already lit candle.

Mala never asked Destiny why she missed her appointment yesterday, and Destiny saw no reason to bring it up. Mala stood and motioned Destiny towards the door, pulling the leather hide aside so she could exit. "Your lessons start now. I have a job for you."

It was bright outside. Destiny shaded her eyes to see. She saw several huts scattered about, most of them smaller than Mala's. A couple huts were larger; one in particular was quite large. The ground around the huts was soft and sandy. Outside the perimeter of the huts, she could see a grassy area that led down to a slow, lazy stream. Beyond the stream, she could see a tall, majestic mountain range. The sky was clear, and bluer than she had ever seen.

Once outside, Mala stepped in front of her and commanded her, "Come."

They walked to the largest of the huts. An arch of woven saplings marked the entrance. Destiny followed her inside, where she found three people lying on fur skins, with two girls tending them. Mala walked around the three individuals and pointed to them. "They have the sickness. You heal them." She passed her pointing finger over the three of them and stopped at the one on the end, the smallest and youngest one. "Him first."

"Are they real? Or did you create them like you created this world for me?"

"They real, and they real sick. You need to heal him. You heal them in this world, and they heal in their own world."

"If he is real," Destiny asked, "and I can heal him, does that also mean I can hurt him?"

"Yes, that is possible."

"Doesn't it bother you that someone like me can come from the future and hurt someone like that? How do you protect yourselves?"

"You don't worry about that," Mala said. "This world exists outside of the real world. It is outside of time itself. To come here, you must be invited. We can't travel through time in the real world. Now, enough questions. Heal them."

"I don't know what to do. I'm not a doctor. What if I make them worse?"

"No matter, you try."

"I'm serious." Destiny's hands trembled slightly. "What if I try to heal them and end up harming them, or they die?"

"They are enemies. We would have let them die, anyway."

"Then why do you want me to heal them?"

"You heal them, you learn why."

Destiny crouched down by the young boy. She held his hand in her own and tried to recall the feelings she had before, but nothing happened. "It's not working."

Mala clucked. "Maybe his hand not hurting."

Destiny put her hand on his forehead. He was burning up. She felt his cheek with her other hand. She ran her hand from his cheek to his throat, and down his chest to his belly. As she reached his chest, she felt her hands tingle, and her head started to swoon.

Mala coached her, "Breathe. Breathe deep and slow. Do not let your head become faint."

Destiny could barely hear Mala, but she heard enough, and regulated her breathing while she probed her hand right and left across the boy's chest. His breathing was shallow, with occasional spasms of coughing. The hand she held to his head began to cool, while at the same time, the hand she held to his chest was alive with sensations. The boy began to stir; he arched his back, kicked his legs, and began to shake with a seizure. His eyes popped open wide, then closed, and he fell limp, his breathing so shallow it was imperceptible.

Destiny withdrew her hands from the boy, terrified with what she might have done to him. Mala signaled one of the attendants to remove the boy's limp body. "Now the girl."

Destiny wanted to protest, but Mala simply motioned for her to move on.

The girl appeared to be sleeping, but she moaned and moved her legs about, holding her stomach with her hands. Destiny started at her head, one hand on her forehead, and the other tracing a path from her cheek to her throat. A bitter taste developed in Destiny's mouth.

"Yes," Mala said. "You can taste the poison. Very good. Continue."

Destiny continued to probe her hand down to the girl's chest. She guessed that the girl was about fifteen years old. Destiny gingerly traced her fingers down the center of the girl's chest.

"Ach! How you going to feel what's wrong like that?" Mala reached down and grabbed Destiny's wrist and directed her hands directly to the girl's breasts. "You must be more thorough."

Destiny wanted to retract her hand, but she was overcome with a new lightness in her head, and the taste in her mouth turned sweet.

"Aha," Mala said, "not so bad, huh? Continue."

Destiny drew her hand down the girl's abdomen over her belly. Her head was filled with noise, like a siren had gone off in her brain. Her hand started to warm and tingle over the girl's belly. The noise in her head had shriveled to a loud, piercing scream. Destiny's mouth fell open as she suddenly realized what she felt. The girl was pregnant, and the baby was dying. She rubbed her hand over the girl's belly. She felt as if she was comforting the unborn child. Her hand tingled and cooled. The baby stopped screeching in her head.

"Very good, young Destiny. She tried to lose her baby with bad medicine."

The girl arched her back and sucked in a sharp breath, then fell silent and limp. She slept soundly, her breathing hardly visible. An attendant quickly dragged the girl away to another bed.

The third victim was older, not yet grey haired, but full grown. He faked unconsciousness and had been watching Destiny through his squinted eyes. He had obvious injuries, and his clothing was soaked in blood. She moved towards him and reached for his forehead, but he sprang to life. He may have been weakened by his injuries, but he had plenty of strength to handle Destiny. He grabbed her by the wrists and stared directly into her face. "You won't find me as easy to kill as those children, witch."

She struggled to free her wrists, twisting right and left, but his grip was strong. He tried sitting up to fight her, but his injuries prevented that, and he remained mostly prone. She came down on his mid-section with her knee. He released his grip, and she stepped back.

He pushed himself upright, rolled over onto a knee, and righted himself again. His legs were wobbly, but managed to stand up full and tall. "You may yet have time to regret killing those children, but it will be your dying thought!" He raised his hands just over waist-high. Balls of flames formed in his palms, and he promptly expelled them in her direction. She instinctively raised her hands to block her face and caught the balls flush with her own palms. Her hands were momentarily hot, then cooled. He threw two more fireballs at her, which she also caught.

Destiny grew confident; she apparently could resist his fire. She moved forward and tried to grab his wrists to control him, but he slipped by her hands and punched both hands into her chest, propelling her backwards. She felt like she was hit with a bat. She screamed, not out of pain, but out of anger, and shook her fists at him. The flames he had thrown at her were now racing back to him. He raised one arm and quickly wiped it across the space in front of him from right to left. The flame balls impacted in front of him where he had just wiped his arm.

She was furious. She repeated what she had just done and flung two more fireballs at him. They, too, impacted on the shield he had just drawn in front of him. She was beside herself. She stretched her arms out to the sides and spread her fingers, screaming out of control. She thought she might get fireballs to sweep outside his force field. Instead, she saw thick bolts of blue lightning spring from her hands around his field. He was shocked, literally, and surprised. He fell to his knees, unable to control his movement.

Mala started screaming, "What was that? We don't know that magic. Where did you learn that? What did you do?"

"I don't know what I did! He was throwing fireballs at me! I just tried to block them and then, without knowing what I was doing, I was throwing them at him."

"Not that," Mala yelled. "I can teach you to turn his own magic against him, but you made the skybolts by yourself."

"The skybolts? You mean the lightning? I saw a boy do that in a memory. I guess I picked it up, but I still don't know how it works."

"I think you may be too old to teach. Now you are dangerous to us all. I should gather the elders to discuss your fate."

"My fate?" Destiny asked. "Are you mad? This is all just a dream. Maybe it's been a dream all along. Maybe I'm as mad as my mother, and I'm actually in a hospital strapped to a bed somewhere."

"Wake up, little girl," Mala said. "This is no dream you are in."

"Sure it is, and since it's all just a dream, I should be able to do anything I want. If I wanted to lift that spit over there into the air, I probably just have to wave my hand." She waved her hand as she spoke, and the spit fell over, covering the roasting meat with dirt.

"Argh!" Mala screamed. "Look what you've done now."

"I'm sorry. I didn't know I could really do that. I'll go now, before I do something else wrong."

"I think you will have to stay now. We'll see what the elders say."

The message was short and to the point. Blake was to pack his things. He would be taken to the airstrip the following morning. Packing light for this mission was a snap; he had little enough belongings. Everything he needed was in his head, anyway.

After throwing some clothes into a small backpack, he took a walk through the compound, hoping to see some envy on the other boy's faces, but, evidently, they weren't even told. He amused himself with the thought that they weren't important enough to know about his mission.

He couldn't resist pulling one last prank before he left. He sat outside the classrooms under an old redwood tree. He closed his eyes and pictured his shiny seagull trinket in his mind. He fell into the quiet, contented state where he could sense the other students inside and start to enter their thoughts. He bounced from mind to mind until he found one of the new kids.

There weren't many girls here, and those that did come usually didn't last very long. The older boys were cruel enough to each other, but they were merciless with girls. They were old enough to be interested in girls in general, and many were quite vocal about their conquests, but when it came to competition, they had absolutely no interest in a girl being trained alongside them. To make matters worse, this girl was a scrawny, unimpressive little thing.

Blake could see through her eyes that this lesson was on trying to ignite candles with their thoughts. Something which none of these boys had ever accomplished, though they often claimed they could sense the wick warming up. Today was no different. They stared at their candles endlessly while the minute hand worked its way around the clock face. Blake could see some of them straining so hard, he thought they were going to give birth. He felt sorry for the girl; sorry enough to reach through her eyes and light her candle.

"Hey!" one of the back row boys shouted and pointed at her candle. "The new girl did it! Look!" All the back row boys were the unpopular kids. The clique sat up front, feeling smug and superior to everyone else.

"Liar! She must have cheated!" one of the boys up front shouted as he jumped from his desk and marched back to hers. He blew out the candle. "There, do it again while we watch."

She stared into her candle, and it erupted in flames.

"Well," the instructor said as he roused himself from his nap, which he always claimed was a trance, "what do we have here? Finally, we have a prodigy worthy of instruction."

The boy from up front stood dumbfounded. Another voice from up front shouted, "No way! Her candle must be defective or something! Here, light mine!" He hadn't even reached her desk before the candle in his hand lit up, startling the poor boy, who promptly dropped the candle on the floor. "Hey watch it! You trying to kill me? This makes no sense. Why would she be able to do it when the rest of us can't?"

The instructor opened his mouth to answer when two other back row boys shouted out in unison, "I did it! I lit mine, too!"

Boys from all over the class now gathered around the two new phenoms, except for the two remaining front row boys, who stared intently at their candles, looking quite constipated. Sweat beaded down from their temples, but not a spark came from their candles. All over the classroom now, unattended candles sitting on abandoned desks began to light up.

Blake felt sorry for the girl and hoped this would take some of the heat off of her while they tried to figure out who the mystery arsonist was. Otherwise, she would surely be expected to perform again, and without him, would end up drummed out as either uncooperative or another dismal failure.

This was so easy for him. Even being outside the building posed no problem. He didn't know why they found it so hard, and yet, he wasn't inclined to share with his instructors, or even the commandant. Maybe he'd let that important guy know when he met him again.

Brian chose to keep the mission secret and wrote the orders for the mercenaries himself, without involving any of his staff. As far as he was concerned, the less people that knew about this operation, the better. He sent a wire transfer from his discretionary funds to cover the deposit, and faxed the orders to a dank biker bar located just off the interstate outside of Mobile. The last thing he arranged was a flight for himself to meet the team and the boy in Alabama. He picked an abandoned air base north of Talladega.

With all the preparations made, he went home and packed for his trip. A plane would be ready for him at four in the morning. They should converge in Alabama by ten.

Destiny was escorted to a smaller hut, where she was told she would wait for the elders' decision. Her mind was ablaze with options. She should be able to just close this memory and wake up back home in

Cricket Bend, but even if she couldn't leave, the fear in Mala's eyes told her that she could probably defend herself if she had to.

She sat on a cot in the hut. It was magnitudes more comfortable than the time she was burned at the stake. She closed her eyes and tried to concentrate the way she did when she connected to these memories. She hoped she could reach that point where she made the connections and disconnect it there. She let go of her surroundings and felt like she was floating in a void. She started to hear the familiar sound of the voices that she used when getting into these memories. She strained to hear if one of the voices was her nana leading her home.

"Destiny," A voice rang clear in her mind, but it was not her nana. It was a man's voice. It was familiar to her, but she couldn't place it. "Destiny. I'll have a word with you."

She followed the sound of the voice and found herself in a small room surrounded with candles. It appeared to be some kind of chapel. She sat cross-legged on a plump pillow, and before her sat a familiar face. He was the wizard who had captured Nimisen.

"Hello Destiny, it is good to see you again."

"I'm sorry. Have we met?"

"Many times," he said, "and you do not fool me with your feigned ignorance. I'll grant you that it can be a tad confusing when our meetings are always out of chronological sequence, but I already see that you recognize me."

"I do. I have seen you before, but I was unaware that you had ever seen me."

"Ah. Let's just say you weren't yourself at the time."

Destiny laughed, "True. How is Nimisen? Could she not join us?"

"Nimisen? She is barely twelve years old now. I think I'll let her grow a bit before I send for her."

"You're right," she said. "It is very confusing."

"So, you are growing into your strengths quite fast. You seem to have created quite a stir across several times. I have spoken on your behalf, but I am only one voice, and not all give my voice as much credence as others might."

"Mala called you the Great One. Surely your voice carries some additional weight? Besides, what is so terrible? I never really tried to learn this stuff. It just seems like I experience it in a memory and it sticks with me. I don't even try to use it. It just seems to slip out."

"It is extremely rare for our kind to control fire and lightning like the others do."

"But you do," she said. "I learned the lightning from you when you were just a boy."

"Yes, well, we are rare enough, but you are most extraordinary. Very few people of our kind have ever been able to learn so easily, maybe only three or four. You may find you don't have many allies in the struggles that lie before you."

"Struggles?" she asked. "What am I facing?"

"That's not for me to say. You will get there when you get there. For now, you have enough problems to face with your own people."

"Yeah, like how do I get out of Mala's memory and back home?"

"Whatever happens," he said, "please remember they are good people looking out for all our kind. You may have some trials ahead of you in which it may become difficult to distinguish friend from foe, and I want to give you a gift before that time comes."

"I'm not sure I like the sound of that."

"What?" he exclaimed. "You don't like gifts? I've never heard of a girl who didn't like gifts. Astonishing!"

Destiny giggled. "No, of course I like gifts. It's the trials I don't like. Sounds like a math test with pain."

"Hold up your hands like this." He held his arms out in front of him, slightly wider than his shoulders, with his palms facing Destiny. She held her hands up as he did. He touched his palms to hers.

She could immediately feel a tingly warmth exuding from his hands. "Magic is not about incantations and casting spells, although they do serve a useful purpose for focusing the mind and sometimes even frightening people. Magic is a feeling from inside you. It actually starts up in your mind, but it feels like it comes from the pit of your stomach. Here, feel this. It starts in your stomach and flows out from you like a bubble."

She felt everything he described.

"Now," he continued, "how you hold your hands is not really important, but it seems to make it easier for our minds if you visualize holding a bubble between your hands. You can spread your hands as if you are making it larger, and your mind interprets it as if it were so."

"You're not making sense. What is this bubble?"

"Stand up and do as I suggest. Spread your hands and increase the bubble."

She stood up and spread her hands. She felt kind of like a mime in an invisible box, but she also thought she could feel something, and like he said, it was attached to the pit of her stomach.

"Very good," he said. "Now watch this." He quickly snapped his hand in front of him and flung a fireball at her. It impacted in front of her and dissipated without harming her. "What you have there, young Destiny, is a protective shield. I think you may find it useful."

"But I thought you said it was bad to learn so much, so fast."

"Sure, some believe it is so. But all the same, I think you should know how to defend yourself. You should go now. I believe we'll meet again."

The room faded away, and she was back in the hut, still in Mala's memory, a bit tired, and went to sleep.

Blake had no memory outside the compound. He'd been delivered there as an infant who could sense his mother's thoughts. He never knew anything else. He was driven to the abandoned airstrip where a plane was already waiting. It was a short trip from there to a larger airport where he was directed onto a mid-size jet.

Brian was waiting on the jet as Blake arrived.

"Mr. Grupp, it's nice to see you again."

"Hello, Blake. How have you been?"

The two extended their arms to shake hands, and just as they were about to grip one another's hand, a large spark jumped from Brian's hand to Blake's.

"Sorry about that," Brian said. "I've been having a lot of those lately."

"That's okay, Mr. Grupp. It might have been me, with all that bumpy weather I just went through, I could be full of all kinds of static charges."

"Well, I think you'll find this leg of the flight much smoother. We don't have anyone to staff the galley, and we'll miss lunch, so the best I can offer you on this flight is some poor boys and plenty of junk food."

"Sandwiches are fine," Blake said, "besides, I'm not so hungry right now."

"That's just nerves. Anxiety, really. You're just keyed up to be on this mission, and that's a good thing. I think we're lucky to have you."

"Thank you, sir. I hope I can prove myself to you, and that you will find a place for me in the organization."

Brian appreciated his candor. "I can't tell you how important this mission is to our people. It's probably the most important operation we've conducted in over two hundred years, and even though I am keeping it strictly secret, it is very visible to those that count. You prove yourself here, and there is no telling how far you can go."

Blake sat back, planning out his future, and his meteoric rise to the very top. He pictured himself as a long prophesied king. At his age, of course, it took a sort of rock and roll form where he was surrounded with adoring girls.

He wondered how long it would be before everybody recognized what he could do. He wanted to tell Brian and blurt out all the things he had learned to do, but still remained silent. He would save his new abilities as a surprise and trust that he would know when the time was right to use them.

Brian watched the boy lean back and close his eyes. He flexed his hands, trying to retain the feeling of power and wishing someone could tell him why it comes and goes. He thought back on his youthful days when he had been given the training. He had never distinguished himself as particularly talented in the dark arts, but he proved himself a natural leader and had risen through the ranks on his ability to get what he wanted from people. He'd often fantasized about one day turning into the great grand master of all things magic, and was well on the way to convincing himself that these recent twinges of power were the fulfillment of those dreams.

He opened the palm of his hand and faced it towards the magazine in his lap. His hand tingled. He drew up an energy from within him and flipped the magazine to the next page. He looked up to see if Blake had seen it, but Blake's eyes were still closed. Brian had never planned on actively joining the field team, but he started to wonder if the field would be the most practical place for his developing powers.

Blake breathed in calm, shallow gulps of air. His eyes were closed, but he had been watching through Brian's eyes. He had an almost irresistible urge to help Brian, as a private joke, but he didn't need to. The page flipped on Brian's command. He could feel Brian's excitement over such a simple trick. *Someday, Blake thought to himself, I am going to own these people. If he thinks flipping a magazine page was that exciting, I'm going to blow his socks off.* With that thought, he let himself slip asleep.

Destiny had been dozing and was barely awake when Mala entered the hut. She was immediately followed by three other intense looking people who surrounded Destiny, holding their hands in defensive positions as if they feared she might attack them at any moment. Destiny stood up; if they wanted to play, she would be ready for them. She held her hands in front of her, ready to react to their next move.

The youngest, and only woman of the three, didn't like Destiny's posture and shifted into a more aggressive pose. She raised her arms with her elbows higher than her hands. Her eyes widened, and her dark black hair began to rise around her head.

Destiny turned to face her, cocking her head, thinking to herself, *Bring it on, sister.* She was expecting some kind of attack from the girl, but instead, she sensed something new. The dark-haired witch was probing Destiny's mind. Destiny was prepared to fend off fire balls, not this kind of intrusion. She brought her hands together and looked inward with her mind and tried to push the girl out. She spread her hands apart as she pushed and felt the girl's mind leave her own. She kept pushing and pushed back into her attacker's mind. Now she was standing in the circle of witches looking at herself in the center. From the other witch's mind, she looked over at Mala and reached into her mind.

Mala was startled. Her eyes widened, and she shrieked, "Stop it! Look what you have done! Get out of her mind before you teach her more!"

The dark-haired girl had not lost total control to Destiny. She couldn't stop what Destiny was doing, but she could still respond, "I can't stop her. She's in my mind." She was clearly struggling to speak.

One of the others, a much older mage with a thick black beard and dark black eyes, reached into the dark-haired girl's mind and tried to help push Destiny out. The last of the three tried binding Destiny in a special field to interrupt any magical energies coming from her.

Destiny turned her attention to the last witch. She spread her arms wider and imagined her bubble shield encircling and trapping his field. She enclosed her field onto his, like gripping a foam rubber ball, and absorbed his energy somewhere in the pit of her stomach. She didn't understand his field, but she felt it, and turned her attention to the old witch, casting the same field around him.

Mala was furious. "What did I tell you? Now look what you idiots have done!"

Destiny had tapped, at least partially, into everyone's mind, and made a startling discovery. One of the witches was carefully hiding something from everyone, and he was desperately fighting to keep her out. He was spending almost all his energy on preventing Destiny from discovering his secret and only pretending to aid the others in controlling her.

The room started to fill with every kind of assorted mage, and every one of them started casting the same confinement field around Destiny. She tried encircling them like she had before, but their combined power was too great for her to pierce.

Destiny knew that even if she could fight off all of them, it would accomplish nothing. She reached into Mala's mind and tried to share what she sensed from the black-haired witch to her left. She pulled back her fields and stood tall, facing Mala. "Don't you people realize that I'm not even here? You are all long dead in my time. I don't know why you are getting so worked up. Why do you insist on holding me to this place? If you just release me, I'll be long gone from your time and you can live your lives as they were meant to be."

An old mage, much older than any she had yet seen, entered the hut and stood next to Mala. "She is strong, very strong, but I haven't seen anything to suggest she is anything other than what you thought she was in the beginning."

Mala pointed a crooked stick at Destiny. "She controls fire and air. I saw lightning from her hands."

"You aren't suggesting that she is one of the others, are you?"

"I am. I didn't want to believe it, but I can't deny what I have seen with my own eyes."

"I haven't seen it," the old mage responded. "We haven't seen it. Faced with this many adversaries, you don't think she would use all her abilities to elude us?"

"She doesn't want to escape. She learns our magic every time we go up against her."

"Have you ever known any of the others that could learn our magic?"

"No," Mala responded, "she's the first. You know they have been trying to develop this ability throughout the ages."

"And you think they have finally succeeded?"

"Yes. We never stopped them, and with time on their side, it was inevitable that they would eventually succeed."

"Ahhh." The old man stroked his beard. "Well, that's one theory, anyway."

"If you don't have the heart for what must be done," Mala said, her voice harsh and unfeeling, "then maybe you should go and leave it to the rest of us."

"Sharp tongued to the last," the old mage responded, "but I haven't heard a vote from the other Elders yet. I will hear their decision on this matter before any action takes place.

Mala didn't want to put it off, but she didn't dare go against the Elders.

Destiny couldn't believe the hatred she felt from Mala. She didn't know anyone could turn so quickly or so powerfully against another person.

CHAPTER 9

B lake found himself wandering in a forest. It was nothing like the camp where he was raised. The hills were green instead of brown. The trees grew in thick stands, and he could clearly make out an edge dividing the trees from the meadows.

He started climbing up a hill to get a better look around. It was larger than he first thought and grew steeper as he climbed. The ground was soft and his feet sunk into it and made a plopping noise as he pulled them out of the muck. The soft ground slowed his ascent, and sometimes his feet would stick, landing him on his hands and knees.

As he neared the middle of the hill, he could hear a commotion coming from somewhere on the other side. He thought maybe he had stumbled across a playground with a ballpark or soccer field. He could hear cheers and whistles. He couldn't make out any specific language, but there was clearly a large throng of people yelling and screaming. He thought he saw something flash just over the rise of the hill, but he couldn't make it out. As he neared the top of the hill, he clearly saw glimpses of fireworks rising over the hill's horizon.

At the top of the hill, he found two enormous boulders. They stood as big as buildings, separated from each other just enough to leave a single path between them. Their sides were tall and slick, and they extended off as far as he could see. The only way for him to see what was going on was to pass between the massive slabs.

It was cold and dark between them. The path was no longer soft and now crunched beneath his feet. The commotion echoed through the narrow rock canyon until he emerged on the other side, where it was peaceful by comparison. The sound came from far below him in a wide valley.

He found himself standing on the edge of a large cliff. There were stairs carved into the rock on either side of him, one to the right and one to the left. He leaned forward to survey the valley. He wanted to see what was going on down there, and he also wanted to see if either path would be a better descent than the other.

What was going on, however, was something he never expected. There were thousands of people down below in the valley, perhaps tens of thousands. They were split into two groups. To his right were men and women wearing dark robes, some black, and some a bloody red color. They were moving in circles, groups of them would move up towards the center of the valley. They would fling lightning and fire to the other side, then rotate to the back again. On his left side, they were dressed in earthy browns and light blue colors. They weren't moving around, certainly not approaching the center of the valley, but as lightning bolts or fire balls crossed the center section, they would move into action and cast what looked like a glowing net into the air to catch the attack and slam it into the ground.

If this was a sport, it was sure the coolest sport Blake had ever seen. Several rounds went by with neither team gaining an advantage over the other, until the red and black team tired of the stalemate and split up into three groups, one sending an initial attack up the middle which was intercepted by their defenses, while the other two groups circled around to the sides and aimed their attacks at the defenders.

The defenders were busy wrestling the first attack to the ground, and were blindsided by the flank attacks. Blake could hear them scream, and he could see the smoke rising from their twisted bodies. The defenders then sent a small squad across the valley to a position right in the middle of the attackers. Lightning and fire descended upon them from all directions, but instead of striking them, it went right through them and struck down attackers on the other side. They, too, screamed and fell in smoldering heaps.

After these attacks, they would fall back into their patterns of volley and defend. The pattern repeated. As time went on, the volleys became smaller and smaller. Eventually, after both teams suffered considerable losses, the attacks lost their meaning. The teams were too small to pose a meaningful threat. They just stood glaring at each other, hurling insults instead of fireballs.

Blake was getting bored with the lack of action and remembered that he still hadn't decided if either descent was better than the other. He started to focus again on the two paths, when he heard footsteps on his right. He stood to face the right and heard footsteps from the other side. One man from each side had raced up the path and now stood at the tops of their paths and faced him. They said nothing but seemed to expect something.

Blake held up his hands, showing them he was unarmed. "Look, I don't know who you are, but I don't want any trouble. I was just out for a walk when I heard all the noise."

They spoke together, in unison, "Choose."

"Choose? Choose what?"

Destiny sat down on a mat in the center of almost two dozen witches. The old man had given them strict orders not to take any actions until the elders had deliberated on the matter. They surrounded her, holding their hands in aggressive positions that appeared both defensive and offensive to Destiny. Some cocked their heads and watched her through the corners of their eyes, while others preferred to bow their heads and stare at her through their eyebrows. As far as she was concerned, it was all posturing to make them look scarier. She made herself comfortable, conserving her energy while still maintaining a protective bubble around herself. She tried putting on her most innocent face and said, "I don't know why you people are getting so worked up. I'm one of you. Yesterday, I was to be trained because I might be our people's savior in the future. Now look at us, and all because of one crazy old woman."

The black-haired witch responded, "Do not speak so. We have a great deal of respect for Mala."

"So does my nana, and I did, too, at least, until she went mad."

Mala was clearly displeased with the conversation. "Hush! All of you! She is just trying to trick you and create distrust amongst ourselves. We must remain united." Yet, even while she spoke of being united, Mala tried to enter, undetected, into the black-haired witch who spoke on her behalf. She heard his words, and yet had memories of his words being deceptive, concealing his true feelings. She could not sense anything out of the ordinary in his mind. Not because there was nothing in his mind for her to discover, but he wouldn't allow her to sense it. He had already been in her mind for quite some time, filling her with distrust and anger over Destiny.

"Mala's right," Destiny said, "you don't want to listen to me. I could be wrong. Maybe she hasn't gone mad. Maybe she is acting completely normal right now. She probably always gets worked up like this."

Some of those in the circle glanced at each other.

"For all I know, the elders are always warning her not to do stuff without their prior approval. This is probably all perfectly normal behavior."

A couple of witches in the circle relaxed their posture slightly.

Mala shrieked, "Do not listen to her! It is a trick! She was sent here to destroy us!"

One of them dropped his hands and turned to Mala. "But there is truth in what she says. You are not acting like yourself."

Another in the group also relaxed. "I agree. You have not been acting like yourself, and you have made some very serious accusations. How can we trust your judgment under these circumstances?"

Others relaxed. Some left the hut. One offered Destiny a tray of food and water, leaving them just outside her protective bubble.

"Stop!" Mala was beside herself. "Come back, I cannot protect all of us alone!" She turned to Destiny and screamed, "You! You did this! You tricked them! It was all your doing! You made them turn on me!"

One by one, hearing Mala's ranting, the others left, until only Destiny, Mala, and the black-haired witch remained. Mala screamed, "I won't let you destroy our people, even if I have to stop you myself!"

Destiny had no idea what Mala was hurling towards her, only that they were some kind of magical energies, and they were effectively absorbed by her shield.

The old man, Ishun, returned to the hut with some others Destiny assumed to be the elders. "Mala! Stop at once!"

Mala was out of her mind with rage. She may not have even been aware of the elders' presence until they started attacking her. She went crazy and started attacking everyone in the room.

Destiny watched the insanity for a moment. Boils formed on Mala's arms and face. Her hair turned white. Destiny could swear she was aging before her very eyes. Blood dripped from her ears and mouth. Their attack on her was brutal and merciless. Destiny felt sorry for her.

She sprang to her feet and cast a protective bubble around Mala. "Stop, she needs help. She's not evil, she's just gone a little crazy."

The elders' attack on Mala was intense. Destiny had to dig deep to create a shield strong enough to hold them out. Mala fell limp to the ground inside the bubble Destiny had created for her.

Destiny had put too much energy in Mala's shield, leaving her own shield weakened. The elders quickly circled around Destiny. They held out their arms at the sides. They weren't close enough to touch, but a blue filament of light stretched from one elder to the other, completing a full circle around Destiny. It was all too quick. She had no time to respond, and the room faded away as she passed out of consciousness.

Blake stood facing the two men from below. They were both very short men, but had fierce expressions on their faces. They stood on either side of the crack in the boulders, which he had traversed to get here. They hated each other and continually tried to hurl magical attacks at each other, but neither of them could muster much more than a harmless little spark.

"Quickly," one said, "kill him now and we can win!"

"No," the other responded, "Kill HIM and WE will win!"

"Why should I kill either of you?"

"Choose!"

"Maybe I should kill both of you and then I would win? What do you think about that?"

The two men turned their attacks on Blake but were equally ineffective. They took on a comical appearance, arms waving, occasionally producing a spark or small puff of smoke, but mostly arm waving and dirty looks. He turned to see what was going on below, but he could see nothing. "Where is everyone? Are they resting while the two of you came up to entertain me?"

"There are no others, just us. Now choose!"

"You two are all that's left? How pathetic. Why would I want either of you to be declared victorious?" Blake looked from one man to the other, sizing them up, drawing out the suspense. "I choose to be uninvolved. You can settle your own affairs."

"But we cannot! As you can see, our magic fails us."

"Then use your hands. You can kill each other, and then I will win because I still have my power. Or if one of you lives, then I will win because I have the power and I will be your lord. On the other hand, if you both live, I will still be the one with the power, and I will still be your lord. In either case, you will serve me. Your only escape is through death."

Blake watched the two men puzzle out the implications. Blake exhaled loudly and said, "I can see that intelligence is not a requirement for either of your duties. I'm wondering how it is you might serve me?"

They turned on each other with their bare hands, electing to kill each other rather than serve Blake. They locked together, each with his hands around the other's neck. They rolled around until eventually they rolled down one of the stairs leading to the valley below.

Michelle was worried sick. Destiny had been in her trance all day. Her candle had burned out long ago. Night was setting and Destiny's body finally slumped over the table, unable to stay upright on its own. Michelle wasn't strong enough to pick up her granddaughter and carry her, but she couldn't leave her like that. She dragged her off the chair and over to the sofa. It was old and overstuffed with lots of cushions and extra sofa pillows. Once she pulled Destiny up onto the sofa, she stretched her out and covered her with a light blanket. The weather wasn't too bad, but she didn't want her getting a chill during the night.

She wet a cloth and squeezed it on Destiny's lips, hoping she would be able to sip some. She did manage to wet her lips, but the young girl didn't respond at all.

Michelle went to the table and lit a new candle. She was going to track down Mala and find out for herself what was going on with her baby.

Brian didn't dream of being an administrator when he was a child, but when he finally faced the reality that he wasn't faster, smarter, or more magical than everyone else, he found that managing and manipulating other people was as good a way as any to get what he wanted and climb to the top. When he first started to rise in management, he fantasized about being the one that made all the right decisions, hired the right people, and led the way to answering the centuries old riddle of where the magic had gone. After the first incident, he convinced himself that this was fate unfolding before him. It was happening, and it was on his watch. He thought finding the boy and using him would be his claim to glory, but now, he was seeing things differently. He saw a new future for himself.

The boy was sleeping soundly while Brian practiced his craft. He turned pages back and forth with his mind, and refined his ability to turn the number of sheets he wanted. When he tired of turning pages, he tore off small pieces of notepaper and put the pieces in a small bowl, and one at a time, ignited them using a power from within. He wanted to make the fires bigger and hotter, but forced himself to wait until he was off the plane before he did that.

He had only planned on delivering the boy to the mercenaries, along with their final instructions. He had been concerned that they might not treat Blake well. Now, of course, he would be going with them. He would still present the boy as a kind of bloodhound. He would try to protect him, but this way, Blake would be the one they resented while Brian just went along for the ride.

Michelle entered the realm of memories and searched out Mala. Ordinarily, this was not a difficult thing to do. Mala had always been very receptive to her, but not now. Michelle could find no sense of the old woman.

She shifted her focus to locating Destiny. She tried focusing on the voice of her granddaughter, but she kept getting hit with other strange voices. She felt like she was in a large crowd walking the opposite direction and continually getting bumped into by the many people. She stopped and focused beyond the crowd, searching for Destiny. She thought she heard a stray thought, but was immediately swept away. The voices spun around her a few times, then retreated far away and the image popped. She was back in Cricket Bend, staring into the candle.

Something was wrong. She knew she was ejected from all memories, but didn't know why. Destiny still lay limp on the sofa. Michelle was near frantic, and went to the cupboard where she kept her special herbs, hoping something would jar her memory about any herb or medicine that could help her Destiny.

Blake watched the curious little men roll down the stairs. They gripped each other's necks like vices, and never let go, no matter how much they tumbled. When they reached the bottom, they rolled around, each trying to find an advantage over the other, but they could not.

Blake never heard the old man emerge from the crack which brought Blake to this ledge. The old man silently walked up behind Blake, looked over his shoulder and said, "Neither of them will win without your help."

Blake spun around, startled out of his skin. He raised his hands to defend himself, but the old man raised his own palms to calm him. "Fear not. Had I meant you harm, I would have done so rather than speaking to you."

Blake saw that the old man had the advantage over him, and nodded, accepting his reasoning.

"Besides, I am such an old man. What danger could I present to a young, strong man such as you?"

Blake nodded again.

"You don't say much," the old man continued. "I think that is good, especially for someone as young as you are. I guess most young folk these days will find that most of their troubles start with something they said."

Blake felt compelled to speak, but now he thought he would be embarrassed to speak as if the old man had goaded him into it.

"So, why didn't you help them?"

Blake pointed his thumb down the hill. "Who, them? Why would I help either of them?"

"You're one of them, aren't you?"

"One of them?" Blake asked. "I don't think so. For one thing, they're both morons."

"That may be a bit harsh. They are both enemies to each other, and they are both from the magical community."

"If you say so. They don't look very magical to me."

"Perhaps not now," the old man said, "but you've been standing here long enough to know that there was a considerable amount of magic flowing around back and forth down there."

"Why do they hate each other?"

"They always have. Their people have hated each other for thousands of years."

"That's stupid." Blake shook his head. "I've heard of it before, wars lasting hundreds of years, but I don't see why anyone would hate someone enough to go to war over something that happened centuries ago."

"There's more to it than that. They have been enemies so long now that they can't stand to be around each other. Just being near each other can make them feel sick to their stomach and aggravated beyond reason."

"Then I can't be one of them," Blake said. "I felt no such illness."

"They wanted you to choose."

Blake turned his attention back to the two men rolling around in the mud below. "There is nothing left to choose."

"Perhaps you aren't ready."

"Perhaps I wish to choose a third option."

"Oh, right," the old man said, nodding his head. "You were going to be lord of both sides. I suppose you're going to start your own branch of magicians. Be sure and let me know how that goes."

Blake spun around and asked, "Hey, who are you, anyway?" The old man was gone, as suddenly and silently as he had appeared.

Michelle continued tending to Destiny's body. Her knowledge of healing consisted of a combination of herb lore which she learned from Mala and her mother, and good old country know how, like all the residents of these parts knew. Destiny lay completely motionless. A sleeping person rolls over, or pulls up a knee, but Destiny didn't even twitch. There was little Michelle could do for her granddaughter. Ten hours had passed since Destiny had gone into her trance. Michelle tried administering water to her lips, but Destiny didn't even swallow, something that Michelle had hoped would have been automatic.

Chapter 10

Destiny opened her eyes and found herself still locked in the dream world, in the large hut where she had encountered the three patients that Mala had wanted her to heal. This time, Destiny was on the fur, lying on her back with her hands and feet firmly secured, and a leather strap bound across her chest, holding her to the fur. Her head was free, and she could see that Mala was also strapped down in a fur to her left. The room was filled with the scent of burning herbs. Destiny couldn't tell if it was just incense, or if it was for medicinal purposes. More likely, she thought, it was intended to keep them calm.

Two men entered the room. Destiny recognized the elder, Ishun, followed by a witch she thought was too young to be an elder.

"I agree with you, Ishun. I, too, am satisfied that I have seen enough, but you know the rules. The verdict must be unanimous, and I don't think there is anything to be done to change Migul's mind on this matter."

Irritation was evident in Ishun's voice as he growled back, "Whoever suggested it had to be unanimous, anyway?"

"You remember as well as I," the younger man said, "that it was Migul's suggestion. And the suggestion was passed unanimously, as you also recall."

"And who demanded that we put her to the test so soon? Surely you realize that she was not yet prepared for it."

"Again," the young man said as he nodded his head, "I agree with you, and again you know perfectly well that it was Migul who had insisted that the test be administered immediately."

"So," Ishun said flatly, "Migul arranges that the verdict must be unanimous instead of the customary majority, then he demands the test be administered prematurely, and now he is the only dissenting opinion in the matter. Does that not suggest anything to you?"

"It suggests to me that Migul is very cautious and was thinking ahead of all the rest of us."

"Does it?" Ishun squatted down beside Destiny and stroked his beard. "It suggests to me that Migul has orchestrated this whole affair, but I know not why."

Migul entered the room. "Ishun, how is she?"

Fearing Migul might have overheard some of their conversation, the younger witch quietly but swiftly excused himself from the room.

"She's just coming to, but I expect she will be quite confused."

Migul walked around the room and saw that Ishun was next to Destiny. "Not her. I was asking about Mala."

"Her wounds are healing, but I detect something more serious is going on inside her mind."

Migul wagged his finger and said, "I told you this one was vicious. She throws a protective shield around Mala, pretending to side with her, and all the while she is doing damage to her mind."

"That certainly would be one possible explanation, but we don't really know that it happened like that, now do we?"

"What else could it be? It is what I saw. It is the only explanation."

"It is not the only explanation," Ishun said flatly. "It is but one of many. You know we don't make life and death decisions based on guesswork, Migul."

"Of course, Ishun. The council of elders has already begun assembling near the Dawning stone. I believe Minister Palig wanted to speak with you before the council convened. Please tell them I'll be along shortly."

Ishun stood, nodded politely to Migul, and left the room.

Migul stood over Mala, alone in the room except for Destiny. His eyes were as dark and black as his hair, and his face showed no sign of empathy. He stared down at the old woman; her body was mostly limp with occasional involuntary jerks and spasms. "Mala, why did you let her get to you? If you only could have stuck to the plan, then you would have avoided so much pain."

Mala could not form a coherent thought. Her eyes were open, and she saw him standing over her, but her mind was complete chaos. Migul had already seen to it that her mind was sufficiently scrambled so she could not speak, but now he wished to push her past the point of healing. As he had done before, he created an energy bubble in her brain. The effect was like a seizure, with several parts of her brain being over stimulated simultaneously. She had random thoughts firing off right and left and was completely incapable of focusing on any single thought.

Destiny reached into Mala's mind and was flooded with a cacophony of unrelated images. The only constant she could sense was Migul's field. She thought about the feeling she experienced in her hands when she healed someone. She tried to extend that feeling into Mala's mind, to heal and soothe her pain. She tried to encircle Migul's destructive field with a protective field of her own, to cut him off from her brain.

Migul turned his attention to Destiny. "You are a clever little bitch, aren't you? You know, I was only sent here to stop her so she couldn't prepare you for your destiny, but, imagine the headlines on the six o'clock news if I get rid of both of you at the same time!" He started to form a twin field in Destiny's mind, but not before she slammed a fireball into his abdomen. He flew backwards off his feet, but had managed to escape significant harm. "So," he said as he stood up and brushed himself off, "you can fight even with your hands tied down. I'm impressed."

He stood now at Mala's feet and fired a large bolt of lightning into Destiny's protective shield. Destiny responded with another large fireball, which Migul caught with his hands. He held her fireball like it was a child's toy, turning it this way and that, trying to show as much disdain for Destiny as possible. She responded with a barrage of fireballs aimed high and low at him. She knew he couldn't resist showing off how powerful he was and how little her fireballs affected him. While he was catching and deflecting her attack, she reached into Mala's mind and fired a large bolt of lightning into Migul from Mala. He was so completely focused on Destiny at the time that he was knocked off his feet once again. This time, he got up more slowly, obviously winded and disoriented from the attack.

Destiny focused fireballs on the straps binding her hands to the ground. Her wrists burned from her own attacks, but she was able to burn through both straps. She removed the third strap that was binding her chest and sat up. She tossed fireballs and bolts of light-ning all around Migul. Migul had recovered enough to throw up a shield, and eventually started returning volleys.

With Migul so distracted, and his disruptive field out of her brain, Mala had regained just enough of her senses to sit up and cast some spells on Migul, but she was too weak.

Migul was very strong and started attacking Mala alongside Des-tiny. Destiny threw a bubble around Mala, but she wasn't able to muster up much of an attack while protecting both of them. Migul's attacks started to penetrate her shield. Her skin burned from the flames, and her muscles contracted spastically from the lightning bolts. Migul succeeded in surrounding Destiny's head in flames and started pelting her with an unrelenting series of lightning bolts. She couldn't see or hear what was going on, and she was paralyzed from the lightning bolts. Migul created a new fireball deep within Destiny's chest, burning her from the inside out.

Freed from Migul's hold, Mala turned to Destiny and mustered up her last bit of energy, and cast her last spell, sending Destiny home, but leaving her tortured form here to hide her escape from Migul.

Destiny's mind exploded with pain. She sat up and screamed. Michelle nearly fell off the chair where she had been sitting all night next to her granddaughter. Destiny was in agony. Michelle felt her pain. Once again, like before, a wave emanated from Destiny and spread across the state, across the country, and around the world. Her mother felt it.

All the captive inmates in all the secret asylums felt it. Some of the doctors sensed it, and this time they had it on tape, and the time was synchronized.

Blake bolted upright in his seat and grabbed his burning chest. Brian felt something, too, but not nearly as much as Blake, who had unbuttoned his shirt and was panting heavily before he sensed that Brian was watching him.

"Wow!" Blake exclaimed. "That must have been some nightmare. I thought I had swallowed lava or something."

Brian nodded his head. "I think we just had another event. We are probably getting closer to them, too. I wonder if that makes them affect you more?"

"Well, that one was definitely not cool." Blake noticed that Brian did not seem to suffer as much as he did. "Are you saying you didn't feel the same burning?"

"I felt it, but I guess not the same."

"That makes no sense. Are you sure this is coming from the witches?"

"It's not coming from us."

Blake thought about it a moment, then asked, "Do they know about me? Do you think they are targeting me?"

Brian studied Blake's face and was suddenly aware of just how young he really was. He shook his head and said, "I don't know if they are aware of you, but I don't believe they are targeting you. Remember, the first event burned their own kind, not ours."

"No way! They are attacking their own kind? Why?"

Brian shrugged his shoulders. "I'm not sure. I'm going to let our researchers figure that one out."

"Maybe one of the witches is learning how to use our people's magic, but can't figure out how to aim it?"

"Anything is possible," Brian said. "Right now, I'm concerned about how we are going to protect you long enough to find them. The team I hired can certainly protect you from other weapons, but they won't be able to protect you from this."

Blake hid the amusement he felt inside; as if he needed any protection. "That's OK. I'll keep my head down. Once we find them, I think I'll be able to take care of myself."

"I appreciate your confidence, but I've decided to go with you all the way."

"Cool," Blake nodded. "Maybe when we find this witch, some of her power will rub off on one of us so we can save the day."

"Like I said, anything is possible. You better bring your seat up. We're about to land."

Blake straightened his seat back and looked out the window. The sun was still fairly high in the west and he reckoned it must be midafternoon. He unwrapped the sandwich that was on the seat next to him and took a bite. As the sting from the burning dissipated, he began to recall the strange dream he just had. He stared out the window, reminiscing about the battle, the strange little men, and the mysterious old man, while absentmindedly chewing off pieces of his sandwich.

***

Destiny remained on the couch, panting in short gasps, while Michelle wiped the sweat off her face with a damp cloth. Her eyes were wild and glazed over until her breathing calmed down, and she regained some of her senses and started to focus on her nana.

"What am I gonna do with you, child? You kept me at my wit's end all night. Then you let out a scream that makes my blood run cold, and oh, the pain! You're lucky your ol' nana didn't keel right over on this very spot, or you'd be speakin' with a ghost right now."

Destiny tried to sit up, but was too weak.

Michelle pushed her back down on the couch. "Stop that right now, ya hear? Lie back and relax a spell. Have some water, just sip it."

Destiny lifted her head just enough to sip the water. She was disoriented, but she was glad to be back home. She sipped the water, trying to clear her head and recall what had just happened.

"I don't think I like what Mala has you doin'," Michelle said. "You shouldn't be gone so long, and coming home like this."

Destiny tried sitting up again. "Oh my god! Mala! I must go back and help her!"

"You ain't goin' nowhere. I won't allow it."

"You don't understand; she's in grave danger!"

"Sweetie, Mala's dead. There ain't nothing you gonna do to change that. You ain't got that kinda power to heal."

Destiny's expression shifted from fear to sorrow. "No!" she cried. "You mean he really did kill her? I was sure I would be able to stop him."

"What you goin' on about? Mala died thousands of years ago. You can't change the past."

"Why not?" Destiny cried. "What makes you think you can't change the past? Has anyone tried it?"

"Because it tain't real. It's like an echo from long ago. Even if you could change the echo, you just cain't change what made the sound you hear echoin'. It be like adding a mustache to a photograph. You cain't change the real person that way."

"But he did, and I think he was from the future."

Michelle tossed the damp rag aside. Destiny wouldn't sit still long enough to accept her care. "Who you talkin' 'bout now?"

"A witch. He was one of the elders. His name was Migul, and he was very powerful. But I got the feeling he was really a sorcerer from the future."

"Just a feeling, huh?" Michelle asked. "Tain't much to go get yourself killt over."

Destiny pulled herself up and twisted around, landing her feet on the floor. "No," she said, "he didn't act like the others. He was too confident."

"Lots o' people is confident, that don't make them from the future."

"No!" Destiny's voice revealed the panic in her heart. "Lots of people might act confident, but he really believed he knew how things were going to turn out. I'm talking about deep inside of him. He knew all along how things would turn out. He knew just when and where to be."

Michelle nodded and smiled, trying to exude calmness to her granddaughter. "Lots of us have the sight. We can see the future, but that don't mean we is from it."

"No, you're not really listening to me. He didn't just think he knew what was going on, he really knew it. The only thing that seemed to surprise him was me!"

"And what makes you think you surprised him?"

"Because he said so." Destiny searched her memory and continued, "He said he was only sent to kill Mala, but that I was a bonus!"

"Someone's trying to kill you?"

"You're not listening to me! I'm talking about him!"

"I heard you!" Michelle said. "He's a bad guy. That still don't make him from the future."

"I surprised him because I'm from the future, too. He knew everything that happened in the past, but he didn't know about me!"

"You be thinkin' about this way too hard, Cherie. You needs to get your rest now."

"No!" Destiny yelled. "I have to go back and help Mala!"

"I thought you didn't even like Mala."

"I don't. I mean, she's hard on me, but that don't mean she has to die like that. Besides, it wasn't all her fault. He was making her crazy. If he can go back and hurt her, then I should be able to go back and protect her."

Michelle was never more than a voyeur in the memories. She had come to trust them as a safe and even fun pastime. The thought of them actually being able to hurt Destiny bothered her, but she knew Destiny would never see reason. "Yes, child," she said, "I see that. But you don't have to go back just yet. It's in the past, you can go back anytime to save her. Right now, you needs to rest and recuperate."

Destiny leaned back against the couch. Her nana was right. She should still be able to go back and save Mala after she regains her strength. Maybe it would be a good idea to learn some way to counter Migul's magic.

The plane landed on the remote airstrip, where it let off the two passengers and their meager baggage, then immediately took off for a nearby airfield that was actually named on its flight plan. The runway itself was a mixture of broken concrete and patches of asphalt. Weeds sprouted from the cracks in the concrete, and the numbers at the end of the strip were painted by hand with a can of spray paint.

Two Hummers were waiting for them in the shade of the abandoned tower that sat midway down the runway. One of the three men standing around the cars stepped forward as Brian and Blake approached. He extended his hand to Brian and looked over Brian's shoulder to Blake. "My orders were to pick up one, not two."

"It's Okay," Brian said. "I'm the one that gave the orders. I've decided to accompany you on the mission." Brian tossed his bag in the back of one of the vehicles and peered inside one car, then the other. "I thought there were supposed to be four of you?"

"Yes sir. One of our recruits went all superstitious on us and bugged out."

"Superstitious?"

"He was nuts. We knew we would be taking on a civilian who was supposed to guide us. We don't usually take on civilian trackers, and the guys started joking about what made this guide so special. Well, sir, I figured it was just someone who could recognize the target on sight. Gomez thought it was probably some local Indian guide, but Johnson joked that it was probably some Voodoo witch doctor and that the target was either vampires or zombies. He said his mother was a big Voodoo priestess from Haiti and he knows about these things. It was all pretty funny, but Ray, the guy that left, didn't seem to get the joke. He mumbled a lot. I couldn't make out most of what he said, but it sounded to me like he was talking about Horoscope mumbo-jumbo and Tarot cards."

"I take it you don't believe in psychics and stuff like that?"

"No sir," the soldier explained, "I don't suppose I do. I believe in what I can see and feel, and in what I can do with my hands and my gun."

Brian looked the man up and down. He wasn't especially large, certainly not built like a wrestler, or a Hollywood hero, but he did appear physically fit and unafraid. "What if I told you the mission relied heavily on information provided by psychics, would that affect your ability to perform your duties?"

"It would not affect my ability to follow orders, sir, but I can't honestly say that I could comfortably plan an attack based on intel if it didn't seem reliable."

"And," Brian continued, "if the intel proved accurate, but you couldn't explain how or why?"

"Well, sir, I can't explain how a heat-seeking missile works, but I trust that it does. So if someone were to show me any information with a history of being accurate, I guess I don't need to know how it was obtained to take advantage of it."

Brian looked directly into his eyes and said, "Very well, then. I appreciate your candor. There is a strong likelihood that at one time or another on this mission, I might not be able to reveal our source."

"No problem, sir. I will assume that any intel sent down the chain of command is good intel."

"Excellent. I'd like you to meet my young associate, Blake. He is a unique and gifted young man. He has been selected to infiltrate our objective. His insight may prove useful in locating them as well."

"How do? I'm Sergeant Hughes. You're a little young for a spook, aren't you?"

Blake shook his hand, grateful that he didn't take it as an opportunity to squeeze the life out of it. "A spook?"

Brian smiled and said, "He means a spy."

Blake thought about it a moment, then smiled and said, "I like that."

"Sending Blake in was my idea," Brian said. "I believe we will find our objective is a religious cult. I think a younger person will be less threatening and more easily accepted."

Hughes simply nodded his head. "Sir, my initial briefing indicated that this would be a search and destroy mission. Has it been reclassified to a recon mission?"

"Our mission has three parts. First, we need to track and locate the target. Second, we need to infiltrate and gather some data on whether the target is an independent cell or part of a much larger organization. Third, will most likely be the termination of the target, although we may choose to capture depending on what we have learned to that point."

"Understood." Hughes looked like he had more on his mind, but was hesitant to continue.

Brian broke the silence, saying, "Let's move out. We can grab a bite at the Motel and plan out our search pattern there. I'm expecting some new data in the morning."

The battle in the hut had attracted everyone's attention. Fire and lightning escaped through the door and the small chimney at the top of the hut. Ishun was one of the first to return. He waited outside the door for two more that had followed him. The three of them joined hands with their arms crossed, each with their right hand joined to the fellow on their left and vice versa. They created a powerful shield around them and entered the hut. Flames and lightning hit their shield and turned to embers, falling to the floor with a sizzling sound. As a unit, the three men entered the hut and worked their way around the divider that served to create an entryway before reaching the main room of the hut.

Migul recognized the sizzling sound coming from the entrance. Mala was dead, Destiny was escaping, and he was desperately trying to get his attacks to follow her to her own time, but now it was too late. Thinking fast, he slammed a lightning bolt into himself, knocking himself back against a wall of the hut.

Ishun and his companions entered the main room. The fire and lightning had ceased. They dropped the shield. Ishun went to Destiny, while his companions split up between Mala and Migul. He put his hands on Destiny's head. He could hear his companions performing healing spells on Mala and Migul.

The man at Mala's side stopped ministering the healing magic. "We are too late. Mala is dead. Ishun, you do not even try to save the stranger?"

"She is gone."

Migul was feeling better. "I had no choice. She was killing Mala. I had to stop her. Good riddance, I say. I only wish I had been soon enough to save Mala."

The man at Mala's side winced at Migul's harsh remark. "Let us hope she is not the chosen one who was prophesied."

"No," Ishun corrected him, "let us hope she is. She is not here, but she did not die. She lives."

Migul hung his head. "Again I have failed."

"Perhaps you did not hear me, Migul. I said she may still be the one."

"That cannot be. She killed Mala. I saw her with my own eyes. She knows the power of fire and lightning."

Ishun held his hand on Destiny's forehead and said a prayer for her safety. With his head still bowed, he answered Migul. "That she does, as it was prophesied she would."

Migul's voice began to betray his desperation. "Does the prophesy state that she would kill one of our own?"

"No, it does not. Nor does it state that she would try to take her own life."

Migul was silent. He bowed his head and closed his eyes for a moment, then popped his head up. His eyes burned with rage. "Why do you question me about her death? I told you what happened."

Ishun stood and faced Migul, staring deeply into his eyes. "Forgive me, I forgot that you already told us you killed her."

"And now you hold me here against my will?"

Ishun stepped aside so Migul and the other two witches could view Destiny's remains. "Perhaps you can explain why her remains are scorched? Did she fire flames upon herself?"

Migul was frantic. The pace of his words accelerated as he tried to explain himself. "You know perfectly well this is not the real world. You can't collect evidence in this world. She may have performed a glamor to disguise her remains as she left. For that matter, why are her remains here at all if she is not dead? You know as well as I that only the dead leave remains in this world. She clearly means to trick us!"

Ishun took three slow paces towards Migul. Still staring into his eyes, he stroked his beard and asked, "You are suggesting that she had the presence of mind to do this to herself?"

Migul believed he finally had found the logic to support his explanation. He mastered the panic in his voice and calmly said, "She may have. She was quite clever, you know."

Ishun closed the gap between them. He was now directly in Migul's face when he asked, "Why are you here, Migul?"

"Ishun, my good friend, you know well why I am here, the same as any of us. We gather here to preserve the future of our kind."

"Am I your friend now? Because I certainly do not feel that we are friends. I'm going to ask you again. Why are you here? Not on this plane, but in this room. Why are you here in this room? Why is it that this tragedy has taken place now in your presence?"

Migul recognized that his cause was lost. "How dare you question me like this? You may be here on some noble cause to protect the future, but I am here on a more desperate mission to protect my present."

"Why did you kill her?"

Migul arched his eyebrows. "You confuse me. I thought you said she lives."

"Not her. Why did you kill Mala?"

Migul bowed his head again and closed his eyes.

"Hold him!" Ishun bellowed.

"He is not alone," said one of Ishun's companions. "Someone else helps to pull him away from this world."

Ishun reached out and tried to hold on to Migul's spirit before he escaped back to his own world. "Now, more than ever, we could use Mala's help."

"Yes," the same companion said, "she was good at these spells."

"And strong too," the other companion added. "Her strength equaled three of ours."

Ishun reached into Migul's mind. He searched for understanding, for some kind of identity. He sensed Migul's fear, but he also sensed that Migul was not alone. He had help. Someone was pulling him from this world. His spirit escaped the memory they constructed, and the form before them faded away.

The two witches who had held his arms looked to Ishun for an explanation. One of them asked, "How can this happen? Our people have never died in this world. How could one of our own become so corrupted as to come here and kill one of us?"

Ishun held them by the shoulders and shook his head. "He was not one of us."

The fear in the two witches doubled. "That can't be," one said. "They cannot come here! They don't have the magic to come to our world unless we bring them!"

Ishun now nodded his head as he filtered through everything he saw in Migul's mind. "He was not one of us, but he was also not one of them, either. I think we may never be safe here again."

"And what of the girl? Is she the chosen one?"

Ishun's last words before fading out of this reality were, "Let us hope so."

Migul returned to his own time. His nearly lifeless body came out of its trance, tired and weak. He sat up with the help of his longtime friend and associate, Peter. Knowing how dry his throat would be,

Peter held up a glass of water and placed the straw between his friend's lips. The water was cool and welcome.

"Thank you, Peter, you are a lifesaver."

"For giving you water? I doubt you were that near death, my friend."

Mark, Migul's real name, sank back down into the pillows. "No, for pulling me out of there."

"That wasn't my doing. The librarians pulled you out. They said something had gone wrong."

"Besides them inserting me in the wrong time-line?"

Peter gave him another sip of water. "I don't know, and I'm not a good enough friend to question them."

"You're a good enough friend. I wouldn't ask anyone to question one of them."

"All I can say is they were really unhappy about something. They kept speaking of 'that fool Migul'."

Mark winced. "Please don't say that name."

"Sorry, bud; I was just quoting them."

Mark looked around the bare room. It held the bed he was on and a couple of chairs, and room for little more. "So, why aren't they here?"

"They'll be back, I'm sure. They tried peeking into your memory while you slept, but your dreams were too chaotic. It was actually kind of funny seeing them so frustrated over their own failures."

"How long have I been out?"

Peter pulled a chair next to the bed and straddled it backwards. "Not that long, maybe five or six hours."

"How long was I gone?"

Peter held the water to his lips again and said, "A long time, not long enough to break the record, but long enough to suffer separation sickness."

"Fifteen? Sixteen hours?"

"Twenty three."

Mark whistled. "Twenty-three hours? I've never been gone that long before. Why did they leave me under that long if they weren't happy with what I was doing?"

"They were happy. They were thrilled, in fact. They seemed to get concerned about something around day six or seven, but they said things could still work out. Then this morning they went hysterical and pulled the plug as fast as they could."

"Oh shit," Mark exclaimed. "That's not good."

"You think? What happened in there?"

Mark pushed himself up a little higher on the pillows so he could punctuate his story with his hands. "For one thing, she was already there."

"Who was already there?"

"Her, the one. She was already there."

Peter rubbed his free hand over his bald head. "Oh my god. Someone sure screwed up."

"I hope it was a screwup, because if it was planned that way and I wasn't told, then maybe I wasn't expected to return."

"How's that?" Peter asked. "Were you supposed to go up against her?"

"I did! I had to! She was like the old bitch's shadow. I couldn't get the old one alone, but luck was on my side. I convinced them to plan this grand, elaborate test where they set up a battle against the girl to see where her true loyalties were."

"Oh my god," Peter repeated himself, "that's not in the historical records, no wonder they were pissed."

"It almost worked. I had hoped that the girl would kill the old woman for me, but instead, both of them were exhausted to the point of passing out. I went to kill off the woman while they slept, but the girl woke up, or maybe she wasn't really asleep. She protected the old woman and battled me at the same time."

"In her condition? Exhausted like you said? She could still battle you?"

Mark took the water from his friend and held it to his own lips. He took another sip and said, "I think I need something a little stronger."

"When you're a little stronger. Tell me about the battle."

"You should have seen her!" Mark continued. "She battled me and protected both of them at the same time. And it's true that she knows fire and lightning. What she doesn't know, she seems to learn in a blink."

"So they pulled you out just as she was about to defeat you?"

"No!" Mark said. "I won the battle. I killed them both, or at least I thought I did. The witches said the girl escaped. That was when they started to hold me there, and that must be when the librarians pulled me out, because I sure wasn't able to leave on my own."

"So, what's the problem?" Peter asked. "You killed the old woman, and that was your objective, after all. If she already told the girl about her destiny, they certainly can't hold it against you, can they?"

A noise behind Peter, a simple cough, alerted the both of them that they were no longer alone. Peter snapped his head around and saw three of the librarians standing behind him. Just knowing they were librarians was imposing enough, but these three were dressed in their formal grey hooded robes, which presented a formidable presence.

"Go ahead," one of them said, "answer his question. Did the old woman tell the girl who she really was?"

"I don't think so," Mark answered. "They hadn't finished the testing yet, but the girl was in the old one's mind. I sensed her there."

"Yes," one of the librarians said, "she was there alright. But the old woman didn't tell her anything. She didn't have to."

Peter and Mark looked at each other, puzzled.

"Come now, Mark," the librarian continued, "don't you remember?"

Mark shook his head slowly.

The elder librarian stepped forward, shaking his head, and said, "Let me refresh your memory, and I quote, 'You are a clever little bitch aren't you? You know, I was only sent here to stop her so she couldn't prepare you for your destiny...' That was enough to turn her around, you fool. What were you thinking?"

"I was thinking I was going to end her there, killing two birds with one stone."

"Had we wanted her killed," the elder librarian barked, "we would have sent someone more capable."

"That's a bit harsh," Mark said. "My record speaks for itself. I have been a very reliable agent my whole career."

The smallest of the three librarians snickered and said, "Well, your perfect record has been tarnished now, in a big way."

"So send me back further. I'll cut down the old woman before they ever meet."

The three librarians responded in unison, "That won't work."

"How can you know that?"

"It's been tried."

Mark nodded his head, thinking he understood. "I see, tried and failed."

"No," the elder librarian said. "Tried and succeeded to kill the woman, but without the desired results. So we undid it and let her live."

Mark felt better knowing they had failed, too. "So we've all made mistakes. We live and learn."

"Indeed. We would like to learn more from you about the girl."

Peter stood at that point and excused himself. "I think I am needed elsewhere."

Chapter 11

B rian woke early and found an isolated spot in the motel parking lot with a boulder large enough for him to sit on. He sat cross-legged, facing into the east where the sun could warm his cheek. He closed his eyes and tried to feel the rising sun. He listened intently to everything around him, hoping to extend his senses beyond the normal reach of his sight and touch. Trucks and busses had distinctive sounds that separated them from automobiles as they rolled by. He could smell the acrid odor of spent diesel fuel as it wafted past him. He concentrated on the environment around him, trying to filter out the five senses. He heard doors closing in the motel behind him. The trees surrounding the parking lot chittered and chattered, creating a constant background noise that lay underneath everything else he heard. He tried reaching beyond what he could hear. These were lessons he had learned as a child. He never had a talent to go beyond his physical senses, but lately, he was feeling a growing power, and hoped that maybe this time he could push past his limitations. It's certainly not unique for his kind to be limited in such a way. In fact, even in the days of power, very few were able to expand beyond their five primary senses. That was something that came easily to the witches, but not his kind.

Blake hardly slept. He was too wound up to sleep comfortably and didn't really make much of an effort. He had this new idea that might come in handy later on. The soldiers made him uncomfortable. They were hardcore serious guys and looked at him like he was a liability. His whole life he'd been pushed around by people who thought they were better than he was. These guys were certainly bigger and stronger than him, but he had a secret weapon, and wanted to keep it a secret. He wasn't even sure why he was so careful to guard his powers. He just had an irresistible urge to keep a low profile, and if one of these gun-wielding soldiers of fortune started pushing him around, he would probably be forced to reveal himself. If he did that, it would probably turn lethal real fast. So he wanted another way to resolve any conflict with them. He thought that maybe if he hung out in their dreams, he might learn something they didn't want to share, and he could use it as leverage to persuade them to treat him differently.

Sergeant Hughes, the lead guy, had a fear of tunnels, dating back to some traumatic bunker collapse in Iraq. Blake tucked that bit of information away, but didn't see how it was going to help him any. Anyone buried in rubble for a couple days would probably have the same fear.

Gomez dreamed mostly of women. This in itself wouldn't be so unusual, but Blake sensed that they weren't just fantasy women, but real women that Gomez would visit now and again during his travels. Blake tried to sense if there was a wife among these women, but he couldn't detect anything to suggest that one was more important than the others. Blake just didn't see how a man with so many girlfriends would care if one of them found out he was cheating on her. He wasn't even sure if it could be considered cheating if they weren't married. This was not going to be much help.

Johnson offered up a pretty good morsel. Blake had to sift through his mind some to tell which of the dream images seemed more like memories than random dream sequences, and found that his dreams of the time he spent in the stockades was real. According to the images Blake saw, Johnson had been brought before a tribunal regarding some friendly fire that resulted in the death of several officers. Apparently, he had a reputation as a hothead and had visited the guardhouse several times for insubordination. His jail time was usually long enough for him to sleep off his intoxication. His temper and drinking were well known. He couldn't keep them secret if he wanted to, but he harbored a secret fear that someone would discover the truth about the friendly fire. He was cleared of any wrongdoing, but the truth was that he killed his commander and two other officers intentionally. He recognized that his unit was drawing down on friendlies, and instead of alerting them, he took advantage of the mistake to eliminate his commander. His commander was an idiot and told Johnson that he was going to file an official court martial recommendation against him. It never happened. Blake hoped that if this was the only thing he could hold against these guys, then maybe Johnson was all he needed, and he could persuade Johnson to side with him should one of the other soldiers become a problem.

Destiny slept peacefully, despite the ordeal she had just been through. While she slept, her nana kept busy. She wished there was more she could do for her granddaughter, but she didn't have Destiny's abilities. So she busied herself doing what she could, and spent the night brewing special potions and weaving talismans out of the local herbs, saplings, and her collection of ancient bones which had been handed down for generations. They were ancient talismans, and she had no way of knowing if they would protect Destiny from modern dangers, but it was comforting for her to do something to help, no matter how small.

She surrounded Destiny with herbs said to ward off inquisitive minds. She burned incense to reveal the presence of astral projections. She hung mobiles inside the windows and doorway to act as alarms should any magical fields enter the home.

Outside, in the yard, she burned a small bonfire. She sprinkled herbs and ground stones over the fire. The herbs burned, some giving off a pleasant fragrance, others not so pleasant. Most of the stone powders and pieces fell into the embers and grew warm. Some grew warm enough to glow themselves, but some of the powders burned bright and flew up into the air, sparkling brightly above. The fire was a beacon, but rather than a beacon to attract attention, the properties of the ingredients combined to emanate a powerful and dangerous magical warning for strangers to steer clear of this area. Michelle put larger stones into the glowing embers. As they warmed, they emanated feelings of fear. She was already frightened enough, but she could not ignore the feeling of doom they generated in the pit of her stomach.

She returned to Destiny's bedside, and was relieved that the dread she felt outside was warded off by the charms she placed around the inside of the room. There was still a couple hours before daylight, but she didn't dare sleep. The truth was that she couldn't sleep. She sat by her sleeping granddaughter, getting up only to refresh the incense burners arrayed around the room.

<hr>

Blake remained in bed while the men woke up and started the morning. He feigned sleep, all the while listening and probing. The soldiers were used to waking up and jumping directly into their routines. Blake felt as powerful as ever, and didn't need to open his eyes to see what they were doing. If he had ever entertained the notion that he was being stupid and paranoid, that thought was quickly quelled as each and every one of the soldiers looked upon him with disdain. They saw him as an unpredictable risk. As mercenaries, they accepted orders without question and viewed him as part of their mission, but orders don't build trust. They would be responsible for protecting him, but they would not be able to rely upon him to pull his own weight in a fight. No one was ordered to like him.

Blake couldn't help feeling paranoid, and their feeling towards him certainly warranted his fears. He couldn't identify the source of his concern, but he felt uneasy. The feeling grew inside of him, like a vulture standing over him, waiting for him to die before eating.

He opened his eyes and saw Gomez sitting across from him, staring. "Morning, Princess. Hey everyone, the Princess is up. We can get going now."

Blake sat up, incensed by Gomez's comments. His tone was bitter and demanding. "What'd you say?"

Johnson stepped between them. "Down boy," he said, "he didn't mean no offense. Princess is just a term we use for anyone that's privileged and sleeps late while the rest of us are working." They didn't know Blake well enough to tease him and were genuinely upset that he would waste the morning for them.

Blake's mood wasn't appeased. He wasn't even sure where it came from. Maybe lack of sleep, maybe something else, but he lashed out at Johnson, "Who you calling 'boy'?"

"Listen, sunshine," Johnson still tried to maintain his position between Blake and Gomez, "you're with the big boys now. You'd best watch your tone, you hear?"

Blake was losing control of his emotions. He couldn't help it. It felt like someone had flipped a switch and turned on his irrational anger. "The big boys?" he asked. "Is that what your kind call themselves these days? Or is that just the 'don't ask, don't tell' name you use?" He looked over Johnson's shoulders at Gomez and said, "I guess all the women are just to hide your true homo tendencies from your friends."

Johnson didn't know where the hostility was coming from, but he still managed to maintain some control over his temper. Gomez, on the other hand, was ready to explode. He shoved Johnson aside and lunged at Blake, circling his hands around the boy's neck. This is exactly what Blake wanted to avoid. Even as Gomez's hands tightened around his throat, he reached out and grabbed his shirt on either side of his rib cage. In moments, Gomez was going to be a pile of ash and his secret would be out.

"Gomez!" Johnson wrenched his paws off of Blake and stepped back between them. "Gomez! We got a job to do!" He turned to Blake. "Are you trying to get yourself killed?"

Blake stood his ground, staring right back into Johnson's eyes. He spoke in an even voice loud enough for only Johnson to hear clearly, "Why would you guys kill me? I thought you only murdered your commanding officers."

Johnson started to form a question with his mouth, but staring into Blake's eyes, he understood the message loud and clear. The boy was a spook, and he came armed with Johnson's best-kept secret.

Sergeant Hughes poked his head in the room and barked, "Ladies, if you are all done with your chit chat, we'd like to get this show on the road."

Johnson pointed his thumb over his shoulder towards the door and Sergeant Hughes. "See what I mean? The name calling and teasing are like a term of endearment."

Blake regained some semblance of control and nodded to Johnson. He threw on some clothes, ran his hands through his hair, and headed out the door.

Brian was still outside trying to pick up any kind of intuition he could, but he had nothing. The team was gathering outside the entrance to the motel. Blake saw Brian meditating in the sun and crossed the parking lot to join him.

"Morning, Blake. Did you sleep well?"

"Yeah, I guess. You?"

"Me too. So, you got any special feelings about what direction we should head out?"

Blake looked around him. He could see some mountains far off to the north, past the highway. He turned clockwise, hoping he would get some kind of sign. After completing his spin, he looked to the south, and then started frowning and turned back north, pointing towards the mountains. "I think we want to head that direction."

"North it is. I'll tell Hughes." Brian hopped off the boulder he had been sitting on and headed off towards the vehicles.

"Wait!" Blake turned around and looked south.

Brian turned back and asked, "What's up?"

"It's hard to explain. I want to go south, but every time I think that I want to go south, something inside me turns me around and points north."

"We're too small to split up, so we'll have to pick one or the other."

"South," Blake's voice quavered as he said it. "I don't know why I pointed north. It's almost like something was MAKING me say north when I really meant south."

Brian waited a moment, unsure what was ticking in the kid's head, but then, stepped back towards the cars, and with less conviction than he had before, said, "Okay. We head south."

Blake settled into the back of the forward Humvee, right behind Brian. Sergeant Hughes drove while his men followed in the second vehicle with all their gear.

Brian and Hughes talked about everything and anything. Baseball, politics, the weather, no topic was too small for them. Blake sank down into his seat, with nothing to add to the carrousel of conversation in the front seats. He hadn't slept during the night. His stomach was feeling uneasy, and with the steady drone of the wheels on the road and the wind past the windows, he fell into a nice, soothing sleep.

Destiny could have sworn she had made it home. Her mind was a jumble of out-of-sequence memories. The one clear memory she had was of Mala dying. Less clear was her belief that Mala had somehow sacrificed herself to release Destiny from the memory. She tried retracing her steps through her memories to see if she could piece together what was real and what was dream, but she found it difficult to determine one from the other.

She was certain she remembered returning home to Cricket Bend, but when she opened her eyes, she was surrounded with a variety of odd talismans made from bent wood and a variety of herbs and stones. They swayed in the breeze and hung from the trees all around her. She took deep slow breaths, something Mala had taught her, and tried to clear the fog from her mind so she could better focus on the talismans around her. As the fog lifted, the talismans faded away, and in their place she saw flowers and fruit hanging from the trees. The sun poked between the trees and struck her in the face. She sat up and looked around. She didn't recognize where she was, but it sure wasn't home.

She could hear water splashing in a brook somewhere beyond the trees. The sun was hot on her face, so she headed off towards the sound of the brook. She found a path heading in the same general direction and followed it. The path took her into the cool shade of a thick stand of trees. Just inside the trees, she found a small fawn lying on its side, quivering.

Destiny was filled with empathy for the poor thing. She knelt down beside it and placed her hands on the side of its head. She could feel its pain, but she could also feel the warmth well up in her hands and draw the pain away. The young fawn jumped up on its feet, and stared at her a moment, then bounded off into the woods.

She returned to the path. The brook did not seem far off, yet, still she had not reached it, and not much farther into the woods she came across a small pack rat. It was injured and could not run away from her. Again, feeling for the poor animal, she knelt beside it and drew away its pain, healing its broken limb. The rat sprang up and ran away a few feet, then stopped and looked at Destiny. Quick as a snake strike, it sprang back to where it had lain, gathered up the shiny bauble it had left behind, and scurried off into the brush.

She returned to her quest, for she now considered the brook to be a quest. She walked into the woods, through the trees and past flowers and brush alongside the path. She came to a spot that was littered with twigs, leaves, and flower petals. In the center of the mess she saw the remains of a small bush, its limbs twisted and torn from its trunk. The twigs and flowers were mutilated and scattered all around its bare core. Destiny searched the ground around the mess for signs of what had caused this mess. She thought maybe she would find bear tracks, but she had no skills at tracking wild animals, and the ground was probably too hard to leave footprints, anyway. She wondered if she could heal the plant, and knelt down beside it to offer what relief she could. The tattered pieces remained on the ground, yet she thought she could feel some relief and some hope in the plant's roots.

Having done what little she could, she returned to the path again. The sound of the water was growing louder, but she also heard something else. There was a loud splashing sound which came at odd intervals, and usually in sets of three or four splashes. She continued walking until she finally came upon the brook.

A small boy stood beside the brook. He had a large pole in his hands. The pole was a couple inches thick, and two to three times taller than the boy himself. He held the pole on his shoulder and stared into the water. She stepped quietly, trying not to disturb him. He raised the pole up high over his head and then swung it with all his might, crashing it down onto the brook. He repeated this a couple times, then scowled at the water.

Destiny lightly tapped him on his shoulder and asked, "Whatcha doin?"

The boy nearly jumped out of his shoes. "Where'd you come from? You're not supposed to be here!"

"I asked you first. What is that?"

The boy held the rod in front of him and said, "This? It's just a stick."

"Why are you attacking the river?"

"What? That's stupid. Why would I attack the river?"

Destiny shrugged her shoulders and said, "I don't know. Seems to me you're the crazy one doing it."

"I'm not attacking the river. I'm fishing."

"Wouldn't it work better if you put a hook and some string on your pole?"

"Sure," he said, "but where's the satisfaction in that?"

"Have you caught any fish like that?"

"No."

Destiny smirked and asked, "Then where's the satisfaction in that?"

"Hey!" he shouted. "You didn't answer my question. What are you doing here?"

"I dunno. I woke up a ways back there and was thirsty, so I came this way."

The boy struck the end of the rod against the ground next to him, holding it tall by his side. He pointed directly at Destiny and said, "You shouldn't be here, and you ask too many questions. Just go back the way you came."

"I like it here. I'd rather stay. Why do you want to hurt the fish?"

"Who says I'm trying to hurt the fish?"

Destiny sat down on a boulder that was lining the brook and asked, "Why did you hurt the rat?"

"Since when do you need a reason to hurt a lousy rat?"

"Gosh, what did the rat ever do to you?"

"I told you," he said, "you're not supposed to be here. It was a dirty, stinking rat. Rats are nasty vermin, you know? Now stop asking so many questions."

"Oh, okay. Rats are vermin."

"Yeah, now go away."

Destiny watched the boy return to thrashing the river a few times before she continued. "What about the fawn? It was kinda cute. You didn't have to hurt it."

"Look, I already told you that you're not supposed to be here. What I do here is just plain none of your business. Go away before I lose my temper."

"I didn't wake up this morning hoping to find some silly little boy torturing innocent animals, not to mention the bush, and now the river!"

He stopped thrashing the river and pointed at her again, shouting, "Not that it's any of your business, but I only come here when I'm really upset! It helps me release some of my anger so I can behave properly when I return home."

"So you admit this is not proper behavior?"

"Of course I do!" he shouted at her. "I'm not stupid!"

"Then why do you do it?"

"I told you. I have to. It's really important."

"No, you don't." Destiny frowned and shook her head. "You never have to be cruel to nature. You just choose to be cruel. You're probably trying to compensate for being a boy instead of a man."

"Oh, aren't you clever? You sound like one of my grandfather's wicked advisors, twisting his own words to do their own bidding even when it goes against his best interests. If you're so wise, advise me what you would have me do instead of whacking some stupid animals?"

"For one thing," she said, "you could simply look around you. Listen to the water. Don't you find it all very relaxing?"

"I don't have time for all that girly stuff. I think my grandfather's advisors have him bewitched. They're magical, you know, and now they are trying to hex me, too."

"Sounds to me like they failed."

"But they keep trying," he replied, "and each attempt they try harder."

"Look around you. The answer is all around you."

He looked around. A perplexed shadow crossed his face. "Where?"

"You're standing in it."

"I'm standing in the river."

Destiny nodded.

"How is the river supposed to be my answer?"

"If you build a dam, the river just builds up until it can go over or around the dam. If you build it bigger, the river just gathers its strength and goes around again. It doesn't waste time getting angry or feeling defeated."

"That doesn't help my grandfather any. I have to defeat them." He raised the rod high over his head and brought it crashing down on the water one more time. "I have to be mean and tough to defeat them."

"Why don't you just tell him? Show him what they are doing to him?"

"Oh, sure, he probably spends most of his day hoping his grandson would show up out of the blue and advise him. Stupid girl."

"Make up your mind," she said. "A moment ago, you said I was clever."

"I said you sound just like his advisors. Maybe you should talk to my grandfather for me, since you have skill twisting people's words."

"I can't do that," she said. "If they really have him bewitched, then only someone close to his heart could break the enchantment."

The boy nodded, then sat down next to the river. His face grew dark and sad. His eyes glistened with wetness and his nose sniffled.

Destiny could feel the sadness overtake him and asked, "Now what's wrong?"

"Nothing." He paused a moment. "It's just that if I'm not going to be mean and tough for my grandfather, then I feel real guilty for what I did."

"Every choice has its consequences. Fortunately for you, all of this is just a dream."

"That doesn't change what I did."

"But still," she said, "you don't need to worry. I healed them all."

"If you know it is just a dream, why did you bother to heal them? They're not even real."

She thought about it a moment, then said, "Because I wasn't healing them. I was healing you."

The boy paused and digested what she said. "Thank you. That was really thoughtful of you, but it doesn't matter. You still aren't supposed to be here. You need to go now. You need to be somewhere else."

Destiny cocked her head. "Where am I supposed to be?"

"Not here."

"I didn't choose to come here. I was brought here. That usually means something."

"Fine," he barked, "and now you're done here. Go!"

She didn't like his tone, and started to say so, but he reared back with his stick and whacked her on the head. She found herself floating in a void. She could hear the different voices around her. She listened for one to call for her and wondered if she had really helped the boy, or if he was back to destroying nature with his stick.

Chapter 12

A sharp poke in the ribs roused Blake from his nap. He straightened up in his chair and looked around him. About half the faces were amused and laughed out loud, but the rest looked irritated and annoyed. The juror next to him leaned over and whispered in his ear, "You might get away with resting your eyes, mate, but not if you starts snorin' the way you was!"

In the front of the room, a judge was furiously rapping his gavel to gain control over the laughing crowd. "Order! Order!" The din died down, and the judge turned his attention to Blake. He put his gavel down and adjusted his robes around his collar, all the while staring and scowling directly into Blake's eyes. "Well, son, I must apologize for my colleagues. I'm sure that in the future, they will try much harder to maintain your attention. Actually," the judge started shuffling papers in front of him, feigning to look up some spec of information, "I think you have set a new record. Normally, we don't start losing jurors until the afternoon, after lunch, but you've nodded off before mid-morning. Didn't you bother getting any sleep last night?"

Blake was fully aware that he was expected to answer, but he was still trying to figure out where he was and what the hell was going on. He tried to open his mouth, but completely without his control, the answer offered itself through his mouth, and in someone else's voice. "No, sir," he said. "I mean, yes, sir. That is, I tried to sleep, but the awesome responsibility of serving on this panel was just too much for me, and I had a little trouble sleeping."

"I see," the judge said. He curled his lips into an insincere smile and continued. "We'll just have to make sure to help you out tonight, but in the meantime, it's far too early for me to call a recess. Do you think you could possibly keep awake a while longer?"

Blake's host pushed himself further upright in the chair and nodded his head. "Yes, sir," he said, "absolutely."

"Thank you," the judge said. "Should you have any trouble, I assign the job of waking you to the juror on your right."

"Yes, sir. It won't happen again."

Blake heard the conversation, but was not actually part of it. He tried to look around the room, but he didn't have control over his head, and had to wait for it to turn around on its own so he could get a better look at where he was. It was obviously a courtroom, but not the fancy kind you see on TV. The chairs in the jurors' box weren't fixed to the floor; they were office chairs wheeled in for the occasion. There was no ornate wooden fence and gate separating the participants from the audience. A series of velvet ropes hanging from brass pedestals, like what you might find in a movie theater, separated the audience from the business end of the court. The audience sat on folding chairs that squeaked and rattled. The judge sat behind a nice walnut desk, but instead of a tall desk built to the floor, it was setup on a raised platform with bunting hanging down to the floor. This, Blake decided, was no real courtroom. It was some kind of temporary, or possibly emergency, make-shift courtroom.

The judge rapped his gavel again. "Let's proceed."

A tall, well-dressed man, standing between the prosecutor's table and the judge, tugged on the sleeves of his coat and said, "Your Honor, in light of the fact that the prosecution has not had a chance to depose the coroner yet, and considering this young man's tiredness, perhaps a recess would be in the best interest of justice."

The judge snarled back, "Mr. Tangiers, justice has its own demands, and one of those is swiftness. So, for the sake of justice, Mr. Prosecutor, please ask your questions."

"Yes, Your Honor, right away, sir." He turned his attention back to the smartly dressed woman in the witness box. "Doctor Mc-Mann, you were telling us what you found at the crime scene. Please continue."

Dr. McMann had her dark hair pulled tightly into a bun on the back of her head. She wore dark-rimmed glasses. The lenses were not terribly thick looking. Blake did not doubt that she wore them as a prop to look more credible. Her face was thin, almost gaunt, as was her pencil skirt and tightly tailored suit. "We sifted through the ashes and collected hundreds of bone fragments."

"Tell me, doctor, have you been able to determine how many victims there were?"

"Objection." A lawyer popped up at the defense table. "The prosecutor has not offered any evidence that these bone fragments represent victims at all. He hasn't even established if they were human."

"Sustained," the judge replied. "Please rephrase your question."

"Dr. McMann, were the bones human?"

"Yes, most of them were human."

"And were you able to determine how many human's bones were in the ashes?"

"We performed DNA analysis on the bone fragments to see if we could identify them. So far, we have identified over a dozen different remains."

The prosecutor smiled smugly. He was finally getting somewhere. "Were you able to determine why they were so fragmented?"

"We've identified hundreds of nick marks that indicate the use of tools, perhaps a knife of some kind. Some displayed breaks and cracks that probably resulted from the fire."

"You are certain the scratch marks were from a sharp edge, something man made?"

"Yes."

The prosecutor turned towards the jury. He gripped the lapels of his coat and puffed out his chest, saying, "So then, you would conclude that we have definite signs of foul play."

"No, I would not."

"I'm sorry," he said, "please explain yourself."

"The bones were certainly cut up, but we can't conclude foul play from that."

"Since when do knife marks not suggest foul play?"

"Since," she said, "the knife marks are over twenty-five thousand years old. Most of the bones were quite ancient, possibly religious relics. We haven't determined that yet."

Mr. Tangiers turned towards the judge and asked, "Permission to approach the bench?"

The judge was clearly annoyed, but waved him up. Mr. Charles also rose from the defense table to join Mr. Tangiers before the judge.

"Your Honor," Mr. Tangiers pleaded, "not only have I not been given the forensic reports in time to review them, but the coroner has not even concluded their investigation. How can we proceed with this trial when they are still investigating the cause?"

The judge was clearly agitated, but maintained his cool. He turned to the witness box and coolly asked, "Dr. McMann, how long do you think it would take for you to complete your examination of the evidence?"

"There are a lot of bone fragments, Your Honor, it could easily take many months, possibly even years."

"In your expert opinion, Dr. McMann, do you think the remaining evidence would alter your conclusions regarding this case?"

"No, sir," she replied. "I think that would be highly unlikely."

"Just highly unlikely?"

"No, sir." She leaned forward into her seat and spoke directly into the microphone. "In my expert opinion, I would say that the remaining evidence would have absolutely no effect on my current conclusion regarding this case."

"Thank you, Dr. McMann, I think Mr. Tangiers may still have some more questions for you, but we should be done shortly."

Dr. McMann adjusted the glasses on her face, smiled slightly, and nodded her head.

The judge turned his attention back to the prosecutor. "Mr. Tangiers, you see those twelve people sitting over there? I think they all have lives waiting for them. I know I do, and how about that little girl over there? I think she would like to return home to her grandmother. Now, as the lovely Dr. McMann has so eloquently stated, there is nothing to be gained from delaying this trial any further just to examine the remaining evidence. Do you think we could continue this questioning and finish up this trial?" His voice was sweet and lyrical, but his long face and dark eyes were threatening.

The two attorneys left the bench. Mr. Charles returned to his seat, and Tangiers returned to the witness.

He was clearly frustrated with his witness. Forensic reports were always slanted to favor the prosecution, but there was something wrong here. He suspected supernatural influence. He wasn't especially surprised. If he were in the witch's position, he would tamper with the minds of the witnesses, too. "Dr. McMann, can you please confirm that we still do have two corpses from the ashes?"

"Yes."

"And they were human?"

"They were," she said. "Two human male remains were found in the home."

Once again, the prosecutor thought he had made some progress, but this time he endeavored to suppress his emotions. "And were you able to determine their ages?"

"We guess their ages are between twenty-five and thirty-five."

"And did you carbon date the remains? We want to make sure they aren't also ancient."

The defense attorney stood up timidly. "Your Honor, the prosecutor is badgering his own witness."

The judge politely asked, "Is that an objection, Mr. Charles?"

"Not really, sir. I just felt bad for the witness."

The judge rapped his gavel. "Noted. Mr. Tangiers, get to the point, and do it quickly, and try to tone down the sarcasm."

Tangiers threw his hands in the air and returned to his table, saying, "I'm through with this witness."

At the other table, the much younger attorney shuffled some papers and stood up to approach the witness. "Dr. McMann, I'll try to be brief. Can you tell us how the victims died?"

"They burned to death."

"In the fire?"

"Yes, and no," she said. "There is no doubt that they were in the fire, but it didn't kill them. We've never seen anything like this before, and we are unable to determine the exact cause, but they burned from the inside out."

"Can you speculate on what kinds of things could cause this type of burning?"

The prosecutor sprang up. "Objection, calls for speculation."

The judge waved his hands at the prosecutor, motioning for him to remain seated. "Sit down, Mr. Tangiers, I'll allow it. I'd like to hear what she has to say."

The prosecutor was stunned and sat down quietly.

Dr. McMann continued, "I suppose if someone ingested a powerful incendiary substance and ignited it, they would burn from the inside out."

"Are you aware of any such substance that could be ingested by accident?"

"None. I don't believe you could hide it in food."

The young attorney knew what he was going to ask, but pretended to think about it anyway, for the jury's sake. "So a person would have to ingest it on purpose."

"Yes," she said, "or be forced to ingest it somehow."

Mr. Charles, the defending attorney, paused for a moment, letting that answer settle in with the jury. "Dr. McMann, were you able to measure the deceased weights for us?"

"Adjusting for fluid and tissue mass lost in the burning, we estimate their weights to be almost two hundred pounds for the smaller one, and two forty for the bigger guy. They may have weighed an additional five or ten pounds, depending on their fitness."

"Thank you," he said, "and have you also measured the weight of our defendant?"

"She's about one hundred and fifteen pounds."

"Hmmm. So the victims were both much larger than the defendant, and one of them was even twice her weight. Let's not forget that there were two of them."

Dr. McMann nodded her head and said, "Yes. That's about right."

"Could you detect any drugs or chemicals in the remains that could have been used to incapacitate them?"

"None. We checked for drugs and poisons. They were spotlessly clean."

Mr. Charles walked over to the gallery behind the defense table and pointed to two men. "Could you two please stand up?"

Mr. Tangiers started to object, but a quick glance from the judge stopped him.

Mr. Charles faced the jury and pointed to the two men with his left hand, and the defendant with his right. "Dr. McMann, can you explain how a small one hundred and fifteen pound girl could force two grown men, both weighing over two hundred pounds, to ingest a deadly incendiary chemical?"

"No way," she said. "Besides, I only speculated that an incendiary substance could be used to cause that kind of damage. We detected no such chemical in their remains. How they burned is a complete mystery. We only know they did, and we are estimating their internal temperature was over two thousand degrees."

"Thank you, doctor. No more questions."

The prosecutor stood up to call the next witness. "The prosecution calls Captain Gerald Polin."

The bailiff echoed through the court and out into the hallway, "Captain Gerald Polin?"

A large man entered the courtroom. He was tall and fit, with full dark hair and a bushy handle-bar mustache. He wore a dark uniform with a shiny badge over his left pocket, and "F.D." clearly printed on the back of his shirt. He climbed into the witness booth and raised his right hand. There was no Bible present.

"Do you swear to tell the truth, the whole truth, and nothing but the truth?"

"Yes, I do." He sat down and adjusted the microphone in front of him.

The prosecutor took his place in front of the witness and said, "Please state your name."

"My name is Gerald Polin, captain, Lafayette Fire Department."

"Lafayette is pretty far from the location of the fire. Why would you be involved?"

"We don't respond to fires here. They have local volunteer firemen for that. I am the regional arson investigator, so my involvement is purely after the fact."

"Have you concluded your investigation of the fire?"

Captain Polin both nodded and shook his head, saying, "I have completed my investigation, but I was unable to draw a conclusion and have not closed the file."

"Why is that?"

"The cause of the fire is still unknown. We exhausted all the evidence, and further investigation was not warranted."

"Have you been able to rule out any common causes for the fire?"

"It was not caused by a gas leak. There was no evidence of gas or kerosene or any other kind of accelerant. We ruled out every known cause of arson."

Mr. Tangiers nodded his head and made eye contact with the jury. He wanted them to follow along. "What about natural causes? Did you rule out the weather?"

"The temperature was around eighty-six degrees, with over seventy percent humidity. There were no lightning strikes that evening. I can't attest to the whereabouts of fire ants or lightning bugs."

The courtroom laughed at the last remark, but quickly quieted before the judge had to go to his gavel.

"Very amusing," Tangiers said. "Were you at least able to identify the location where the fire started?"

"Yes. I have a map of the property, if you would like to see. I identified twenty-seven sources where the fire started."

"And you are quite certain that there was no lightning?"

"Absolutely certain," the captain said decisively.

"Twenty-seven sources where the fire started? My, my; doesn't that suggest foul play to you?"

"Sure," he replied, "it suggests foul play, but I deal in evidence, and there was absolutely no evidence of foul play."

"Thank you, Captain. No further questions."

The attorney for the defense stood for his turn. "Captain, just a couple questions. How large an area did these twenty-seven hotspots ignite?"

"They were all over the entire property; over three thousand square feet."

"Were there any signs that a remote control device was used to ignite these fires?"

"None," the captain said. "I found no evidence of any kind of electronic devices, or even of any accelerants."

"Could you determine when the fires started, and in what order?"

Polin's face grimaced slightly. "I can't give you an exact time, but I can tell you which ones had been burning longer, which should give us the approximate order in which they ignited. They did not start up in a straight line that we usually see when an arsonist lights a fire. One would ignite on one side of the property, then another a hundred feet away, then another seventy feet away from that one, all within about three seconds."

"Wow," Mr. Charles mused, "one hundred feet, then another seventy feet in three seconds. That would be one really fast arsonist. I think maybe the NFL would like to recruit him."

More laughter; this time, the judge succumbed and snickered.

"And you are quite sure there was no lightning?"

Polin nodded his large head, "Believe me, I wanted lightning to be the cause. It made the most sense, but I double and triple checked with the weather bureau. There was absolutely no lightning."

"Thank you. No more questions."

The fire captain stepped down.

"Your Honor, the defense fails to see any evidence that links any loss of life to my client. I respectfully request that the charges be dropped so we can all go home and let this poor young girl get on with her life."

The prosecution sprang to his feet. "I object!"

The judge coolly replied, "I knew you would."

"The prosecution is allowed to present its full case before the defense can make such a motion!"

"I'm fully aware of procedure, Mr. Tangiers, so if you'll just settle down a bit, I'll explain it to Mr. Charles." The judge turned to the defendant's table and smiled warmly. "Son, I know this is your first jury trial. I also know this is a pretty important case for a young man who just passed the bar. You did pass the bar, didn't you?"

"Uh, yes...yes, sir," he stammered.

"That's good," the judge replied, "and you are doing just fine, under the circumstances. But right now, we're just gonna let the prosecution finish up all their talking and ballyhooin'. Then after he rests his case, that's when we can entertain motions to throw this case out of the courts. Okay?"

"Yes, sir," the young attorney said, blushing broadly, "thank you, sir."

"Mr. Tangiers," the judge said, the smile now evaporated from his face, "do you have any further witnesses? Perhaps someone who actually witnessed a crime?"

"Yes, sir," Tangiers stammered. "Well, I mean sort of, Your Honor. At this time, we would like to enter this video recording into evidence."

"You are aware, Mr. Tangiers, that in capital cases, the court prefers to have real live witnesses instead of recorded depositions."

"Of course, Your Honor, but this is not a deposition. This is from a security camera. Really, sir, it would be much easier for me to explain while viewing the recording."

"Very well." The judge motioned for a clerk to bring in a video player, which was all done very quickly, and the disk was inserted.

The screen came on, showing a handful of people sitting in a room wearing robes and pajamas.

"Mr. Tangiers," the judge asked, "where was this shot?"

"Your Honor, this is from the St. Austin Mercy Hospital. It is a home for extremely troubled mental patients." Tangiers turned to the bailiff and asked, "Can we increase the audio, please?"

The bailiff stood across from the video stand and pressed the volume button on the remote.

"Thank you." Tangiers said. "Now please watch the woman sitting on the couch. She becomes very agitated and starts to speak. Just listen to what she says."

The judge motioned to have the recording stopped; the bailiff pressed pause on the remote.

"Mr. Tangiers," the judge said, "I asked for relevant evidence about this case. What can a security video from a mental hospital possibly have to do with this case?"

"Please bear with me, Your Honor. Just a few moments, I promise you."

The judge snarled and frowned, but motioned to have the recording played.

On the screen, the woman on the couch started to rock back and forth. "Watch out, baby! Look behind you! Duck!" She got up from the couch and moved to the window. "Yes! Burn him, baby, burn him! That's my baby, my little girl! Make him pay. Watch out for the other one! Duck! Burn him! Light him up! Go, baby, go!"

Mr. Tangiers motioned for the bailiff to pause the player. "Your Honor, please look at the date and time on the recording. It matches exactly with the time of the fires and the death of the two men."

The judge rolled his eyes. "Mr. Tangiers, how does the babbling of a crazy woman have anything to do with our case?"

"Your Honor, can it be a coincidence that this woman accurately described the death of two men at the same exact time it occurred? How can a woman hundreds of miles away know about these things as they happened? This woman was admitted to the hospital with symptoms that included hearing voices in her head. I submit that she does hear voices because she is psychic, and she witnessed the events that occurred in Cricket Bend just as clearly as if she were there herself. What's more, I think you should know that there is a connection between this woman and the defendant." He pressed play on the tape player.

The woman in the window raised her hands to her mouth and shouted as loud as she could, "I love you, Destiny! I love you!"

The girl at the defendant's table stood up and cried, "Momma?"

The crowd clicked and clucked over the turn of events.

The judge banged his gavel and shouted, "Lunch!" He turned to both attorneys. "In my chambers!"

Blake found himself staring at the girl. She was pretty, like the woman in the video. He did not doubt that they were mother and daughter. She wasn't very old, maybe his age. He already figured out what happened. She was like him, and these idiots didn't even believe in magic. He wasn't one of a kind anymore.

Another poke in the ribs woke Blake from his nap. He wished people would stop doing that to him. He sat up and wiped the sleep from his eyes and saw Brian leaning in the car from outside the door. "Lunch time, kid. Then let's see which road feels best to you."

Blake cleared his throat and climbed out from the back seat. "Sure thing." It was hot and muggy outside the car. The sky was slightly hazy but relatively free of clouds.

Through lunch, the guys talked about various adventures from their past, but Blake kept to himself. His mind was locked on the face of the girl he had seen in his dream. He didn't know why; he didn't normally remember dreams in any detail, but this girl's face was etched in his mind as if he'd actually met her somewhere. He nibbled on his lunch, thinking that if she was real, he should be able to reach her mind. He cleared his mind as he had done on hundreds of occasions before. Instead of focusing on her location, this time he focused on her face. He imagined actually knowing her and tried to lock onto her spirit.

Destiny was still bobbing around, listening for a memory that called to her, but none came. She found herself losing her focus when she finally heard someone calling her. The voice was very far off and was definitely a woman. She tried to narrow her focus and sweep through the voices before her, but the one she heard sounded even farther off. She took slow deep breaths, trying to let the voice come to her. The other voices started to fade away and dissolve around her.

"Well, it's about time you come around," Michelle said. "You already missed last night's supper and this morning's breakfast. You need to get some food in you before you waste away."

"Oh, Nana, you just don't know what I've been through out there."

"Out where? That was yesterday that you was viewing them memories, you been sleeping it off ever since then."

Destiny sat up in her bed and rubbed the sleep from her eyes. "First of all, you know there's more to these things than just someone's memory. Things got changed by someone from the future. A memory would be like a movie. The ending stays the same every time you watch it."

Michelle headed back out towards the kitchen saying, "You best throw some clothes on and I'll fix you somethin' to eat."

Destiny grabbed the first shorts and t-shirt she could find and followed her nana out to the kitchen. "Are you even listening to me?"

"Sure, I hear ya, but I don't see nothin' that's changed round here. You still the same. I'm the same. So they sends someone back there to hurt you, he be from the future, you be from the future. So he puts the hurt on you. That taint the same as changin' the past."

"He killed Mala! That sounds like changing the past to me!"

Michelle pulled some ingredients from the fridge and sliced a couple pieces of bread. "Mala died thousands of years ago."

"Yeah, she was killed by a sorcerer from the future!"

"Oh, nonsense," Michelle laughed weakly as she said it. "How do you suppose he done that?"

"Magic, of course. The things we can do are miniscule compared to what they used to do."

Michelle put the sandwich on a plate with servings of potato salad and baked apples, then turned to face Destiny. Her face went from stern to soft as she said, "No, the things I can do might be miniscule, but you, child, be one of them. Somehow, you has the real magic in you."

"That's why I have to go back and warn Mala."

Michelle set lunch on the table while she talked. "Maybe we should let the candles rest a while. You been through a lot lately."

"Oh yeah, something else you should know. I'm not sure I really need the candles anymore. I don't think they was all dreams I was having while I slept. I was having the memories."

"I feared you would reach that point, but didn't expect it quite so soon."

Destiny pulled herself to the table and started eating. It wasn't until her first bite that she fully realized how hungry she was. Her nana wasn't an extravagant cook, but she set a nice table when she wanted to.

Blake could still see the girl's face. It was clearer than ever in his mind. He reached out with his feelings and thought he found her a couple times, but the feeling was snatched away. His head started to hurt. Each time he came close and wasn't able to lock on to the girl, it felt like someone rapped him on the side of the head.

Blake's head stung from the last rap, and he sat up straight in his chair. Sergeant Hughes was standing over him with a newspaper rolled up in his hand while the others around the table laughed. "Hey kid, the waitress wants to know if you want something sweet to top off your meal?"

Blake saw that they were already getting slices of cake and pie. "Yeah, sure. How about some apple pie?"

Hughes slapped Johnson on the back. "See that? You're not the only all-American boy eating apple pie after all."

Johnson looked over his shoulder. "So the kid has good taste after all. Y'all could learn something from him, especially you, Gomez. That French Silk stuff is way too feminine for a real man."

"Yes, it is," Gomez snapped back, "and there ain't hardly a woman in the world who can resist a rich, chocolaty, French silk pie."

Brian switched seats and sat next to Blake. "I figured you for banana or lemon myself."

"Yeah, actually, I do like banana cream and lemon meringue better. In fact, I never really cared for apple that much before, but she's eating apple. I know she is."

"You've found her? You know where she is?"

Blake saw the astonishment in Brian's eye. "Who? Oh, no, not her, someone else."

Brian frowned a bit. "I need you to focus on our target, not some girl you saw on the road."

"She's not just some girl. I think she's a witch."

Brian's mood perked up again. "A witch? You found someone, but it's not her?"

"I don't know who she is. I don't know for sure that she is not the one we are looking for. I just saw this girl in a vision. I think she was on trial for witchcraft."

Brian's mood dipped back down. "Oh, a witch trial? You can tune in on visions of the past now?"

Blake shook his head. "It wasn't the past. Not like the Salem trials or anything like that. It was a modern courtroom."

Brian rubbed his chin. "Hmm. After we finish eating, see if you can give us a heading. Then I want you to try and get back to that vision until we can identify who it is."

***

"So, tell your nana about them visions you been havin' while you is asleep."

"It was the strangest thing. I think it started out as a dream. I found a boy who was beating up everything in sight. He knew what I was doing and kept telling me to get out of his memory. I thought maybe I was supposed to help him get over whatever made him so angry, but then he whacked me on the head to get rid of me."

Michelle cleared the dishes to the sink and shook her head, saying, "Some people just don't want to be saved, no matter how much they need it."

"You mean like Mama?"

"Yes, your mama be one."

Destiny pushed herself from the table and went to the screen door, looking out on the bayou. The trees were swaying gently in the breeze, but all she saw was her mother sitting expressionless in the hospital. "You suppose maybe my powers of healing could help my mama?"

"I reckon if your mama was really damaged, you possibly could fix her up. I just don't think there's nothing wrong with her 'ceptin' she don't wanna accept being what she is."

"Can we try? It's worth a try if I can help. I doubt it could hurt. Can we?"

Michelle went to Destiny and put her arms around her. "You are a good girl. I just don't think it's a good time right now for you to be goin' out into the world."

"Is that why you've been decorating everything with all this stuff?"

Michelle backed up and pointed around the room. "This 'stuff,' as you call it, be some powerful and ancient charms to help protect you."

"I don't think I need charms. Besides, some of them are kinda creepy."

"It's the creepy ones that has the most power of them all. If someone out there aims to hurt you, I means to make it as hard for him as I can."

"Well, I can't just sit around here doing nothing. I have to do something to make things right again." Destiny returned to the table and set a candle in front of her seat.

Michelle folded her arms and watched. "I thought you didn't need the candles no more."

"Yeah, but I like the candles."

"I wish you wouldn't rush back into it. Why don't you just settle down and spend the day with me? We could play cards instead. You used to love playing cards."

"I love you, Nana, but I have to do this."

"It just ain't safe."

"Nana..."

"Maybe I forgot where the matches was."

"That's okay." Destiny reached out and held her hand near the candle. A small spark leaped from her finger to the wick, lighting it.

"Oh my, I guess you won't be needin' them matches after all. I ain't never heard of no one able to do that before."

"I think you mean any of our kind," Destiny said. "The others did it all the time."

"So, where'd you learn that?"

"I don't know. I just learn stuff. Others do things to me, and I learn how to do it back to them."

"But how? Why would you suddenly be the first of our kind who can do that?"

"I'm not the first. There have been others, but they are rare; we are rare. I've met a couple. Well, actually just one, but at different times."

"So," Michelle said, "you meets with this rare witch and she shares with you how she does the other's kind of magic?"

"She was a he, and he didn't show me. It was just a memory. But he did the magic, and I learned how it was done. His mother was one of us, and his father was one of them."

Michelle sat down at the other end of the table, defeated. "Is that so?"

"Makes you wonder about my father, don't it?"

"Only thing I ever wondered 'bout him was if I could pull the switch when they strapped him in the chair."

"What if it wasn't all his fault?" Destiny asked. "If he was one of them, he was probably crazy with the sickness. You just don't know what goes on inside them! Just being around us makes them go completely mad."

Michelle had never heard this kind of compassion from her granddaughter. "Are you gettin' soft in the head? We talkin' about your mama and the man that hurt her bad and put her in the hospital."

"No, Nana, we're talking about my father. Mama was already going crazy from the visions. I'm as sorry as you are that I can't have my mama here with me, but I also don't have my daddy too. If he was one of them, maybe that's why I am the way I am."

Something twisted up in Michelle's heart. "I thought maybe you was the way you is because of me."

"Sure, Nana, you made me who I am, and you taught me the vision, but you didn't teach me to make fire and lightning. I must have got that from my daddy."

"Shoot, if it were that easy, we'd have lots o' witches making fire. You ain't the first child born from them bastards."

"No, I'm not the first. That just means it's more complicated."

Michelle sighed. "You certainly be more complicated. I just don't get you sometimes."

"It's okay that you don't get me."

Destiny took a deep breath and focused on the candle, tuning her nana out.

Michelle sat and worried about her granddaughter; she also closed her eyes and said a little prayer.

Destiny entered into the void where she could hear the voices from the past. She tried to sort them out in her mind to find the oldest ones. She wanted to find Mala early enough to warn her. She hadn't learned how to tell what time period the voices came from. She tried to find something in the voices, or even a feeling inside of her that would be different.

Blake pointed Brian in the opposite direction that his fear wanted to go. Once he settled back into his seat in the back of the car, he immediately focused back on the girl. Brian turned down the radio a bit, claiming he had picked up a slight headache. They continued to talk, but in pleasant, subdued tones.

The sound of the road under the tires lulled Blake directly into a calm, relaxed state of mind. He tried to concentrate on the image of the girl, but he was far too drowsy to control his mind.

Destiny strained for a hint of Mala's voice. There was plenty of chatter, but it was as if Mala was hiding from her. Unable to locate Mala, she tried finding the old wizard, the one that was like her. Maybe he would know how to find Mala. She had just started to focus on his face when she heard her name coming from the mist. She followed the voice calling her name until she was out of the mist and into a well lit room.

"State your name, please."

"Destiny Faith Boutin."

"Where do you live, Miss Boutin?"

"Most recently, I've been staying at the Lafayette Parish Correctional Facility." Unlike any other memory Destiny had ever visited, this time she heard her own voice and her own answers coming from her own mouth.

The smartly dressed young lawyer turned to the jury and feigned exasperation. "I mean, before you were arrested, Miss Boutin."

Destiny recognized the old meeting hall that was part of the diner in Cricket Bend. It wasn't used much anymore, except by evangelists holding travelling revivals now and then. It was dressed up now to look like a courtroom. She seemed to have landed right in the middle of a trial. "I guess you'd say I'm between homes at the moment."

"Well then," the lawyer said, "Miss Boutin, perhaps you can tell us," he spread his arms dramatically, indicating the jury and the audience, "tell us where you used to live, before you were between homes."

"I grew up in Cricket Bend, Louisiana."

"Can you narrow it down a bit from all of Cricket Bend?"

Destiny turned towards the jury and explained, "Cricket Bend doesn't have any streets, except for Main Street, and I don't live on Main Street. We never had no address to speak of, so I guess I can't really narrow it down much more than Cricket Bend."

"Did you have a home, Miss Boutin, in Cricket Bend?"

"Of course I had a home. I lived with my nana, in the house you been talking about all morning. That's the one that burned down, as if you didn't know."

Mr. Charles exhaled a deep breath. "Thank you, Miss Boutin. Can you tell us, please, how long you lived there?"

"Since I was a baby, I guess, pretty much since I was born."

"And during all that time, your nana has raised you?"

Destiny looked over at her nana in the gallery and smiled. "Yes, sir," she said. "My mama is in the hospital."

The lawyer turned the pages in his tablet, going over his notes. "How old are you, Miss Boutin?"

"I'm sixteen."

"Where do you go to school?"

"My nana gives me my lessons."

"You're home schooled?"

"Yes, sir. I take the tests at the end of the year to prove that I've had the right lessons."

"So, you've been with your nana pretty much all the time for the last sixteen years?"

"Yes, sir," Destiny said, "pretty much."

Mr. Charles stepped away from Destiny until his back was to the gallery. He held out his left hand, indicating Michelle, and asked, "And you would know more things about your nana than anybody else?"

"Yes, sir, I suppose so."

He stepped slowly towards the jury, nodding his head as he walked. Before reaching them, he turned back to Destiny and started to say something, then stopped and laughed to himself. He looked at the jury and grinned, then turned back towards Destiny and asked, "Is your nana a witch?"

"Excuse me?"

"I'm sorry," he said. "I'll rephrase. Does your nana believe she is a witch? Does she practice secret rituals?"

Destiny laughed. "A witch? Well, she doesn't fly around on a broom, if that's what you mean. I suppose you could say my nana taught me about many different religions. I think maybe she respects most all of them, and even though she doesn't go to church on Sundays, she's a Christian, like most everybody in these parts. At least, that's how she raised me. As far as secret rituals are concerned, they wouldn't be very secret if I knew about them, would they?"

He smiled and nodded his head. "That's a very clever answer, only you never really answered my question. Does your nana believe herself to be a witch?"

"Are you asking me if I know something that she believes?"

"I am asking you, since you know her better than anyone else in this courtroom, probably better than anyone else alive, if you can share with us whether she believes she is a witch."

"Of course she is! She is a witch. I am a witch. My mother is a witch. We come from a long line of witches. Excuse me a second, I'll read her mind." Destiny waved her hands around her head and rolled her eyes backwards. "You know something? She does believe she is a witch."

The audience roared with laughter, nearly rolling in the aisles.

"Order! Order!" The judge rapped his gavel until the din died down.

"Miss Boutin, did your nana kill those men?"

"What? You think she chanted some incantations, and those men burst into flames? Or maybe she brewed a magical potion and teleported it into their tummies?"

"Did she?"

"Of course not. She doesn't have those kinds of powers."

"What kind of powers does she have?"

"She's pretty good with local herbs and homemade remedies. You can ask just about anyone around here. She sells lotions and stuff at the General Store."

The prosecuting attorney stood up. "Your honor, how long must we endure this magical carpet ride to nowhere?"

Mr. Charles turned to the prosecutor and showed him his palms in surrender, then turned back to the judge and said, "I'm through, Your Honor."

Destiny watched her court appointed defense attorney return to his seat. They had cooked up the line of questioning together to foil any attempt by the prosecutor to tie her or her nana with supernatural powers. It may have worked. The prosecutor was shuffling his papers around before he approached her. She glanced over at the jury to see how they accepted her testimony. Most of them were watching her attorney seat himself. She thought she could detect some humor in their eyes. One juror, the third from the left in the front row, was watching her. It was more like he was staring at her. He was an odd-looking boy. A shiver went up her spine, and she felt like something was not right about that boy.

The prosecutor finally stood. "Miss Boutin, where is your mother?"

"She's in St. Austin Mercy Asylum. She was the woman on the recording you saw, remember?"

"Why is she there?"

Destiny shifted in her seat and said, "I'm probably not the best one to ask, but I believe she was diagnosed with schizophrenia and paranoia."

He approached the witness stand, pretending to study the medical charts in his hand. "So she hears voices?"

"Of course she does. She's not deaf."

"But she hears voices that aren't really there."

"Well, I guess we don't really know that, do we? She might just hear voices that others don't hear."

He dropped his arm with the papers to his side with a half-smile on his face. "Miss Boutin, how do you suppose your mother had prior knowledge to the events of June 3rd?"

"Maybe the voices in her head told her what was going on."

"So, you believe the voices are real and not imaginary? We've already heard testimony about whether or not your grandmother believed herself to be a witch. You made a very clever joke that you were all witches, but I wonder, was it really a joke? We've seen your mother on the monitor, as if she were watching what was happening from clear across the county. How do you explain that?"

"My mama is in a crazy hospital. She probably has been saying the same thing every day for the last 15 years. You know what I think? I think maybe you might be crazier than my mama is."

Destiny's defense attorney stood up. "Your Honor, where is the prosecution going with this? If he is suggesting that this crime is truly of supernatural origin, then I wonder if it is out of this court's, and his, jurisdiction?"

The judge rapped his gavel.

***

Blake snapped out of his slumber just as the car was pulling over to the side of the road. He sat up and peered out the window. "What happened?"

Hughes pulled the car to a stop on the side of the road. "Flat tire." He got out to fix it.

Brian asked, "So, any more info on our girl?"

"It could just be a strange dream. I swear, it's hard to tell who is on trial, and even harder to tell which side the attorneys are on. The girl is smart, though, and she is making the prosecutor look like a fool."

"Do you have a name or location on her?"

"Some place called Cricket Bend, but she doesn't have a street address."

"How can we find her without a street name?"

"I don't know, but I think her mother is in a hospital, St. Austin Mercy Asylum. Her last name is Boutin."

"Excellent. That is something we can check. If there is a female patient there named Boutin, I think we can take a closer look at your dreams, and this place, Cricket Hollow."

"Bend, Cricket Bend."

"Right." Brian turned forward in his seat, pulling out his cell phone to have his office check on Ms. Boutin.

The courtroom dissolved from Destiny's view and she found herself sitting at the table in her nana's house once again. She looked around nervously to see that everything was in its place. "Nana? What's the date today?"

"Today? Lemme see; it's the first of June."

Destiny leaped from the table and dashed to her room, screaming, "Oh my God, we have to go now!"

Michelle followed her to her doorway and asked, "What are you talking about?"

Destiny was throwing clothes into a backpack. "It's not safe here. We have to leave now! Something bad is going to happen, right here, the day after tomorrow."

"Nonsense child. Put that stuff away. I have all the protections up in place."

"You're not listening to me! Something happens here in two days, and we end up being accused of witchcraft. They say we killed some people."

"That's ridiculous. We wouldn't kill no one."

Destiny stopped packing and faced her nana. "Maybe you wouldn't, but I might. I think I am the one that did this. I mean, will do this."

"Was they bad men?"

Destiny threw her packed bag on the table and ran to her nana's room. "Of course, they must have been."

"Then you was just protecting us."

"Fine, then why am I on trial for murder?" Destiny started going through her nana's clothes.

Michelle wrapped her hands around Destiny's and said, "Instead of rifling through my drawers, maybe you should find out why you was on trial, and do it different."

Hughes finished changing the tire and wiped the sweat off his face, leaving a dark smudge on his cheek. He tossed the tire and the tools into the back of the car and climbed back behind the wheel. The car started up, but the back wheel spun and dug a small hole under it. "What the hell now?" He shut off the engine and slammed the door on the way out. He looked at the tire, hopelessly dug into the dirt on the side of the road. Pulling a wooden back board out of the vehicle, he placed it under the tire and climbed back into the driver seat. He turned the key, but the car wouldn't start. He pounded his fist into the steering wheel.

Brian asked Blake, "Do you sense anything? Is anyone watching us?"

"I still feel what I felt before. It's like a fear. Maybe dread is a better word."

"The old texts tell us that the witches can make magical barriers to keep our kind away. I think maybe we've stumbled onto one and it doesn't want us going any further."

Gomez and Johnson had pulled up behind them when their tire had gone flat. They had been waiting patiently for Hughes to finish the tire change, but now he just sat there. Gomez honked the horn at them; their car was working fine. "Need a lift?"

Brian, Hughes, and Blake poured out of the car and climbed in the other one.

Johnson considered himself an automotive expert and wanted one last look at the car. The first thing he did was turn the key to see what it sounded like, and it fired right up.

Gomez climbed in with Johnson. "It's okay, boss, we'll take this one."

Brian and Blake glanced at each other and nodded. It could be a coincidence, and the rest of the world would believe it was, but they didn't think so. This had to be a magical warning, trying to slow them down.

Brian reached to pull the car door shut, and the door pulled itself closer to meet his hand halfway. He could feel the power surging through his body and rubbed his palms together. When he separated his hands, he could see dozens of thin blue electric filaments undulating between them. He quickly closed his hands before anyone else could see them, and marveled at his own growing power, which was gaining strength with each passing day.

With the car back on the road again, Blake settled back and closed his eyes.

Chapter 13

"**S**on, you gotta choose. If you ask me, it's not even that hard. You only got two options to choose from."

Blake looked around and saw the other jurors seated at a long table, as was he. He could see the anticipation in their faces as they all stared at him, waiting for him to cast his ballot.

"Jeez Louise, son, it's not that hard." The old man picked up the pencil in his shaky hands and pretended to write on the pad in front of Blake. "You just pick up the pencil and write down that she's guilty or not guilty. I'll even make it easier on you. She's guilty. Just write down guilty. Then we can get on to seeing that she fries for what she done."

Another juror put his hand on the old man's shoulder. "Settle down, Edgar. We don't fry people in the chair no more. We injects them like they was dogs bein' put down."

Blake tried to write down guilty. One less witch in the world was one less witch in the world. Instead of writing down guilty, he watched his hands write down "not-guilty".

"Son of a bitch," Edgar bellowed, "are you stupid or something? We's gonna be here forever if you doesn't get your head on straight."

Blake felt the words come from his mouth, though it wasn't his voice. "Has everyone in this room lost their mind? The prosecution barely mounted a case, let alone proved that she had done anything? Are you all buying that crap about her magically turning those guys into crispy crunch? What were they doing there, anyway? Seems to me it was her home, and they were intruders. Don't any of you pay attention to the facts?"

"Facts - Schmacts," the old man said. "I know when someone is guilty. I seen it in her eyes. She done it, mark my words, and it's our duty to make her pay."

"Our duty," Blake's host explained, "is to weigh the facts and determine if she is guilty beyond a shadow of a doubt."

"But, her eyes." Edgar cried. "Didn't you see her eyes? Tell me they weren't guilty!"

"Yeah, her eyes," a few other jurors echoed around the room.

Blake shook his head. "Her eyes? I can't believe you people. Sure, I saw her eyes. They were pretty if you ask me. There was nothing menacing or guilty about them."

"Oh, I get it," Edgar went on. "You think she's pretty. You fancy her and want to be her protector. Why don't you try explaining what happened then? How'd those guys die?"

"I don't need to explain it. I don't even need to understand it. The medical examiner couldn't explain it, and the prosecutor certainly didn't explain it, and all you have said is that you didn't like something about her eyes."

Edgar's face darkened as his exasperation turned to anger. "So that's how it is. You never even looked at her eyes. Where were you looking, you sicko pervert?"

"Honestly, Edgar," Blake's host stood to make his point, "I don't know how you manage to find your way out of bed in the morning. If anyone should be put down like an old dog, I can think of someone more deserving than Miss Boutin."

Edgar already shook from old age, now he shook from rage, too. He raised his cane about shoulder height and would have knocked Blake on the head if the foreman hadn't stopped him.

Ellen, juror number four, a heavyset woman in her late thirties, had been watching Blake throughout the vote and the arguments. He caught her staring and returned her stare, deep into her eyes. "You know," she said, "I thought she looked guilty too, but now that I think about it, maybe he's right. There really wasn't much evidence against her. I don't know why I was so wrapped up in how guilty I thought she looked."

"Noooo!" Edgar reached up and grabbed the few remaining locks of hair on the sides of his head. "Not you, too! We'll never git nowhere with this clown, and now he's infecting Ellen, too. I move we call it a hung jury and be done with it."

The foreman set Edgar's cane out of reach in the corner and said, "We can't call the judge and tell him we're deadlocked, Edgar. We've only been in here twenty minutes."

Ellen stood up and said, "Sit down, Edgar, and shut up for a minute. If everyone at this table eliminated how they felt about the girl because of her looks, how would they vote? And what exactly was it about her eyes? I saw it, too. I felt all the same things I think everyone else did, but I just can't put it into words. They weren't beady eyes. They weren't shifty eyes, either. They were kind of sad, but look what she's gone through here. Someone explain to me what was so bad about her eyes?"

A stockbroker two seats to Blake's right cleared his throat and said, "Well, they were, I mean, that is, they had this, you know, this thing about them."

"What thing?" Ellen asked. "I sure can't nail it down."

"They were, that is, they were..." The stockbroker stopped stammering and sat down quietly, unable to find the right description.

"Anyone else?" Heads around the room scanned right and left. Some shrugged their shoulders.

Destiny took a deep breath and focused on the candle in front of her. She wished someone would teach her how to target a specific memory. She repeated in her mind, "Take me to the trial. The trial, take me to the trial." Her eyes lost focus for a moment, and she found herself hiding in an outcropping of rocks, looking down on a clearing with a pile of timber in the center. This certainly wasn't her trial, but she recognized the center of the circle from her first memory when she was burned at the stake.

Outside the circle, which surrounded the stake, there was another circle. A safe distance away, people were collecting. The clearing between the outer circle and the unlit pyre was smoothly raked dirt and sand.

A stern-looking man with flowing black robes entered into the clearing, followed by two burly, hooded men escorting a much younger person between them. The first man, a priest professing the new Christian religion, walked around the pile of timber, inspecting the quality and shape of the stacks of branches. The two henchmen proceeded straight up to the top of the pile and held the young man with his back to the stake. His hands were stretched over his head, and a nail was hammered in through his chains, holding them in place.

"Oy," said a voice from the crowd, "what happened to the trial?"

"Aye, where's the trial?" echoed other voices.

The priest raised his arms to calm the crowd. "My Lords and Ladies. I know not why we persist in this charade, for we know the outcome already. But if we must, we must. We can hold the trial right here."

"What?" A large man of some importance stepped forward. "You mean to try him while he is already nailed on the stake?"

"Sir Hammond. I knew you would be here, and there you are. How wonderful to see you."

"I thought I was to speak at his trial," Sir Hammond growled, "not his burning."

"And so you shall." The priest stepped between the two rings and spread his arms dramatically wide and said, "I declare this trial commenced. I will deliver the charges myself. I charge this person of questionable blood, son of unspecified parentage, known to us as only as Marvalaine, with convening with the Devil and with being not of human origin. I further charge him with casting magic charms and hexes against nobles and members of the royal house. What say you, young Marvalaine?"

Destiny's mouth fell open at the mention of his name. She should have recognized him.

Marvalaine tried to answer, but was unable. His mouth was fitted with a leather gag that pressed down on his tongue, covered his lips, and held his jaw from moving.

"No answer? I thought not."

"Bort," Sir Hammond bellowed, "you pretentious charlatan. You weren't satisfied with being a ridiculous buffoon masquerading as a priest. Now you must escalate to an intolerable jackal usurping the King's power! I should just cut you down here and now and do the entire kingdom a great service."

The crowd swooned at his response. As hated as Bort was by all, few would dare speak to him so boldly. So scared were they that most would not even show support for Sir Hammond, and many backed away from him, lest they be caught up in his reprisals.

Sir Hammond was not without charm and civility, but he was a man of action. He had every intention to make good on his threat, but something prevented him.

"Perhaps, Sir Hammond, instead of demonstrating your intolerance, you would speak on the boy's behalf."

"I shall speak then, since you have so graciously offered me the floor, but I need not speak on behalf of the boy. I must, however, speak on behalf of the kingdom. Our laws have been crafted to protect us from single-minded individuals such as yourself. Why do you hasten this so much? I know why, and I will tell why. I know someone who will speak for the boy; someone who is not here with us now."

"How will anyone not with us speak for the boy? Do you profess to be a witch also? Will you conjure up a spirit to speak on behalf of the boy?"

Sir Hammond tried to grip his sword to slay the bastard, but could not. "You know as well as I that he who would speak for the boy is away on an errand, and that is why you hasten to conclude this business with the boy's death before he returns and grants his leniency."

"Irrelevant. This is a trial. If you have no evidence to speak on the boy's behalf, then I'm afraid we can only draw a single conclusion."

Hammond found it difficult to respond to such blatant disregard for the King's laws. His mouth opened to speak, but no response came forth.

The crowd was restless. Everybody wanted to support Sir Hammond, but they feared Bort's reprisals if they did. A voice hidden in the crowd cried out, "Let the boy speak!"

"I'm sorry. Who was that?"

Another voice from the other side repeated, "Let the boy speak!"

"Out of the question; he is far too dangerous, but I am not without compassion. I will ask him a question and let him respond by blinking. One blink for yes, and two blinks for no." He climbed up and stood to the side of the boy so all could see. "Young Marvalaine, I will ask you a question; you may blink once for yes and twice for no. Do you understand?"

He blinked once.

"Very well. Do you swear to answer the truth to my questions under pain of death if you lie?"

Once again, a single blink.

"Excellent. You have been charged with practicing evil witchcraft in league with the Devil himself. Tell me, are you still visited by the Devil?"

He didn't blink.

"Do not trifle with me, boy. Your life lies in the balance here. You would do well to respond. Are you still visited by the Devil?"

Again, he didn't blink.

"I must conclude that his lack of response is evidence of his guilt. But I will give him one more opportunity to respond. It's quite easy, boy, are you still visited by the Devil? You must choose! Choose one blink or two. Are you still visited by the Devil?"

Marvalaine looked at Sir Hammond for help, then back at his accuser, and blinked twice.

"That is good. We would not want him here with us, now, would we?"

Two blinks.

"Can you swear for us that you will never again practice evil, black witchcraft?"

A single blink.

Hammond found his voice. "What kinds of questions are these?"

"Too late, Sir Hammond. Although the poor lad has repented, he has admitted that he has been visited by the Devil and that he did practice evil black magic. I have no choice but to find him guilty." He jumped down and addressed his two henchmen, "Light it."

The two hooded men selected one torch each and approached the center of the circle, holding their torches out in front of them to light the blaze.

Destiny jumped up from behind the rocks that hid her. Her plan was to shock those two oafs with lightning bolts, but it was she that was shocked. Marvalaine looked over his right shoulder directly at her. His eyes stared directly into hers, and she heard his voice in her head. *No, wait and watch.*

She was no longer hidden behind the rock, but only Marvalaine had seen her. Everyone else was intent on the scene in the center of the circle. Sir Hammond was clearly unhappy, but did not protest any further.

As the first torch touched the base of the timber, a powerful gust blew through the circle, and the timbers puffed out with only a few puffs of smoke remaining behind until they followed the gust out past the outer circle. The two men looked at each other and shrugged their shoulders. When they tried to relight the timbers, the sky grew dark with clouds. The clouds were low in the sky and immediately burst into rain, soaking the entire circle, dousing the torches.

Bort jumped back to the center of the circle. "What more proof do you need? He is a danger to us all and must be killed."

Hammond had regained some of his composure by this time and asked, "Does not the rain fall from the heavens?"

"What does the rainfall matter to these proceedings?"

"Are not the heavens the province of your one true God? Perhaps he has spoken."

Bort puffed out his chest and proclaimed, "He does not speak through the rain. He speaks through me."

"Ah, yes, well, we have only your word to attest to that, and damn few who are feeble enough to actually believe it."

"You come perilously close to blaspheming the one true God, Sir Hammond."

"Not at all. I merely suggest that He has something to say and you either aren't listening, or perhaps you are twisting His message for your own purposes."

"You think this rain is a sign? A portent from God? Nonsense."

Hammond stepped forward between the two circles with Bort. "You aren't listening. He who is above all wishes to speak to all of us, and you deny Him His voice."

"I deny no one."

"Invite Him to speak."

"To speak? The Lord does not speak like that."

"Perhaps He would if you invited Him."

Bort threw his hands in the air. "Very well." He looked up into the heavens and sang out loud and clear, "Lord of all. Creator and Father. Do You wish to speak?"

The wind rushed through his hair while a lonely clap of thunder reverberated through the circle, but no voice fell from the heavens.

Bort stood with his arms outstretched, looking straight at Hammond, and asked, "Are you happy now?"

Two claps of thunder clearly crashed directly overhead.

Bort's stare lifted from Hammond up to the heavens.

"There's your answer, Bort! Go ahead and ask Him if the boy should be spared!"

"Should ... "

A single clap of thunder, louder than all the others, descended upon them, not even allowing him to finish his question.

This clearly stirred the crowd. "Let the boy go! Free the boy!"

Bort didn't believe for a moment that this was a message from God, but he had been preaching the power of the One God to the people, and they clearly believed what they heard. If he denied what they witnessed for themselves, he would lose them. "Very well, then.

The Lord has spoken. Let the boy go." It would be days before he realized that he had already lost his flock.

The clouds lifted, and the evening stars twinkled overhead. The crowd loitered for a while, congratulating Sir Hammond on both his daring and his restraint.

The circle eventually emptied, leaving only Marvalaine and Hammond. When they were alone, they approached Destiny. She was sitting on a stump watching everything from her hillside.

Hammond bowed low at the waist and declared, "Good evening, young maiden. My Godson tells me you were about to come to his rescue. I thank you for your good intentions."

Destiny giggled. "While I suppose it is possible that I may have saved him from the fire, I suspect that my solution would not have been nearly as elegant, and may have even complicated things. The thunder was quite brilliant."

"He's a talented lad, I'll give him that."

Marvalaine stepped up to Destiny. He was a year younger than she, but already several inches taller. "What are you doing here?"

Destiny was a bit confused. He talked to her like they were old friends, but he shouldn't have known her. "I'm sorry, how is it you seem to know who I am?"

"We have met before. You were a bit older I think, I mean, I was younger at the time. That's why you don't remember, but you do know me."

"I remember you, and we've actually met when you were much older, but I didn't think you would know me."

Hammond coughed to get their attention and said, "I think I'll be seeing to the horses. Don't be long, son. The weather has been a bit unpredictable lately."

"So, the King still hasn't acknowledged you?"

"Not publicly, but he did assign Sir Hammond as my godfather. Even that is kind of hushed. Hammond is not allowed to raise me as a son, at least not openly, but he does look after me."

"I saw that."

Marvalaine sat down on a stump next to Destiny and said, "You still haven't answered my question. What are you doing here?"

"I guess you could call it bad aim, but I prefer to think of it as good luck. I'm glad I was here to see what happened."

"What were you aiming for?"

"Oh," she said, "my own trial in the future. I was trying to peek at my own trial. Apparently, I'm being tried for some murder. They'd probably accuse me of witchcraft…"

"Except that in the future, they'd get laughed at for suggesting magic."

Both laughed.

Destiny asked, "How did you make the thunder?"

"It's kind of like lightning, but that's not important. You need to learn to aim your travels. I'm guessing that you had your head focused on the trial instead of your heart. Our brains are kind of tricky, and they like to play tricks on us that end up getting us in the wrong place. You need to feel where you are going with your heart."

"Thanks, I'll try that. Where did you learn all this?"

"My mother has guided me. She is far more powerful than any of them ever realized, but I still have to figure a lot of this stuff out on my own. It's funny how things have changed. Before the Christians came, we were faerie folk. There were some people that hated us, but they were the types that hated everyone, anyway. Many more believed themselves fortunate to know one of us, but the Christians changed everything. Now instead of being faerie folk, we're witches working for the Devil."

"That Bort sure seemed like a piece of work."

Marvalaine laughed. "Your speech is funny to me sometimes, but I like what you say. Bort is a selfish man. He is not typical of the Christians, but he is typical of the scoundrels using Christianity for their own advantage to rob the people and usurp the crown's control."

"In my time, we call them conmen. They gain the people's confidence and talk them out of their possessions."

"Aye," he said, "that would be him alright. I should be going now, but I would like it if you would come see me again sometime. Perhaps you can catch me on a good day when I'm not being tied to a stake for burning."

"I think I'd like that."

Blake sat at the table, surrounded by his fellow jurors, locked in somebody else's body, unable to explain the truth to them about witches and witchcraft. He could have explained how witches would be able to confound their minds and make them focus on how guilty she looked, or how evil her eyes were. Clearly, however, she was not the one filling their heads with her own guilt. So, how could he explain what a witch was without admitting that a witch was trying to convict the girl? Perhaps he was fortunate that he couldn't communicate with the jurors. He had his own dilemma to worry about. His duty to his people was clear; convict the witch. But he did not see evil in her eyes. Like his host had said, she had beautiful eyes. He'd like to have more time to look into her eyes. He felt a connection with her, almost as if she knew he was there.

Down at the head of the table, the foreman had been poring over the trial transcripts. He looked agitated about something, and when he finished reading a page, he would hand it over to the woman to his right, who passed her finished pages across to the man at the foreman's left. Each of them seemed to grow more disturbed with each page they read. Occasionally, they would lift their eyes from their pages and confer in private about what they had just read. Finally, the foreman stood and rapped his glass on the table as if he were holding a gavel. "Ladies, gentlemen, can I have your attention for a moment, please?"

It took a few moments before people finished what they were saying and were willing enough to offer their attention to him.

"Thank you. After the question was raised about whether we were basing our opinions on the girl's appearance rather than the evidence, I asked the bailiff if we could see the transcripts, and we've spent a few minutes here reviewing them. I don't know what went on in there, but reading these is like reading a different trial from the one we attended. According to the transcripts, the prosecutor sounded like he was about to accuse the girl of witchcraft."

"Nonsense!" Edgar roared. "He said no such thing."

"Ease up now. Didn't you hear what I just said? We reread the transcripts. It's in the transcripts."

"I don't need the transcripts. I was there and I remember what I heard."

The other two jurors, who had helped the foreman read the transcripts, now stood beside him to show their unity. He put his hands on their shoulders and said, "We remember what we heard, too, but it doesn't quite match up with what we are reading here."

"What are you saying?" Ellen asked. "You think they have altered the records?"

"No, I don't think so." The foreman picked up one of the pages and showed it to them, saying, "After reading them, it seems as if I can sort of remember it that way."

"Now what are you saying?" Ellen walked over to see the transcripts over their shoulders. "You must have read them wrong. You can't possibly think they hypnotized us all into remembering something else? Show me; let me see those transcripts."

"I want everyone to review the transcripts and see what they remember after reading them."

Thoughts, dreams, and voices swirled around Destiny like she imagined balloons at a prom would fall around her. She wanted to get back to her own life, and her own trial, and, as instructed, tried not to focus on it with her mind, but with her heart. She found that as much as she didn't always like Mala, she still worried about her, and now she felt lucky to have found someone else who could help her. Even more than with Mala, because she felt he had something in common with her. She still didn't know if Mala genuinely feared her skill with magic from the other clan, or if maybe Mala was just pushing her to discover her own power. Marvalaine shared her gift for both kinds of magic, and he lived hundreds of years ahead of Destiny. Despite the fact that she just witnessed how much some people of his time feared and hated their kind, she couldn't help feeling envious that he lived in a time when people accepted magic instead of classifying it as a delusion or some other brain disorder.

She remembered how he called up the thunder. His hands were tied, his mouth gagged, and still he could control the weather. He was truly blessed and very powerful. She should visit him again from time to time and see what she could learn. She should follow his life and see where it led him. Surely, he grew too powerful to be defeated by another. Some things made no sense. Magic disappeared from the world with no apparent victor. Certainly, neither of the two families of magic was left dominant. Maybe she would ask him when he was older, certain that he was probably very smart. He certainly was cool and calm at his own attempted burning. He probably had already seen the outcome before he went there. That's pretty smart. He was almost her age. She would probably be as powerful as he was, if she had grown up in his time, where she could have started training at a much younger age.

The voices around her dissolved away, and she found herself in a garden looking into a deep, dark pool of water. She was drawn to the pool. She sat on the edge, which was built of mortar and stone, and stared deeply into the black-bottomed water.

"Careful you do not fall in," said a voice from across the pool.

Her focus shifted to the surface of the water, where she saw the reflection of a strapping young man. He wore luxurious purple silk robes with bright orange piping on the edges. The robes had a satin finish and changed hues as they undulated around him. A jeweled clasp secured the robes around his shoulders.

She thought she recognized him and asked, "Marvalaine? Is that you?"

"Tis I. I wasn't expecting you."

"Once again, my aim is off."

"Oh," he asked, "am I to be insulted because your being here is an accident?"

She shook her head. "No! Not at all, I'm sorry. I didn't mean it like that. It's just that I was still trying to find my future trial. I haven't quite mastered aiming myself with my heart."

"Your heart?" He put down the contraption he had been studying and started a slow walk around the small pool. "You can't aim yourself with your heart. It only takes you where it wants to go. Who in the world told you to follow your heart?"

"You did."

"Did I? Well, I must have been very young, and not yet experienced with matters of the heart. No matter, I'm thrilled to see you again. How are matters in your time?"

"I don't know," she said. "I just left you at the stake. Remember when Bort tried to burn you?"

"Ah, yes. I do recall your visit. So you just left there and ended up here? I must have made quite an impression upon you, and you couldn't wait to see me again."

Destiny rolled her eyes and replied, "I think only a man could come to that cockeyed conclusion. Probably I landed here so you could fix your previous advice on how I might aim myself to my own trial."

"Perhaps," he said, "but I prefer to think you are denying your own heart's true desires."

"Wow, you've sure changed. But I can see you are busy, and I don't want to interrupt you in whatever you are doing."

He saw her looking at the tangle of wood and wire he had been working on and said, "That thing? It's just a curious device. I've become quite the student of engines and mechanics."

"From the looks of things," she pointed at his luxurious robes, "I guess you must be quite the celebrity these days. You must have your pick of the ladies."

"It is true. I have met with some success and notoriety. And more than one lady has made herself available to me, but as you say, I have my pick and none of them were selected."

"You do like girls, don't you?"

"What a scandalous question!" He stretched his back to appear taller and adjusted his robes. "Of course I like girls. I just have a very high standard, which most of them fail to meet."

"I think if you set the standard too high, nobody will ever be good enough."

"Yes," he said, "I see your point. That is excellent advice. Perhaps you can help me. I will introduce you to some of the ladies I might choose from, and you can tell me what is wrong with them."

She stood and brushed the debris from her jeans. "And if I don't see anything wrong with them?"

"Then perhaps they are the right ones for me."

"Okay. What if I find something wrong with all of them?"

Marvalaine considered her statement while he stepped around her and looked deep into the pool. "Then maybe I am looking in the wrong place. Or, possibly, I was correct all along and there are no suitable candidates."

"There has got to be someone. You're too good looking to be on the market for too long. I'll help you. It will be fun."

"You think I am good looking?"

"Sure, well, for some girls, anyway. Some girl is certain to think you're cute."

"But that was not the question. Do *you* find my features pleasing?"

She bit her lip and shrugged her shoulders. "You're okay. I mean, there's nothing drastic we have to change."

"But I'm not perfect. I see that. If you were a girl, I mean, you are a girl, but if you looked at me, what would you see that is all wrong for you?"

"For me?" She giggled. "Well, for starters, you're too old."

"Too old? I'm only in my twenty-first year. How is that too old?"

"I'm sorry," she said. "I didn't mean to hurt your feelings, but for me, you're a bit too old."

"How can I be too old? There can't be more than five or six years between us. I thought you were about the perfect age for a man such as myself."

"Five or six years? Try maybe about a thousand years between us. Sorry, but you're way too old for me."

Marvalaine was stunned for a moment, then figured out what she meant and laughed.

"You're a handsome enough man," she said, "and if I lived in your time, I would definitely want you for a suitor."

"If you find me attractive, then with your help, I am certain we could find someone perfect for me."

"Absolutely," she said. "I'm convinced that we can find someone who will go for you."

Try as he might, Blake was unable to induce his will upon the body which confined him. His host dutifully read the transcripts. He made small guttural sounds every time he found a small point to support his opinion that the girl was innocent. Blake tried to correct his thought process, to show him that just because the evidence did not point directly to the girl, it did not mean she was innocent. After all, it did not point to anyone else either.

Blake's host kept reading. Others around him, especially Edgar, objected, stating that his opinion did not need to be changed, but he kept reading. Every word he read was entered into Blake's mind as well. He tried to ignore it. He knew the girl was a witch and did not want to confuse his mind with facts. He also knew that someone, somewhere, probably in the courtroom, was casting a spell on the jury to get her convicted, only it wasn't working and he couldn't do a thing about it.

The medical examiner's report was especially damning. The victims were burned from the inside out. Nothing natural could cause that kind of damage, yet instead of concluding that the girl was unnatural and used unnatural powers to kill the men, they concluded that there was no evidence connecting her with their unnatural demise.

The arson investigation report proved that damage was recorded all over the yard, at nearly the same time. She was certainly a very capable witch. If only she weren't one of them, he could have taken her on as a partner and ruled the world.

An idea hatched in Blake's mind. He couldn't influence the juror's minds, but this was the future. Maybe he could influence the event and plant evidence pointing to her.

"Time!" One of the jurors hit him in the head with a wad of paper. "Let someone else review the transcripts."

His host handed over the transcripts, but kept the diagrams that came with them. Blake watched and memorized the layout of the home of Destiny Boutin in Cricket Bend, Louisiana.

Another larger wad of paper landed aside his head.

"Wake up, sleepyhead."

Blake opened his eyes and saw that the car was stopped and Brian was standing outside with the door open.

"We're probably close enough to break for the night and go in early. You learn anything new?"

Blake rubbed his eyes. "Her name is Destiny Boutin. She lives in Cricket Bend, Louisiana. It's a real small place; might be hard to find on the map. I don't have an address for you, but I've memorized a layout of her home and property. All we have to do is find Cricket Bend."

Brian pointed across the car to the highway. Blake got out and saw that the hotel was right on the highway. He could see the signs with a rural route pointing to Cricket Bend, 150 miles. "Wow, what a lucky break."

Brian shook his head and said, "I don't believe in luck. We'll leave early. We'll take you as far as we dare go for now and drop you off. You check the place out, verify that they are who and what we think they are, and return to us with your report and directions how we can get in there. If we don't hear from you after three days, we'll have to go in anyway."

"If something happens to me, you'll lose your advantage of surprise."

"I know, so don't let anything happen to you."

Blake wasn't worried. He felt he could handle anything that came up.

CHAPTER 14

Destiny followed Marvalaine along a path which circled around the main courtyard. She always thought medieval times were dirty, but the view before her was as beautiful and clean as anything she had ever seen. The walls were a pristine white stone, meticulously pieced together. She couldn't see any grout or seams between the stones. It was as if entire walls were carved from a single stone.

Enormous elm trees in the corners of the yard created a canopy over the top, providing shade and filtered light to the entire courtyard. The yard itself was a series of crisscrossing stone paths surrounded by beautiful flowerbeds. Here and there, she could see ornate stone benches along the paths, many of them occupied.

Marvalaine smiled with pride as he watched her expression and followed her eyes around the courtyard. "I can see that you like my home," he said. "You have come at a good time of year, too. The trees are as beautiful as ever."

Her mouth fell open a bit. "This is yours? All this? Oh, I forgot, you are the King's grandson, aren't you? So, is it Prince Marvalaine now?"

He stood tall and grand. "Why yes, of course. Well, sort of. I am the King's grandson, and I am a prince, but I am not in line for succession. In fact, I hold no official title, even though the secret is out there, that I am a member of the royal family. It will always be a family matter and never official to the rest of the world."

"Oh, I'm sorry."

Destiny followed Marvalaine up a stone staircase that lead to a balcony, looking over the courtyard. "I'm not sorry in the least," he said. "I'd much rather be the King's advisor and grand wizard, even if it is mostly in secret. Matters of state would only interfere with my studies. It is enough that I am part of the family, and if not heir to the throne, I am at least heir to the royal fortune, or some share of it."

"So you are rich. That should make finding a woman easy."

He stopped in the middle of the stairs and exclaimed, "Ow! Now you think I must buy my bride!"

She hit him playfully in the arm. "No, you don't need to buy your bride, but you may have to pay off her father."

"Now you have me paying the dowry?" He continued climbing to the balcony. "Is that how things are done in your time? How strange your world must be."

"Do you really need any woman's dowry? Or do you have all that you need?"

"Put that way," he said. "I have no need for a dowry, but it's not just a matter of need. There is pride and principal, too."

They reached the top of the stairs, and Destiny looked down from the balcony at the immaculate scene. "So look at it from the father's point of view. Anything he offers you would be a paltry, embarrassing offer. Wouldn't he be better offering it to someone who would think it a princely sum? He probably has pride and principle, too."

"But wouldn't any father wish his daughter to be wed to the royal family?"

She turned around and leaned backwards against the stone railing. "Perhaps he would, so long as he didn't view the prospective groom as a half-breed wizard and bastard."

"Ah, yes," he replied, "there are those. So you think I should offer the father horses to overcome his prejudice?"

"No, you can't buy him like that. Maybe you could offer him a royal assignment with a stipend befitting the father of a royal bride. Perhaps he could use a home in the castle. Make him feel like the marriage will elevate him to royal status."

Marvalaine grew quiet for a moment and surveyed the court below them. "Your advice is sound. There are sure to be many who would be swayed by such an offer, but perhaps we should find the right girl first. She may not even have a father, and I, for one, am not going to stand on ceremony about the girl's parentage."

"So she doesn't have to be a royal? Does she have to be noble-born? Or would you be content with a commoner?"

"I would like her to be educated, but an intelligent woman with a thirst for knowledge would also do. I can provide all the education such a woman could digest."

Destiny turned to face the courtyard again. It was like a fairy tale garden filled with trees of every color. People milled around the yard. Couples could be seen having deep conversations while appreciating the roses. Occasionally, a small group of boys would run through, heading off to some adventure outside the courtyard. Girls in finely tailored clothes could be seen exiting the castle and walking through the yard. They spoke privately in soft whispers, but could be seen to laugh and carry on as they headed towards the exit across the way.

"What about them?" She pointed to three finely dressed girls crossing the courtyard. "The one in the middle looks very pretty."

"She is very pretty, but looks aren't everything. I can see that this is not the best vantage point for you. You need to be closer so you can know them a little better."

"Where does that exit go?" Destiny asked while pointing to the great doors where the girls had exited. "The girls all seem to be heading that way."

"Then so shall we. Outside those doors is the finest market in all the land. In addition to our regulars, we have vendors from all over selling their crafts and wares."

Destiny smiled at the familiarity of it all. Even though her remote existence in Cricket Bend rarely included a mall, she had read enough books to understand how many girls of her age went to the malls for no more reason than just to be there and watch boys, and there were a few occasions when she and her friend Anton would sneak out of the library to watch boys at the nearby mall.

Marvalaine led Destiny to the stairs. She stopped before descending them and asked, "What about my clothes? Won't I look conspicuous?"

He waved his hand before her and she was wearing a beautiful blue gown in the place of her own shirt and blue jeans. She gathered up the full skirt in her hands and swished it right and left. "How did you know my size?"

"Lucky guess."

"But you don't believe in luck."

He shrugged his shoulders and smiled impishly, then led her down the stairs and through the courtyard towards a large archway with two huge oak doors. The doors were opened in the morning and closed in the evening. A smaller door built within one of the large oak doors still permitted passage under the scrutiny of one of the many guards when the main doors were closed.

Destiny leaned in close enough to speak softly to Marvalaine. "Maybe you should tell me what kind of girl you are looking for. Are you looking for someone to tend to your home and prepare meals for you?"

"No, we have servants to handle the chores."

"Well then, you said you would like an educated woman. Are you looking for someone you can talk to about politics and the sciences?"

He stroked his trim beard while he considered her question. "That would be nice, but I was just wishing out loud. I doubt you'll find many educated women in my time. Some girls are raised in the convents and taught to read and write, some are even taught Latin, but I think the only politics they might learn would be the affairs of the church. We'll probably have to settle for an intelligent woman, even without an education."

"But your auntie was educated, and not in a nunnery."

"Yes," he snickered, "but she's already married."

She hit him again. "That's not what I meant. Surely, she can't be the only educated woman in your world."

"As you already know, my grandfather was a very enlightened individual. There are very few as open-minded or modern thinking as he. Sadly, no, there are few women of such an upbringing."

"What about sports?"

"Sports? Why would you ask me about sports? I certainly don't train for the tournaments, and if you did manage to find a girl who jousted, I would probably want to stay far, far away."

Destiny growled at him. "We will never find your woman if you keep making jokes! Do you ride a horse? Do you like to swim or fish? Certainly you must have some activities that you could do together."

"I must say, swimming sounds intriguing, but I doubt that the family would appreciate the scandal if I were to bathe in public with a woman. I confess I have never fished, but it certainly sounds like a fine, gentle activity. Horses, however, are a necessity, I think. I can't abide a woman too dainty to sit on a horse."

They exited the courtyard into the marketplace. The market was merely a street, albeit a finely cobbled street, lined with carts and tables. Some vendors setup small tents to protect their wares from the sun and dust. Behind the vendor stalls were small corrals where the more successful merchants tethered their horses and oxen. Destiny could see a couple spots, where there were cross streets that ran through the row of vendors. Hardly more than alleyways, she imagined they led to roads heading off to other parts of both the city surrounding the castle, and on to the neighboring townships.

The motel was a dingy, run down little place. It only remained in business because it was the only motel within sixty miles. Its one and only attractive feature was its vacancy, which was brightly flashed on the sign overhead. It serviced only the most desperate people, tired truck drivers who didn't want to sleep in their cabs, and the unfortunate motorist who was too tired to drive through. Many tired motorists looking for lodging were sure to give it one quick glance and move on. It was clearly a magnet for serial killers and sex offenders, and tonight, it would be host to a small band of mercenaries.

Brian entered first and rang the bell on the registration desk.

A heavy unshaven man came into the office from the adjoining room. He carried a chicken leg and spit bits of food when he asked, "Can I help you?"

"Five rooms, please."

Hughes came in behind him and said, "Three rooms; we thought we'd bunk together and play some cards before lights out."

The proprietor put his chicken on the counter and rubbed his fingers on his already greasy t-shirt before handing Brian three registration cards. He watched the men stretching their legs outside the car and wondered why three men wanted to share a room with only two beds. Somewhere in the recesses of his mind, he wanted to tell them he didn't want any monkey business, but in truth, he didn't care. Still, he would have liked the extra two rooms of income.

They took their keys, said their goodnights, and went to their respective rooms. Blake closed the door behind him and sat on the edge of the bed. It felt like the thinnest mattresses available, and instead of box springs, it just sat on a box. The room had a television, but no cable. Unfortunately for Blake, he had already slept most of the day while driving here, and didn't feel like he could sleep any more. He tried finding a station on the TV, but the best he could get was a snowy version of the news. He left the news on just to drown out the crickets chirping outside and propped up the pillows on the bed so he could kick back and eat. A 24hr diner next to the motel provided room service, so Blake ordered a steak sandwich, which almost made up for the condition of the room.

He regretted not knowing the outcome of the trial in his vision, but he didn't really want to go into it again. He wished he could influence it and speak his mind, but he was only a voyeur watching it unfold before him.

The weather was on the TV, and he chewed on his steak while watching the forecast. It would be clear and sunny. He was glad it wasn't expected to rain. He hoped there would be something more interesting to watch after the news. He didn't want to slip back into the vision; it might leave him too tired in the morning.

Marvalaine led Destiny down the cobbled road, past the food merchants hawking baked breads on one side, and roasted meats on the other side, to a festive-looking tent with many colored ribbons adorning the doorway. Immediately inside the doorway, she found a table covered with jeweled pins and hair combs. Next to it was another table with silver and gold Brooches, necklaces, and bracelets. She also saw the girls who had just left the courtyard at one of the tables pawing over some beautiful scarves.

Marvalaine stepped forward and boldly said, "Good morning, ladies. How are you this morning?"

The three girls turned, the outer two curtseyed, and the middle one barely nodded her head.

"Have you met my cousin Destine? She is here on holiday. Cousin, I would like you to meet Melody, Vivian, and Phoebe."

Again, it was the outer two who smiled warmly while the middle one scrutinized Destiny up and down. Melody stepped towards Destiny and said, "That's a lovely..." but Vivian interrupted her.

"Careful Melody, we don't know who she is. I've never heard of her. She's probably just another bastard half-breed."

Melody sucked in her breath. Her eyes looked at Destiny apologetically, but she retraced her step backwards, cowing to Vivian's authority.

Destiny bristled and adjusted her posture to adopt the carriage and appearance of a regal. "Well, cousin, I see that ill manners have spread from London ahead of common sense." She stepped closer to Vivian, with only disdain visible on her face. "In the future, you should learn to whom you are speaking before you bare your teeth. I just don't know how such poor breeding ever passed itself off as nobility."

Vivian had never been spoken to in this manner before, and could only respond, "How dare you?"

"Silence!" Destiny barked. "Henceforth, you shall speak to me only when spoken to!" Destiny turned and left the tent with Marvalaine right behind her.

Marvalaine stopped Destiny a short way outside the vendor's tent. "That was well done. Very well done. I dare say she doesn't hear that nearly often enough. I almost thought you performed a glamour upon yourself, the way you changed your bearing, but I sensed no magic."

Some of Destiny's anger still lingered, but she couldn't stifle a small giggle from escaping. "Oh my God, I don't believe I pulled that off. Do you think I was convincing?"

"Convincing? You nearly scared the color from my hair."

"Well, once the shock wears off, I doubt that what I said will still mean anything to her."

"No," Marvalaine admitted, "not a bit. But she won't forget being spoken to with such disdain. That was brilliant."

"I could set her hair on fire, but I doubt it would woo her any."

"No," he laughed, "and it probably wouldn't even be enough to melt the ice from her heart."

"Too bad she has so much influence over her..." Destiny didn't finish her sentence, but instead turned her head back to the tent they had just left, where an argument was growing in volume and creating a bit of a scene. She and Marvalaine both listened to what was coming from the tent.

"I'm just saying you don't even know her and you treated her so rudely. What if she was someone important?"

"Then I should have heard of her before," Vivian's distinctive voice rose in pitch, "and keep your voice down."

"You may have inherited your nobility from your parents, but sometimes you act like a common, spoiled little child."

"How dare you?"

"Why shouldn't I dare? My blood is as noble as yours!"

"Your blood may be noble, but just barely. My bloodline is pure going back three generations!"

"Maybe your blood is pure, but your heart is black."

"What?!" Vivian shouted. "Are you really defending that half-breed's harlot cousin? You must be mad!"

"Why must you always be so hard on him? He's never done anything to hurt you!"

"He's a half-breed. Half man, half faerie. What more reason do I need?"

"You are blind to what is good and true in the world!" Melody stormed out of the tent and froze in her tracks when she saw that Destiny and Marvalaine had been watching and listening.

Vivian screeched from within the tent, "Where are you going? I haven't dismissed you!"

Phoebe was inching her way out of the tent.

"Where do you think you're going?"

"Sorry," Phoebe said as she slipped out of the tent and followed Melody.

Seeing that everything had already been overheard, Melody marched straight to Destiny and Marvalaine. "I want to apologize for anything and everything Vivian has ever said or done to you. I should have displayed more backbone long ago and stood up for what I truly believe."

Destiny crossed her arms and looked coolly into Melody's eyes. "And what do you truly believe?"

"I don't care if he is half faerie. I wouldn't care if he were all faerie. I was raised to believe that nobility came more from a man's actions than from his lineage."

"I'm sorry," Destiny asked coolly, "who are we talking about?"

"Him." Melody nodded towards Marvalaine.

"He has a name. If you truly believe what you say, you wouldn't be afraid to use it."

Melody blushed slightly and curtseyed, saying, "Begging your pardon, Lady Destine, but I'm not exactly sure how we are supposed to address him."

"How about 'Prince Marvalaine'?"

Melody looked pleadingly at Marvalaine, unsure if it would be acceptable.

Marvalaine interceded, "Really, cousin Destine, nobody calls me prince around here. It's quite enough that they know."

"No, it isn't. You really should be addressed as Prince Marvalaine."

Phoebe had been standing shyly behind Melody, but stepped forward and curtseyed. "Let me be the first, Your Highness. It is good to see you, Prince Marvalaine."

"Now, let me stop you right there. You may be permitted to call me Prince Marvalaine, but none of this 'Your Highness' nonsense. I'll never be king."

Melody curtseyed. "Very well, Prince Marvalaine."

Destiny clapped her hands together. "Excellent, but now that I have heard it said a couple times, Prince Marvalaine sounds too formal, and it is quite a mouthful. I think the prince's friends might be allowed, in private, to address him as Marvin. What do you think, cousin?"

He raised his eyebrows. "Marvin? You don't like my name? Hmm. Marvin would be less taxing on my ears."

"Pardon me, Lady Destine," Melody asked, "but did you just include us as the Prince's friends?"

"I did, and judging from the look on Vivian's face, I think you should make a big show of it, if you know what I mean."

Marvalaine glanced over at Vivian. She stood all alone at the tent's entrance with no one left to hear all the venomous, back-biting, little comments she wanted to sling at her former friends. "Yes," he said, "she looks like she was asked to wash her own feet."

Melody roared in laughter, gesturing right and left, occasionally touching Marvalaine on the arm.

He was astonished by her response. "It wasn't that funny, I didn't think."

Phoebe caught on and roared in laughter herself, then leaned close to the Prince and whispered, "Yes, but then, Vivian doesn't know what you said, does she?"

Phoebe hooked her arm around one of his arms, Melody took the other, and they started escorting him down the promenade. He stopped after a few steps and turned to ask, "Cousin, will you be joining us?"

"Another time, perhaps. I think I must return home now."

"As you wish." He nodded towards her and turned back down the road with the two girls.

Morning came and went, and Blake did not rise with the others. Regardless of how much Blake had slept throughout the previous day, he did finally fall asleep, but when he woke up, he felt tired, as if he hadn't had any sleep. He forced himself out of bed and out of his room. He found Brian and Hughes standing by one of the vehicles, having a slightly animated debate.

"Hey, guys," Blake said, "what's up?"

Hughes was clearly annoyed with the late start. "Nice of you to join us!"

Brian raised his hand and signaled for Hughes to back off. "You okay?"

"Yeah, I had some trouble sleeping. Then, once I finally fell asle ep..."

"That's just nerves," Brian said. "Listen, Hughes was thinking that it might be a good idea if you were armed."

"Nothing fancy," Hughes added, "just a small twenty-two caliber handgun."

"Thanks guys, but if this is the right place, I don't think a pistol is going to help me."

Hughes scratched his head. "I'm not sure what that means, and I don't need to know. I was thinking more about snakes and gators. This is bayou country. I thought you might want a small gun with some snake shot, just in case."

"Thanks for the thought, but these people are probably wary of strangers. I don't think they will accept me if I am carrying a gun."

Brian nodded his head and handed the pistol back to Hughes. "Blake's right. He needs to look like a lost hiker who just stumbled onto their property. In fact, we probably shouldn't have fed him so well. A hungry look might work better for him."

Hughes just grunted, "You're the boss."

"You're a good leader, Hughes. I appreciate that you are concerned for Blake, but he's not going into battle. He's just going in. We need to wait for him and hope for the best. I just wish there was some way we could track him."

Hughes' spirit brightened. "That, we can do. We have a transponder hidden in his backpack, another in his shoe, and I have a special watch for him to wear. Unless they strip him naked, we'll be able to find him, no problem."

Michelle saw that Destiny had finally returned from the memories. She was sitting across from Destiny sipping a coffee and didn't want to wait for the focus to return to the girl's eyes. She put the coffee down and asked, "So, what did you learn from your trip?"

Destiny was glad to see her nana's face. "Mostly, I learned how awful my aim is. I tried twice to find that trial, and both times ended up somewhere else."

"Let me fix you something to eat; you must be starved inside."

"Now that you mention it, I am hungry."

Michelle went to the fridge and grabbed some bacon and eggs. She lit a burner on the stove and said, "You just relax a spell. Then, after we get some food in you, you can go head off to wherever you is lookin' for."

"Some other time, maybe. I think I need to stay here for now; someone is coming."

Michelle dropped the eggs and went straight to her potions and powders. She rifled through her herbs, looking for anything she may have forgotten.

Destiny went to her and wrapped her arms around her. "Nana," she said softly, "I really am hungry. Can't you finish breakfast before you play with your chemistry set?"

"My chemistry set?" Michelle was hurt, but looked into her granddaughter's eyes and saw only love and confidence. "Oh, you're just foolin' with me," she said. "Sure. I'll fix your breakfast. Wouldn't mind some food for my own self anyhoo, but maybe you can tell me something about who you think it is that be coming."

The car ride was uneventful. The highway took them straight to Cricket Bend, where they found the General store, the gas station, and the post office. Gomez tried the post office, and Johnson tried the general store, but people in these parts weren't too likely to share much with strangers, especially when they were so obviously not family.

Blake had been leaning against the car, staring across the street into the bayou.

Gomez returned first. "There's nobody there, it's just post boxes."

Johnson returned and said, "Sorry, Boss. This guy's not talking. I'm not sure we'd understand him if he did."

Blake pushed himself away from the car. "It's okay. I just need a small boat. I can find her."

Brian handed Gomez some money and said, "Get him a boat."

Hughes stepped in. "Wait a second. I thought he was supposed to be some kind of hiker that just stumbled onto their land? How's it going to look if he shows up in a boat?"

"For one thing," Blake said, "it'll look like I'm on a pilgrimage. It'll also look like I'm not stupid enough to try and walk through the swamp."

Hughes shook his head. "It might look like you have more money than most pilgrims."

Brian nodded his head. "Make it an old, used boat. Rundown even."

Destiny poked a bacon strip into her yoke and stirred it around. She nibbled off the end and said, "Nana, I'm worried about Mama. Don't ask me why or how, I just have a bad feeling."

"Your mama's safe where she is. You don't need to worry about her."

"But I do," Destiny said, still toying with her food, "and I'm learning to trust my feelings. I think you should go see how she is, and make sure she's okay. If you hurry now, you can make the mid-day bus to the hospital."

"What?" Michelle cleared her plate to the sink and exclaimed, "Are you crazy? You said someone was coming. I ain't leaving you here alone. Why is you trying to get rid of me?"

"I'm worried about you. I've seen things that are going to happen here, maybe not today, but maybe so, and I don't want you to be hurt."

"Nonsense. I'm not leaving you to face them alone."

Destiny cleared her plate and left it on top of Michelle's in the sink. She went to the screen and stared out into the bayou. "Don't you remember the bones? You said someone near me was going to die. If you get hurt, it will be my fault."

"Forget about it. I ain't leaving you."

"What if I need Mama? She's strong, even if she doesn't want to admit it."

Michelle returned to her herbs and said, "Your mama is crazy. Maybe she warn't really crazy in the beginning, but she's been fed them drugs for so long now, she's lost to us."

"We can save her."

"You don't think I've tried?"

"Sure," Destiny said. "You've tried, but I can heal people."

"Well, if I'm going to get your mama, you be goin' with me."

Destiny barely heard her nana's last argument. She stared out way past the dock. The morning sun twinkled through the trees and glittered on the water. Destiny felt the world slip away.

Gomez returned from the general store empty-handed. "Sir, no dice. He doesn't have boats for sale, and he refuses to sell me his boat. He says we have to go on up the road where there's a hardware store that might have boats, unless you want us to be more persuasive."

"No," Brian said, "let's go up the road. Blake will have to go in at sunrise."

"Wait a minute," Blake said. "Let me try." He straightened out his hair a bit and entered the store, leaving Brian and Gomez looking at each other and shrugging their shoulders.

Hughes patted Gomez on the back and said, "Don't take it so bad, you just don't look trustworthy."

Gomez simply nodded his head.

Hughes looked up at the sun, which was already well past high-noon. "I'm still wondering if sending him at sunrise is the best plan. Early morning might look too staged. If he's really a pilgrim, then he gets there when he gets there."

Brian nodded his head and said, "That's if we don't have to head up the road to find a boat."

Blake emerged from the store swinging a small key chain on his finger.

Brian asked, "How much money did he want? Did you have enough?"

Blake grinned widely and said, "Money? He didn't want any money. He wanted to help us out of civic responsibility."

Brian followed Blake to the dock, and leaned in close so he could whisper, "Civic responsibility? Can you influence people?"

"What do you mean? I've always been a pretty good negotiator."

"Uh-huh."

"What are you saying?" Blake asked. "Are you suggesting that I have some kind of supernatural power to bend people to my will? I'm not the Shadow, you know."

Again, Brian had nothing substantial to add. He watched Blake with a new keen interest and repeated his earlier comment, "Uh-huh."

Blake reached the middle of the small dock and pulled a red rope, which brought a small boat close to him. The boat was covered with a green tarp. He pulled off the tarp, crumpled it on the dock, and climbed in.

"Remember, Blake, try and make friends with them, but don't reveal who you are, or that we are here. Identify which one is our girl and excuse yourself to come back here. We don't know how long it will take you to find them, but if you've only got a couple hours of light left, try to spend the night and start back in the morning."

Marvalaine entered the atrium with Melody on his arm. They circled the courtyard and stopped short when they found Destiny sitting on a bench, staring into the pond. "Ah, cousin Destine, there you are."

"Lady Destine," Melody said softly as she curtseyed.

Destiny was balling her fists. She didn't want to be here right now. She continued to stare into the water and barely even acknowledged Marvalaine's presence.

"Cousin," he said, "you may be surprised to know that Melody here has a great deal in common with you."

"Oh, yeah?" Destiny responded. "That's nice."

"She, too, has been raised by her grandmother."

Melody's attention remained locked on Marvalaine. Her eyes twinkled, and she smiled broadly as he spoke.

Destiny's voice was distant and hollow as she said, "Good."

Marvalaine wrinkled his brow and said, "Her mother moved to a convent and has not left it in years."

"How sweet."

"Her father was an invading conqueror who raped and pillaged her mother's village."

Melody released her hold on Marvalaine and gripped her mouth with both hands to prevent any laughter from escaping and breaking the moment.

"Yeah," was all Destiny managed to say.

Marvalaine swung his arms wildly through the air to accentuate what he was saying. "Her sister was swooped up by dragons and forced to marry a dwarf prince."

"Good for her."

Marvalaine sat down on the bench next to Destiny. "When Melody was young, she was promised to an ogre king, but before the nuptials, she seduced him into her room and poisoned him with fruit, then sliced him up into small bits and fed him to the crows."

"That's good."

He gripped Destiny by the shoulders and gently shook her, singing out, "Destine? Destine? Helloooo? Where are you exactly?"

"Huh?" She shook her head and looked blankly up into his face. "I'm sorry," she said, "what?"

"You're obviously preoccupied. Perhaps you should return to wherever you left your mind."

"I'm sorry, you're right. I'll see you later."

"Are you listening to me?" Michelle's voice was pitched with concern. "Don't ignore me," she continued, "If you wants me to go visit your mama, then we both is gonna be on that bus."

Destiny's focus returned to the bayou outside their home. "I have to stay, Nana. It's my destiny."

"And I be stayin' with you! It's my duty!"

Destiny turned to look her grandmother directly in the eye. "Very well," she said, "but it might get ugly. There's gonna be a group of men trying to get us, and something really bad happens to them."

"How bad?"

"Like catching fire and burning to death from the inside out bad."

Michelle looked around the house at all the various charms she had hanging everywhere. She looked out the window to some of the charms in the yard. "I don't remember makin' any charms that would burn a man like that."

"You didn't, Nana. It was a different kind of magic. A magic our people aren't supposed to know." Destiny held out her hand and created a ball of flame in her palm. "It's a kind of magic I must have learned how to do."

Horror spread across Michelle's face. "What is you telling me? You gonna burn those men? You burn them to death?"

"Yes, Nana, and they catch me and put me on trial, too."

"Then maybe you is right, we should go. We can go see your mama like you said. There's nothing here as valuable as your life."

"I'll be fine, remember? I survived and went on trial."

"How dat trial come out?"

"I don't know yet."

"Maybe you don't come out so good? If I can't make you go with me, then maybe you better go find out how it comes out. I'll wake you if anyone comes."

Chapter 15

Blake waved goodbye as he pushed off from the dock. The boat was a small, weathered, wooden craft, skinny like a canoe, but otherwise built like a cheap rowboat with a small motor attached. There were three seats, front, middle and rear. The wood was old and grey, but thankfully, did not appear to be laden with splinters. The bottom of the boat was stained with both watermarks and dark oil stains.

Blake took a final inventory before starting the small motor. His backpack was sitting on the front seat. The old guy from the store said the gas can was already full. There were two oars secured to each side of the boat, and a small anchor sat next to the gas can in the back. The motor was a small gas engine, much smaller than a lawnmower engine. Blake turned the key, as the man had instructed, and pulled the chord. The engine sputtered to life for a moment, then died back. The old man stood on the porch of the store signaling with his right hand in a push-pull motion. Blake remembered what he had said and pulled the white knob that was clearly labeled "choke" out and in. He pulled the chord again, and after the third attempt it sputtered back to life and kept running.

It made a low puttering sound, and as it warmed up, slipped down to a low guttural growl. He gripped the handle and gingerly turned the throttle. The engine drone rose to a higher pitch, similar to a model airplane. It also engaged the propeller and gently pushed the small craft forward. He swung the handle right and left, getting accustomed to steering the boat.

The dock shrunk behind him, with only his wake and a small silver thread of smoke trailing behind the small motor to show that he had come that way. He piloted the small boat between the shallow sandbars that lay just below the surface of the water.

He could feel the path before him. He could still sense the dread warning him to turn around, but found, quite by accident, that the more he admired the skill of the caster of the spell, the less it affected him. He just had to get himself into character, for after all, the plan was for him to infiltrate them as one of their own, and it was as if that character was a key granting him access through the waves of fear and panic urging him to turn back.

The water he had crossed, so far, was like a narrow clearing between the mainland and the real swamp. On one side, where the dock stood, the shore stretched up and down for miles. But on the far side, a thick wall of cypress trees stretched up and down as far as he could see. The trees were an impressive barrier. Blake couldn't help thinking of childhood tales of enchanted forests and hidden monsters within.

He pierced the barrier and was immediately surrounded with trees. Vines stretched between them, and moss hung from the vines. Some trees projected up from the water, while others were on small outcrops of land. The trees nearly blotted out the sun, yet grasses and reeds still surrounded them. Something stirred to his left. He could feel eyes on him everywhere. He didn't belong here, and all those eyes seemed to know it. The water around him, which had been bright and alive, turned dark and murky. Bits of tree bark and decayed leaves now floated on the surface of the swamp, where moments ago there had been a thin veil of tiny green leaves surrounding him. He found patches of afternoon sunlight that penetrated the canopy in thick shafts of dusty light, separated from each other by the overwhelming gloom where the trees blotted out the sky.

Cricket Bend didn't have a motel, but the general store had a small apartment on the second floor. Brian offered the store owner a generous fee for their stay, which the gnarled old shopkeeper considered to be a small fortune. He leaned back in his chair, counting his money, wondering why in the world anyone would want to stay in Cricket Bend, and especially why they would pay so much to stay there. But he was smart enough not to say anything, except with Old Nate, who came over from the filling station to play checkers in the afternoon. They whispered and snickered about why four grown men would want to share one cramped room.

Brian called his office and left instructions detailing where they were and how they could be reached. Schaefer wasn't available when he called, but he had left a message for Brian that he was developing some new device which might be able to detect the witches' magical energy.

***

Destiny couldn't hide how she felt. Her nana looked at the worry on her face and asked, "What's wrong?"

"Someone's coming."

"Now? The bad men from your dream?"

"I don't know, and it wasn't a dream."

"I know that, child. This be no time to pick on my words."

Destiny swung the screen door open and said, "I'm going out to see."

"What if it's them?" Michelle asked. "It's not safe."

"If it is them, then it's not safe in here either."

"It be dark soon. I'll get a lantern and the shotgun."

Destiny's instinct was to stop her nana from going with her, but she knew it would be futile to argue with her. The old woman gathered up the kerosene lamp, the shotgun, and a handful of shells.

"I guess we don't need no matches. You can do that thing with your fingers when we wants the light."

They headed out to the point where their own small dock floated in the waterways of the swamp. It was the nearest spot to the mainland, and it was where Destiny expected the intruder would land.

Michelle's eyes were sharp as ever, and she spotted the small boat first. "Stop! Who dat?"

Blake thought he heard something and idled the motor, letting the boat drift.

"I said who dat!" Michelle repeated louder. "I gots a shotgun pointed at that melon you calls a head and if you doesn't answer me..."

"Okay, okay," he said. He didn't have to act afraid, the fear was already evident in his voice. "You don't know me. My name is Blake, and I'm a stranger here. I'm lost."

"You ain't lost," Michelle argued. "Lost gets you lots o' places, but lost don't bring ya here."

"No, you are correct, but I'm not that kind of lost."

Michelle kept the shotgun trained on Blake as she stepped in front of Destiny. "Don't talk in riddles. Either you is lost, or you isn't lost."

Blake had already thought of different ways he would try to talk his way in. "I don't know where I am. I don't know why I'm here, but I was drawn here."

"You was drawn here?" Michelle almost snickered. "Boy, you is lost. Now turn around and go back where you come from until you ain't lost no more."

"Yes, ma'am. Only...but..."

"What you stammerin' about, spit it out. My patience is drawing thin."

"It's getting dark soon, ma'am. Is there someplace I could stay till morning? I swear I'll leave in the morning."

"Nana? He can sleep in the smokehouse."

Blake's mind reeled. It was the witch. He fought back the impulses to kill her now. He had to learn what she was doing, and why, after hundreds of years without witches, why she was able to perform magic.

"Okay," Michelle relented, "we let you stay the night. But might be you find you be safer with them snakes and gators."

A chill ran up and down Blake's spine. He wondered if the old woman was suspicious of him already. He hoped it just meant they were suspicious of everyone that came around this way, but then, he had also hoped his 'being drawn here' ploy would have won them over.

He tied the boat to the hook, next to their boat, grabbed his bag, and followed them up a small path. He continued to feel the pangs of dread, which grew stronger with every step, but he focused on being like them, which still seemed to help. The old woman was scary, not scary-looking, just serious looking, and very unhappy that he was here. She talked like she wasn't well educated, but she acted just the opposite. Blake tried catching a look at the girl. He thought she seemed younger, closer to his age, but he couldn't get a good look at her.

Michelle stopped in front of an old, small shack next to the chicken coop. She held out her arm, pointing to the door. "This be our smokehouse. We ain't used it in ages, but it could be you might still smell the cured bacon. You can wait here. I'll fetch you a blanket."

Blake swung open the door and poked his head inside. The shadows were already looming outside, but inside the tiny room, it was positively dark. There were some small openings in the roof and the tops of the walls, and he was pretty sure the holes in the roof weren't supposed to be there. A few thin shafts of light found their way into the room, enough to see that, thankfully, it wasn't full of cobwebs, but not enough to really see anything. Soon it would be pitch dark, he was sure. Fortunately for him, Hughes had packed his backpack with all the essentials, including a battery-powered lantern.

Destiny waited in the shadows while her nana retrieved a blanket. "So, what's your name?" she asked.

Blake pulled the lantern out of the sack and inspected the smoke house while he answered her, "Blake, you?"

"Hi. I'm Destiny. You traveling alone?"

"Yeah, just me."

The smoke house looked even less inviting than a barn, but it was shelter, and at least didn't seem infested with rodents.

Michelle returned with a blanket, a sandwich, and a glass of water. "Here, in case you get hungry durin' the night."

"Thank you, ma'am."

She headed back up the hill and signaled Destiny to follow.

When she was comfortable they were out of Blake's earshot, Michelle said, "I don't like strangers showin' up jest when you's expectin' trouble. It don't feel right. Maybe we should pack up and go see your mama like you was sayin', and just leave him here."

"No, Nana, it's too late for that. Whatever's gonna happen has already started. Besides, I've learned how to tell their kind when they approach. I didn't feel any of them bad feelings from this boy."

"I hopes you is right, but just the same, I'm putting up some extra protection spells."

Brian was looking over Hughes' shoulder at his laptop when his cell phone rang.

"Grupp."

"Hey, boss, it's Schaefer. I think I've narrowed down the center of the disturbances as far as we can go with our current data. I'd put it around two or three hundred miles south of Lafayette in Louisiana."

"Good. Then we're in the right place."

"You're in the right place? How did you know?"

"Magic, Dick. That's what we do."

"Very funny. How did you really know?"

"I'm serious. It's a little early to be sure, but I think magic's coming back. Our power, theirs, too, I'd say. We could sort of feel our way here. I want you to check with the schools and see if there has been any improvement in our younger candidates."

"Sure, I can do that." Schaefer paused a moment, and Brian could hear him taking notes with his free hand. "If it's really back, we should probably start retesting our senior members, too."

"Do that, but try to keep it quiet for now. I don't want to alert anyone who is not on board with us until we know for sure."

"You got it. You want me to have security renew the loyalty lists?"

Brian shifted the phone to his other hand as he walked over to look out the window at the road and the bayou. "Are you after my job?"

"Of course I am, but I'm loyal to you. I want to promote you out of the job so I can slip in."

"Good answer. I don't trust anyone who isn't ambitious."

Brian closed the flip phone and asked Hughes, "Any change?"

"None. The beacon is working fine. He just hasn't moved for the past half hour or so."

"So he either found them and is staying the night, or he found them and they killed him."

Hughes pointed to the screen and said, "They didn't kill him; we'd know if they did that."

"You don't think a gator ate him?"

"We'd know if that happened, too. The watch includes heart rate telemetry. His heart is still ticking."

Brian leaned in close to see the heartbeat on the screen. "How long would the beacon work under water?"

"It's not waterproof at all, maybe an hour or two."

"So, if his heart stops and the beacon dies, we assume he was dragged under by a gator."

"That's about the size of it."

Brian clapped his hands together and said, "I'm hungry; let's see what this diner has to offer."

Destiny wasn't very hungry. She could feel something happening around her, and it was twisting her stomach into knots. Her nana was too busy tying bones together into talismans to even notice when Destiny said she was going to bed early.

Her head sunk deep into her pillow. She stared up at the ceiling. Stick figures were hanging all around her bed. They had feathers and pieces of yarn hanging from them and shiny little beads tied to them. The beads twinkled as they reflected the light from the many candles that were lit around the room. As she drifted off into that middle state that lies between consciousness and sleep, the twinkling beads began to look like the stars outside.

"For heaven's sake, will you make up your mind?"

Destiny opened her eyes and saw Marvalaine pacing back and forth while she lay on a rather large cushion. "I'm sorry, what?"

"You can't be in two places at once. Either you're here or you're there, but this popping back and forth is not getting us anywhere."

"Why am I here? I was going to sleep!"

"I thought you were here to help me find a bride?"

Destiny sat up and wiped the sleep from her eyes. "A bride? I thought you just wanted some companionship! I didn't know you were interested in marriage."

"Companionship? How disgraceful. What sort of man would do such a thing?"

Destiny rolled her eyes and said, "You might be surprised."

"Wait, are you saying it is so in your time? I think I would very much like to witness your time for myself."

Destiny patted the cushion, testing its firmness, and asked, "Do you think that if I go to sleep here, I'll wake up back in my own time?"

"I can't say. You're the one traveling back and forth in time. I don't know where you learned that trick, but I know Mala didn't teach you."

"Mala! I got so wrapped up in my own problems, I forgot all about saving Mala!"

Marvalaine gripped her shoulders and pulled her to her feet. "Never mind Mala, you are here now. Help me with Melody and Phoebe. They both seem interested in being my wife."

"Melody and Phoebe? Are you kidding me? Melody is a major kiss ass. She's only interested in furthering her own title, and Phoebe is a shy little lamb following Melody everywhere she goes. And her voice! Can you stand to listen to that voice the rest of your life?"

"In truth," he said, "Phoebe is not as shy as you may think, and she does not follow Melody in all things."

"What do you mean?" Destiny caught a twinkle in his eye. "No! You didn't! You and Phoebe?"

"I tell you, she is not so shy as you might think."

Destiny pushed him away from her. "And is that the kind of woman you desire as a wife? How disgraceful. What sort of man would do such a thing?"

Marvalaine pretended to be wounded. "Now you use my own words against me. Why shouldn't I enjoy Phoebe's company? And don't act so shocked. From everything you say about your time, this is nothing to raise your eyebrows at. Besides, I'm not promised yet, and perhaps these are good qualities in a prospective wife after all."

"What does Melody think about you and Phoebe?"

"She wasn't pleased at first, but she has made it clear that she is willing to try harder for my attention."

"Great. They're going to keep outdoing each other."

Marvalaine looked pleased with himself. "Yes, it is rather clever, isn't it?"

"No! It's not clever," she screamed. "It's repulsive! You're using them against each other. You're taking two friends and manipulating them to do things they might not ordinarily do."

"I don't force them to do anything they don't already want to do!"

Destiny punched him in the chest. "Do you really believe that they want to throw themselves at you?"

"Well then," he said, "I don't force them to do anything they aren't willing to do! How's that?"

"ARGGHH!" She turned her back on him and stepped to a window, unable to see through the stained yellow glass. "It's still pathetic. You're going to break up their friendship."

"You'd think so, but when they are together, they act like nothing has happened."

"You need to move on. They are both too needy for my tastes."

He joined her at the window and showed her how to open it. "There are not many suitable candidates as fair as they are."

"Typical! All you care about is how pretty they are!"

"Not true! I would also like someone who is learned and can hold up her part of a conversation."

"As long as she is pretty."

Marvalaine pushed open the window and tossed some bread crumbs from a bowl he kept by the window, out onto the outer sill, making little cooing noises to attract the pigeons. "It would not hurt if she were attractive. I can ask a wife not to speak in public if she has an irritating voice, but I cannot ask a wife to not be seen if she has a homely face."

"So why have them compete? Just stand them side by side and choose the prettier one."

"That's not so easy. Melody has a more handsome face, but Phoebe..."

She shoved her hand in his chest, pushing him away again, and walked away from the window. "Stop right there! I don't want to hear about it. I have to go. How do I return?"

"Don't you know?"

"How would I know? I'm still pretty new at this."

"But you're the master at it."

She threw her arms in the air and asked, "What am I the master of?"

"Haven't you even noticed?" he asked.

"Noticed what? You're speaking in riddles!"

He held up a finger. "For one thing, you no longer need to go into a trance to travel here."

"Yeah, okay, I noticed that, but it's still been by accident."

He held up a second finger and said, "Another thing, you appear as yourself."

"What do you mean?"

"How long has it been since you traveled back and found you were somebody else?"

Destiny's mouth fell open. She hadn't noticed, until now, that she was no longer piggy backing on somebody else's memory. She was actually interacting with real people, asking her own questions, and hearing her own voice. "So, is this a dream world? Mala had taken me to a dream world where we could talk to each other and I could do things as myself."

"If this is a dream world, it is quite excellent. No witch before you has ever traveled through time to the real world."

Her eyes and head rolled around as she took in the splendor and detail of the world around her.

"I thought you had to go," he reminded her.

She nodded and focused on home.

Chapter 16

Blake fought the urge to sleep. He should have brought a book. He stared at the walls and roof of the small smokehouse, which were rough, weathered planks of wood covered with pegs and hooks. A moth in the corner caught his attention for a minute or two, but no more. He tried focusing on his job. He pictured the many ways things could go in the morning. The old lady would surely want to see him on his way, but maybe he could appeal to the girl. Too bad they never trained him in the ways of women; she was pretty. He shook the thought from his mind and tried to focus on his task. He could not afford to see her as pretty when he might have to do some very ugly things to her.

He finally decided that staring at the walls was of little use to him, so he shut off the lantern and was immediately enveloped in darkness. In fact, it was pitch dark, at least for the first few minutes. As his eyes adjusted, he could see some faint signs of light where holes were cut in the walls. *At least I won't suffocate*, he thought. His eyelids were heavy, and drooping on his eyes. He had hours before dawn, but he could not afford to be vulnerable to them. If he slept, he would be at their mercy.

He spotted a star through one of the ventilation holes. He focused on the star and wondered if there was a planet orbiting that star, and if there were people on that planet looking up at his sun wondering the same thing. He wondered how far the star was. It grew brighter and larger until it filled the small opening and a shaft of light pierced the dark room, ending directly on his face and his eye. The room filled with a dazzling white light until all was whiteness and the room disappeared.

He held his hands over his eyes and tried focusing on the room around him, but when the light faded, he wasn't in the room. He was lying on a sandy beach facing a vast ocean. The sand was hot; burning hot, except for his feet where the surf rolled up on the beach, cooling the sand and kissing his feet before slipping back into the ocean's depths. He sat up and looked around. There was nobody in sight. In fact, there were no birds, or animals, or any kind of life except for the palm trees and thick vegetation behind him.

Blake stood up and turned to survey the palm trees behind him. He was barefoot and wearing only khaki shorts and a tattered top. The sand was hot on his feet, so he headed towards the palm trees. The sand burned the soles of his feet. He picked up the pace to a jog, and then again to a full run. The closer he came to the tree line, the more the sand was littered with small twigs and rocks. He quickly learned just how painful the rocks and debris were to his feet, so he started picking his way through the rocks until he found some shade. He found a spot under a group of coconut palms where the ground was slightly damp and blissfully cool. He sunk his toes into the earth and took a deep, soothing breath. The air was damp and salty.

Sheltered from the blistering sun, he could now feel the occasional mild breeze whip up and swirl around him. Clouds were rolling in. The sun became a patchy spot in the broken clouds. Soon it would be completely overcast. It might even rain, not that rain would be significantly damper than the oppressive humidity.

Looking around, Blake saw no reason to stay where he was. He didn't like walking through the burning sand, and he pondered whether mud and rain would be an improvement. He thought he saw an opening to his left where the jungle might be thinner and easier to cross. As he approached it, he saw that it actually was a small path cut through the jungle. He still had not seen any people or animals, and wondered who, or what, had made the path.

The world darkened around him as he plunged deeper into the jungle. He couldn't tell whether it was the jungle or the clouds that shaded him from the sun, and he didn't care. He could no longer tell where the sun was, and as the path took large winding turns through the hills, he found he had lost his bearings, a slave to the path. He couldn't hear the surf behind him. Even the wind could barely penetrate this deep into the wild. He thought about turning back, not knowing how far this path would lead, but there was nothing behind him but burning sand and precious little shade from the burning sun. For all he knew, the path could end in another thirty paces. It was during one of these reflective moments, when despair had him questioning what he was doing, that he saw something up ahead. It was just a brief flicker through the many leaves and vines. He thought he saw the glint of something shiny, and pushed forward, hoping to catch another glimpse, but the path turned away and was taking him farther from where he had seen the flicker. He knew he had seen something, yet he had no clue what it would be and had sinking doubts that it would be of any use to him. He walked faster. Something was out there. He was still heading in the opposite direction, and just when despair was once again replacing his hope, the path turned around and he could see something again.

The path before Blake must be exceptionally straight now, because he could definitely see a distant flicker. He walked even faster.

He continued to see flickers far off in the distance. He had to reach it. He was running now, nearly in complete darkness, except for the light at the end of the path. He couldn't see the edges of the path and ran into palm fronds hanging on the edges. Some fronds had sharp points which stung his face. Blake's lungs were burning now, yet the flicker remained far off. The burning in his lungs spread throughout his body. He was getting too hot, and would have to slow down, but he couldn't slow down. A rain started to fall onto the canopy over his head, dripping onto him. The rain was a warm rain, but to him, heated up from so much running, it felt cool and refreshing. He finally felt he was getting closer, the flicker turned into a flash and a glow. The path dipped downwards, and the light disappeared over the horizon. He reached both arms out and followed the dark path by feeling the plants with his fingers. He completed the descent and started climbing back up again. He could see a faint glow at the top of the hill where the light hit the jungle surrounding the path. As he approached the top of the hill, he realized that the path he was on was more like a tunnel cut into the dense jungle.

Blake finally reached the top of the rise. There before him, at the end of the road, was a tall torch. Underneath the blazing flames of the torch were two signs: one pointing left and one pointing right. Most amazing of all was what he saw beneath the signs. A woman, blond, perhaps twenty or thirty years old, was sprawled beneath the sign. Her eyes were lined with dark dramatic makeup. She wore bright blue and white eye shadow that extended from her eyes to her temples like wings. He thought she looked like a showgirl or an exotic dancer. She licked her dark red lips and cocked her head to the side, viewing Blake like a predator might view a meal.

He no longer ran, but walked the remaining paces as he approached her. He cleared his throat and croaked out, "Hello."

She nodded her head and rose to her feet. She wasn't particularly tall, but she was thin. Her thin, bare legs and her short skirt made her look taller than she was. Her top was short, baring her belly. It fell off one shoulder and clung to her skin.

Blake was still catching his breath. "What's your name?"

She raised up an arm and pointed a long red fingernail to the sign behind her. Pointing to the left, it read "*Pleasure*," and pointing to the right, it read "*Knowledge*".

He closed the remaining distance, stood directly before her, and asked, "What should I do?"

She giggled and placed one finger at the top of his chest, tracing it down to his belly, but she did not answer him.

"Can you come with me?"

She shook her whole body right and left, instead of just shaking her head. Her smile was intoxicating. He turned to the left and started down the path labeled "*Pleasure*". She raised her hand, giggled again, and waved goodbye with her index finger.

Barely three paces onto the new path, and he was surrounded by the jungle again. She continued to giggle behind him. The path darkened. It was a gloomy darkness. He shuffled his feet, feeling his way along the path. The jungle closed in around him with every step and started to slope downwards. The jungle was quiet. The absence of birds and insects punctuated the oppressive silence. He thought he heard something behind him, but it was a fleeting sound. The only thing he heard for certain was the sound of his feet sliding across the ground. He stepped down the descending grade a few more paces and was sure he heard something. He spun around in the direction he came from. The torch was a distant memory already. He listened intently and thought he heard it again. It sounded like the girl was sobbing, but as he stood there and listened, it became apparent that it was more of a whimper than a sob, and could even be mistaken for moaning.

Blake turned his back on the girl and stepped down further. The ground became moist and slippery. If it weren't so dark, he would have thought it were moss or algae; it felt too slimy to be mud. The jungle continued to shrink around him. Vines and air roots, suspended from the canopy, brushed him in the face. The path steepened. He could still hear the girl moaning. Distance and jungle did nothing to fade her utterances now. He thought her moans were developing a regular cycle; on, then off, then on again, but it wasn't a cycle. The rhythm he heard was from her panting. The path was becoming radically steep. Blake was clinging to the vines to his right and left and gingerly stuck his right foot out in front of him. It sunk into something soft, something that did not feel natural to him, something that made him gag. He jerked his foot back, believing he discovered something truly vile on the path. It was pitch black and getting far too steep to proceed any further. He could hear the girl clearly now. She had been screaming, "Oh...Oh...Oh..." and then, much like a baby at the end of a period of crying, she calmed down into panting, then deep breathing and sighing. Blake turned around and climbed his way back up the dark slope. His heart was pounding. For all he knew, one slip could have led him straight down a cliff to his death. He reached the sign. The girl was lying down below the sign. Her hair was mussed and her skin glistened with perspiration. She smiled wickedly and nodded her head at him as he walked by.

He left her behind and started along the *Knowledge* path. Someone has a strange sense of humor. There was nothing pleasurable about that path.

The knowledge path was smooth and level. The dirt floor was replaced with a smooth cobblestone. If it weren't for his bare feet, he would have considered that a reward for taking the right path. The vegetation sprawled around him, but the pathway was open and roomy. It was dim, but not the wretched darkness of the other path. It turned right and left in lazy s-curves. The many turns made it difficult for him to sense how far he had gone, and made it impossible to see the end. The path straightened out, and for a moment he thought he had gone full circle and landed right back where he had started. He could see the flickering torch with the girl sprawled out below, but as he approached, he realized it was not the same girl, though she looked very similar to the other girl.

This girl wore a light blue sarong and a flowery headdress. She had a wide band around one ankle, and it was attached to a heavy rope securing her to the sign behind her. Blake stepped around the girl to view the sign. This time it read "*Freedom*" pointing to the left and "*Understanding*" pointing to the right. He paused for a moment, pondering whether *Freedom* could be another trick. He chose the *Freedom* path, but this time, he would be extra cautious and move slowly.

The path remained paved with cobblestones, which he figured was a good sign. It didn't darken or shrink on him, or dive down some steep grade, which he also considered to be good. It wound around like the other paths, hiding his destination from him, until it directed him straight into the walls of a cliff rising up through and beyond the ceiling of the jungle canopy. There was a hole dug into the cliff, with a door blocking the entrance. A familiar "*EXIT*" sign was over the door. Blake opened the door and stepped through. He found himself not in a cave, but in front of another "*Freedom*"/"*Understanding*" sign, identical to the first, except there was no girl at this one. He looked behind him and saw a path instead of the door he had gone through.

He liked mazes and briskly followed the *Freedom* path. It wound around like the other path until it reached an exit door identical to the first. He stepped through the door and was once again facing an identical "*Freedom*"/"*Understanding*" sign. Suspicious of whether he could believe what he was seeing, he pulled some leaves off a plant on the edge of the path. He placed the leaves in a triangular pattern where the paths met, and trotted off down the *Freedom* path again. A moment later, he crossed the threshold of the exit door and there at his feet was the pattern of leaves he had left behind.

He turned the other direction and started down the *Understanding* path, scratching his head. Something strange was going on. None of this made any sense. He tried to clear his thoughts and focus on why this place felt so unnatural to him, but he couldn't. He sensed that this was some kind of elaborate game, but he could not see through it. Perhaps his thoughts were blocked from seeing beyond it. He had little choice but to continue and see where it led him.

The path was gritty beneath his bare feet. It was dimly lit, a vast improvement over the first pitch-black path he had seen. His feet brushed up against roots spilling onto the path, looking for fresh sources of water. At the end of the path, no surprise to him at this point, was a girl, a sign, and a torch. The girl was dressed in rags. Her clothes were old, filthy, and worn to tatters. Her hair was a matted, dark mass. Her skin was dark from too much sun and streaked with dark stains and dirt. In stark contrast to her clothing was a large ring on her finger. A gemstone on the ring caught and reflected the light of the torch magnificently. The girl stood tall, with her head held high.

Behind the girl, the sign pointing to the left read "*Fortune*" and "*Truth*" pointed to the right. Suspicious of the game he was playing, Blake thought the smart move would be to take the *Truth* path. He didn't, however, because he wanted to see what cruel joke remained at the end of the *Fortune* path. Besides, if there were a fortune to be had, he didn't want to overlook it.

The *Fortune* path didn't dive into oblivion, or turn dark and ominous. It simply wound around and ended at a large wooden chest. The hairs on the back of his neck told him it was a trap. He walked around the chest, checking all sides. He tried the jungle around it, but the jungle was impenetrable. He stood squarely in front of the chest and scratched his chin. If it was a trap, and it probably was, he would never know unless he opened it. Nothing bad happened on the way to it. If he chose not to open it, then he wasn't playing the game anymore. It would be like skipping a turn or something. Whatever was in the chest was surely not a fortune. That would be too easy, but the chest must contain something for him, or else it would not be there.

He bent down on one knee, opened the latch, closed his eyes, held his breath, and pushed the top of the ornate chest open. It was heavier than he'd expected. Nothing happened. There were no explosions or flying darts, or poison gas clouds. He stood and peered inside. It was mostly empty. At the bottom of the chest was some cloth. He reached down and removed the cloth. As the cloth unfolded, he realized it was a dress. This was far too obvious. He was supposed to give the dress to the girl wearing the rags, then he would get another clue to his quest.

The return trip seemed faster and shorter. He found the girl still standing before the sign. He gave her the dress. She accepted it, but appeared ashamed.

Blake saw the shame in her face and said, "It's okay, don't feel bad. It was really meant for you all along. In fact, you could say it really is your dress already. It's not charity or anything. It's not like I could use it. It's really meant for you."

Nothing he said seemed to have any effect on her mood. "Oh, I'm sorry," he said, "I get it. I'll turn around so you can put it on." He turned and faced the opposite direction. She never spoke, but when she had the new dress on, she used the old rags to wipe her face and then threw them at his feet so he could know she was done.

He turned to see her in the new dress. She was stunning. The dress was a long white gown with sequins on the bodice. It draped from her left shoulder, and fit her like a second skin. Her mood hadn't changed, however. She held her hands out slightly, so he could better see the dress. She felt he deserved that, but her head hung low. After showing him the dress, she collapsed to her knees and sobbed.

Blake was confused. He wanted to console her, but knew nothing at this point would help. He turned and headed down the *Truth* path.

The path curved and undulated through the jungle, but was relatively smooth and free of drama. Like the others, it led him to a torch, a sign, and a girl. The girl bore a remarkable resemblance to all of the other girls. She was dressed in a very plain white dress. It was hardly more than a white sack with holes cut out for her head and arms. Unlike the other two girls, this one was scared. He could see it in her eyes. The sign behind her said *"Life"* and *"Death"*.

He was beginning to understand their game. They obviously wanted him to choose the *Life* path, but that would only lead to a catastrophic end, so he turned toward the *Death* path. The girl gasped loudly. Her eyes were wide and wet with tears. Her lips trembled. She reached her hands to him pleadingly, shaking her head. He stopped and asked, "You want me to go down the other path?"

She put her finger to her lips and almost imperceptibly nodded her head yes. He started to ask another question, but she shook her head no, her finger still placed over her lips, so he remained quiet. He nodded his head back to her and headed down the *Life* path.

The *Life* path was shorter than the others. It wound around enough to hide the destination from him initially, but it quickly dumped him off in front of the next test. They were tests; he realized that. He had no idea who was testing him, but he thought he was beginning to understand how he was supposed to answer their tests. This station, like the others, had the tall torch with the flickering flame. The signs read *"Victory"* and *"Humility"*.

This girl was stronger than the others. She was dressed in leather, with a leather skirt, not unlike what the Roman legions wore. Her leather sandals had straps winding up and around her legs. On her wrists were leather bands, but they bore a hardened leather shield on top of the supple leather strap that encircled her wrists. Her chest and her helm were further adorned with metal bands sewn to the leather. She was every inch a warrior, right down to the short sword hanging from her belt and the staff on her back. As strong and dangerous as she looked, her face was soft and feminine. Blake was particularly intoxicated by her eyes, which looked deeply into his own eyes.

Blake looked at the signs again. They were trying to trick him. She was obviously dressed as a warrior, and he was supposed to go down the *Victory* path for her benefit. But that would certainly end disastrously for him, leading him back to the *Humility* path and some sort of moral lesson. He wasn't falling for it and turned toward the *Humility* path instead.

Faster than he had made up his mind, she moved past him and stood before the *Humility* path. He nearly ran into her, his mind dizzy from her speed. He dodged to his right, but she moved to her left, blocking his path.

"I need to go down this path."

She crossed her arms and planted her feet.

This was new. None of the others had interacted with his decision like this. It was a test; he remembered. He had to be humble. "Please, may I pass?"

She didn't budge.

He reminded himself that they weren't just tests; they were also games. He had to find some combination of actions to earn passage. He dropped to one knee and bowed his head low before her. "I know I am not worthy, but I am on a quest which lies down this path. I humbly ask you to let me pass."

She bent forward and lunged at him, slamming both hands into his shoulders and shoving him backwards. He rolled backwards and landed sprawled out on the path in front of the sign. He hadn't quite realized what had happened to him. He started to get up, but she had run up to him and kicked him hard in the chest, launching him backwards again. She pulled the staff off her back and pelted him with a flurry of attacks from right and left. He held his hands up over his face to block the blows. She cracked her staff against his wrists, his knuckles, and occasionally she snuck a blow through to his face. Each blow knocked him backwards down the *Victory* path. Every time he was nearly back to his senses and nearly remembered how to defend himself, another blow would slip through and knock any thoughts he had clear from his mind, until finally one last blow landed him on his back, and he did not have the energy or sense of thought to fight back. He cried softly. His face was split and bruised. His fingers were gnarled and broken. His ribs were cracked, and his knees were sore and swollen. His tears came more freely. She stood over him and pulled the sword from its sheath.

"Please," he sobbed, "no more. Please don't kill me. You win. I can't beat you. I'll go wherever you say, just don't kill me, please."

She put her sword back in its sheath, nodded her head, and stood aside, motioning that he could now take the humility path.

He climbed gingerly to his feet and hobbled down the path. Blood splattered from his mouth as he said, "Thank you. Thank you." He could barely walk. He was surprised how far down the *Victory* path she had forced him. It was slow going. He dragged his left foot through the dust and gingerly took baby steps with his right leg. Once he had finally reached the original sign and moved past it, he could see the next station was just around a single bend. He wasn't sure if he could survive any more tests like this one.

"Any change?"

Hughes looked over his shoulder and saw Brian's long, drawn face. Brian looked genuinely concerned. "No change."

Brian scanned the laptop display and asked, "Are we still getting a signal?"

"Loud and clear."

"Maybe he dropped the transmitter?"

"No, sir," Hughes replied. "The telemetry indicates his heart is still beating."

"You're sure it's his heartbeat?"

Hughes turned his back to the computer and looked Brian directly in the eye. "Yes, sir, but I don't know exactly what's going on with him. His heart rate has been through some unusual changes, but it keeps coming back to his normal rate."

"So why hasn't he moved?"

"I can't say. Maybe he is still asleep."

Brian checked his watch, and his worry deepened. "It's ten o'clock now, and he's out in the open. He wouldn't sleep that late. What if they drugged him?"

"What if they just gave him some wine?"

"What about the heart rate changes? Maybe they have him tied up and are torturing him."

"That's possible," Hughes admitted, "but it seems pretty unlikely. He might be hurt, though. A snake bite or even just an insect sting could cause fever and shock."

Brian paced back and forth, wringing his hands. "Let's go in."

"You want to go in guns blazing, or just to take a look-see?"

"Guns blazing." Brian started to leave to pack a few things, but stopped at the door. "No, we recon first, but have your guns ready, just in case."

"Affirmative. I'll get the guys ready."

Blake approached the next checkpoint slowly. Not out of any caution, he was simply slowed by the pain from his injuries.

The girl was righthanded and landed the most damaging blows on his left side. His left knee was swollen and could only barely hold his weight. His left eye was swollen shut. He didn't want to think about the pain in his ribs, and how many bones may have been broken. Both hands were mangled, and his left arm, which he held with his right, was bent where it shouldn't bend.

His vision was blurred with tears, but he could still tell that the next station was close. He kept most of his weight on his right leg, quickly limping on and off of his left one. The girl at the next station wasn't a girl at all, but an old woman with long white hair. Her face was ravaged with time, but her eyes were clear and bright. She held up a frail arm and beckoned him to come closer. The sign behind her read "*Sympathy*" and "*Empathy*". His mind reeled. What the hell was that supposed to mean? Aren't they the same thing? He could be dying for all he knew, and they wanted him to understand the subtle difference between sympathy and empathy?

As he finally closed the gap to the old woman, her expression changed from concern to a deep sadness. She reached out and touched his face. Her hand felt good. He closed his eyes and focused on the softness of her hand. His body was wracked in pain, but his face felt good, really good. He opened his eyes and took a closer look at her. She was weeping, and her eye was swollen like his. She removed her hand from his face and held his broken right arm. He jumped when she straightened his arm, but he had no need to fear.

There was no pain. She held the arm straight and rubbed her fingers up and down its length. His arm never felt so good. She released his arm when she could no longer bear its weight and her own arm snapped between the wrist and the elbow.

Blake was horrified. He backed up from the old woman, holding up his hands in protest. "No! I can't let you do this." He looked back to the sign behind her. He still wasn't sure which path to take, but he couldn't allow her to transfer his injuries to herself. She was too old and wouldn't survive.

Still limping, he hobbled down the path labeled *"Empathy"*.

"Why is he still here?" Michelle's face scowled at the stranger's presence.

Destiny was already in the smokehouse, watching Blake writhe in his sleep.

Michelle stood in the doorway. "I thought I told him to leave at sunrise."

"Something's wrong with him. He sounds like he's in a lot of pain. Maybe I should help him."

"You wanna do what?"

Destiny turned sharply and faced her nana. Michelle's face was dark and angry. "Nana! What did you do?"

"Me? I didn't do nuthin."

"Nana?"

"I don't believe I care for that tone in your voice. You think I done something to this boy? Child, you know I got no powers like that. Only thing I done was hang up some charms to protect us. But they is only gonna protect us from someone what means us harm. Do you think he means us harm?"

"I don't know," Destiny said. "I'd ask him if he weren't unconscious! Can you stop your charms?"

"I suppose I could, but then we'd be exposed to harm from him or anyone else if he's not alone."

"Fine then. I'll heal him, and we'll leave the charms in place."

Destiny knelt down next to Blake and placed one hand on his forehead and the other on his chest. Blake continued to moan out in pain. Destiny moved her hand around his forehead, trying to identify the source of his pain.

"What's wrong?" Michelle asked.

"I don't know. I usually can feel where the problem is, but I don't feel anything."

Michelle slapped her hand against her forehead and started laughing.

Destiny thought her nana had taken leave of her senses. "It's not funny. Why are you laughing?"

"I'm laughing cause I'm so stupid. We assumed he was hurtin' because we heard him cryin' and moanin', but he's just havin' himself a whopper of a nightmare. That's why you can't find nothin'."

"I don't think so. His pain is real enough. I just don't know why."

Destiny shifted her weight to a more comfortable position, closed her eyes, and reached into Blake's mind.

Blake's vision was sharper than ever. He could see the next station clearly. The sign read *"Torture"* and *"Collaborator"*. He didn't like the sound of either of those options and stopped where he was. The girl standing in front of the sign was the same girl that had just beaten him nearly to death. She had taken off the warrior costume, but it was the same girl, he was sure of it. He stood frozen, not choosing either path. She stepped out to meet him. He couldn't outrun her. He couldn't even out walk her. He stopped to take stock of his condition. His eyes and his arm were healed. He would have to fight her this time. He would probably die, but he was probably going to die, anyway.

He flexed his right fist. He thought maybe he should try a fireball. Why didn't he use his abilities before? He thrust his fist towards her and opened his palm. A round, red ember appeared before his palm and flew in her direction. She waved her arms in circular motions and the ball of flame impacted on an invisible shield surrounding the girl.

She continued to approach him. He wished he could create a barrier that would keep her out, but he didn't know how. He tried making a larger fireball instead, but it just made a bigger flash around her. She continued to advance. He wouldn't have much more time. He snapped his hand downwards and shot bolts of lightning into the ground. The lightning slithered just below the surface of the ground and shot up around her feet, only to find itself dancing outside her protective barrier.

She reached him and grabbed his wrist with one hand and his opposite shoulder with her other hand. He was frantic now, nearly hysterical. Thoughts came to him in short bursts. Something was happening to him. It was her. She was doing something to him. He could feel tingling from her touch. It must be electric.

He didn't have the strength to fight her off completely, but he was inside her safety shield. He concentrated his energy on freeing the hand she held by the wrist. He leaned his weight on the bound wrist and twisted it. Her grip weakened, but she did not let go. He twisted again and was able to loosen her grip enough to twist his hand around and grab her wrist. He wasted no time releasing a stream of electricity into her arm. Her eyes widened as she felt the bolt stream through her arm.

She released him and shoved him away from her. He fell backwards, hitting his head against the ground. He struggled to get up, but he was finished. She knelt down beside him and placed one hand on his head and the other on his chest. He could actually feel the world slip away from him. His vision went out of focus, then turned grey, and finally black.

Blake could resist no more and let go of his final remaining hold on the world around him.

Chapter 17

Hughes and his men gathered down by the dock. They had hoped to leave unnoticed, but as soon as they had crossed in front of the General Store, the old shopkeeper had poked his head outside the door and motioned for one of them to come in.

"I'll see what he wants," Brian said as he started up the front steps. "You guys go ahead. I'll meet you at the boat."

Brian stepped into the store. The old guy was pretty excited about something.

"Coooh! But you be fixin' to start a early day! You run off without ya chu-chut."

Brian cocked his head and tried replaying what the old man said in his mind, but still couldn't make it out. "What was that?"

The proprietor was clearly excited, but speaking to the foreigner was rubbing the shine off his mood. He picked up a cardboard shipping box and plopped it on the counter. "Where put dis?"

"What's that?"

The old man was annoyed now. "Dis come for you."

"Oh, I see. Thank you." Brian took the brown box. "Sorry if it woke you up."

The old man watched Brian carry the package across the street, where he joined up with his friends. He closed the door to the store muttering, "Idiots."

Rather than ask for a boat, and risk being turned down again, Hughes and his commandos simply took one of the two boats left at the dock. It was a shoddy, wooden rowboat with a small outboard engine, not much different from the one Blake took out. It wasn't intended to carry four men, let alone four good-sized men, but they squeezed in. Hughes packed Brian's box and three bags of gear into the front of the boat. Gomez and Johnson took the rowers seat, which was really meant for a single man to row both oars. Brian, being the smallest, sat up front in the bow of the boat with the laptop, while Hughes manned the motor. They pushed off from the dock and drifted as far as they could before Gomez and Johnson tried to row them to the edge of the tree line. Rowing was nearly impossible. With the two of them in the one seat, they didn't leave much room to maneuver the oar handles, and even when successful, the coordination between them was comical.

"Okay, boys," Hughes said, "you can stop rowing now. We should check the monitor and set a bearing."

Brian flipped open the laptop; it woke up automatically and up-dated Blake's relative position. Hughes already had a compass sitting on his knee; he turned a dial on the compass to point in the general direction of Blake, started up the small motor, and headed off.

"Gomez," Hughes said, "keep your eyes sharp looking for snakes and gators in the water. Johnson, I want you to monitor any water we take on and bail us out before we become gator chow."

Even before he opened his eyes, Blake could feel someone holding his head down. He could feel the electricity flowing into his body. It wasn't hurting him, certainly not killing him, but he had already blacked out once, so, in one swift move, he snapped open his eyes, grabbed Destiny by the wrists, gave her a mild electric shock, and rolled free. He held his arms up, poised to attack her again.

"Ow!" Destiny bellowed. "What'd you do that for? I was only trying to help."

Blake wasn't listening to her. His mind was numb with an overwhelming feeling of dread. He shot a fireball at Destiny. She slapped it with the back of her hand, deflecting it into the ceiling, where it popped into embers, falling and sparkling like a fireworks display. He shouldn't have been surprised by anything she did. She was the same girl as the one in the leather armor that nearly killed him. He knew she was strong, but the way she deflected his attack was humiliating. He sent another larger fireball her direction. This time, she caught it in her hand and held it up to show him. "Are you sure you wouldn't rather just tell me what's bothering you?"

Blake was outmatched. He looked around him, but didn't recognize the room. He was disoriented and tired. He relaxed his stance. He couldn't match her in a fair fight. He would have to think of another way to defeat her. "Why were you trying to kill me?"

"Kill you? I wasn't doing anything to kill you."

"Then what were you doing to me?"

"Me?" She clapped her hands together, popping the fireball between them. "I wasn't doing anything. You're the one that went all battle crazy for no reason."

"I thought you killed me once already. Then I woke up again and thought you were still killing me!"

"You were moaning and crying all night. I was just trying to make you feel better."

"No," he said, "you were doing something else. You were doing something to me."

"Really, there wasn't much I could do. I tried to heal you, but you weren't really sick or injured, so there wasn't anything I could fix. I just tried making you feel better, so you'd stop moaning."

"So it was magic then?" he asked. "I mean, of course it was magic. I just never met anyone like you before. I mean, like me."

"I never expected to meet another like us neither. We're supposed to be very rare. As far as I know, there has only ever been one or two like us. Who trained you?"

"Trained me?" Blake asked. "How could anyone train me?"

"No training? You learned all that without training?" Destiny smiled and let out a small laugh. "Me too, sort of. I mean, I had some training, but I learned most of my stuff outside of training, especially the good stuff."

Blake's mind was working full speed ahead. He couldn't beat her, but maybe he could trick her into teaching him what she knew, so he could. "How about if you train me?"

"Me? I can't train you. I'm just learning this stuff myself."

"Who trained you? Maybe he can train me, too."

"First of all, he's a she, and she's dead."

"Oh, I'm sorry," he said. "That must be tough. Just learning this stuff and losing your teacher. How long ago did she die?"

"That's a good question. I guess she must have died about twenty-five thousand years ago."

Destiny enjoyed the look on Blake's face as he puzzled that one out for a moment. "How could you be trained by someone who died twenty-five thousand years before you were born?"

"Magic, silly." She enjoyed not giving him the full answer.

***

"Shhh," Brian said, "stop the boat. I think I saw some movement."

Hughes stopped the small outboard and leaned forward between Johnson and Gomez while Brian held up the laptop so he could see it. "Looks like he's moved about two meters. That's not much."

Brian was still concerned. "That would fit in with the scenario where he was hurt or trapped somewhere. Let's continue."

Hughes settled back in his seat, grabbed the throttle, but then released it. "We're getting too close. Let's go to oars."

"Dang, boss," Johnson complained, "you know we can't pull the oars right with both of us sitting here like this."

"You're right," Hughes said, "you swim alongside; Gomez can row."

Johnson's eyes widened as he peered out on the swamp. "Are you serious?" Seeing no indication that Hughes was joking, he started removing his holster.

Brian cleared his throat, not wanting to interfere with the military chain of command. "You could both sit in the middle, the one in back straddling the one in front like you were on the back of a motorcycle."

Gomez pointed his thumb at Johnson and said, "I don't think I know him well enough for that."

Hughes looked back and forth from Johnson to Gomez and ordered, "Gomez, in the back."

"That's right," Johnson added. "Bitches in the back."

"And Johnson will man the oars," Hughes continued. "Now let's keep the chatter down from here on in."

"Sheeet. The brother always gets to do the manual labor."

"Damn, Johnson," Gomez whispered, "I never noticed how plump and round your butt was before."

"And you can just go on not noticing."

"Firm too..."

"That had better be your gun..."

"Quiet you two."

Destiny was leaving the small smokehouse, but stopped at the door. "Oh yeah, I almost forgot. My nana is a little upset you didn't leave at sunrise like you said you would, but being that you weren't feeling too good, I'll ask her if maybe we can give you a bite to eat before you go."

"Go? I can't go now. We've just met."

Destiny knew exactly what he meant, and truth be told, she'd like to see him some more, but she continued to toy with him. "It wasn't that great a meeting. You tried to kill me."

"But that was before I got to know you."

"No, that was when you thought I was the girl from your dreams, you know, the one that kicked your butt..."

"But you are the girl of my dreams, I mean..."

Destiny giggled. "I know what you mean, but what do you expect? You think my nana is going to let me keep a boy like he was a stray puppy? No way. Besides, she don't like strangers."

"But I'm not a stranger. I'm like you. Does she know about you?"

"She knows about me. She used to train me."

"Then," Blake pleaded, "maybe she'll like me. Maybe she can train me even. I can stay here in this shed even. I don't mind."

"She won't trust you enough to let you stay here."

"Why not?"

"For one thing, you're what, about seventeen, eighteen? And worse yet, you're a boy. She'll never want a boy as..." she had to stop herself and regroup her thoughts, "that is, she'll never want a boy like you living here with us."

"You think I'm cute," he said, "you were going to say she'd never let a boy as cute as me stay here with you."

"Was not! I was going to say she'd never let a boy as young as you stay here. She could get in trouble with the authorities."

"It's okay," he said. "I know what you really meant. I heard you think it. Maybe you should try to hide your thoughts when I ask her if I can stay."

"You're crazy."

"Crazy, but cute. I can be pretty persuasive when I want to be."

"You better not pull any funny stuff on my nana, or I might have to fry you. And when I kill people, they don't wake up like it was just a dream."

A shiver ran up Blake's spine. He wondered if he would ever be able to match her.

Hughes used hand signals to tell Johnson to pull the boat up alongside a large cypress tree. The tree was tall and firm, growing straight out of the water. More hand signals told Gomez to shimmy up the tree and take a look. Gomez balanced himself on the edge of the boat and tossed a large belt around the tree. He caught the belt as it swung back around to him, and swiftly began climbing up the smooth trunk. The boat rocked a bit as Gomez transferred his weight onto the tree. He reached the first limb, about thirty feet up, and let the belt hang from his waist, and climbed up three more limbs, then whipped his leg over the limb and steadied himself, straddling the branch. He pulled field glasses from a pocket on his pant leg and scanned the horizon.

He clicked a button on his headset and whispered into the mic, "I see four structures, a house and three smaller buildings that could be chicken coops, or maybe some kind of a shed. There's smoke coming from the house."

Hughes whispered back, "Look for movement. The kid's moving roughly northwest."

"Roger that. The vicinity is obscured by the trees, but I can see the kid's boat tied to the dock. Wait a sec, I saw something." Gomez zoomed the glasses in on the house. "Got him. It's your boy. He looks fine. He's with a girl; kinda good-looking if you ask me. They're going inside the big building. I'd say he looks fine."

"Good, send down a rope." Hughes turned to Brian and asked, "Can you reach that silver bag? The one with the orange tape on it?"

Brian reached down and picked up the bag for Hughes.

"Great," Hughes said, "if you don't mind, can you pull the dish out and attach it to the rope he sends down?"

Brian opened the bag and removed the contents. "A satellite dish?"

"No, but it looks pretty much the same. This one's for audio. We should be close enough to pick up some of their conversations from here."

Brian found a hook on the end of Gomez's rope and attached it to the eyelet on the back of the dish, and watched it rise up above them. Gomez pulled the dish up and strapped its belts around the tree trunk, aiming it in the general direction of the house. He plugged his phones into the base and fiddled with the aim until he heard a metallic clank followed by a thunk. He kept the dish steady until he could make out some voices.

"But, Nana, he's like us."

"We don't know nuthin' about this boy. He showed up here outta the clear blue and says he be one of us?"

Hughes gave Gomez a thumbs up, and Gomez shimmied back down the tree and into the boat. Hughes reverted back to the hand signals and told Johnson to turn the boat around and put some more distance between them and the cabin.

Brian was confused. "We're not going in?"

"The boy doesn't appear to be in any immediate danger. You sent him in to infiltrate them and he's doing that. We can monitor what's going on from a safer distance; that is, far enough we don't have to whisper and tiptoe around."

Brian nodded his understanding.

***

"Oh, Nana! When are you going to learn to trust me? I'm not a little girl anymore. I've grown up! I'm old enough to make my own decisions."

"You might be growed, buy you ain't full growed yet. When you is a bit older, you'll see how it be, but for now, you just has to trust me a bit longer."

"Trust you? Let you choose my friends? Let you run my life just because yours didn't turn out so good? I bet your momma asked you to trust her too when you ran away from home."

Michelle was stunned. Destiny had never spoken to her in such a tone before. She was stung by what she heard. She walked slowly to her most comfortable, overstuffed chair and sank into it. Her eyes were wet, on the verge of creating tears. "So, you think my life is not so good? That must mean your life is not so good, too. I try to make a good home for us. I tries teachin' you all the special things you needs to know. What was I thinking? You has all the answers, and I is just a miserable failure. How was I supposed to teach you anything?"

Tears formed small streaks down Destiny's cheeks. "I didn't mean you were a failure. You've been a wonderful nana to me. You're the only mother I ever knew. You raised me to be what I am."

"What be you then? What is you that can't listen and learn from me no more?"

"You raised me and I love you. I'm still the girl who will come to you for comfort and advice, but I'm also the witch you never were. You'll never know what I see and feel around me. How can you ask me to ignore my own feelings?"

"Cherie, it's not your powers I question, it's your judgment, and that don't come from your high and mighty witch powers. I never was the witch you has become, but that ain't my failure, it be your great success. There ain't been a witch like you in hundreds, maybe thousands, of years. I'm so proud of you I could bust. But you is still a girl, and you thinks like one."

"That's the problem! You still think I'm a little girl! How can I listen to anything you say when you think you're talking to a ten-year-old?"

Michelle couldn't hold back the tears any longer. Her eyes overflowed, and she wiped the back of her hand across her face. "Very well then, if you can't listen to me, then you should at least consult an elder. I'll just cook and clean for you till you don't needs me no more."

Somewhere in the back of Destiny's mind, she knew the last statement was just to elicit guilt in her, but knowing this didn't ease the sting any. She stormed out of the house and ran up the pathway to a stand of trees where she could finish crying in private.

Blake had remained frozen at the table during the entire scene, but after Destiny's departure, he pushed himself from the table. "I guess I should get going."

"No." Michelle stood and went to the stove. "You stay. Sit down. Eat something. When she returns, we'll see what we do with you."

Destiny stood inside the hollowed out base of a large cypress tree. The tree had been there for as long as she could remember. Its base had been burned out by fire, creating a small cave, but the tree survived. As a little girl, she would play house in it, but now, she just wanted to hide her face in the shadowy corner furthest from the entrance.

It'd been years since she and her nana had disagreed so strongly about anything, and the guilt thing was working. Her nana had taken care of her since she was a baby. She used to cry for her mama, but her nana always saw her through the sad times. When she was sick, it was her nana that took care of her. Now, she was just tossing her nana aside. No! She couldn't think that! That was her nana talking. For whatever reason, her destiny was revealing itself to her, and her nana could not see it. She had to follow her own path, even if it meant going against her nana's wishes.

She stood stiff as a statue, with her back facing the entrance, as her mind reeled through her thoughts over and over. In her mind, she could hear her voice repeating the same arguments over and over. She stood there, in the darkness, transfixed by her thoughts, until a tiny sliver of light bouncing off a drop of morning dew caught her eye as it bounced around on the blackened inside of the tree. She stared at the bouncing light through her tears. She traced the sliver of light back to the dewdrop. It was a perfectly formed drop sitting on a broad cloverleaf. She thought she had never seen such a perfect clover leaf in her life. It was the most brilliant green color, and its leaves were broad and strong. Even when it was rustled by the breeze, it stood strong, thrusting its leaves up towards the sun. Destiny leaned in closer and the light flickered across her eyes.

"Oh, there you are!" Marvalaine exclaimed. "Where have you been? I've been looking for you for days. I've even tried to summon you, but I guess I haven't quite worked out how that works yet."

Destiny blinked her eyes to clear the vision of the clover and looked up to see him pacing and prancing. He was in the private courtyard, a small garden where only family, very close friends, and staff were allowed.

"Get up, get up, you needn't bow to me."

She stood up and straightened out her clothing. "I wasn't bowing to you. I was inspecting a flower, if you must know, and popped in here quite by accident."

"Accident?" he asked. "No, it was no accident. You came here because it is where you are needed the most. I require your assistance."

"I really don't have time. I need to consult an elder about a rather important problem plaguing my own life."

"Nonsense," he said, "that will wait. You created this problem, and you must help me sort it out."

"What problem have I created for you?"

He continued to pace and wave his arms about wildly. "Well, for one thing, because of you, I am now being hunted by two very skillful trackers. I don't think I can continue to elude them much longer."

"What? What do I have to do with hunters? Do they mean to kill you?"

"Most definitely," he said, "they mean to be my total demise."

"Both of them?"

"Yes, both of them. Now, what are you going to do?"

"What am I going to do?" Destiny asked. "First, you tell me who they are and how this is any of my doing."

"Phoebe and Melody, of course! You set them on me like hounds on game."

Destiny burst out laughing. She tried to speak, but could get nothing intelligible out of her mouth until her laughter died down. "Melody and Phoebe are the hunters who mean to kill you?"

"Do not laugh! This is serious! You must help me!"

"How can I help you? What do you expect me to do? Protect you from them? Kill them first?"

"Would you?" he asked. "No, no, I don't want them dead. Just help me choose."

"Choose? You want me to help you choose between them?"

"Precisely! Help me choose between them."

Destiny found a bench and seated herself. "How is that going to help you? If you choose Melody, won't Phoebe hunt you down and kill you?"

"No. They have both agreed to honor my decision."

"How sporting of them. So, how do you feel about them? Which do you like?"

"I don't know. I like them both, but I don't think I want either of them."

"Let's start with Phoebe."

Marvalaine sat down next to Destiny. "Phoebe is an incredible woman. No doubt she will make some man very happy. In fact, she has promised to pleasure me in ways that no man has ever been pleasured by a woman before."

"And how do you feel about that?"

"How would any man feel about that? But it seems to end there. Shouldn't there be something more to a marriage?"

Destiny laughed and said, "You mean besides goats and cows?"

"Now you jest me."

Destiny forced the smirk from her face. "Sorry, go on."

"Phoebe is certainly an attractive woman, and would make me the envy of many men."

"So, if she'll make you so happy, what's the problem?"

"I never said she'd make me happy, neither did she. She said she'd pleasure me."

"Yeah," Destiny said, "I heard. Like no man before."

Marvalaine stood and paced again. "Only I suspect that other men have been pleasured thus before."

"I see, so what about Melody?"

"Melody is an intriguing woman. She is thoughtful and surprisingly intelligent."

"Weren't you looking for an intelligent woman?"

"Yes! I love intelligent women, but she's always fussing about fixing things her way. She constantly adjusts my hair and my collars, as if I couldn't dress myself."

Destiny giggled again.

"There you go again!"

"I'm sorry, but I've often wondered who dresses you."

"Why, you little…" Marvalaine lunged for Destiny, but she was too fast. She leaped from the bench and dashed around an elm tree. He chased her around the tree, followed her around a bench twice until he leaped over the bench, caught her, and pulled her down onto the well-manicured grass.

"How…dare…you?" she asked, her words broken into small syllables punctuated by her laughter. She hit him lightly on the chest, but he held tight to her waist. "I don't know what those poor women see in you," she proclaimed. "You are just a common ruffian."

"Common?" he asked.

"A brute. You're a bully."

Destiny pushed him off of her and rolled to her right, but he rolled over and landed right back on top of her. "Did you say I was common?"

"I think you should do the right thing and tell both Melody and Phoebe that they are far too refined for the likes of you and should forget all about you."

He rolled off her and looked up at the sky. "I like that, but I don't think either of them are concerned about me. Phoebe believes she would gain a title so she can look down her nose at her friends, and Melody, well, I think Melody believes that she could one day acquire a country to rule."

"How ambitious."

"So you see, you must find some way to get me out of their hooks."

Destiny sat up and brushed the grass from her hair. "It's not for me to say. You must either marry one of them, or marry no one at all, and keep looking for someone else."

"But where am I to look? I've been all over the countryside looking for suitable girls."

"Then stop looking so hard. You're not buying a horse. You just want to find someone you like, preferably someone who likes you back."

He sat up and leaned towards her, staring deeply into her eyes. "How do I know if someone likes me?"

"Argh! Why are men so stupid?"

"You know about girls. You can talk to them. I can't tell the right one from the wrong one. You must find her for me!"

She jumped back up on her feet. She turned to face him, but walked backwards away from him. "I won't do it! You must find your own path. You need to find the right girl for you, and you will. I have seen it. You will find her, and you will draw her to you, and when that day comes, YOU must choose what to do about her. Besides, I have my own problems to deal with."

"You've seen this?" he asked. "Now you can see the future?"

"Do you forget who you are talking to?"

He stood up and followed her. "Oh, you think so much of your abilities now?"

"No, but I don't need to look into the future to see your future."

"Ah, so you have seen it."

"I'm not saying anything more," Destiny said. "I've said too much already! You need to find her yourself."

"You must help me. It is your destiny."

"What is my destiny?"

"To guide people and set them on the right path. You are the chosen one."

Destiny stared at him blankly. His face was suddenly thoughtful. She had never seen him like this before.

"It's okay," he said. "You go home and deal with your problems. There is still time for you to help me choose. Others need your guidance now."

"But..." she objected.

"Shhh." He put his finger to her lips. "Never question your calling. You are what you are, and you will become what you will become. Nothing more, nothing less. You must go now."

Destiny's form shimmered into nothingness, and Marvalaine pressed the finger which he had held against her lips upon his own.

CHAPTER 18

The mood around the camp was mixed. They had located their target and were able to monitor the situation before they swooped in, but it was a gloomy spot to set up camp.

Hughes spent most of his time monitoring the listening device. Even though everything was recorded digitally, he didn't want to miss anything. Gomez was boiling some water for lunch while Johnson had strapped his knife to a stick and promised to return with some real meat.

Brian opened the box that had been shipped to him that morning. He pulled out the note that was on top and read it silently, then began sifting through the parts and pieces inside.

Hughes' interest was piqued. He pulled the headphones off for a moment. "More equipment? Anything good in there?"

"Possibly, but it would be hard to explain."

Hughes knew that Brian had been keeping secrets all along. They were hired knowing that, and he really didn't care. But he couldn't help himself from being curious. Normally, he would think secrets were about hiding some crime, or keeping someone's identity unknown, but they had just sent some young boy with no combat experience, or even training, into a potentially hostile environment. He'd seen Brian and Blake whispering between themselves, and knew there was something he didn't know, but he couldn't figure out what they had going on. Now, they had some kind of equipment that was shipped to them in a damn near secret location and it appeared to be some kind of ultra-new technology. He wasn't sure what to think. "You don't have to explain anything more than where to put it and what to look for if you want us to use it."

Brian pulled some pieces out of the box. They were spindly metal rods that looked to Hughes like UHF antennas. "Where to put it, would be up in the tree by the eavesdropper. It will transmit a Wi-Fi signal to the laptop. This disk needs to be installed. It will display a graph of how much radio energy it detects."

"I don't need to know your business, but I hope we're talking microwave and not radiation. We didn't pack any hazardous material suits for this trip."

Brian put his hands up and smiled his most reassuring smile. "Don't worry. It's not a radioactive zone. This equipment isn't a Geiger counter. It measures Alpha and Beta waves. My security chief thinks we can use it to determine if things get hostile, so we can go in and get the kid."

Hughes' bull meter told him that he still didn't have a straight answer, but he still didn't care. "Okay, fine."

"Look," Brian added, "I know you've had questions about how we found this place. And this stuff looks kind of weird, so I'll tell you what's up. You remember back in the cold war, how the soviets were experimenting with psychics to spy on other nations?"

"I remember. I think I remember them trying to find a way to make assassins who could kill psychically, too."

Brian put the gear back in the box, but carried the disk over to Hughes. "Exactly. They did a lot of experimenting with psychic powers. We did, too, only, we pretty much gave up on it."

"Yeah, better to stick with what's real."

"Don't blow it off, Hughes. It's real enough. It's just not as reliable as we would like. We didn't have their tolerance for unreliable technology."

Hughes accepted the disk and set it next to the laptop. "So, what are you saying? These are some escaped Russky psychics?"

"Something like that. And this equipment should detect if they are up to something."

"Good. Killing Russkies is something my men and I can get behind."

"Excellent! So, maybe we can put this detector up this afternoon after lunch."

Hughes put the headphones back on and returned to monitoring the audio, but his mind was still on their conversation. He pulled the phones off and turned back towards Brian and asked, "So, the boy is one of ours, then? That's how he found this place?"

"Yes. Blake is one of ours. He's very special, though. We believe he can hide his true allegiance from them and make them think he is one of them."

"And you think this equipment will help tell you what they are doing?"

"I honestly don't know how much it can tell us, but I doubt it can determine what they are up to, but it should tell us how hard they are trying."

Hughes nodded. He didn't have to understand. He was a doer, and this was something they could do. "Hey, Gomez, where's that lazy s-o-b partner of yours?"

"He's probably swimming to the general store to buy a fish to bring back and claim he caught it."

"I heard that." Johnson's voice came from behind Hughes. He was carrying two smallmouth bass in one hand and his makeshift spear in the other. "And Cap'n, please don't call us partners. You make it sound like we was domestic partners."

Hughes looked at Gomez slaving over the steaming pots, and Johnson carrying the fresh catch. "I'm sorry, Johnson. I don't know where I could have gotten that impression."

Brian had followed Hughes' eyes and laughed along with him.

Blake was still sitting at the table when Destiny returned. It was a most uncomfortable position for him. He sat at the table, under the stare of Michelle, eating the plate of potatoes and eggs. The food was quite good, and he was certainly hungry enough, but the tension hung on his fork like lead weights. He forced himself to eat, but as he came closer and closer to the end of the food on his plate, he ate slower and slower, until he was just pushing the remains of an onion around.

Despite their earlier argument, Michelle brightened considerably when her granddaughter returned. She immediately went to the stove and prepared a plate of food for Destiny, placing it on the table.

Destiny sat at the table. "Thank you, Nana." She started eating and gushed, "This is good! Really good!" She turned to Blake and said, "Isn't this really good?"

Blake was caught off guard, but caught up quick enough and responded, "Oh, yeah. Really good."

"You don't need to shine ma boots child, you knowed my cookin' since you was just a baby, but thank ye anyway. I'm glad you likes it."

"I love you, Nana. I always have, and I always will. And, I know you figured you'd have more time to train me before I left out on my own, but my destiny seems to have fallen in my lap already, and I'm the only one that can choose what path I take."

"I know, child, but I canst help worryin' about you. I'm just scared you gonna make a wrong turn on that path you be on and find yourself down a dead end."

Destiny was too busy eating to answer.

Michelle showed the pan to Destiny and asked, "You want some more?"

She nodded her head. "Yes'm."

Michelle scooped some more potatoes and onions onto Destiny's plate, then turned towards Blake. "How 'bout you?"

Blake nodded his head, looking a bit like a deer in the headlights. "Yes, ma'am, thank you."

Brian and Hughes sat staring at the laptop screen. A small, ripply line was on the bottom of the screen. It had the faintest undulations, barely visible, but made no significant movement.

Hughes clicked the talk button on his headset. "Gomez, you sure you hooked it up correctly?"

"Yes, sir. They didn't give us schematics, but the instructions were pretty clear."

"You might need to boost the signal."

"No can do, sir. The wireless signal is fine. Any adjustments would have to be made before the signal is converted to digital. The installation script doesn't specify those adjustments."

Hughes turned to Brian and shrugged his shoulders. "Maybe it just doesn't work. It looked like a prototype, and the instructions don't include any kind of diagnostic to see if it's operating correctly."

"Let's give it some more time," Brian said, "and see if it changes."

Destiny placed one of her nana's candles on the table in front of Blake. Michelle had her hands in the dishwater, but was mostly pretending to do the dishes. She saw Destiny take out one of her candles and saw where this was leading. She didn't approve of this at all, but bit her lip, preferring not to drive Destiny away.

Blake knew what Destiny had on her mind, but continued to play dumb and learn everything this girl knew.

Destiny placed her hand on the candle, holding the wick between her thumb and forefinger. The wick came to life, sputtering and dancing as the new flame warmed the kerosene infused wax.

"Stare into the flame." Destiny spoke slowly and in a low monotone voice, partially to create a calm, soothing atmosphere, but mostly because she was trying to remember how her nana had taken her on her first visit into the void. "Let the rest of the world fade from your sight until only the flame exists. See the flame as if it were inside of you. Imagine you are looking inwards behind your eyes, and it is there that you see the flame. Follow the flame. Let it guide you."

Destiny let the world slip away. She was in that strange place where she could hear voices from different places and different times. Blake was with her; she could sense him as if he were standing behind her. She listened for a familiar voice. She wanted to find Marvalaine, but she could not sense him anywhere. She tried calling out to him, hoping maybe she had some latent ability to summon him at will, but he did not materialize.

"Are we lost?"

She heard Blake's voice as clearly as if he had spoken out loud. "No," she replied, "not lost, but I can't find someone I wanted you to meet."

"I hear so many voices. Who are they?"

"Those are the voices of our ancestors. We should go meet some of them. Bear in mind that these voices are like echoes, and what you will see will be someone else's memory. It's like watching a movie, except you are one of the characters in the movie, but all you can do is watch and listen."

Like the trial, Blake thought to himself. He asked, "You mean we can't really talk to them?"

"No, not here. There are other places where we can talk to them."

Blake listened to the voices, some near, some far. "What should I do?"

"Pick out a voice you would like to meet and let it draw you in. Once you are in, you just need to observe and remember."

The voices swam around his head. Some of them were strong, others were soft. Some seemed to call him, as if aware of his presence, while others seemed to float along as if they were suspended in the surf, completely oblivious that they were there.

"How do you choose?" he asked. "I can't sense anything from them. Which voice will make me more powerful? How can I tell which is the best voice to listen to?"

Destiny thought the exploration of his ancestry would be exciting enough. His zeal to find the most powerful surprised her. She thought it might be insightful for him to ask such questions, but at the same time, it worried her that he would be seeking more power this way. "Don't you think this is an amazing opportunity to learn something about where you come from? Why would you be so focused on your own power?"

"Of course, you are correct." Blake immediately recognized that he had pushed too fast, and may have revealed himself to her. "Sorry, it's probably just a 'guy thing'. Bigger, stronger, you know?"

His explanation was plausible.

He continued, "I'll just pick one at random." But he didn't pick one at random. He picked a weak voice. It was a meek-sounding voice. It was a woman, crying.

<hr>

Blake focused on the weak woman's voice, but it was a loud, brawny voice that bellowed in his ears. "Stop your bawling. It's over for you. The sooner you accept it, the sooner you can just rollover and take what's coming to you."

Blake was stunned. His vision was blurry, and he felt like he was squinting, but through it all, he could make out the unmistakable form of a large man standing over a young woman. He held a slender rod in his hand, which he raised up over his head and brought down hard across the back of her head. Blake tried bringing his arms around to form a fireball to fling at the brute, but it was as if he had no control over his hands. In fact, they were bound and hanging from a hook over his head and his feet dangled off the ground. He felt his mouth forming words and incantations, completely without his awareness, but only a vain muffled sound came out. His mouth was gagged.

The brawny beast looked up from the whimpering woman and pointed a big meaty finger at Blake, "You can just wait yer turn. I'll be gettin' to you soon enough."

The poor woman on the floor below managed to spit out her gag, which had become loosened from the fierce whipping. She began muttering incantations. Her voice rang out surprisingly clear but short-lived. The monster standing over her thrust his arms out towards her. He locked his elbows and spread his fingers, then gathered them into two tight fists. "Oi! I told you there'd be no magic during this here interrogation, but you had to break the rules now, didn't ya?" Deep violet veins ran across the floor below the woman. They wove their way outwards, splitting into two branches here and there, until the woman was surrounded by a sparkling purple circle. Her body was surrounded with a faint yellow glow. She writhed around for a few seconds. She started to scream, but only for an instant before her voice went silent forever.

Blake had never seen anything so powerful. He was mesmerized. Clearly, he thought, he had only scratched the surface of magic with his puny fireballs and lightning. He was completely awed and thrilled by what he had just witnessed, until the interrogator turned and walked to him.

"Ain't you just the prettiest little thing?" The man leaned in close. His breath was putrid. He put his hand on Blake's cheek. "I'll be knocking off for lunch now, but when I gets back, you an' me are going to have a go at it. I think we'll just have a real special time, you and me. Don't go nowhere now, darling."

When the man left the room, Blake could hear Destiny laughing to his left. He tried unsuccessfully snapping his head towards her. "What are you laughing at?" he cried. "Do you think this is funny?"

She stopped laughing long enough to answer, "No, this room is horrible, but your reaction was pretty funny."

"Stop laughing. This isn't funny at all. That creep plans to get all freaky with me, and I can't seem to do anything to stop him!"

"Of course not. This is just a memory. You can't change anything, just like it's not really you he was looking at. You've probably popped into one of your great-great-great-great-grandmother's."

Blake's host turned her head towards Destiny's, but Blake and Destiny saw each other. "So how come you are yourself?" he asked.

"I'm not. I'm probably in some other witch's body too, but I guess you and I can see each other, just like we can talk to each other."

"I see. So we're just watching. We don't really feel anything, we just watch and listen."

"Not exactly," she said. "We get to feel all their stuff, too. Did you smell that guy?"

Blake didn't like that answer and tried vainly to will himself out of this situation. "So, how do we get out of here?"

"We just ride it out till it comes to an end, kind of like a movie."

"Don't tell me that. This guy's coming back to have his way with this chick, and you're telling me I have to feel all of it? Why'd you bring me here?"

"First of all," she said flatly, "you chose this one. Bad choice. Second, I think you should be more concerned about the torture and the killing than the other stuff."

"Easy for you to say."

"I'm also hoping that when you get to the end of your memory, it end's for me too, and I don't have to wait for my own ending."

"Hey, boss, look at this." Hughes was pointing at the monitor. A wavy line wriggled across the screen. It wasn't a sine wave; it rippled up and down in irregular ways. A window had popped up on the screen with the inscription, "*Signal Detected...Please wait for lock.*"

Brian glanced at the screen, then ran his finger down the single page instruction that came with the equipment. "It's supposed to identify some parameters about the signal's strength and frequency. The theory is that we might be able to jam those frequencies when we go in, but that's never been tested."

"So, you think we can jam their brain waves?"

"Not exactly. We just don't want their brain waves to escape out of their heads."

Hughes just nodded his head, still not sure how much he believed in this stuff, but certain that he wished none of it were true. He'd prefer living in a world of physical power rather than mental power.

The message on the screen changed. *"Unable to lock on signal."* Four buttons appeared on the window below the message: *"Save"*, *"Apply Fourier Transforms"*, *"Ignore"*, and *"Cancel"*.

Brian was thumbing through the instructions. "Hmmm, save just stores the signal to process off site. Ignore and cancel are pretty self-explanatory, but this transform thing only says it will apply some kind of mathematical analysis."

"I've heard of these before," Hughes said. "I don't know what they are, but I think the signal corps engineers called them their best friend. I have no idea how they work, but those guys swear by them. They used them for all kinds of signal processing. I got the impression that they could use them to separate two signals, like when they were breaking encryption schemes."

Brian glided the mouse across the small box the computer sat on and clicked the transform button. The screen responded, *"Fourier analysis will try to demodulate two or more overlapping signals. This may take several hours. Are you sure?"* The two men looked at each other and shrugged their shoulders.

"What the hell." Brian clicked the continue button and sat back, watching. Nothing happened on the screen. "Well, I guess we wait now."

Blake couldn't stop thinking about what he had seen. As terrified as he was about that guy's return, he couldn't help admire his power. The ground was still glowing, long after he had left the room, when Destiny had spotted some movement on the floor.

"Blake, did you see that?"

"Yeah, what kind of magic was that? Can you do that?"

Destiny was watching a wispy form rise from the witch's remains. "I don't think that's magic. I think that's the witch's spirit."

Blake refocused his eyes and saw the thin, transparent image of the dead girl rise from her pale corpse. "Woah," he said, "even if it isn't magic, it sure is pretty cool."

The girl's figure looked at them hanging on the wall, then knelt at the spot where she had died and bowed her head.

"What's she doing now?" Blake asked.

Even though she didn't believe their conversation used real voices, Destiny lowered her voice to a whisper, out of respect for the dead witch. "I think she's praying."

"I know that, but why? She's dead already. Is she doing some kind of resurrection spell?"

Even though she could not control the behavior of the body she inhabited, Destiny rolled her eyes on the inside and bowed her head. "Honestly, are you going to tell me that stupidity and rudeness is a 'guy thing' too?"

"Well, yeah. At least, that's what most women think."

Destiny remained silent.

"What did that guy do? I mean, how did he kill her? What kind of magic was that? Can you do that? Can you teach it to me?"

"Shhhh."

"What? I thought you said it was just a memory? They can't hear us."

"I said shhhh!"

"Look, I'm the one facing unspeakable torture, and worse! You said yourself that I should learn something from these memories."

"Then learn some respect and keep quiet."

Blake gave up and remained quiet, not out of respect, but because she clearly was not going to answer him. Well, if she wasn't going to help him, he'll have to help himself. He had plenty of experience invading his classmate's minds and learning what they failed to learn, and that didn't require free hands like fireballs. He'd just apply the same techniques to their captor and pick his brain a bit.

He didn't have to wait long. The far door opened and the big beefy guy entered the room. The ghostly figure in the center of the room stood up, facing him. She gracefully swung her arms up into the air, holding them in a V formation with her palms facing upward, and her fingers pointed like a ballerina's. As she stood over her body, she tilted her head upwards and vaguely focused her eyes somewhere beyond the ceiling. A faint green mist wrapped around her remains, and then was absorbed into her corpse until it disappeared completely. Blake wasn't waiting for what came next. He closed his eyes and focused on his captor.

The sounds of the room changed, and when Blake opened his eyes, he was looking at himself from across the room. He didn't really hear the brutal wizard's thoughts, but he could feel his passion. He didn't feel the passion of a man staring at a beautiful woman, but rather, it was the surging brutality of an animal wanting to tear another living being apart piece by piece. Calling it an animal is probably unfair, because animals would not feel the pleasure from the sheer destruction of a life. He took a few lumbering steps towards Blake and said, "Soon, my dear, soon." He turned around and picked up the corpse from the floor, easily flinging it over his shoulder. He took three steps towards the door and the room began spinning around Blake.

Blake knew immediately what was happening. He could feel his stomach knotting up and his throat tightening. The big brute threw the lifeless body to the floor. He raised his arms into the air, arched his head back, and let out a horrific scream. He flung his arms downwards, towards the witch's remains. Silver blades of light shot from his hands into her body. Thousands and thousands of blades pierced, punctured, and lacerated her remains.

Blake was ecstatic. He was in his mind. He should be able to sense the spell. He searched his mind, but could only pick up guttural growls. He found no sign that there was ever any sort of thought or reason anywhere in that mind. He felt the anger and hatred, and he felt an undeniably wonderful sensation when the blades minced the body into little pieces. He couldn't imagine how such an unorganized and chaotic mind could possibly focus enough attention to cast such fabulously powerful magic. He might as well try reading a chimpanzee's mind for all the intelligence he found there. He retreated out of his mind, back to hanging from the hook.

A misty green cloud leaked now from the perforated flesh. The great brute stood back, keeping clear of the escaping green cloud. "Clever witches." He then turned and stared directly into Blake's eyes. "But not quite clever enough, eh?" A maniacal laugh bellowed from deep inside his enormous girth, "I guess you'll have to wait yer turn whilst I get this green goo out of me system. Don't go nowheres lover, I knows yer dying to see wot I got fer yeh." He laughed again as he headed towards the door, then turned once more to Blake and said, "Behaves yerself." He passed his hand in the air and Blake was hit with a purple light before blacking out.

Brian sat cross-legged on the ground, staring at the computer screen. There was no indication of how long the analysis would take. Hughes set a fresh cup of coffee on the log Brian was using as a table for the computer and said, "Here, time to give your eyes a rest."

Brian blinked and focused on the cup. "Thanks."

Hughes settled down on a log behind Brian and asked, "Any change?"

Brian sipped the coffee. "Every now and then, two of the waves seem to come into focus, but then they always slip back into a mass of squiggly lines."

"How long is it supposed to take?"

Brian turned away from the computer screen so he could face Hughes. He unfurled his stiff legs and pulled himself up against a tree. "I don't know. I'm not even sure how many waves there are going to be."

Hughes studied Brian for a moment. He could see that he was dead serious in what he was doing. Hughes never really believed in anything that much, at least nothing he couldn't see or touch. "You really believe in all this stuff. This psychic power stuff, I mean."

"Yes, I do. My parents did. I guess I can't help it. Besides, look for yourself. We're tracking something."

"Sure," Hughes said, "we're tracking something, but who knows what that is? Could be some alligator tagged by fish and game, or a communications tower bouncing signals across this God-forsaken swamp."

"So, you think that if we randomly aimed our antenna somewhere else, we're likely to get multiple readings wherever we point it?"

"I don't know, but that's not a bad idea, for a test, I mean."

Brian didn't think that would be necessary, but he thought about it, anyway. "I don't share your skepticism, but I agree. We can call it our control group, but not yet."

Hughes was already nodding his head. "Yeah, better let this job finish first. If the control group is empty, or even just noise, we'll want to know which frequencies to tune back to."

Brian was impressed. In his world, there wasn't much room for open-minded people. Their belief in magic and the old ways was largely based on faith, like any religion. Hughes was a non-believer and was willing to wait for the current test to complete.

A young, squeaky voice pierced Blake's brain, whining, "Is this how the great Hogur questions his prisoners? He snores until they spill their guts just to get some peace and quiet?"

Blake snapped out of his slumber and turned towards the voice that had sliced so cleanly into his sleep. He saw two figures, a boy who glared upon him contemptuously, and a man of some years who rolled his eyes at the young boy's remark.

"Quiet, son," the elder man said. "Hogur has been interrogating witches since before I was born. He is the greatest interrogator there has ever been."

"Look at him, Father. He barely knows where he is. I've seen wharf rats with more life behind their eyes."

"He's old, son, and deserves our respect many times over."

"So," the boy sneered, "we'll show our respect and put flowers on his grave, which is where he should be, from the looks of him."

"That's enough." A flash lit the room as the father struck his son in the back of the head with a static bolt.

The son spun around and poised menacingly at his father. "Do not presume to treat me as a common child!"

"Then do not act like one!"

Hogur cleared his throat and asked, "Can I help you?"

"I very much doubt it!" the young one quickly responded. "We came to check on your progress, only to find you asleep without having even begun your investigation!"

Blake wasn't sure what the young brat was referring to, but he didn't like the boy's tone and was ready to respond when he heard the words form in his mouth, "What makes you think I haven't begun the interrogation?"

"Look at her, not a scratch on her!"

"Ah," Hogur said, "I see. I suppose you think you could do better?"

"Of course I could! You've done nothing! A dung beetle could do better!"

Blake's host chuckled. "So, you must think yourself as good as a dung beetle. Fancy that."

"How dare you! I compare you to a dung beetle!"

"Frank, my friend," Hogur said, "your son here seems quite well spoken and sure of himself. Perhaps the elders should send him to the front so he could sling insults at the witches. I'm quite sure he could win the war for us."

"Father! You let him speak to us that way? He insults me and speaks to you as an equal."

The father sighed, feeling fully the disappointment that was his son. "No, son, he doesn't speak to me as an equal. He speaks to me as a friend."

The boy was indignant and on the verge of rage. "Well, he's not my friend. I don't like the help speaking to me that way."

"Judging from the way you spoke to him, I would not expect him to be your friend. Besides, I thought his remarks rather humorous, and you were most deserving of them."

"But you are the King, and I am a Prince; he must not be allowed to trivialize us!"

Frank sat down next to Hogur so he could speak to his son, eye to eye. "Just because I am king does not mean I am his equal. In here, he is my master."

"If he is such a master, then why hasn't he even begun the interrogation? He's had the girl since yesterday and I don't see a mark on her!"

"He is the master, son, and you don't see a mark on her because you are a petulant child who doesn't understand what it means to be a master."

"Why hasn't he begun the interrogation yet?"

The father exhaled slowly, shaking his head. His eyes wetted with disappointment while he said, "Let me speak plainly for you. His technique doesn't make marks on the subjects. You would know this if you didn't believe you already knew everything from birth. Let me speak plainly some more. You are my son, and therefore a Prince, and I will always love you, but it is clear to me that you will never rule. I will never put the future of our people in your hands. Was that clear enough? You may be my son, but you will never be my heir."

The boy glowered at his father, but did nothing.

The King turned to Blake, recomposed himself and asked, "So, tell me, Hogur, have you learned anything yet?"

Hogur cleared his throat and said, "Nothing tactical, I'm afraid, but it seems there is a new prophet among the witches. He believes that the great war will end with us victorious, but the price of our victory will be the loss of our powers; all of our powers, ours and theirs."

"Father, you can't believe this. The witches don't have the power to do this. They can't strip us of our abilities."

The King replied, "We don't know where our power originates, but already, I get reports that the range of our war spells is decreasing. Perhaps it's true that the witches have found a way to strip our magic from us."

"All the more reason," the boy said, trying to sound like the leader his father claimed he wasn't, "for us to step up our efforts and wipe out the witches, before they have stripped us completely."

The King sighed. "Maybe we should not be so hasty, young Prince, for that would run us full speed into the witch's prophecy. Winning the war could lose us our heritage." The King scratched his short, white beard. "I must find a way to save our magic. I need to convene a council to discuss this." He turned to Hogur and said, "Carry on, my old friend."

The two royals left the room, and Blake turned his attention to the young witch strapped to the table in the middle of the room. She turned her head and looked at him, eyes wide with fear. Only then did Blake recognize Destiny behind the gag, covered in a wild mane of hair. Even with her mouth gagged, he clearly heard her say, "So, you are one of them. How did you hide it from me? I can feel your kind from far away. Why did I not sense it in you?"

He was relieved that she knew. He wouldn't have to pretend any longer. He was about to respond when the room dissolved around him and whisked him off to somewhere else.

CHAPTER 19

The message on the screen was short and sweet, "*ANALYSIS COMPLETE*". The window showed three different waves; two rather large waves dominated the screen and displayed continuous activity, while a third smaller wave remained relatively inactive. A legend under the graph read: *three signals detected*. Brian clicked on the save button, turned to Hughes, and nodded his head.

Hughes found Gomez and said, "Okay, you're on."

Gomez paddled the boat out to the tree and climbed up to the receiver package. He cut some tie straps and turned the antenna ninety degrees off axis. He clicked the talk button on his mic and said, "Okay, boss, how long you want it like this?"

The results on the screen were instantaneous. The screen went blank and a message read, "*No Signals*".

Hughes said, "Hang on a second. I don't think it will be long."

Brian was thumbing through the instructions. He held the page up for Hughes and pointed to a diagram.

Hughes said, "Gomez, there should be a small hole on the transmitter box with a triangle next to it."

"I see it."

"That should be the initial gain control. Insert a flat-head screwdriver and turn clockwise to boost the gain to the digital converters."

Some activity now showed on the scope, near the zero line. It could have been noise. Brian pointed his thumb up and Hughes said, "Boost the gain again."

"Okay, Cap'n, boosting to max."

The zero line showed some very limited activity, but it was barely readable. A small panel on the computer screen flickered, *"Signal Detected"*.

Brian pointed at the flickering panel. "It's detecting the same signals we had before. Maybe you were right after all. We're getting the same patterns, only they're farther away this time."

Hughes was pointing at the same panel. "No, I think you were right. Those are the exact same signals. They're lower power because we're only catching reflections." He engaged the mic again and said, "Gomez, point it back to the original target."

The signals were now loud and clear.

"Thanks, Gomez." Hughes said. "Dial the gain back half-way, strap it back in, and return to base."

———

Blake found himself running briskly through a sparse forest. A full moon overhead lit the world around him. Ahead of him, a young woman swayed seductively through the trees. His host followed her. He wasn't chasing her, they were running together. They were swift and silent. Occasionally she would turn slightly right or left, but always, they traveled in a generally southern course.

They broke free of the woods and across a meadow. A settlement could be seen atop a hill. A small castle overlooked the collection of thatch-roofed homes. A handful of goats and cows roamed freely around the village. Blake and the girl came up to the settlement, slipped through an alley, and down the main road to the castle. Nobody had noticed them until they had arrived at the large gate blocking their entrance to the castle.

They could almost knock on the door when a guard finally stopped them and barked out, "What are you doing here? Hold it now, what the hell are your kind doing here, anyway?"

The girl fell prostrate to the ground, holding up a basket she carried with her, and pleaded, "We seek an audience."

Blake fell next to the girl.

The guard asked, "Why should I let you in?"

"We come in peace and bear gifts."

The guard took the basket and poked about inside. "Don't mind if I do."

The girl asked, "You don't think he minds if you do?"

The guard looked at her warily. He was inclined to keep the basket and dispatch the two witches like the vermin he thought they were. "And what makes you think he even knows you're here?"

Blake's host asked, "You really think he doesn't know we are here?"

It was clear from the clatter coming from inside that he did indeed know, and had ordered someone to see what was going on this late at night. The gate swung open from the inside. "What's all the racket out here?"

The guard, whose back was conveniently turned to the gate, extracted his hands from the basket, and spun around to face the secretary at the gate. "They seek an audience." He thrust the basket towards the secretary. "They bring gifts."

"Who seeks an audience?" The secretary stepped out through the gateway and gasped, "My god, they're witches! Did you not notice they were witches?"

The guard stammered, "I did, sire. I was just questioning them to learn their intention."

"Who cares their intention?" the secretary bellowed. "We don't admit witches, we kill them!"

The guard bowed low and said, "They said they comes in peace. I thought it might be bad form to kill them that comes in the name of peace."

The secretary stepped around the guard and pointed at the girl. "You there! Witch! Why do you bother us?"

Destiny raised her head. Her voice quavered as she said, "We have important news. We wish an audience to share what we have learned."

The secretary said, "I can't grant you an audience without knowing what you wish to discuss."

Blake said, "We know why your people are losing their powers."

"What? That's preposterous," the secretary said. "We aren't losing our powers." He turned to the marshal of the guards who had arrived behind him. "Kill them. When you are through with them, discover their route and kill anyone they snuck past."

The marshal grunted and nodded his head.

Blake's host raised his hand. In it he held a rolled parchment. "Wait!" he shouted. "We bring a prophecy. You need us. Killing us will only hasten your own demise."

The secretary had not quite returned inside. He turned and saw Blake pleading for his life. "Why aren't they dead yet?"

The guard went to do his duty, but Blake continued, "What will your masters say when they learn you were presented with a prophecy to save magic for both our kinds? Only you killed the messengers?"

The marshal was clearly hesitant to continue.

The secretary grew more annoyed. "Why do you hesitate? Must I kill them myself?"

"No, Your Lordship."

"Then do it, and give me that scroll, and the basket."

Blake raised his voice so all could hear. "The prophecy says that if you extinguish all the witches, you will be stripped of all your magic and will be doomed to live mundane lives with the simple folk."

The secretary turned his back on them and said, "Idle threats from two pathetic witches."

The secretary waved his hand in the air, dismissing them, and the marshal nodded to the guard and it was over.

Destiny recognized when a memory changed. Her vision cleared, and she found herself focused on Marvalaine. She looked around the room, but Blake was nowhere in sight. "What are you doing here?"

Marvalaine was rummaging through a large trunk full of clothes. "I am trying on hats. I have a rather important speech to make and wanted just the right hat."

"No," she said, "I don't mean what are you doing. I want to know why we are here? Why am I here with you?"

"I live here. You are visiting me, remember?"

"Where's Blake? I was traveling through some memories with him."

Marvalaine continued digging through the trunk while he asked, "Who is this Blake? Should I know him? Is he your new trainer?"

"No," she said, "actually, I was training him, sort of. That was, at least, until I found out he was one of them."

Marvalaine pulled his head out of the trunk and straightened up. "Them?"

"Yeah," she said, "he's one of the bad witches."

Marvalaine chuckled. "They may not mind that you call them bad, but I don't think they like being called witches. They prefer you call them sorcerers and wizards."

Destiny threw her arms up in the air and screeched, "Who cares what we call them?"

"They care," he said. "Why were you training one of them, any-way?"

"I didn't know, of course. I thought he was one of us."

He pulled a tall purple hat that rose to a point and tried it on. "Does this make me look taller?" He threw the hat back in the chest and asked, "You couldn't tell he was one of them? Can't you sense when they are around?"

"I thought I could, but he was different. I thought he was one of us, but then he jumped into a memory of them. That's how I knew. They were his ancestors."

"Did he have any other memories?"

Destiny sat down on a cushion. "Yes, but he was a witch in those. That's why it is so confusing."

"Why is it confusing to you? Clearly, he must be descended from both lines."

Destiny bit her lip. She wasn't sure why she didn't trust him. "Well, I think he knew it all along and hid it from me. I suspect his loyalties are with them."

"Has he killed you yet?"

"No, of course not."

Marvalaine stopped rummaging and sat next to Destiny. "Then perhaps he is not so loyal after all. Enough talk about him. On your last visit, you said I had to do something to find my mate. Is there any more you can tell me about her?"

Blake's vision swirled around him. The entrance to the castle
faded out of view and was replaced with the view of an open field.
At first, he thought it was overcast, but he came to realize that
it was smoke that blotted out so much of the sun. It wasn't dark
as night, but the sun, hidden behind the smoke, was little more
than an orange glow in the sky.

Blake crouched behind a large boulder on the south side of the
field. He had a clear view all around him, and he continued to
scan the area ahead of him. The field was mostly dirt. What little
vegetation was there had long ago been flattened. Blake didn't
know why the field was so much concern to his host, but he could
feel the tension as he checked and rechecked the ground around
him. His curiosity was satisfied when he saw a ripple in the
ground. It was barely more than a slight distortion of the field,
but he felt his host spring to action. He blasted all manner of destruction towards the sliver of distortion. He sent fireballs right
and left of the spot and lined up a powerful bolt of lightning down
the middle. Blake was thrilled by the fireballs that now issued
from his hands. Nothing in his experience compared to releasing
those fireballs. Much more than the fireballs he had ever let
loose. These came with a magnificent sensation of satisfaction.
It was an overwhelming physical sensation unlike anything he
had ever experienced before. It felt so good, he wanted more. The
lightning left his fingertips tingling. His heart seemed to stop
with the exquisite pleasure of sending that bolt.

Once struck, the targeted distortion turned into a man. He waved his arms and took a defiant stance. Blake felt a horrible sadness grip him. He wanted to fall to his knees sobbing, but his host did not. He could feel his host fighting against the sadness, and focus a fireball inside the man he faced. The man erupted in flames from the inside and quickly burst into cinders. It was better than the fireballs and the lightning combined. This was what magic was all about. His new goal in life was to learn how to recapture those feelings.

The field spun around him and disappeared. Blake found himself in what appeared to be a small stable. He saw wooden stalls with gates and hay scattered around the floor. He did not know how, but he could sense that time had advanced since his previous vision.

Blake heard a horse stamping in a nearby stall. He couldn't see the beast, but he could sense its anxiety. Someone had entered the barn. Blake couldn't see or hear anyone, but he knew the horse could. Maybe it was the intruder's smell, but the horse was getting quite agitated. The shadowy figure entered the barn and hid in the stall opposite the horse. The horse was frantic now, kicking the stall door and spinning around in circles, bucking and kicking its rear legs.

A young girl entered the barn. "Easy, Snowball," she said. "What's the matter, girl?" Snowball reared up on her hind legs. Her eyes were wide with fright and her nostrils flared. She stood on her hind legs as if shadow-boxing with her front hooves.

Having heard Snowball's warning, the girl spun around and faced the other stall and commanded, "Who is there? Show yourself!"

She already knew the answer, and she had already called out, in her mind, for help. Even before her mother answered her call, the hounds were already running full speed. Blake could feel his host ready to leap from the stall, but hesitated, preferring to pounce simultaneously with the dog's arrival.

A weak, sinister voice came from the stall. "No need to be afraid of me, little girl. I'm too old and tired to be a danger to you. I was just looking for someplace to curl up for the night. I didn't know anyone would be here. I'll just be going on my way."

The girl unlocked Snowball's gate. The white horse streaked out of the gate and poised to pounce on anything leaving the stall. Blake's host decided to wait no longer, and jumped out of the stall, facing in the intruder's direction. The hounds arrived a moment later. One of them took an immediate stance outside the stall gate, while the other took an interest in Blake, but then, deciding he was not an enemy, joined the other dog at the gate.

"Show yourself," the girl commanded, "and don't try anything. I'm not alone out here."

"I can sense that, miss." He cracked the gate open and held his hands outside the gate. "As you can see, I am unarmed."

Three goats scrambled into the barn and took positions behind the dogs. The girl's mother arrived seconds later. She took a position in front of the girl. "Go back to the house, Kate."

"But, Mother," the girl pleaded, "I was handling this."

"You did fine, but it's time for me to take over now."

"Aw, mom, you know Snowball wouldn't let anything happen to me."

"I see that," the mother said, "and you have Jericho and Dusty, plus the three goats. Quite an impressive little army."

"And I have that nice man over there."

The mother pointed at Blake and said, "That man over there is why mommy wants to talk to this bad man over here. If you aren't going to leave, then at least stand back behind mommy, okay?"

"Yes, Mother." The young girl stood directly behind her mother, but could see from the look on her face that it was not far enough, so she backed up another five paces. The hounds remained behind the mother, and the goats gathered in around Kate.

The mother turned her attention to Blake. "I assume he was chasing you?"

"Yes, ma'am."

"And you led him here? Couldn't you tell there were children here?"

"No, ma'am," Blake's host said. "I apologize for that, but when I saw the barn, I only sensed a horse inside. I didn't even know we had people here."

"What does he want with you?"

"I was being held prisoner, ma'am. I managed to cloud one of the guard's minds and escaped. He was just trying to get me back."

"What do you know about him?"

"Not much," Blake answered. "He's a nobody, a lackey they send out on errands."

She turned to the shadow in the back of the stall. "Come out now."

"No, I don't think I will," said the squeaky voice from the stall.

"Come now," the mother said softly, "let us get a look at you."

"So you can kill me? I don't think so."

"If I were going to kill you, don't you think I would just step in and do so?"

"Your point is well made. If you could kill me, you would have done it already. All the same, I think I'll stay right here."

She waved her hands over the dogs. They glowed now with a protective seal. "Perhaps my hounds can convince you to come out, then."

The dogs entered the pen and growled menacingly. The shadowy figure emerged with his hands held high. "Okay, okay, I didn't do nothing to them. You see? I'm not such a bad guy!"

She eyed him up and down. He had no weapons and was, as Blake had described, just a lackey. "Kate, you can join us now."

The young girl pulled up beside her mother, and held one of her mother's hands, and one of Blake's. Blake held the mother's other hand, forming a circle around the intruder. Blake and the young girl could hear her mother's plan in their minds. They focused on what she said, and together, they made it so. "The man you are chasing has turned himself into a magnificent owl." An owl flew down from the rafters and sat on Blake's shoulder. "You can never return home without him. You must catch him. You must follow him to the end of the Earth and catch him. You cannot live without him. Nothing can ever distract you from your mission."

The owl flew through the barn door and perched on a post just outside. The man looked at the mother and said, "Begging your pardon, ma'am, but I have to go. He's getting away." She let go of her daughter's hand and motioned towards the door. The intruder shot out of the barn after it. The owl flew off and landed on a fence at the edge of the property.

"Kate, wash up for dinner." The mother turned to Blake and asked, "Would you like something to eat?"

Blake never heard the answer. The room dissolved around him. He carried with him a warm afterglow from the experience. His first impulse would have been to kill the man, but setting him on a new task was something he had never considered. He laughed at the absurdity of it all. He was sorry it ended so soon; he enjoyed the feeling and would have liked learning more from the mother.

Blake found himself crouching behind a boulder again, poised to attack a witch that was sparsely protected by a bush. He could feel a tight, tingling sensation in his brain. The witch was trying to enter his mind.

"Just what do you think you're doing?" his host asked. "Do you really think your feeble attempts to control my mind could ever succeed? You're pathetic! I should blast you on the spot just to save your people from the embarrassment of your failure, but I won't. Just stop your probes and come on out from behind that bush, and I will let you live. I have some questions for you, but I'm really far too tired to deal with all the paperwork required if I bring in a prisoner, so I'll just let you go."

The witch remained hidden behind the bush.

"Come on now," he continued. "I just want to go home and see my family. I'm sure you do, too." He put on his most reassuring smile and opened his hands in a gesture of peace.

His smile was captivating. The witch stood up and stepped around the bush. She stepped timidly toward him and said, "My name is Ilyana."

"That's a very beautiful name. My name is Bob." He waited for her to cover over half the distance to him. "But most people call me the Butcher." He reared back and blasted her with a variety of spells. Blake was unable to identify everything he had thrown at her. He recognized fire and lightning, but the array of multicolored clouds and light effects that emanated from the man's hands was mesmerizing. Blake thought the interrogator was powerful, but this man was far stronger. As before, Blake tried to retain what he could, hoping he could recall these powers when he returned to his time.

The girl glowed like a hot ember. Her body lifted up and hung in the air as if it had been placed on an invisible spike. The Butcher moved in on the girl and reached into her chest. His hand entered her as if she were smoke. He gripped his fingers around her heart, but before he could rip it out, he was frozen in place. He felt his mind surrounded by intruders piercing his skull like thin daggers. He was completely paralyzed. The girl disintegrated before him, not by his doing, and he was suddenly aware that she was never there. She was just a clever illusion, a decoy.

A large man lifted the Butcher's paralyzed body over his shoulder and headed off towards the far forest surrounded by witches.

Marvalaine was charming as ever, yet as much as Destiny had found herself attracted to him, she couldn't clear the image of Blake running amok through his ancestor's memories.

"You seem distracted." Marvalaine had selected a hat and was now adjusting the lay of his coat. "Perhaps you are thinking of him?"

"Him?" she asked. "Oh, you mean Blake? Yes, I guess I was thinking of him."

"I thought you didn't like him. I thought he was one of them."

She nodded. "He is one of them..."

"Yet," he said, "you devote so much of your thoughts to him, you must see something in him."

"In him? No! It's not like that. It's just that I..."

"Why do you help him, then?"

"Help him?" she asked. "I didn't say I was helping him."

He sat down on a cushion next to her and said, "I just assumed."

"Well, don't assume, you know what they say..."

"I know, I know. I know something else, too. He likes you. You do know that, don't you?"

"What? Him?" Her face blanched. "Why should I care? He is one of them. Or did you forget?"

He took her hand in his. "I trust your judgment. If you see something in him, he may not be all bad."

"He's not all bad. It's hard to explain."

"Maybe he's not really one of them, but just with them."

"What difference would that make?" she asked. "He's either with us or he's against us. And if he's against us, I may have to stop him."

Marvalaine arched his eyebrows and cocked his head. "And yet you help him now."

"It's no big deal. I only showed him his ancestral memories."

"How is that possible? They are not able to contact their memories, only the witches can do that. Perhaps he's really a witch?"

"But I've seen him use fire and lightning."

Marvalaine chuckled. "Do you not see the irony in your own words? You can do fire and lightning, too."

"Sure," she said, "but I'm special. Wait, that didn't sound right. I'm a unique case; you know what I mean. Besides, I learned them from you!"

"We are rare, for certain, but we are not entirely unique. It would seem that he might be like us. Perhaps you should work to ally him with you. You would make a formidable team if you could turn him from their way of thinking."

Destiny contorted her face as if that were the most disgusting thing he could have suggested, but inside, she thought it was a wonderful idea. She thought of how much easier two people could deal with the evil society of sorcerers. She most certainly did not think, would not allow herself to even consider, how cute she thought Blake was, and how nice it would be to have him at her side. She did not think about that, or so she told herself.

"Now," Marvalaine said, "about this woman I am supposed to find."

"I've told you too much already. You'll have to set your own traps for her."

Blake remained frozen in the Butcher's memory, who was himself paralyzed, nearly head to toe. His eyes remained functional, as did part of his brain. He scanned the scene around him. There was a large circle of witches, perhaps thirty or more, all focused on him. In the center of the circle was a roaring fire, but he was not placed upon the fire. He deduced their intention was to question him. He had always known that they might find a weakness in his attacks and eventually capture him, so he was prepared. He knew nothing of consequence and kept it that way. No matter how much the elders might want to keep him in their confidence, which was more for their vanity to consort with his celebrity than actually holding council with him, he refused to know any more than where and when they wanted him to be somewhere. The witches would be disappointed. He drew some comfort in that and considered it his last victory.

Blake could feel the witches enter the Butcher's mind. Individual witches entered and gripped different parts of his brain, like men would grip the arms and legs of a stronger captive. He could feel them slither around like snakes until they found a piece of his brain that had not yet been conquered. They would then wrap their power around that part of his brain, segregating it from the rest. He was defenseless and became even more so with each piece they captured.

A tall, thin man stepped forward from the circle of witches and faced the Butcher directly. His eyes were a clear, bright-blue color shadowed under wild salt and pepper eyebrows. His gaunt face was largely hidden behind a long, bushy beard. A white stripe, almost as wide as a hand, divided his faded black beard into two equal halves. His overall appearance was more of a wild man raised by wolves than that of a solicitor. He smiled menacingly at the Butcher and said, "So, you are the infamous Butcher."

Without need of signal from the interrogator, one of the witches relaxed her grip on part of his brain so he could respond. She was careful to only let him respond, and would instantly paralyze his mouth should he attempt an incantation.

Blake couldn't tell if he could hear the Butcher forming his reply in his head, or if he actually heard the spoken words return through the man's ears. He tried hiding in the unused recesses of the man's brain, like a child hiding in the back of a dark closet.

"Me?" the Butcher replied. "You think I'm the Butcher? Oh no. Not me. I'll grant you, I may have tried to impress a lass here and there by pretending to be the infamous scoundrel, but I'm just a harmless cobbler."

"So," the inquisitor said, his deep baritone voice remained calm and soothing, "you would have us believe that your attack on Ilyana was to impress a girl?"

"What? Who? Oh, do you refer to the ghost? I confess I have no love for ghosts. Vile creatures, if you ask me. And, as far as I know, there are no laws against hunting ghosts."

The witches continued to probe his brain, even while the inquisitor paced back and forth, questioning him. "A ghost, you say?"

"Ah, yes, I knew she was a spirit right off. I must admit, she had a very well formed corporeal body."

The inquisitor stopped pacing. His face looked like he had just eaten something very old, something he fully intended to spit out. "You're not what I expected. I am disappointed in you. Your sniveling cowardice is quite repulsive. Although your ability to lie in the face of defeat is not surprising, considering the spineless nature of your people. No matter, however, we know who you are, or should I say we know who you were. You say your name is Bob, and you are a lowly cobbler who is afraid of ghosts, so be it."

"I never said I was afraid of ghosts," Bob argued. "I just don't like them."

"Forgive me," the inquisitor said while he bowed low in feign apology, "consider it poetic license. Soon enough, you will fear ghosts, to the point of paranoia even. And, so you will never be lonely, you will see ghosts, whether they are there or not."

Blake could already feel it happening. Pieces of the Butcher's mind were being rewritten. Some pieces holding spell knowledge were completely destroyed, while others were modified, some slightly and some greatly. He could feel the fear build, as the man was rendered harmless, yet filled with an irrational fear of ghosts. It seemed a cruel fate for the man. They could have simply made him a cobbler, but Blake admired them for their cruelty, subtle as it was.

One of the witches approached the inquisitor and whispered something in his ear. The inquisitor nodded his head, glanced over at the Butcher, and stroked his beard, then abruptly closed the gap to the Butcher in two long strides. He leaned in close, face to face, staring eye ball to eye ball. "Leave us!" His blue eyes were so light, they looked almost white, until they turned grey and then faded into blackness.

CHAPTER 20

Blake's vision returned, and he was someone else. The Butcher was gone. The pale blue eyes, which had been staring so deeply into his own, were now replaced with eyes so black, the pupils were almost impossible to detect.

Blake's host shied away from the dark eyes, and he now stared at a weathered face that was as intimidating as his breath. "Your mother," the face said, "is worried about you, son. She tells me your friends don't take you with them on their hunts any more. Is that true?"

Blake felt his host quiver before croaking out his answer. "Father, it's no big deal."

The thin man with the dark black eyes stepped back and turned away as if to think, then turned back and asked, "No big deal? Your place in this world has less to do with your actions and more to do with those you associate with."

Blake felt the exasperation in his host's heart as clearly as he heard him say, "Those so-called friends aren't exactly the cream of the crop. They are mostly dull witted thugs who only know how to inflict pain."

The father turned to the boy; his face grew more stern. "Have they inflicted pain on you? Is that why you keep away from them? You should not allow this from them. This is most unacceptable."

"No, Father," Blake said, "they never did anything to me. They just are different from me."

"Of course they are different. You are a bright boy, a leader. You will be their superior one day."

"I don't think they see things that way. In their minds, the superior one is the one who can hit the hardest, or spit the farthest, or kill the most birds with a single spell. They don't respect intelligence."

"I see your point," the father said. "Boys their age haven't always learned their place in society. Perhaps you should rejoin them and assert yourself as their leader."

"No thanks," Blake replied. "I get nothing from them. They couldn't hold a conversation if you handed it to them contained in a sheep's bladder. I have no need for them."

The father's face turned soft and loving. He reached out and held his hand at the back of the boy's head. "But you do need them, son. A leader is nothing without followers. When it comes time for leaders to emerge, it is the ones with the most loyal followers that come out first."

The boy heaved a sigh of resignation, "Yes, sir. I suppose you are correct. I will find them and join them on some stupid crusade."

"That's a good boy. But, you must somehow treat them as if you were willing to follow them into battle, while never, ever treating them as if they are your equal."

<hr>

Hughes was a light sleeper, a desirable trait for a man of his profession. His eyes popped open and he cocked his head to the side. A small, low beep emanated from the computer. It was a low volume siren. He rolled over and crept to the screen. It displayed three sharp signals.

Brian had also heard the signal and was behind Hughes, looking over his shoulder. "What is it?"

The screen clearly displayed two larger busier signals, and a third, lower intensity one. Hughes shrugged and said, "Looks the same as it did before to me."

As Hughes was pointing at the screen, one of the active signals disappeared and it emitted the same low beep.

Neither man could hide the surprise from his face.

Brian sunk to his knees next to Hughes and muttered, "What the hell?"

The computer beeped again, and the third signal was back.

Hughes tapped the screen on the side like he would to a gas gauge. "Are they supposed to do that? The signals are strong, but it looks like one keeps flipping off and back on."

Brian was scratching his head. "Can't be that. Are you sure this thing is working correctly?"

"It's your gear," Hughes said. "We might be able to run a diagnostic on the transmitter and receiver, but if that was going to fail, I would think all three signals would be blinking off."

Brian just shrugged; he had no better ideas.

"This may take a while," Hughes said. "You might as well head back to sleep."

<hr>

After leaving Marvalaine, Destiny floated through the void, trying to locate Blake. Every time she tried focusing on any one memory, she felt herself being pulled to another. When she peered into the one pulling her, she saw only dark, gloomy despair. She tried pushing it out of her mind. She wanted to put distance between her and the despair, but try as she might, the gap closed, until finally the void was replaced with a grey haze that slowly focused before her.

She found herself in a room. It was a square room, only twelve feet on each side. The walls were grey and there were no windows, only a single door in the center of one wall. There was no furniture either, only women, all witches. Women of various sizes and ages filled the room. They stood shoulder to shoulder, vaguely facing the center of the room with their arms hung loosely at their sides. Every face wore the same deathly pallor. Gloom and despair permeated Destiny's every sense. It was morbidly quiet. She smelled death with every breath.

The door popped open, smacking one woman on the side and shoving her away. A man pushed in, grabbed the nearest girl, and pulled her out of the room. Her mouth formed an oval as if to scream, but no sound was heard. She lifted an arm to grip the doorway, but the man simply threw her out. Destiny heard her slam into the wall across the hallway, and then the door was closed and locked.

The women pulled together in the middle of the room and bowed their heads. Those who could pressed their heads together while others were satisfied with laying their heads on someone's shoulder. They breathed in unison as they joined their minds to search the world for a kind soul to save them. There was no other reaction from them, and eventually they drifted back to their original positions until the next woman was taken from them.

Still in the young boy's body, Blake bounded out the door into the bright sunlight. The father's voice still reverberated in his brain. Blake was confused over the boy's reaction. To Blake, the father's words were very reassuring, but he could feel the boy's humility, as if his father was berating him.

It was a long way from the house to the gate. Outside the gate, the boy skipped down the road. It was a well-cut dirt road surrounded with trees and hedges on both sides. The boy hummed a bit as he skipped. Blake wasn't sure why, but his mood had improved tremendously. In fact, the boy's mood was a bit contagious, and Blake found himself kind of happy inside without really knowing why.

He could see up ahead where the trees ended, and the sky opened up. Reaching the end of the lane, he quickly rounded the corner to the right and stopped dead in his tracks.

"RAWRRR!" was the sound from the large, brown, furry shape that stood before him. Blake's instincts told him to turn and run, but the boy didn't react at all. He waved his hand and said, "Hi, Roofy; hi, Artie."

"Aw man!" Artie, the smaller of the two, unwrapped the bearskin that he held. He looked down from where he stood on top of Roofy's shoulders and asked, "Weren't you even scared a little bit?"

"Not really," Blake said. "Well, maybe just a little bit. I was kinda scared I might crash into you and come out smelling as bad as that nasty old rug."

Roofy could not control himself. He burst out laughing and started shaking all over.

"Roofy!" Artie yelled. "Stop that!" Still perched atop Roofy's shoulders, Artie tried keeping his balance, but ultimately ended up falling over backwards.

Blake's host joined Roofy and laughed until tears filled his eyes.

"I'm okay," Artie said. "If anyone still cares, my head broke my fall."

That was too much for Roofy; he fell to the ground in a laughing fit.

Artie got up off the ground, brushed the dust out of his hair, and asked, "Hey, Billy, watcha doin?"

"Looking for you guys, actually. You wanna play stones?"

"Nah," Artie said, "stones makes my head hurt."

Roofy, who had barely stopped laughing enough to get back on his feet, said, "But playing bear makes your head hurt, too."

Roofy started to laugh again, but Artie balled up a fist and punched him in the arm. "Oh, yeah?" he said. "Well, not when you do it right!"

Billy didn't really expect them to play stones. It was a thinking man's game. "Then if not stones," he asked, "you wanna go down to the shore and pull sea urchins out of the rocks?"

Roofy made it to his feet. "That sounds good to me, but I don't think Artie wants to go."

Billy asked, "Why not, Artie?"

"Nothin'," Artie said, "I just don't think it's much fun."

Roofy said, "He means it wasn't fun last year when he got stung by one."

"I didn't get stung by one. I just don't like them."

"Did too!"

"Did not!"

"Well then, what do you call it?" Roofy asked.

"Nothin!" Artie bellowed. "I don't call it nothin!"

Roofy turned to tell Billy the story. "He was pulling the spines off of an urchin last year, but he dropped one of the spines in his chair and sat on it."

"That's it!" Artie said as he lunged for Roofy. "You're dead now!"

Even while Artie chased him around the road, Roofy finished the story. "Then he ran around crying and asking everybody to pull the thing out of his butt! It was hilarious."

Artie caught Roofy, but instead of hitting him, he yelled out, "Next time, I'll hit you double!"

"Fine," Billy conceded, "no sea urchins then."

Artie slumped his shoulders and said, "You never wanna do anything fun, Billy."

"Sure I do." Billy searched for the right answer. He couldn't say they just weren't smart enough to enjoy the same games. "I just think exploring stuff is more fun than pulling the stingers off of urchins."

"I have an idea," Artie said. "Let's go down to your father's lab and check out the prisoners."

Billy started to object, but then he thought, if his father saw him playing with these boys, he would be pleased. If he didn't like what they were doing, then maybe he would not want him to play with them anymore. "Sure," he said, "I suppose we can do that, but they don't like to call them prisoners; they're subjects."

"Whatever."

The witches in the small square room were motionless again. They sensed when the jailer approached to remove one, and only then would they break their formation. Destiny tried searching their faces and their minds, but her host wasn't very cooperative. She didn't understand where or even who she was, or who any of these witches were.

Any one of these witches should be able to reach out telepathically to their free comrades for help, but she could sense no such action from her host. They were linking together, bonding their minds, and they were doing nothing with the link. They were just feeling sad and humble together.

The door swung open, and three boys came in. The witches remained in formation. Two of the boys swiftly started walking the perimeter around the witches, inspecting them, while the third one hung out at the door. Destiny recognized Blake in the third boy by the door. She called to him, but he was more intent on what the other boys were doing.

The boys stopped and grabbed a young girl next to Destiny. They started to pull her out when Blake said, "No!" He had seen Destiny, and walked around to their position. "This one." He tugged on her wrists to lead her out of the room.

The two other boys looked at each other and shrugged their shoulders. They tied her wrists together and helped direct her out of the room.

<hr>

Brian was lying on his back staring up at the stars when Hughes came to him with the results of the signal analysis. "You know," Brian said, "the universe is an amazing place. And we, as humans, have not even tapped one billionth of its potential."

Hughes stopped for a moment and craned his head upwards. "Yeah, for everything we think we know, there are another billion things we know nothing about."

"Not to mention," Brian added, "that half the things we think we know get proved wrong at some point when we learn something different."

"Yeah? Well, here is something that I think we know. We aren't losing one of the signals. Two of the three signals we identified occasionally lock in phase with each other, making it look like a single signal."

Brian sat up. Two of them were doing something, probably together. He had no way of knowing if it was his kid with one of the witches, or if it was the two witches. If Blake was involved, he could not tell if it was cooperative or adversarial. In either case, Blake might need their help. "Let's move in. How soon can your men be prepared?"

"We can abandon the camp in thirty seconds, or we can pack in fifteen minutes."

"Packing is fine."

Brian started to gather his things when Hughes stopped him and said, "We have no reconnaissance, however, and don't know what terrain we are moving into. I'd recommend flanking the target on two sides, but we'd have to scout it first."

Brain asked, "How long would that take?"

"We can send Johnson in to recon while we break camp, and then when he reports, maybe add an additional fifteen minutes to assess the situation."

"Excellent," Brian said, "let's do that."

The three boys walked Destiny away from the stand of buildings and out toward the shore. They had a favorite spot where a local river fell into the ocean. Between the waterfall and the surf beating on the rocks, the area was loud and difficult to hear one another. It was also difficult to hear what they were doing.

Artie pushed the girl to the ground and started unbuttoning her shirt. "All right, I'm first."

"No, you're not." Billy stepped in and commanded, "She's mine. You two can go stand watch on the road."

"But we want to watch!"

"What did I just say?" Billy yelled. "You get to watch...the road!"

Billy leaned in close and whispered in the girl's ear, "Act like this really hurts." He stood up, raised his arms like he was about to conduct a symphony, and then swung them down together. The girl was immediately enveloped in a purple shroud. She screamed and cried. She kicked her feet and writhed right and left.

"Damn, Billy!" Artie's jaw dropped to his chest. "I didn't know you could do that!"

Billy turned to his friends. His eyes quivered in their sockets. "Why are you still here?"

Artie and Roofy scurried up the hill to the road. They couldn't see or hear anything from there.

Artie hung back and turned around, trying to peer over the hill.

"Artie," Roofy said, "don't. Did you see his eyes? He's gone crazy. I wouldn't test him if I were you."

"Yeah? Well, he should've told us and we could have grabbed another."

"Next time. Did you see what he did to her? I never seen that before."

"Yeah, I know. Who knew he had that in him?"

Johnson waded across the swamp and circled the home while the other men packed the camp into duffel bags and stacked them on the small island waiting to be picked up after the men completed their mission. The remaining three had approached halfway in the boat when Johnson radioed in. Hughes spoke quietly into his headset, using mostly short cryptic words until he had a clear understanding of the situation.

"It's like an island," Johnson said. "There's the four buildings we scouted before and a dock on the southeast side. It looks like another island off the western shore goes on at least a couple miles. About a mile up, there's a burned down farm of some kind."

"Roger that," Hughes said into the headset. He turned to Brian and said, "Their dock is dead ahead. We need to split up and circle around left and right, then come in from the West and the North. Since Johnson is already setup, I'll send Gomez in to join him, then you and I will make a wide path around the dock, and come in from the Northeast."

Brian nodded his approval to the plan.

Billy fell lightly on top of the girl. "Are you alright?"

"I knew it would be you," she said. "I saw you in my dreams."

"Yeah, me too. My name's Billy."

"Hi, Billy, I'm Diane. So, I was wondering, are you going to untie me? Or do you plan to do me while I'm still tied up?"

"Oh, I'm sorry." He loosened the bonds on her wrists. "I'd never do that to you."

"This is a little weird. I thought you would be older, but I've seen you in my dreams so many times. You are always the one that rescued me, and well, here you are now." She closed her eyes, sucked in her breath, and said, "Okay, I'm ready."

"Ready for what?"

"For whatever you have to do next."

"I'm not sure I can now."

She opened her eyes and propped herself up on her elbows. "Why not? Is something wrong with me?"

"Wrong with you? Are you crazy?"

"Well then, why can't you do what you were thinking?"

Billy smiled warmly and said, "Because I thought I would stare into your eyes, but you had them closed."

She blushed slightly and said, "Wow, that was kind of sweet. I wouldn't expect a kid like you to say anything so romantic."

"Romantic? Maybe I just wanted to see if your eyes were different colors, like they are in my dreams."

"Oh," she pouted.

"I'll tell you a secret. I am not as young as I look. I was always a bit smaller, so my father hatched a plan to make me look younger, which meant I would be more powerful than other boys my age."

"I see," she said. "How clever of him. So how old are you then?"

A smile stretched broadly across his young-looking face. "Old enough." He leaned forward and kissed her on the lips.

"Hey! I won't let you do that again until you tell me how old you really are!"

Billy thought about it a moment and decided he wanted another kiss. He cupped her cheek in his palm and said, "Almost sixteen." This time, when he leaned in, he kept his lips pressed against hers. He felt her lips pressing back.

Their lips parted, and she sucked in a cool breath of air.

His mind was spinning. "You better go now."

Her voice softened into a husky whisper. "No, Billy, you have to finish."

"I don't have to do anything."

"I know what your kind..." she said, "I mean, I know what your friends expect you to do, what they would do."

Billy sat up and picked up a stone from the ground and tossed it. "I know what they would do, but I'm not like them, and you're not like anyone I've ever met before. I'd really like to get to know you before. I mean, I was hoping to see you again. You will meet with me, won't you?"

Her eyes twinkled. A single tear slowly traced its way down her cheek. She pulled him back to her and reached one hand up behind his head, and lifted her lips to his. Her passion entered through his lips and filled his body with warmth. The hairs on his neck and arms stood straight out. "Yes," she said, "I will most definitely meet with you again."

"I think you better go, before I'm not strong enough to send you away anymore."

"But what will you tell your friends? Won't you get in trouble?"

"No, if there is anything my father taught me, it's how to really destroy stuff. I won't get in any trouble. Go."

"I won't go far," she said. "We'll find a way to meet again."

She ran off down to the bank and along the shore, turned once to wave at him, then disappeared into the woods.

Billy waited until she was completely out of sight. His body still tingled from her kiss, but he had to empty himself of the wonderful feelings flowing around inside of him. He stood and looked down upon the spot where she had lain. He raised his arms into the air and thought of his father for a moment, then brought his hands crashing down and created a mighty explosion with a large impressive orange cloud, and a pile of smoldering ash blowing away in the breeze.

CHAPTER 21

Blake and Destiny found themselves back in Cricket Bend, sitting across from each other with the candle between them. Their hearts raced from the passion between Billy and Diane, which still lingered in their minds and in their young bodies. Their skin prickled with goose bumps and shivers shook their spines. It was dark outside, and at best, the inside could be called dim.

Blake's head was woozy from the experience. He had just emerged from a series of dreams that all felt real to him. He thought he was back in the real world, but his head spun and the room wobbled. He wasn't sure.

Destiny had no such doubts. She knew she was back home and something terrible was brewing outside. She tore her eyes from Blake and found her nana flitting around the room, setting up talismans and charms.

Michelle paused when she saw they had returned from their trances and said, "'Bout time you comes back to me. It be plenty dark outside and I got the fear in my bones telling me it's time we gets out. You pick a fine time to go gallivanting about leaving me to watch over things. Where was you that was so important you should be gone so long anyways?"

Destiny glanced nervously at Blake, and then they both looked up at her, but said nothing. The blush still lingered on their cheeks and Michelle said, "Never minds. I don't wants to know." She went to the bedroom and started throwing clothes into an overnight bag. "You know, Cherie," she yelled, "if we leaves now, we can catch the early bus to go see your mama. You'd like that, wouldn't you?"

Destiny rose from the table and went to the window overlooking the entrance from the dock. The bayou was a beautiful place at night, with the moon casting slender beams through the cypress trees and the wind rocking the surface of the swamp into a glittering reflection of the moon, but an ugly pall was gathering outside and descending upon their peaceful home.

Michelle exited her bedroom with her carry-on bag stuffed with just the essentials. "Come on, Cherie," she said, "you too. Pack a few things and we can slip out of here."

"It's too late, Nana, you need to hide."

Michelle dropped her bags and sprang to Destiny's side, peering out the screen door. Destiny pushed her away from the door and said, "Go find a safe corner to hide in. They're here."

Michelle froze for a moment, then cast a trembling thumb towards Blake and asked, "What about him?"

"Don't worry about him."

Michelle started mumbling complaints about Blake, but Destiny told her, "Shhh! Get in the corner like I told you! They have us surrounded."

Michelle sank into the corner, scanning the room for her talismans. She felt lost and alone, helpless to protect her child.

Brian's voice boomed in from outside. "You in the cabin. We have you surrounded. Come out with your hands in the air and nobody will be harmed."

Michelle grabbed a couple nearby charms and sank lower into her corner, muttering protective incantations that she hoped would enhance their effectiveness.

Destiny waved her arms in front of her, creating a protective shield.

Brian bellowed, "We aren't going to wait forever. Come out with your hands in the air."

Destiny crossed the tiny kitchen to the screen door and yelled out, "Who are you? What are you doing here? You're trespassing on private property. You best either show yourselves or get the hell outa here!"

"We're with the government," Brian said. "Didn't we say that?"

"Oh yeah? Whose government would that be?"

Brian barely refrained from chuckling at her answer. "Why, yours, of course. We're out here searching for an escaped convict. We thought maybe he might have gotten kind of cozy with one of the locals out here. He's a dangerous boy, and we are searching homes in the vicinity for him, so kindly come on out so we can know he's not with you."

Destiny glanced her eyes over to Blake. His condition when they found him could have been that of an escaped convict, but she didn't buy it.

"Just send the boy out," Brian continued, "and we'll be on our way."

Blake's head settled enough for him to recognize Brian's voice. He wasn't sure what their plan was, but he would just play along until he could figure out the winning side. "It's true," he lied. "I'm sure that once they have me, you won't be in any trouble."

Destiny peered out the screen again and yelled, "You're going to have to show yourselves, and you better look like who you say you are."

Hughes stepped forward into a pale patch of moonlight. He looked military and governmental. Brian stepped into the light next to him. "Now you can see us. Come on out now, you first, then the boy."

"Me first?" she asked. "Don't you just want the boy?"

"So he is with you, then."

"To hell with you," Destiny barked. "If you want to know who's up here, you're just gonna have to come up to the porch like civilized human beings!"

"Destiny, honey," Michelle said in a weak trembling voice, "these men be lyin' to you. They is so deep in lies, I don't think they would know the truth even if they was drownin' in it."

"I know, Nana, I can feel it, too."

Brian also felt something. Ever since they had stepped onto the island, he felt a growing surge of power. A tingling sense of energy more powerful than anything he had ever felt before. He knew in his mind no one had ever felt this kind of magic in thousands of years. He was going to be the Messiah that ushered magic back into the world and lead his people back to the forefront of human kind. He stepped forward. "Of course, you're right. We'll come to the porch, and you will see we are who we say we are. In fact, we thank you for the invitation."

Hughes tapped his earpiece and whispered, "You hear that boys? We're going to the porch. What's your twenty?"

Johnson's voice returned, "I have the back door covered."

Gomez was breathing heavy as if he'd been running, "I'm north. I can see you and Mr. Grupp. I have coverage of most of the porch and have some visibility inside through a window."

Hughes put his hand on Brian's shoulder to hold him back and whispered, "They're in position." He tapped his earpiece again so Gomez and Johnson could hear everything that was going on and said, "Let's watch the crossfire. These walls look paper thin."

Hughes took a step forward, but Brian put his palm on Hughes' chest and said, "Tell them to be prepared for anything. I mean, they might see some pretty strange shit. Don't freeze up on us."

"They won't freeze up, Mr. Grupp."

"And one more thing." Brian looked Hughes directly in the eyes. "The boy, we think the boy is with us, but be on the alert in case they changed him."

"You hear that, boys?" Hughes said. "We're in for some crazy voodoo shit, and the boy we brought with us might be compromised now. Stay frosty."

Hughes stepped forward to take the lead, but Brian stopped him and whispered, "I got this. I know their kind." In truth, he only knew legend, but he wanted the glory and history for himself.

Brian spoke loudly to the cabin; "I'm coming up the steps now. Remember, we have the place surrounded. Keep your hands where we can see them."

Destiny backed into the room, away from the screen door. She was ready. Ready may be an understatement. She had spells prepped. She felt as if the spells were stored in her wrists and would fly out at the very first thought of using them.

Michelle remained back in the corner. She sat, crumpled on the floor, with her hands in constant motion, as if she were using sign language, or possibly knitting without needles and thread.

Blake sat with his hands on the table, waiting to see how things developed.

"Okay," Brian said, "I'm on the porch and I'm approaching the door. We don't want any trouble, we just want the boy. Why don't you and your grandmother come on out while we get the boy?"

"Liar! Liar!" Michelle stood up straight, still in her corner. "You ain't for the boy. You has murder in your heart! I see it in you. I sees plenty in you, Mr. Boss man. I sees that you does know the boy, and you may even like him some. You brought him here with you. You brought the boy to come kill us, but you don't really care if he lives or dies. What's that you was thinkin? Awe, now that's not very nice, Mr. Boss man. You really think that just acause you raised the boy, that you owns him? That ain't how things work, Mr. Boss man. They grows up and does what they does. We gots to let them do what be in their own heart. But you're thinkin' that if he's not with you, you gonna kill him? That's not right, Mr. Boss man, that's just not right."

Brian couldn't stand it. He hated her tone. He hated that she was in his head knowing his thoughts, but most of all, he had that age-old hate in the pit of his stomach for all witches. He threw back the screen door and burst into the room with his right hand cocked back, ready to throw fireballs at the old woman, but Destiny was ready.

Lightning streaked out of Destiny's right hand, slamming Brian directly in the center of his chest and throwing him backwards against the screen door. At the same time, her left hand hurled a protective bubble that expanded to surround her grandmother. Brian's hand came down as he slammed against the door jam and a giant fireball completely engulfed Michelle.

Blake was shocked. He thought that he was the only one of their kind that could marshal that kind of power. All the time on the plane, he had laughed at Brian's pathetic little displays of magic. He thought he was the only one in the whole world, except of course for Destiny, who could do what he now witnessed.

Destiny hit Brian with something Blake could not see. It was some kind of invisible power that threw Brian off the porch and back outside into the yard.

Hughes entered the room, pointing his gun around and finally resting his sights on Blake. Blake lifted his hands, showing Hughes his palms and gesturing that he wasn't his enemy.

Brian surrounded Destiny with flames, but they merely danced around her protective field and died into either embers flying up into the sky or ash sliding off to the ground. Destiny followed him out across the porch and into the yard, all the while firing back giant flames at Brian. Brian had no protective field, but his rage had reached epic proportions and the flames didn't hurt him. He bathed in her flames. He fired one volley of fireballs after another but could not penetrate her shield. Johnson and Gomez fired at her, but their bullets were equally ineffective against her shield.

Brian reached deep inside, gathering up as much energy as he could, creating a huge explosion in the ground below her feet. The blast threw her fifteen feet into the air. She lost her shield and slammed her head into the ground, blacking out.

Brian pointed at her and barked out, "She's not dead yet. Pick her up and carry her inside."

Johnson's knees quivered as he picked her up and carried her inside, with Brian following right behind.

Brian was glowing with pride. He stepped back into the cabin, brushed the few remaining embers off of him, and said, "And that, my boy, is why we are superior to witches. We always have been and we always will be."

"Wow, sir," Blake croaked, "that was sure impressive. I've never seen anything like that."

"Nobody has, not in a thousand years, I think."

"Why now?" Blake asked. "Why, after a thousand years, are we, I mean you, suddenly able to do this?"

"I don't know exactly," Brian said, "but ever since we started hunting for her, I could feel the power, and the closer we got, the stronger it felt. I have people working on it, but for now, however, I want you to witness this whole event, especially the killing blow."

"But, sir," Blake pleaded, "if we don't know what brought the power back, then it couldn't have been us that did it."

Brian asked, "What are you saying?"

"What if the witches brought it back?"

Brian stood puzzled. "Then, if they brought the power back, why didn't they win? It's always been us or them, and we always win."

"Sir," Blake continued, "I've gotten to know them a little bit. They aren't evil, sir."

"Who ever said they were evil? They're witches. That's all we need to know."

"Maybe they have something they could teach us."

Brian laughed. "What could they possibly teach us? How to lose?"

"But, sir..."

"Enough!" Brian barked. "Observe and be quiet."

Brian patted Destiny on the cheek and said, "Wake up, little witch. You won't want to miss this."

Destiny opened her eyes. She was scared. All the talk of her being the chosen one disintegrated from her mind.

Brian reared back as if to throw a spell. Gomez and Johnson trembled and gasped, wide-eyed, as they were still holding her arms.

Brian laughed. "Just kidding, boys. Tie her to a chair, the old biddy, too."

Michelle looked deeply into Johnson's eyes and yelled, "Keep your grubby paws off her!" Her voiced boomed in his mind. It was a voice she had never used before, a voice only he could hear, and a voice that hadn't been used in this world for centuries. Johnson backed off of Destiny, leaving Gomez to tie her to the chair.

After tying her arms, Gomez felt most comfortable standing behind Brian, near the door, but Johnson backed his shivering body out the screen to the porch.

Brian was quickly acquiring control over his spells. He spread his arms at shoulder height and thin blue filaments of electricity sparked out from his fingers, slowly encircling Destiny in glowing coils. She tried thinking her spells without using her hands but could not muster up a proper shield. The coils squeezed in around her torso. They were like hot razors against her skin. Her spine went cold and the inside of her mouth tasted like metal. She screamed. At first it was one long, agonizing scream, then it was panting gasps and sobbing.

Johnson and Gomez had little stomach for torture and they were terrified by the power that was emanating from Brian. Gomez sprinted out of the room and ran with Johnson down to the dock.

Destiny was helpless. She writhed in pain, gripped by Brian's coils. She could sense her nana behind her, and knew she would be next. There was nothing Destiny could do to save her. She looked around the room one last time through tearful eyes. Her gaze fell upon Blake, begging for help.

In that one instant, staring into her eyes, he saw everything. He saw the past and the future. He still felt the kiss of her lips from their last memory. Here she was, helpless to Brian's attack, yet Blake saw a different outcome. He had seen her on trial. She could not lose like this. He remembered the little men asking him to choose sides, and the old man who also questioned his allegiance. He stood up, balled his fist, and cocked his arm as if he were doing curls with a dumbbell. Brian's attack weakened for a moment, then stopped.

Brian started screaming and Hughes knew something was wrong. Hughes did not like Brian's methods, but he was all about duty. He was paid to do a job, and now he sensed a cause and reaction between Blake and Brian, so he raised his weapon to Blake. Blake repeated the same curling motion to him and he doubled over in pain.

Brian's stomach was glowing red from the inside, and his skin was turning tan. He doubled over, fell on the floor and burst into flames next to Hughes, who was also on fire.

***

Blake went behind Destiny and Michelle and cut them loose, then went to the window and said, "There are still two more of them out there."

Destiny finished pulling the ropes off of her and jumped into Blake's arms, wrapping him in a hug. "What took you so long?"

"I don't know. I was so confused."

Michelle looked around her. The house was in flames. She pushed them out the door and said, "Come on, you two, we gotta get out of here."

Blake started to sprint down the path towards the dock, but Destiny lassoed him with a force field and pulled him back to her. She leaned forward to kiss him, but Blake pulled back. "Didn't you hear me?" he said. "There's two more of them out there!"

"Let them go." She leaned forward again to kiss him.

He pulled back again and asked, "How can you kiss me after what I almost did?"

She sighed. "You didn't do anything. You were just dazed from the memories. It's my fault you were so confused. Searching ancient memories can be real hard on you at first. I never meant to keep you out there so long."

"You didn't keep me out there," he said. "I was totally thirsty for it. Besides, that's not the confusion I mean. There was some of that, but it was mostly me. Partly the way I was raised, and partly these dreams I have been having. The dreams showed me that I am from both clans. They wanted me to choose sides. I thought that to fulfill my destiny, I had to wait and choose whichever side was winning."

She pushed him away. "That's awful! You mean you were going to let them kill us?"

"That's just it. I didn't understand my dreams correctly. You know the signs are never really clear. It wasn't until your eyes locked on mine that I realized you were my destiny and I didn't have to wait to choose the winning side. I could make the winning side by joining with it."

"Don't be playing games with my name. You were going to let me die. You must be waiting for some other Destiny."

"Look around you. Do you think I want to go through this again?"

Michelle rapped each of them on the back of the head. "What's wrong with you two? The house is burnin' down and you two pick now to spoon?"

"What?" Destiny argued. "Are you nuts, Nana? We're not spooning."

"Shush, child. Let's get outta this place first."

Blake fell behind Destiny and Michelle and asked, "What's spooning?"

"Oh, Nana, the whole woods are on fire; what do we do now?"

"Your mama is waiting for us. We go gets her and starts over. Then, maybe we be done with this business."

Destiny's eyes were staring off into space a bit. "I think we're going to need Mama, but I don't think this business will be over yet. I still have to save Mala and figure out who that Migul guy was from the future."

Blake tapped Destiny on the shoulder and asked again, "What's spooning?"

Destiny giggled and grabbed Blake by the back of the neck. They stopped walking long enough for her to pull his face to hers and kiss him softly and passionately on the lips. "That's spooning."

Michelle shook her head in disgust and walked ahead of them.

They continued down to the docks. Michelle's boat was missing, but thankfully, Blake's boat was still there and in one piece. Michelle took the pilot's seat, Destiny got in front. Blake took the center and gave a good shove off the dock.

The small motor puttered quietly as they meandered through the tall Cypress and occasional sand bars.

Blake leaned forward in his seat and asked, "Is Destiny really your name?"

"Of course it is. Why? Is there something wrong with my name?"

"Nothing, just wondering. I like it."

Darkness had set fully onto the bayou. The moon was full and created a flicker on the boat as they passed under the boughs overhead. Michelle knew the way with her eyes closed.

Destiny turned in her seat and asked, "So, is Blake your real name?"

"Why? Don't you like Blake?"

"Blake's a fine name, I guess. You just don't seem much like a Blake."

Blake detected a mischievous twinkle in her eye. "What's a Blake supposed to be like?"

"You know, rich and snobby. An ivy league type, I'd say."

"Hmm, I hadn't thought of that. What name should I have?"

Destiny turned back to face front. She wiped some ash off her lap and shrugged her shoulders, saying, "Blake's just fine. If your mama chose Blake, then you'll just have to live with it, won't you?"

"Not necessarily," he said. "As far as I'm concerned, if you don't like your name, if it doesn't suit you, you should be able to pick one you like."

"Wait a minute. Are you saying Blake's not your name?"

Blake stared off into the swamp and calmly said, "My name is Blake."

"But, is that what your mama named you?"

Silence followed.

Destiny turned back around again and asked, "Well? Did your mama name you Blake?"

"No. My mama was insane."

"Mine too," she said, "so I won't hold that against you. What did your mama name you?"

Blake looked up into the sky. "It doesn't matter. Is it true that you can read the future in the stars?"

Destiny hit him on the shoulder. "Tell me."

Blake turned his head and asked Michelle, "Hey, how much farther do we have to go?"

Michelle just chuckled and kept her mind on the path before them.

Destiny leaned back so her face was close to his. She batted her eyes and smiled wide. "Tell me, pleeeeeeeaaaasssseeee!"

"No, really, my mama was crazy, or she hated me, or both maybe."

She stared intently into his eyes and said, "Tell me. You know I can enter your mind and pull it out of you."

"Please don't. It's a really stupid name."

"I want you to know," she said. "I'll never leave you, no matter how stupid your name is."

"Okay, but don't tell anyone." He leaned close and whispered into her ear, "My mama named me after my great-great-great-somethin'-or-nuther grandfather, Marvalaine."

The End

Jonni Jordyn was born in Oakland, California in 1957. She started writing at an early age, writing music, poetry, short stories, radio, film, and stage scripts. She didn't start writing novels until later in life, after she retired from playing music, and found herself travelling away from home for extended periods.

She currently lives in Denver, Colorado.